THE
HERMIT

THE
HERMIT

THOMAS
RYDAHL

Translated by K.E. Semmel

ONEWORLD

A Oneworld book

First published in North America, Great Britain and
Australia by Oneworld Publications, 2016

Originally published in Danish as *Eremitten* by Forlaget Bindslev, 2014
Copyright © Thomas Rydahl, 2014
Translation copyright © K. E. Semmel, 2016

Published by agreement with the Nordin Agency, Sweden

The moral right of Thomas Rydahl to be identified as the
Author of this work has been asserted by him in accordance
with the Copyright, Designs and Patents Act 1988

A CIP record for this title is available from the British Library

ISBN 978-1-78074-889-4
ISBN 978-1-78074-890-0 (eBook)

Typeset by Tetragon, London
Printed and bound in Great Britain by Clays Ltd, St Ives plc

Oneworld Publications
10 Bloomsbury Street
London WC1B 3SR
England

CONTENTS

Luisa
1

The Little Finger
10

The Whore
53

The Corpse
132

The Flat
203

The Cargo Ship
272

The Liar
364

Lucifia
397

Lily
464

LUISA

31 December

1

On New Year's Eve, under the influence of a triple Lumumba, Erhard decides to find a new girlfriend. New is probably not the right word. She doesn't need to be new or attractive or sweet or fun. Just a warm body. Just one of those kinds of women who potters about the house. Maybe she'll hum a song or curse at him because he's spilled cocoa on the floor. What can he ask of her? Not much. And what does he have to offer her? Not much. But it won't get any easier. In a few years she'll also need to empty his piss pot and shave him and pull off his shoes after an entire day in the car – if he can still drive, that is. In a few years.

The mountainside near the house is invisible; the darkness is complete. If he sits still long enough, he'll suddenly be able to see the stars. And if he sits even longer than that, he'll see a narrow band of shooting stars growing brighter and brighter. The silence grows, if one can put it that way. Grows like the sound of nothingness drowning out the heat of the day still whining in the rocks, and the wind's relentless C major, and the beat of the waves lashing against the coast, and the blood that's seeping through his body. A silence that makes him want to weep into the New Year. A silence that's so convincing, so satiating, that it blends with the night and his wide-open eyes which feel closed. This is what he loves about living out here. Out here where no one ever comes.

Just him. And Laurel and Hardy. And here come the stars. They've always been there, but now he can see them. First all the specks, then all the constellations and Orion's Belt and the galaxy like an old-fashioned punch card with messages from the Big Bang.

It's been seventeen years and nine months since the last time. He smells Beatriz's perfume, which practically clings to his shirt right where she'd touched him this afternoon as they parted. She suggested that he come along tonight. A half-hearted attempt, if even that. I've got plans, he'd said tartly, the way only an old man can. C'mon, she'd tried again, sweetly. No thanks, those people are too fancy for me. Which they were. She didn't say anything to that. Instead Raúl said: You are one of the finest people I know. But nothing more was said about it, and when they began arranging the champagne flutes, he gave Beatriz a Happy New Year's kiss and left. Raúl walked him out. *Buen viaje,* Erhard said, when they stood among the distinctive throng on the street. From the opposite pavement, the suitcase salesman, Silón, shouted Happy New Year! to them, though mostly to Raúl, whom everyone knows. Erhard headed to his car, feeling the same pang that struck him every New Year's Eve. Another year gone like all the rest, another year looming.

Cheers, my friend. It's good with cognac. It burns all the way down. The night is warm. His body is tingling hot now. Maybe because he's thinking of Beatriz, her dark place, right where her breasts part and vanish into her blouse, the very source of her aroma. Damn. He tries not to think about her. She's not the one he should be spending his time on.

The hairdresser's daughter. He can think about her. There's something about her.

He's never met her. He has seen her once, at a distance. He's often seen her image on the wall in the salon. He thinks about her. He thinks about simple events. Little scenes where she walks into the salon, the bell above the door chiming. He imagines her sitting across from him at the dinner table when he eats. Or standing in the kitchen, his kitchen, preparing steaming, sizzling food on the stove. In truth she's much too young, absorbed in things he doesn't understand. She's not exactly his type. What could he possibly say to impress a young woman? She probably doesn't even cook. She'd probably rather talk to her friends on the telephone, like all young people do. Maybe she eats noodles out of a small box while staring at her computer screen. In the image at the salon she's a teenager and the very picture of innocence, with thick curls and big, masculine glasses. Not beautiful, but unforgettable. She's got to be at least thirty now and apparently both sweet and quick-witted, according to her mother, whom he obviously doesn't trust. That time he'd spotted her down the street, he recognized her light, curly hair. She crossed the street with her back ramrod straight, a purse slung over her shoulder like a real woman, and she spurted forward running when a car raced towards her. She wasn't elegant, she was even a little clumsy. He doesn't know why he thinks about her so much. Maybe it's just the island eating its way into him. The whistling of the wind around the rocks and corners. Like a note of loneliness continuously rising from a piano.

It's Petra's fault. Her unnaturally high-pitched voice that pacifies her clients in the chair and rules out talk and counterarguments and reasonable thoughts as one thumbs through a magazine or reads an article about the island's football team. She has this firmness about her. For her, love is something to be squeezed out of others. She talks non-stop about the daughter, clawing at Erhard's scalp with her long nails as she tells him that she's moved to an apartment, that she's bought a little scooter, that she's got a new client, that she's broken things off with her boyfriend, that she – not the daughter – would like grandchildren, and so on. And then a few months ago she suddenly said: If only my daughter found someone like you. That's what she said as she stood gazing at him in the mirror. And afterward: She's not like most girls, but neither are you. They'd chuckled at that. Petra mostly.

Erhard had been completely alarmed at the suggestion. She couldn't just say something like that. Wave her daughter under his nose. Did that mean she wanted him to ask her daughter out? Didn't Petra know what they called him about town? Hadn't Petra noticed that he was missing a finger? And what about the age difference? Didn't Petra consider that? They are separated by at least thirty years; he's the same age as her mother, older even. But the symmetry appeals to him. Generations reaching back and pulling the next generation forward, Escher's draw-ings of the artist's hand sketching itself. Five fingers on one hand and five fingers on the other. Five + five.

If only my daughter found someone like you, she'd said. Someone like him.

Not him, but someone like him.

What was that all about? Was she saying there were many like him out there? Carbon copies of men who've done the same things over and over for nearly a generation, without deviation, without asking ques-tions, someone like him, gas from the asshole of the earth, here today and gone tomorrow with only the memory of the stench remaining.

Down in the city it sounds like fireworks booming.

Maybe he should just do it now? Drive over there and invite her out? Right now? Then it'd be over with. He knows it's the Lumumba talking. He knows that his courage won't last more than two hours. Then real-ity will come crawling back. It's quarter past ten. Perhaps she's having dinner somewhere with all sorts of young men who know all sorts of things about computers. But what if she's sitting at home just like him – watching the terrible show they broadcast on TV every year. Her mother has told him multiple times where her flat is. It's in one of the new build-ings on Calle Palangre. Right above the children's-wear shop. It couldn't hurt just to see whether she's home. Maybe he can see if there's a light on in the flat, or if there's a light from the television glowing in the darkness.

He braces himself against the wall of his house and finds a pair of stiff trousers on the clothesline, then jams his feet through the holes. The goats run off somewhere in the darkness.

2

He drives along Alejandro's Trail into the city.

He shouldn't drive on that track; it ruins the car. He's already had the axles repaired twice, and each time the mechanic, Anphil, warned him. You don't drive down the north road, do you? Or Alejandro's Trail? The car can't handle it. You'll have to get a Montero or one of the new Merceros; they can handle it, not this car. But Erhard doesn't want a Montero, and he doesn't have the money for a new Mercedes. Even if he had the money, he would keep his Mercedes from Morocco with its yellow seats and choppy acceleration. All the same, he takes Alejandro's Trail. Drives past Olivia's old house where the surfers have moved in with their boards lying on the roof, and in the darkness he can see their flags: a pair of pink knickers hanging from the end of a long stick that's jutting from the cabin. Two guys and their friends live there. Sometimes when he passes by, in the morning, they're sitting outside, smoking tobacco from large pipes; they wave at him, laughing hysterically. Whenever he stops the car, they're high as poisoned goats and unable to rise from their inflatable chairs. But there's no one home now, and the lights are out. They're probably on the beach or downtown.

He approaches the bend that hugs the coast, a fantastic bend – especially with Lumumba up to his Adam's apple and cheap cognac in every finger joint. It's a pebbly, potholey road, and the entire car vibrates. Swerving when he reaches 70 mph, he feels a tickling sensation that makes him grin. He breaks wind, too, which isn't as funny; he just can't help himself. He's had the problem the last few years. If he squeezes his stomach muscles even a little, a pocket of air lurches through his gut and into his underwear; it's both painful and liberating. From there the trail runs downhill, and he hits the final curve. Through the headlights he sees a goat standing in the centre of the road, and he veers around it before glancing in the rearview mirror; it looks like Hardy, but it can't be him, not here, not this far from the house. The goat has already disappeared in the darkness.

He's so preoccupied that he doesn't see the car driving towards him until it passes on the much-too-narrow road. Mostly it's just sound, a dry whooom. A metallic shadow along the car. The side mirror gets knocked flat against the glass.

– Goddamn amateurs! he shouts, to his surprise, in Danish. He apparently hasn't forgotten how to curse. He continues around the curve, the other car is out of sight, the red tail-lights vanished in the night. There's no point even stopping to inspect the damage. He rolls his window down and fixes his mirror. The glass has splintered into tributaries pointing downward in eight fine lines.

A black Montero. No doubt it was the gadabout Bill Haji, who lives up the road at a ranchlike villa with horses; he's known for taking Alejandro's Trail fast and furious, as if the sea was ablaze behind him. Erhard's heart should be sitting in his throat right now, but instead it's right where it's supposed to be, numbed by the Lumumba and agitated by the prospect of meeting the hairdresser's daughter.

He drives off the trail and into Corralejo. The heat rises from the asphalt. Young people in small cars honk and sing. He heads down the Avenida towards the harbour, then parks in Calle Palangre. He dumps the car when he finds a vacant spot.

He plans to walk to the hairdresser's daughter's place. He wants to knock on her door. He's already red-faced and embarrassed by the look she will give him when he's standing at her door. *Good evening*, he will say, and *Happy New Year*. He's seen her before. *I've seen you in the photograph at your mother's salon.* What if she's wearing one of those summer dresses with the lazy straps that are always falling to the side? Who gives a shit if she wears glasses? He's not picky.

But when he reaches the clothing shop and glances up at the flats above, he sees that the lights are off. On every storey of the building. She's probably watching TV. Drinking white wine and hoping someone will stop by. He needs to fortify himself with a drink. Something really strong. Just something to get his voice box going. It'll do him no good just standing there staring like some idiotic *extranjero*. He walks up the street and down Via Ropia. Towards Centro Atlantico. It's always buzzing there, mostly with tourists, people he doesn't know. He walks into Flicks and goes directly to the bar. He orders a Rusty Nail, and even buys a round for the two gentlemen in the corner. They're olive farmers out prowling for women and unaccustomed to city life, huddled close like mice behind a palm tree. They are practically invisible.

3

Eighteen minutes to go. On the back wall of the bar the TV's showing images from Times Square, fireworks over Sydney Harbour, Big Ben's long hands approaching XII. The bartender shouts *Are you ready for the new year?* It sounds so promising, so simple. As if one leaves behind all the old, bringing only the new into the new year. But new means nothing to him. He's not new. He doesn't need new. He doesn't want new. He just wants the old to behave properly. Seventeen minutes. He can still ring the doorbell and wish her a Happy New Year. Maybe she's wearing a negligee or whatever it's called. She's been sitting there drinking white wine and watching reruns of *7 Vidas*, which everyone loves. Her hair is wet, she's taken a cool bath.

A crowd of people moves to exit onto the street. He's nearly pushed off his stool. He pays with a bill and remembers why he doesn't frequent tourist traps: it costs more than twenty euros for whisky and Drambuie. He follows the throng out and starts back towards Calle Palangre. He crosses the street and enters her building. It was built during the Franco years, and the stairwell is simple and cobalt-blue. On the first floor he reads the names on each of the three doors. Loud music is blaring inside, but there's no Louisa or L.

He walks up another flight. A couple stands kissing beneath the artificial light of the stairwell, but when he passes them they stop, shamefaced, and head down the stairs.

As he stands catching his breath a moment, he looks at the nameplates, then continues to the top floor. Three floors with doors equals nine doors.

On the third floor live one Federico Javier Panôs and one Sobrino. And in the centre, Luisa Muelas. The sign on her door is large and inlaid with gold, her name etched in thick, cursive letters. No doubt a gift from Petra and her husband. It's one of those traditional items parents give their children whenever they, as thirty-year-olds, move out of their childhood home.

It seems quiet behind each of the doors. He puts his ear against Luisa Muelas's and almost wishes her not to be home. But there's a faint noise inside – clatters, creaks, mumbles – but perhaps it's just the TV.

He straightens up and raps his good hand, the right, against the flat chunk of wood above the peephole. It's four minutes to midnight. Maybe his knocks will fade into the raucous noise of New Year's Eve.

Suddenly he sees a face in the nameplate.

The face is indistinct. A pleading, confused face dominated by two eyes wedged between a stack of wrinkles and shabby skin, topped off with a tired beard. A desperate face. In it he can see love and sorrow, he can see decades of bewilderment and alcohol, and he can see the cynical observer, appraising and judgemental. It's an appallingly wretched face, difficult to penetrate, difficult to stomach, difficult to love. But worst of all it's his face. As seen only from the rearview mirror of his car, or in the distorted mirrors above the chipped sinks of public toilets, or in shop windows, but preferably not at all. There's only one thing to ask that face.

What have you got to offer?

In reality there's nothing more frightening than this. The encounter. The moment in a life when one takes a risk. When one says, *I want you.* The moment when chance ceases, when one makes a stand and asks another to accept. The moment when two soap bubbles burst the reflection, merging into one. It doesn't happen during a kiss, or during sex, and not even when one person loves another. It's in the terrifying second when one dares to make a mad claim that one has something to offer another by one's very presence.

He hears sounds behind the door now. Like stockinged feet.

– I'm coming, a soft voice says.

It's two minutes to twelve.

He can't do it, he just can't. He leans over the stairwell and starts down. Down, down. He hears the door opening on the top floor. *Hello?* the voice says. Past the doors with loud music and outside. Onto the street. He hobbles along the wall like a rat, then cuts across the street to his car. Calle Palangre is filled with people now. There's a group of cigar-smoking men standing beside his car, and girls astride scooters, champagne flutes in their hands.

Voices call out from the flats above. He fumbles his way into his car and wriggles it free of its parking spot. Following the one-way street, he parts the throng. A group wants to catch a ride, not seeing that his sign is turned off, but he's not interested. He pays no mind to their hands on his windscreen or their pleading eyes. Happy New Year, asshole!, a young girl wearing a silver-covered bowler shouts at him.

He drives away from the city's light and into darkness. The grey road ends and becomes a pale track. He presses down hard on the old Mercedes' creaky gas pedal. Gravel plinks against the undercarriage.

The image of the hairdresser's daughter opening the door returns to mock him. Now in socks – hair rumpled and a little glass of whisky in her hand. A fantasy only a horny man can imagine. That's something he hates about growing old. Going from the physicality of a youth lacking spirit to pure spirit lacking physicality. To the point where the best moments are comprised of thoughts, of conceptions of the future, of reminders from way back when. For almost eighteen years he's imagined intimacy with a woman. Imagined it. Even when he was with Annette, he imagined it. Back then it had just had a more concrete means of expression, back then it resembled intimacy with everyone else but her, right up until he was no longer near her.

His feet shift from the gas pedal to the brake. In the centre of his headlights' bright yellow cone he sees a giant object lying in the middle of the road.

THE LITTLE FINGER

1 January–3 January

4

At first he thinks it's a fallen satellite, then he sees that it's a car, an overturned car.

It's a bloody Montero, a black Montero like Bill Haji's.

It is Bill Haji's.

It's four or five hundred metres from the spot where they'd passed one another, but how long ago was that? An hour? He can't make any sense of time. Maybe the Rusty Nail went to his head after all.

He cuts his engine but leaves the headlights on, so he can see the car. He hears the ocean and the soft hum of the Montero's motor. The dust settles.

He's about to turn on his CB radio and contact dispatch; it's the best he can do. Then he hears some rapping sounds, as if someone's trying to communicate or get free. He gets out of his car. He calls Bill's name. He calls as though they know each other. Bill Haji. They hardly know each other. Everyone knows Bill Haji. A colourful, obnoxious person. Never at rest, always on his way to or fro. Erhard has driven him a few times. The first time was to the hospital. And after that – upon request: a couple of trips to the airport and home to Haji's villa some miles away. Haji arrived from Madrid with four or five suitcases and a young man who seemed tired. They were the same suitcases both times, but not the same guy. Erhard didn't care about the rumours, or how Haji lived his life. One shouldn't get involved in that kind of thing. As long as the boys are over eighteen and have made their own choices.

– Bill Haji, he repeats.

The car is smashed up. It must have rolled a good distance. Stupid Montero. No better than Japanese cardboard. There's a long trail of glass. Which suggests to him that the vehicle skidded along the road. He calls again as he walks around the car and peers through what might have been the windscreen, but is probably a side window. There's no one inside. Neither Bill nor any of his boys. Erhard breathes easier. Even though he doesn't much care for Bill Haji, he feared seeing him mashed between the steering wheel and the seat like a blood-gorged tick. The vehicle is empty; one of the doors is open, hanging from its hinge. Maybe he's gone after help or was picked up by his sister, who's always close by Bill Haji, whenever he sees him downtown or at La Marquesina. He bends forward and touches the car. It's still warm.

For a moment the darkness and the car fade away, and the entire sky is lit up in shades of green and cyan and magenta, and it's as if hundreds of eyes are looking back at him.

5

The sky above explodes. Erhard stares across the vehicle. More booms follow in choppy rhythm, streaks and flashes of light. At first he thinks that they're emergency lights from a ship. Then he remembers that it's New Year's Eve and he spots the stream of fireworks down in the city. When his eyes adjust to the darkness again, he sees something moving right in front of him.

Sitting on top of what was once the car's exhaust is a dog.

Two dogs.

They're watching him like cute puppies heading out for a walk. They're wild dogs. No one knows where they come from. Maybe from Corralejo seven miles away. Whether they are sitting there or running along the edges of cliffs in the moonlight, they're handsome animals. In the daylight they appear emaciated and beaten, like old blankets. They're a plague to anyone who raises sheep and goats, and among bored young men they've become something one shoots as target practice from the bed of a lorry. And yet somehow there are more of them than ever. Erhard guesses that ten or fifteen of them are out there in the darkness. Maybe Bill Haji hit one of them, maybe that's why he crashed. One of the dogs is drooling. Erhard stares through its forelegs.

Even though most of his face is gone, he can still recognize Bill Haji's remains. There's nothing left to save. Maybe he was dead before the dogs got to him. His famous sideburns look like rabbit fur turned inside out.

Then he sees it.

6

It's lying right behind the left front wheel, in darkness. He only sees it because it sparkles a little each time the fireworks explode in the sky. At first he's not sure what it is. There's heat in the reflection, an amber radiance. He guesses that it's some copper or something embossed in gold, perhaps part of a pair of sunglasses or a cord sliced in half. For a moment he wonders if it's a gold filling, then he sees the fingernail and the small folds around the joint. He notices that the broad ring is surrounded by flesh.

It's Bill Haji's engagement ring. On Bill Haji's ring finger. Ten minus one.

He doesn't want to go around the vehicle, so he reaches for it; he doesn't even know if he can reach it. It's only a metre or two away from him on the other side of the car. He stretches across the undercarriage, but the two dogs glance up from their dinner. One bares its teeth and repositions its front paws, ready to spring. Erhard might be able to snatch the finger, but not without having a dog stuck to his arm.

He walks slowly back to his own car and snaps on the high beams. He blinks the lights on and off a few times until the dogs glower at him in irritation. Then he lays his hand against the centre of the wheel and puts all his weight into it. The car emits a few shrill honks that most wouldn't believe belonged to a Mercedes. He presses the horn until the two dogs on the other car hop sluggishly down like junkies and slink off a few metres into the darkness.

He hurries to the Montero by the glow of his high beams. As fast as he can. It has been several months, maybe years, since he last ran. Although it's only a few metres, it feels like forever. As if the dogs have already seen him and are moving towards the vehicle again. As if his legs are unreliable and can't carry him all the way there and back again in a single evening. He doesn't get as close to the car as he wishes but leans across the overturned Montero to reach for the ring. A mere half-metre away.

He's splayed out just opposite what remains of Bill Haji's head and face, gazing through a red-blue clot at open but extinguished eyes.

Find the boy.

The sentence emerges so loud and clear through the noise of the fireworks that, for a moment, Erhard thinks it's coming from the radio that's still playing. Or maybe one of the dogs, as far as he fucking knows, is suddenly talking. He stares into Bill Haji's eyes and it's almost as if the voice is coming from them, from the dark circles slowly glossing over in death. He's heard the voice before. It's a voice he recognizes. Maybe it's Bill Haji's. Maybe it's just something he said out loud, for God knows what reason. He can't even remember what he said, only that the words were pleading.

Then he sees the finger again and hoists himself forward. The undercarriage is still warm. Not hot, but warm like a rock. The fireworks die out, the final salute blasting above the coast, a green network that sprays silver. Silence follows. Not quite silence. The engine groans. And the dogs' plaintive yips have become a supersonic whine, which must be the sound they make right before they turn vicious. Something rustles just below the car. Erhard crawls forward on his belly, stretches his arm, and clutches the finger. It's cold. Bristly. And incredible.

Nine + one, he thinks.

7

Erhard runs back to his car and hurls himself into the front seat, then slams the door. Since he discovered the overturned car, he's felt perfectly sober, almost hung-over, and now his drunkenness returns with a snap. Not only the dizzying sensation, but also a bizarre elation, a joy.

It's as if his eyes, body, and mind are doing short-circuited mathematics. With his own nine fingers and Bill Haji's one that makes ten fingers. It stirs a pleasure all the way down in his belly, hell, down in his cock – as if having a new finger in his possession has strengthened his libido. He knows that it's wrong, knows he's imaging it, but even though it's not his finger, the sum total of fingers makes him whole in a way he's not felt in a long time. In the same way that losing his finger eighteen years before represented a repulsion, a conscious subtraction, this finger returns his balance to him.

He tosses his socks and plops in bed with a buzzing head. The generator has run dry, because he forgot to turn it off when he left. Tomorrow, tomorrow he'll have a look at it. Although the night is quiet, when the wind shifts direction it sounds like dogs snarling.

If they eat him there will be nothing to bury. If there's nothing to bury, he's not dead. Bill Haji's sister is one hard woman who looks like a man. She'll have to say her goodbyes to an empty coffin.

The finger on a hand, Bill Haji's hand, which once hailed Erhard on the high street. His boyfriend was sick. Bill Haji caressed him all the way to the hospital. What Erhard recalls most of all was the scent of watermelon and the stack of 500-euro notes Bill Haji wanted to pay with. To make change, Erhard had to run inside a kiosk. The finger. Bill Haji's hand. Bill Haji's sideburns. The most Irish thing about the man.

He fumbles in the dark of his bedroom to find the telephone. *There's been an accident. Hurry*, he says. It's like leaving a message. He gives the address, trying to alter his voice so that he sounds more Spanish. *Los perros se lo han comido*. The dogs have eaten him. The man on the other end of the line doesn't quite understand.

– Your name? May I ask who is calling?

A long silence. Erhard wants to hang up, but he can't find the off button in the dark. He runs his hand up the twisted cord until he locates it.

– Hello, the man says.

Erhard hangs up. Once again, the house is shockingly quiet. All that remains is the wind swooshing across the rocks. The new year has already come to the islands. The finger is tucked underneath his pillow like a lucky coin.

8

On Tuesday, he rises early and goes for a drive before reporting to dispatch and picking up his first fares. His first trip is always down to Alapaqa, the fisherman's village, where the seagulls scream and you can get the best coffee on the island. Aristide and his wife Miza brew it themselves, grinding it with Miza's father's old Arabic grinder, which covers the length of a desk. The sweet coffee is practically purple. The island's best. Even though he can't say that he's tried every place that offers coffee, he's probably tried most of them.

– You look chipper today, Erhard, Miza says. Erhard gives her cousin a terse hello. She's staying with Miza temporarily and enters the cafe in her bare feet. She's a motorcycle-girl with a filthy mouth. He doesn't care for that, but he likes her hair. When she's standing with her back to him, he can see it. Dark and long, all the way to her thighs. As Erhard drinks his coffee, the cousin talks about a bodybuilder called Stefano. Not a nice guy, Erhard would say if she asked, but she doesn't. She doesn't ask anything. Instead she prattles on about the bodybuilder's chicken brain and a TV he smashed and all the money he spent on some skanky bitches at a bar in Puerto. Miza cleans the cafe while listening, giving Erhard a glance. Maybe women aren't always worth it, her glance says.

Maybe men aren't, either.

There's also a shower at Miza's that he uses. It's in a small shed where the fishermen clean and dry large fish. Through the years it has become a kind of public shower for surfers, fishermen, and one particular taxi driver who doesn't have his own. On a good day there won't be any fish hanging in the room. Today a huge swordfish dangles from a hook jammed in its mouth.

9

He hauls in a meagre 120 euros. He falls into a good rhythm, with customers turning up just as quickly as he drops them off. He keeps the finger in his pocket, not daring to remove it. He's tried to slide the ring off, but it's stuck, wedged all the way to the bone. Bill Haji wasn't fat, but his finger is either swollen or so fleshy that the ring's now tight. He imagines a young Bill putting it on. When the finger has dried a bit, maybe he'll be able to pry the ring free. As long as the finger doesn't snap in two or crumble like dry clay.

After siesta he heads down to Villaverde. He parks on a quiet road behind the Aritzas' white mansion. Each year, always a few days after New Year, the Aritzas host visitors from the mainland, and their little niece Ainhoa plays Gershwin's 'Concerto in F'.

He arrives half an hour early and tunes the piano while the women drink champagne on the terrace and the men stare into the Steinway, offering commentary. Not to Erhard, but to each other. André Aritza is a friendly man in his late forties with unusually thick glasses. Ever since Erhard blurted out that he knows nothing about computers, nor has any interest in them, André Aritza has been cool to him. The man obviously earned his fortune on computers and ships and navigation. One of the nouveau riche – of which there are more and more. Odd, spineless men with young trophy wives who maintain the household for them and their children.

Today, three of those squinty-eyed inventor types are pointing into the housing at the hammers going up and down, and they refer to Erhard standing right beside them as the Piano Tuner. The brother-in-law says something about a mobile phone, how it can tune the piano. *Very, very smart*, the brother-in-law says. *Tell me, how much do you pay the Piano Tuner?* André Aritza replies: *Way too much for way too little. Then get that app*, the brother-in-law says, *it only costs 79 cents*. The men laugh. *The sad sack will be unemployed soon*, says the youngest of the inventor types. Erhard's busy with the tuning fork, his head all the way inside the housing. He hears a lot of that kind of thing. Also when he drives his cab.

He feels the finger in his pocket. Actually he can't feel it, just knows it's there. It gives him strange ideas. Like the desire to rip the strings out of this goddamn piano. Like the desire to play études with André Aritza's head mashed onto the keys. But it also makes him want to let it go. To be calm and not waste his opportunities.

Reina Aritza tries to gather the company in the dining room. There's a suite behind some closed sliding doors. The entire house smells of overcooked lobster. Erhard takes his time finishing as the party breaks up and begins drinking champagne in front of the windows, where there's a view of the bay and the water. He walks downstairs to the kitchen, washes his blackened fingers, and then heads to the entranceway. Just as he's about to close the front door, he remembers the envelope containing money that's sitting on the small worktop. That's always where he finds it. One hundred euros. He doesn't need the money. If he doesn't take the envelope he can show André Aritza that he's not doing it for the money. That he won't be subjected to commentary for chump-change. But it would just look like he forgot the money. He didn't speak up when they commented negatively about him, and they'd just think the poor, confused piano tuner has forgotten his money. Maybe they would laugh at him even more.

Hell no. He goes back upstairs and past the dining room, where he hears Reina directing the guests around the table, placing men and women. She calls for André, but there's no response. Erhard scoops the envelope off the counter and quickly peeks into the living room through the slit in the door, and he sees the niece leaning against the piano gazing out the window. André Aritza is standing a little too close to her, his mouth a little too close to her ear. He's watching her as if he expects a reaction, but one of his hands is inching up her thigh and up towards the long, silvery blouse that hangs below her waist. She doesn't seem to be enjoying herself, but she doesn't seem ashamed or surprised either. The only mitigating circumstance here is that she's not his real niece, just a good friend's daughter whom they regard as a niece. And she's not a child, she's a young woman, close to seventeen or eighteen years old. For someone like Erhard, who doesn't know anything about sex or seducing women, his advances seem neither sexy nor seductive.

Behind him Erhard hears Reina Aritza on her way down the hallway.

– Señor Jørgensen, she says, when she sees him standing there with the envelope in his hand. Thank you for your help. Happy New Year to you.

Erhard turns swiftly and pushes the living-room door open. André Aritza abruptly removes his hand from his niece and stands stiff as a butler beside her, glancing at Erhard, irritated. The niece still seems indifferent. As if he's filled her with champagne or said something to her that that preoccupies her mind. – Your beautiful wife is looking for you, Erhard says loudly.

– I see, thank you, the man says, looking away.

– The lobster is getting cold, Reina Aritza says into the living room. – Remember the champagne flutes.

– Happy New Year to you and your niece, Erhard says to André Aritza, turning his back to them and heading down the stairs. He sees a lot of this kind of thing, but still he wonders if this will be his last visit to this house. André Aritza may become even more difficult now. On the other hand it'll be a long time before he needs to tune the piano again.

He takes care of the few assignments he has. There's no reason to make a decision now. It'll be another year before he sees these people again.

He snaps on his sign and hopes to pick up a customer before driving home.

10

A man is standing at the door. Before he opens it, Erhard spies him through the tiny peephole; he counts to thirty to see if he will leave. The man, whose name is Francisco Bernal, rubs his eyes behind his sunglasses, as if he's tired or has dust in them. Thirty-one, thirty-two, thirty-three. But the man is still there, staring at the door as if it'll be thrust open at any moment. A handsome young man in his late thirties, he has a couple of kids and a wife who works at one of the hotels. Erhard opens the door.

The policeman looks at Erhard. – Hermit, he says.

– Superintendent.

– I'm not a superintendent.

– And my name's not Hermit.

Bernal grins. – OK, Jørgensen. How are you?

– Fine. You? The kids?

– The youngest one just got over measles.

Erhard nods. He's known the vice police superintendent for a few years. – Your colleague called me yesterday, Erhard says.

– We'd prefer you come to the station.

– I couldn't yesterday.

– Then come with me now.

– But you're here now. I don't understand what you guys need from me. I don't know much. I only know what I've told you.

The policeman removes his sunglasses. He looks tired. – I can drive you in and bring you back.

– Sounds like fun, but no thanks.

Bernal glances at Erhard's car. – What happened to your side mirror?

– That kind of thing happens when you drive a taxi.

– Jørgensen, I was sent here to pick you up. Stop making it difficult for me.

– Call me Señor Againsttherules.

Bernal laughs. An honest laughter. That's what Erhard likes about him. – Why didn't you say who you were? On the telephone?

– The connection was bad, Erhard says. – You know how it is out here.

– As far as I can tell, it's gotten much better with the new cables. Erhard hadn't heard anything about new cables.

– Why didn't you call back? Bernal continues.

– It was New Year's Eve, and I was tired.

– Were you tired when you discovered the body, too?

– Yes. Erhard thinks about the words which escaped from Bill Haji's eyes, but he can no longer recall them. It's not the kind of information that adds to one's credibility.

– When was the last time you saw a doctor?

– Give it a rest, Erhard says, getting out his driver's licence. Taxi drivers have to carry it on their person at all times, but he's never shown it to anyone but Bernal, who checks it every time.

Bernal looks at the date. October 2011. – You have no trouble seeing at night?

– Of course not.

– It happens sometimes. At your age.

– That's called harassment. Two other drivers are older than I am.

– Actually, that's not the case. Alberto Ramirez is sixty-eight, Luís Hernaldo Esposito is sixty-six.

– Impressive, young man. But that doesn't change the fact that I'm a good driver.

– I'm aware of that, but you're also so obstinate that I could have you arrested. All at once his face takes on a strangely serious expression. – Hermit, I have to ask you something.

He can't escape that name. A few years ago it bothered him, and he tried getting people to call him Jørgensen. But it didn't last. There's nothing more durable than a misunderstood nickname. – Let's hear it, he says.

– There's something about… about Bill Haji that we'd like to know. Bernal looks around.

– Easy now. There's no one here but us. And the goats.

– I asked Pérez-Lúñigo to wait in the car.

Erhard gazes at the police car, and only now does he notice the dark shadow sitting in the passenger's seat and grasping the handle on the car's ceiling. Lorenzo Pérez-Lúñigo is a doctor, a very average one at that, but he's also the island's only medical examiner. He's not particularly good at his job, he's just pompous and abnormally interested in corpses. An awful person. Erhard almost reported him to the police a few years back for abusing a corpse, but Bernal talked him out of it.

– What happens in a taxi stays with the cabbie, as the saying goes.

Bernal snorts. – Can we at least go inside?

Erhard enters the living room, which is also the kitchen. He leans against the kitchen table and gestures for the vice police superintendent to do the same.

– You still don't have running water, Bernal says, looking at an empty bottle of cognac on the table.

– Water is for turtles.

– You live like a turtle, too. I'm getting a little concerned.

– No need. I've done far worse.

Bernal shrugs. – On the telephone you said that the dogs had bitten his face.

– I said they'd eaten his face.

– And they sat on top of the car? The dogs. And they were biting him?

– Eating him. Yes, that's what I saw.

– And you're sure of that? It was his face?

– I saw his sideburns, I saw his hair. I saw his eyes.

– Is it possible that you were tired?

– I know what I saw.

– Could it have been his back?

– If he had eyes on his back.

The superintendent smiles. – We can't find his ring. It's a very unique ring that's worth nothing if one tried to sell it.

– Who knows what those animals might have eaten?

– We've shot everything that runs around on four legs out there. We've even shot a few dogs that weren't feral. And Lorenzo has been wallowing in dog guts up to his elbows. No ring.

– Then he's in his element. But maybe they didn't swallow it. Maybe it's lying around somewhere. Who knows where dogs like that hide?

– We would've found it then. We've searched the entire area. The problem is that everything that's been inside the dogs for more than three or four hours is so dissolved we can't tell what it is. Not the ring – we ought to be able to find that. And if the face was the last thing the dogs, um, ate, then we ought to have found it.

– When did you get there?

– We got there as fast as we could. The policeman glances down at the laminate floor, which is torn and fixed with duct tape. – They're calling it a single-vehicle accident. He says it several times, as if it suddenly amazes him.

Erhard is relieved, but afraid to show this relief to Bernal. He turns and arranges some random object on the kitchen table. – How long did it take? he says.

– The man was already dead, of course. Like you said, it was New Year's Eve.

– So what's the problem?

– His family's breathing down our necks. Love makes people unreasonable. They want something to put in the coffin. Not just rocks from Alejandro's Trail. And the ring, the sister's very focused on that.

– Don't try to mess with them. Especially Eleanor. Nothing good will come of that. He remembers the sister as she appears in a rearview mirror. She's twice the man Bill Haji was.

– That's why we're busting our asses here. A ring like that is pretty much, you know, his personality. I'd like to give the ring to his sister and tell her that he's in the coffin. Not just what's left of his shoes or his liver, which for some reason those devils never touched.

Erhard doesn't dare glance over at the shelf where the finger is lying inside a tin of Mokarabia 100 per cent Arabica coffee. – I can't help you.

Bernal peers around as if he wants to say more. His eyes rest for some time on the section of wall where the wallpaper is missing. The bare wood is visible there. Pale plywood marked by the carpenter's scribbled notes. Erhard follows him to his car. Pérez-Lúñigo seems impatient.

– If you hear that someone has found the ring, I'd like to know.

– OK, Erhard says. If he hears that someone has found the ring, he'll call immediately.

– Did I tell you that I knew a girl from Denmark once? Back when I lived in Lanzarote. She was a wild little one, impossible to tame. He climbs into the car but keeps the door open. – She went home suddenly. That's the problem with these islands. All the sensible people go home at some point.

– Don't know her, Erhard says.

11

He talks to the Boy-Man.

Aaz is probably the only one he's unable to read. Aaz may be the first person he's known who is no one and everyone at the same time. Erhard likes that about him. They drive through Tindaya.

Aaz says he should give it a chance. He says: *You deserve it, it'll happen someday.*

But Erhard isn't sure. – It's been eighteen years since the last time, Aaz. Fewer tourists are coming here. And many of them are passionate Arsenal fans who're lookin' for cheap beer and even cheaper pussy, to put it bluntly, Aaz. And the families, the families with their lazy kids who scream for McDonald's as soon as they're off the plane. It's getting longer and longer between good customers, even for me. And even longer between agreeable women.

May I recommend Liana or a couple other sisters?

– That's very kind of you, Aaz. Those girls aren't really my type, or I'm not theirs. If I'm lucky, I'll find an old, used-up, angry widow from Gornjal. The town with all the widows.

They laugh.

– Nah, who wants a rundown cab driver, Erhard says. – A labourer with a handicap and bad teeth and all that.

You also tune pianos.

– It's just a matter of time before only idiots pay for that kind of service. Pardon me, but it can all be done with modern methods, easier, better, and cheaper. For all I know the same might apply to taxis in a few years. You'll have robots driving you around.

What about you? What will you do? Who will drive me home?

– By that point I'll be dead, Aaz. By that point you'll be a grown man and will have forgotten all about me. By that point there will be a tunnel to Africa and you'll be able to drive to the Sahara and ride on electric camels.

Aaz doesn't reply, just stares at the glove compartment's latch, which can be opened with a press of the thumb.

1 2

Grown men with kites.

He turns his sign off and parks out by the Dunes and watches the kite surfers. He decides how much work he wants to do and when he wants to do it. If he wants to work all day, he can. Or if he feels like taking tomorrow off. He just goes to where he'll find customers, then drives them. That's how it feels anyway. It's not difficult; it doesn't require much from him. He just knows where the customers are. It's the same with the piano. Once he hears a few notes, he knows what he needs to work on, whether something is stuck, or whether it's the result of moisture or simply some dust or lint. In the same way, he can see the traffic or kind of feel in the air or hear the sounds from the airport or sense the busyness on the main road. And he knows where a woman is waiting with her teenage daughter on her way back to the hotel after a shopping trip, or where a group of businessmen will soon march a few feet into the road and whistle at him so they can head to the nearest strip bar, or when a surfer with sand between his toes wants to use his dollars to get to the city, his board strapped to the roof. Many of his colleagues hate him for this ability, while some are awed by him. A couple of the Catholics make the sign of the cross when he comes to the auto workshop. Dispatch rarely gives him jobs, because they know he already has plenty of customers. Once in a while there's a young driver who wants to know how he does it. Maybe he sees Erhard sitting at the Hotel Phenix bar, and the young man approaches him wanting to know everything, while his comrades stand there calling out in the background. C'mon now, this guy's a legend, he shouts back at them, he's going to tell me all his secrets. But Erhard doesn't tell him his secrets, it's not something he can explain. All he can say is, Keep your eye on the traffic, think about the people. Where would you want to go if the weather was so and so? Is it a heavy-travel day? And so on. Good advice, but no doubt unusable. The truth, of course, is that he doesn't even know himself how he does it. It's like music, he tries to tell the young drivers, who usually don't know anything about music.

The younger drivers want to learn, but the middle-aged drivers are bitter. They'll never do anything but drive taxis, and they'll never live well doing so. They see Erhard as a parasite, an *extranjero*, who not only takes their customers, but also acts as if he's better than them. He lives alone out in Majanicho, he doesn't talk to the other drivers, and he just sits in his old Mercedes reading books if he's not out stealing the only customers of the day. That's what they think, and some of them even tell him that. And they're right too. Also about the books. In the beginning, reading was something he did to relax and to show the other drivers that he wasn't busy finding new customers. He started driving past potential rides and parking at the back of the queue, doing everything he could to remain there all day with a good book.

In the boot he keeps a box stuffed with paperbacks, which he rummages through and selects from. He likes looking at the covers and touching the raised letters the titles are printed with. Or he riffles through a book and inspects it to see how many dog-ears it has. If there are many, it's good. He buys books, sometimes by the boxful, from a friend in Puerto. She owns a secondhand shop. A few times each month, if he's been out to the airport, he drives past Solilla's and purchases books and maybe some clothes. There's nothing wrong with the books. The clothes smell a little; he washes them before he wears them. Hangs them on the line behind the house and leaves them for a week. Then the smell goes away, and is replaced by the scent of the island's piquant soil. He can stay there all day reading. There should be something left for the others. They all have children and wives, they have to provide for others, and they don't have the luxury of sitting around reading. He doesn't have the same issue. The more he earns, the more he sends to Annette. Every month he transfers most of his salary to her account. Not with a friendly message, but electronically and soullessly. He doesn't deserve anything else, and he doesn't need anything special. He can live on coffee and tinned food that he bought many years ago and which he warms up and eats directly from the tin. It doesn't bother him. Sometimes he goes to the island's finest restaurants and takes a long time choosing expensive wine and cutting a good cigar. That doesn't bother him, either. During the summer he sits in his car and reads with the window open, and during the winter he keeps a reclining chair that he arranges on the sidewalk beside the car. The other drivers, sweating inside their vehicles, hate this.

When one drives through the Dunes and slowly past the quiet hotels with their gardeners and their eager water hoses, one can see the kites out over the water. Back and forth like birds hunting. He parks the car on the road and crosses the sandbanks to the water. Out here the sun is fierce. It feels that way, anyway. The beach stretches endlessly, the sea like a giant air balloon that's suddenly lying at the end of the beige dune. There are no families walking on the beach today. The wind is too strong; the sand is drifting and stinging.

Next to a container filled with surfing equipment, there's a little shop on a couple of pallets. It offers ice cream, music, and shelter from the wind and sun. Erhard drinks a San Miguel while watching the figures being dragged around by ropes. Grown men with kites. Sometimes they're perfectly exposed to the wind, other times it's exactly the opposite. Frustratingly, he hears every sound emerging from the little shop. Every cough or scrape of the coffee machine. The sound of possibility. The woman in the shop is probably around twenty years younger than him, but worn down. She's The Monk, the diligent, silent, labouring, and all-too-affectionate type. The divorced mother of four who had to get a job after her husband bolted. As a potential lover, on the one hand, she's experienced and highly service-minded; but on the other hand, she's scary. She stoops forward to watch the kites through the small window.

– Is that one of your sons out there? he guesses.

She looks at him, surprised. – Do you know my Robbi?

– I know most everyone a little, he says.

13

At 4 p.m. he drives out to the Oleana Cemetery and parks on the opposite side of the road. He watches them walking up the street, a small procession with many flowers. Typically, the wealthiest families like to bear their dead as far as possible, while the poor spend great sums of money on expensive hearses. The Haji family balances the coffin through the cemetery gate and down one of the paths. It doesn't look easy. Maybe they put a few rocks in the coffin after all. Eleanor's at the back of the throng, flanked on one side by a tall young woman whose hair is falling in her eyes and, on the other, by an elderly woman – probably an aunt. The policeman is across the street; he's wearing a nice set of clothes but seems even more tired than the last time Erhard saw him. He nods at Erhard and merges into the procession.

– It's God's punishment, he hears a woman say. She's sitting on a balcony a few storeys above him. – The island's too small for a poof like that.

14

At night he lies in bed with one eye open, staring at the boxlike telephone and its knotted-up cord. In that stage right before sleep, he imagines himself standing and lifting the receiver. In the morning he eyes the telephone while eating his breakfast, and again he imagines it ringing. He considers placing the call himself. It's now been eighteen years. But he can't do it and he hustles to his car.

When he goes to the supermarket, he notices the coin-operated telephone in the corner, or, if he passes an electronics store – Corralejo has plenty of these – he spots, at a distance, an answering machine inside a faded box. Ever since Annette called to curse him out he's been this way at the start of a new year. He was unable to respond to her; she just called to vent. This was in 1997, immediately after he began sending money home. She couldn't take it. Couldn't stomach his goddamn money. She wanted nothing from him. Nothing. You're dead, you're already dead. Then she hung up. The following year she called back. This time she didn't say anything, just cried for twenty seconds. She hasn't called since. But this year marks the eighteenth year since he left her. He's expecting a call. Practically wishes for it. Even if she's just crying into the telephone. But there's nothing. Maybe she's forgotten his number, or him. Maybe she's remarried. There's nothing.

He picks up every customer that comes his way, he works all afternoon and into the evening, and he works until he's so tired that his eyelids stick together. Afterward he heads to the harbour, indiscriminately buys a bottle of wine, and sits on the pier, alone, watching young people leap into the water until the last rays of sunlight vanish from the rocky island of Isla de Lobos and the sea turns black. He staggers to the intercom at Calle el Muelle to pay Raúl and Beatriz a visit.

– Come on up, old man, Raúl says, always ready.

They open the door. She's wearing a sheer yellow summer dress that shows off her long, tanned legs, and he's wearing a shirt unbuttoned at the top. They welcome him like he's their father: pleasant and receptive and happy. They've just mixed some mojitos. The three of them head up to the rooftop terrace.

Beatriz sits on Raúl's lap, and they kiss. Erhard tells them about the kite surfers and Bill Haji and Mónica, the Boy-Man's mother. Raúl says that Erhard's the most unbelievable man he knows, and Beatriz – after mixing more drinks for them and pouring wine for herself – passes next to him, wafting her sublime perfume as she runs her hand and its long fingernails through Erhard's thin hair.

He pretends, as always, that he doesn't care for this, but on some nights it's just such a hand that he fantasizes about. The nails like sharpened pencils drawing long strokes through his hair. It would be a different matter, obviously, if they really were his children, if Raúl was his son and Beatriz his daughter-in-law. But he knows they are not, and his dick knows they are not, and that's all there is to it. He doesn't even feel badly for Raúl. Raúl is Raúl, a real cock of the walk if ever there was one. Raúl may be his father's son and Beatriz's boyfriend, but no one can be sure of anything. He wants it all, but he doesn't want to be tied down. He has it all, but he doesn't want to own anything. Defiant and charming and always on his way into or out of a drunken stupor. In some strange way he was Erhard's most attentive pupil. Erhard's only pupil. At the beginning he was a foolish young man with nothing more than cheap entertainment and American porn mags on the brain, with a pronounced need to avoid additional problems with teachers, police, neighbours, angry young women – and his father. Erhard had to teach him to see the bigger picture, to get past what his father said, to get past the girls' glances. To build a layer of contemplation and preparation in between his spontaneous eruptions and his clumsy attempts at independence. Patience, in short. Some things had rubbed off on the boy, who had since become a man. And rubbed off so well that Raúl has become calmer, less confused, less frightening, happier.

Even his father has noticed his development. Still, he doesn't believe Erhard's friendship was the cause of this transformation so much as the many years Raúl had spent being grounded, his ears boxed, his bank account regulated.

The result is a longstanding friendship, Erhard's deepest and most alcoholic. Perhaps his only friendship. It's a relationship in which Erhard is valued and has a voice, where he feels admired and accepted as the person he has been for the past two decades.

But it's a wrongheaded, bizarre friendship according to TaxiVentura's managing director Pauli Barouki. Because Raúl is on their competitor's board of directors. Rumour has it that there's a shady side to their friendship. They say that Erhard works for Raúl, that he gives him free rides or takes care of Raúl's problems. But by and large they're not even involved in each other's lives. They talk about food, alcohol, arguments at the Yellow Rooster. Erhard tells stories about people from Corralejo or Raúl talks about the rich pigs, as he calls them, and their impossible love-lives, while Beatriz laughs. Neither of them want to know what the other does in his spare time. Raúl doesn't want to hear about life as a taxi driver; every time Erhard complains about dispatch or the new rules for drivers, Raúl waves his hand the way he learned from his father. Nor does he want to hear about the books Erhard reads. And Erhard doesn't ask Raúl about Taxinaria or where all of Raúl's money comes from. He figures it's his father's, even though Raúl repeatedly says that he wants to earn his own money. Only that one time, with Federico Molino and the suitcase, did Erhard go too far for Raúl. It was illegal, but he did it for the right reasons. That's what Erhard now thinks about the episode they haven't spoken of since.

They gaze across the city and the beach. The water looks like marzipan.

Raúl shows him a wound on his knuckle. – Had a little disagreement with a seaman down at the Yellow Rooster, he chuckles. – He said things about my girlfriend.

Beatriz turns away, irritated. – I didn't ask you to do that, she says.

– Was there no another way? Erhard asks, though he believes the three or four louts who fight in Corralejo usually deserve a beating. Erhard knows them; he's driven them all home many times.

– You don't know him, Raúl says. – But he deserved it. He's been bothering me for months, years. But fuck that. No need to discuss it, right Bea? Salud.

He drinks.

They discuss the wine and the sunset and later the sunrise and the new boats anchored in the marina and Petra and her daughter, whom Raúl thinks is perfect for Erhard. To Raúl, it's funny that Erhard has never really seen the girl, only her picture hanging on the wall of the salon.

– What is it with you and these women? Beatriz asks.

Raúl turns serious. – Erhard doesn't talk about his past.

– There can be many reasons for that, Beatriz says.

– Watch it there, Bea, Raúl says.

– Are you afraid of love? she goes on.

Raúl lifts Erhard's left hand so she can see the missing finger.

– Love has many faces, but only *one* asshole, Erhard says.

– Poetic, Raúl says. – Let's just say: Being married is dangerous.

Beatriz shoves him. – You think it's funny? Why do you talk about it like that?

– Tell Beatriz about the hairdresser's daughter, Raúl says. – He's almost met her five or six times, but he's backed out every time.

It was more like four times. Including New Year's Eve. But he doesn't want to mention that.

– It was last year, I think. Or the year before that. The year when it rained the entire month of January.

– The year before, Beatriz says.

– I park the car, taking a break between jobs, and go down the street where Petra and her husband live. The daughter lived with them back then. The son goes to boarding school. I hear Petra through the balcony door. Have you heard Petra's distinct Yorkshire accent?

Shaking her head, Beatriz laughs.

– And then her husband, he's half-Moroccan, owns some electronic shops down in Puerto, among other things. They're arguing about something involving their son's school accommodation. I'm standing quietly in the doorway across the street, looking up, trying to catch a glimpse of the daughter Raúl keeps teasing me about. I probably stood there for an hour. Staring, following every little shadow moving across the ceiling, all the while figuring I'd see her on the balcony or in the big window next to it.

– You're some kind of Hamlet, Raúl grins. Beatriz shushes him.

– You mean Romeo, Erhard says, and continues: – But I'm so preoccupied that I don't even notice a person walking right past me, trailed by this sweet honeylike aroma. She crosses the street and enters the building. It's not until the door of the flat closes and the argument abruptly stops and Petra says, *Luisa, darling,* her voice inflected by wine, that I realize the daughter had just walked past.

– What then? What then? Beatriz sits up.

– Nothing, Raúl says. – That's what makes it so beautiful. It's Erhard. Not a goddamn thing happens! Not a goddamn thing.

– What? Beatriz says. – You didn't go up?

– I'm not meant to see her.

– What? Beatriz shouts excitedly. – Tell me you don't believe that?

– I know a sign when I see one.

– But how do you know it's a sign?

– I can see it. The pattern.

– Salud for Louisa, Raúl says.

– You can't possibly believe that, Beatriz says, and drinks.

Erhard hopes, deep down, that Luisa is a slightly older version of Beatriz, with lips like Kirsten – a woman he shagged in the backroom of a bar in Horsens, Denmark, several decades ago – and an ass like one of the beach volleyball girls he'd recently driven down to Sport Fuerte. But the truth is she's probably a rather average and sweet girl in a floral dress, with pale English breasts like her mother.

– Salud. Erhard sucks the rum and sugar from his glass and picks the mint leaves from his teeth.

– It'll become an obsession, Beatriz says. – In ten years you won't be able to think about anything else, and you'll talk non-stop about her. Just you wait and see. Like those fishermen who finally, at long last, hook some monster fish only to lose it.

– She's not that great, Raúl says.

Beatriz gives him an elbow.

– I've survived without a girlfriend, I think I'll survive a little while longer.

– Seventeen years, Raúl says. – That's because you live in a cave.

– It's not as simple as you make it sound.

– I know that. But what if you only sent half of what you earned home, or a quarter? Then you'd have the money to do something else.

Erhard doesn't want to discuss it.

– The ex-husband in Paradise, Raúl says to Bea. – He sends his entire fortune back to Denmark.

– That's nice of you, Beatriz says.

– It costs money to save yourself. Isn't that what you told me once? Wise words, Old Man. Raúl laughs. – My point is, living out there you don't exactly have a dynamic social life. You need to go out and meet people.

– If I'm meant to meet someone, I will.

– Please stop with all that karma bullshit. If you're so tired of the nickname Hermit, then come out of your turtle shell a bit more.

– His shield?

– Yeah, that too. Meet someone new, meet some ladies.

– Hey, I want to meet new people too. Why don't we ever meet new people?

– We do. On the boat, et cetera.

– Yeah, old men with old money. I mean interesting people, like in Barcelona.

Raúl thinks it's rubbish, that she's just pissed. She has nothing to complain about, he says, his hand slipping under her dress. Erhard sits quietly, staring ahead. His eyes wander across the roofs which appear to be shimmying down and poking their antennae in the water. To turn it all in the right direction, he closes his eyes. When he opens them again, the terrace is empty. The chairs are empty, and everything's tidied up. He's lying underneath a thin blanket, and a small candle burns. The sky is heavy, blue, lifeless. The city light conceals the stars.

15

He picks up a woman. From the harbour in Corralejo, where she stood with her hair poufed out in every direction following the trip on the ferry, to Sport Fuerte, where she can't find the address of the apartment in which she'll live. She's probably close to sixty. Her fingers are long and already brown and ringless. On top of that she's Swedish, and she's confused and nervous about something. They can almost communicate in their native languages, even though he's forgotten much of the Swedish he once knew. She asks him about the necklace that's dangling from the rearview mirror: a small, verdigrised pendant made of silver. It's so dark out here, he says, and she laughs at him. In a wonderful way. She says it's been an interesting ride. Slowly and methodically she drops the money into his hand, and he feels her fingers. That's the kind of thing he misses.

But it won't lead anywhere. He helps her retrieve her suitcase and she squats, puzzled, to rummage through her bag. She doesn't give him her number – as he'd momentarily hoped she would – and she leaves his business card on the backseat along with a few papers from the ferry. He takes this as a sign. What else could it be? He's too old and too ugly.

During siesta, he drives home and eats breakfast.

He lifts the finger out of his pocket. It's light-brown and crooked; his own fingers are pink, except for his nails – they're black. One's nails turn black here on the island. The black dust that hangs in the air above settles onto everything and creeps underneath fingernails. He scrubs them with his shoe brush and washes them in the garden. Just not Bill Haji's.

He uses duct tape to attach the finger to his left hand. The silver-coloured tape covers the joint, so it almost appears as though it's a complete hand. He stands before the mirror admiring himself – hand dangling at his side, hand to his chin, arms crossed, thumb hooked in his trouser pocket. It's a minor change, but it suits him. A new little finger. He almost feels normal, and can't help but keep it on when he leaves.

A couple is standing near the roundabout outside of Puerto. He drives them to a bike-rental shop in Via Panitta. He changes gears and drums the wheel rhythmically. Neither one of them says a word to him. Neither one of them stares at his hand. They just talk about, well, something or other. Then he drives to La Oliva: A man and his dog are heading to the veterinarian. The dog, an old sheepdog, sits stock-still gasping for breath. Erhard's afraid the dog will sniff the finger, but it seems more interested in the hollow space under the hand brake, where there's a balled-up napkin from lunch. The man tells him the animal's going to be put to sleep. There's nothing that can be done, he says repeatedly. One hour later he drives them home. The dog continues to gasp for breath, but the owner is happy. We made it, he whispers to the dog.

16

Then comes the year's first rainy day. Whenever it rains, he likes to be inside drinking Lumumbas. They don't know jack about that down here, so if he's at a hotel – he likes being at a calm, air-conditioned hotel with a bar, where the bartender stands quietly between fags – so if he's at a hotel, he has to tell the bartender how to make a Lumumba. At the Hotel Phenix down on the beach in Corralejo, he once went behind the bar to show the new bartender how to heat up the cocoa with the same nozzle used to foam milk for a *café au lait.*

He's at home today, where he keeps cocoa powder, powdered milk, and cognac on the top shelf of his pantry. The rainy season usually comes in the spring, as far as he's concerned, but there are many different opinions on the matter here. He whips up cream with a fork attached to the power drill. And then he sits, shirtless, in his chair under the tarpaulin, gazing up at the mountain. Into the rain.

He put the finger in a glass of formaldehyde. The glass makes the finger appear elongated and thin. A pharaoh's finger. A finger to make the heavens thunder. Up close, it's just brown and twisted. The ring's loose now; he can spin it, but it still won't come off. It has begun to irritate him. If he can pull the ring off, the finger will seem more like his own. But he can't let it dry out. Then it'll break. Or fall apart. Like a crushed cinnamon stick.

The drops fall so thickly it sounds as if the earth itself is grumbling. As long as it keeps raining, he can't hear anything else. He thinks about the corrugated plastic sheet above the toilet and the kitchen, which makes everything sound much worse. For seventeen years he's considered getting rid of it. It doesn't match the house, and it sticks out like a sore thumb. But he doesn't care about that, actually. It only irritates him when it bangs in the southerly wind and he lies in bed all morning cursing the wind or the roof or himself, because he didn't replace that old plastic sheet years ago or, at the very least, lay some rocks on top of it so that it doesn't bang as much. But when he's outside sitting in front of his house and staring up at the mountain and the silver-coloured sky, he doesn't think about anything.

When someone says, *Isn't it lovely to live in a place where it never rains?*, he says, Yes. But the truth is, those four or five rainy days a year are what he loves most. They break up the monotony of sunshine; they're like instant holidays pouring from the heavens. The entire island comes to a standstill. Everyone looks up or runs around finding the things they've left lying in the driveway, in the window, or on the terrace. And he doesn't drive his taxi on those days. There are lots of customers when it rains, but he doesn't want to waste a good rainy day. He parks the cab and sits under his tarpaulin drinking Lumumbas, until the thermos full of warm cocoa is empty. Then he falls asleep. If he's at a hotel and gets drunk, he loans a room. More often than not, he knows the front-desk clerk. He throws himself fully dressed onto the bed. He doesn't get hangovers from Lumumbas. It's the good thing about Lumumbas.

17

A rapping. The roof's banging in the wind. Or maybe it's thunder.

It's a knock at his door.

– Erhard. A voice penetrates the hard, steady rain. There is also thunder, but someone's knocking on his door. Softly. He throws the blanket aside, stands up, and walks around the house. He doesn't care about the rain. He likes to feel the cold droplets on his skin; they lead him farther and farther out of his ruminations or his sleep, into which he'd fallen. He recognizes the convertible and the figure waiting inside the car, behind the misted glass. Raúl's pounding on the door. – I know you're in there. Put down that Lumumba and come out.

– *Dios mío*, boy, you're going to blow my house down.

Raúl turns the doorknob, then holds up his hand as a shield against the rain to see Erhard. He laughs and embraces Erhard, wetting them both. – Come, he says, and tugs him to his car. – We're going on a little excursion.

Erhard has grown accustomed to this kind of thing from Raúl, so he just follows him. – Just a moment, he says. – I'm coming. He walks around the house and grabs the glass with the finger. He lays it on the top shelf between tins of food and cocoa. He studies the finger for a moment. Then, with a pair of tongs, he removes it from the glass and carefully places it inside a freezer bag before cinching the bag in a knot. It fits in the pocket of his Khaki shorts without sticking out. No one would be able to tell what it is.

Beatriz crawls into the backseat, and Erhard's nudged into the front seat. That's how Raúl is. Beatriz hugs him from the backseat, and he can feel her curls against his neck. Either she always smells different or she never uses the same perfume. Tonight it's vanilla and salt. Raúl backs the car all the way down to Alejandro's Trail and spins around, spattering mud. The music is loud. It's noise. Not really a song.

– It was Bea's idea, Raúl shouts.

– I just said the lightning was beautiful.

– And then you said Cotillo.

– You can see them there.

– That's what I'm saying.

– But why Cotillo? Erhard asks. The windscreen wipers whip back and forth at full speed. – Why not up here?

– Nothing's too good for my friends. We're heading down to the breakers to feel the sizzle of the water. Raúl sounds as if he ordered the lightning himself.

He doesn't drive recklessly, but much faster than Erhard appreciates. All in all, Erhard has grown so used to driving that he doesn't like being a passenger. He glances over his left shoulder each time they turn, and he reaches for the gear stick when they drive up a hill. The road glistens, and the landscape is utterly strange, as though slathered in black plastic. It's the rain – it's everywhere. It doesn't go anywhere. The ground is too dry to absorb it.

– You'd like to go down to the real beach, Raúl says to Beatriz. They splash through Cotillo, water spraying against the houses next to the road. It's easy to sense Raúl's joy. Beatriz likes it too, maybe she's pissed, Erhard thinks. Maybe Raúl's pissed, too. It's possible.

They leave the city behind, heading towards the car park and the flat terrain just before the slope down to the beach. The car park is filled with cars, not in orderly rows like in a drive-in theatre, but randomly chaotic. There are probably twenty or thirty of them, and even a couple of police vehicles. Behind the cars the sky is a grey canvas that lights up bright green every time the lightning strikes.

– Here we are, Raúl shouts. He has opened his door and is standing in the rain, his jacket over his head.

– Can't we see it from in here? Beatriz asks.

Raúl doesn't hear her. He slams his door and runs around the car to open hers. She doesn't repeat the question, but follows him when he offers his hand. Erhard climbs out too. He's quickly soaked, but it doesn't bother him.

They run towards the slope. Almost as though they're searching for the queue to that evening's entertainment. It's not there. Not on the slope in any case. They continue to the water, stumbling down the slope, Beatriz shrieking in excitement. Lightning cracks unremittingly across the sky. The sound is far away, almost buried by the rain. Each bolt forms a unique thread from the base to the top, or vice versa. And in the midst of everything, the sea foams and roars.

Then they spot the throng standing near the beach. Dark silhouettes and a few people with torches or lamps draw attention to the scene. Messages are shouted, and some kind of machine whirls around and around.

– What the hell? Raúl says. – What's happened?

– It's probably some tourist group, Beatriz calls out.

– Not in this rain, Raúl laughs.

They start towards the crowd, which isn't as dense as they'd first thought; it has formed a semi-circle around others. A blue light blinks and a man shouts, Get back, get back. But no one moves. The waves lash at their feet, and some of the people are standing up to their ankles in the foamy water.

– There's a car, Beatriz shouts. – What's it doing here?

18

A policeman is trying to stretch barricade tape around the car. It's a black Volkswagen Passat. A few tall lamps light the vehicle, but the generator can't keep up and the lamps alternately flicker off and on, then fall over in the soft sand.

They pause amid the throng and try to find out what happened. It looks like a terrible parking job or a stolen, abandoned vehicle. Erhard has seen both kinds many times.

– Let's get away from here and watch the lightning, Beatriz suggests.

– We can't do that, Raúl says. – Something awful has happened.

– That's what I mean. We can't stand here watching. Someone was hurt.

A person in front of them says, – Someone drove over the edge and rolled into the sea.

– How do you roll all the way down here? You'd have to want to, another says. – Is it a suicide?

– Who was here first? a policeman tries. A few people raise their hands, but lower them when they see the others.

– Who called us? I can't recall who I spoke to earlier.

A man steps forward. Their conversation is silenced by the rain. The man points up the slope. The policeman tries to write something down in a notebook, but there's so much rain that he's forced to give up. His pen doesn't work, either.

– It must've been stolen. There are no licence plates, someone says. An amateur surfer in a colourful wetsuit.

– They keep looking at something in the backseat, says the other.

– Step back, damn it, step back.

Erhard recognizes the policeman. It's Bernal. He's soaked, his clothes practically glistening underneath an umbrella, and he's shining a torch into the backseat and snapping photographs with a big camera.

– Hassib, Bernal shouts. – I need some help here.

No one comes to his aid. His voice, enveloped in noise, disappears. The other officers can't hear him. One is busy trying to get the lamps to stand upright, another is talking to a paramedic with a bag tucked under his arm. A crane is backing into place on the clifftop, ready to hoist the vehicle up. In the meantime, rain continues to fall.

– Can't we go? I don't feel too well, Beatriz whispers.

– Come here. Raúl pulls her close to him.

– Anyone from the media here? an officer asks.

No one says a word.

– Not yet, boss, the officer shouts at Bernal.

Bernal photographs something on the backseat. They look like papers, newspaper cuttings. A colleague arrives and helps him spread the papers on the seat. They discuss them and shuffle them around as he snaps pictures. Lightning winks across the black sky, as if responding to the camera's flash.

An acrid stench emerges from the car in gusts. At first Erhard thinks it's coming from the bag. From the finger. He feels for it in his pocket, wondering whether the knot's come undone. Maybe running down the slope punctured the plastic. The Lumumba has been flushed out of him. But the bag is right where he put it. At the same time, the smell from the car is more hostile and insistent. Like something that should have been stored away long ago.

– It must be an accident. Did it just happen? Raúl asks the amateur surfer.

– I think the car's been here for a day. Then someone realized that it wasn't locked, he says.

The man who'd just spoken to the officer interjects. – I could tell there was something inside the box on the backseat. Something was sticking up.

– What was sticking up? says the amateur surfer's friend, who is the only one wearing a rain jacket.

– It looked like… He doesn't say anything more.

The vice police superintendent walks past them, an irritated expression on his face. For a moment Bernal and Erhard look at each other. Bernal stops abruptly and returns. Raúl takes a step back. Clearly he's not interested in speaking to a policeman.

– Hermit, Bernal says. – Do you have a nose for drama, or what?

Erhard doesn't know what to say. He wants to tell him that he wasn't seeking out another accident.

– What's happened here? the surfer asks.

Bernal doesn't respond. – I want names of everyone who saw anything. If you're just here for the show and curious, then you need to leave this place, he says, staring at Erhard.

– We came to watch the lightning, Beatriz says.

Bernal just looks at her. – Then watch the lightning, Señorita. He walks up the slope, vanishing within the rain, which has become a kind of dense, black cloud.

– Can we go now? Beatriz whispers.

Raúl stares at the vehicle for a long time. – Of course, my angel.

The water has already retreated a few yards, the waves lashing like savage animals.

– You owe me a Lumumba, Erhard says to Raúl while watching Beatriz, whose dress is so drenched that it clings to her.

19

Once upon a time, the Boy-Man took the bus each Wednesday. It took him most of the morning to get to Tuineje, and most of the afternoon to get back to the Santa Marisa Home. A few times, he'd gotten off too early, in some tiny village, and had to be picked up by the police after he started running up and down the street hitting himself in the head. He's at least 6'7, maybe 6'9, but his face resembles that of a 7-year-old boy, so do his gangly limbs and clothes. His eyes dart around restlessly. As though he's trying to understand the world by reading it as a code or musical notes. In the taxi, he loves to lay his forehead against the window and watch the landscape. To follow the uninterrupted line.

Every Wednesday at 10.15 a.m., including today, he stands on the pavement in front of the broad gate, waiting, his backpack all the way up to his shoulders. Aaz hasn't uttered a word in fourteen years. One day he simply stopped speaking. He can speak, but as Mónica has explained, he doesn't. During the first few Wednesdays, Erhard hoped that he would say something. Each time they spent more than two hours together – one hour out and one hour back. Erhard had hoped such proximity would open up the Boy-Man. That he would show Erhard trust. It became a game, a challenge, to get the boy to say something. Erhard could make him smile, he could make him turn his head. Nevertheless, Erhard was defeated every Wednesday. Finally, Erhard grew so irritated that he asked Mónica to find a new driver. He could no longer take it. The problem was that none of the other drivers wished to drive the Boy-Man. Aaz would have to take the bus again.

Mónica offered to pay Erhard double to continue. You don't need to like him. Just pretend, she'd said. Erhard gave it half a year. He didn't want her money.

And then something happened.

Erhard heard Aaz speak.

They arrive at their destination. He follows Aaz inside. Mónica clutches the boy's large hand. They sit at the piano. It's one of the things they have in common. Aaz loves music. Erhard watches them cuddle like birds. Every other month, though not today, he tunes the piano. Today he just glances around.

It's not an unhappy home like his own, even though Mónica is the same age and, like him, alone. There are fresh flowers, a fish tank, and ladies' magazines in a rack beside the sofa, a small chest of drawers with madonnas, and an entire wall of framed portraits showing a little girl in black-and-white ballerina skirts, men in military uniforms out near Calderon Hondo, and two young women on a Vespa in front of an office building. Probably twenty photographs in all. All of them black and white, beautiful, sad. A life passed by. There's not a single image of her son. Erhard looks around. Not even on the shelf above the TV, or on the chest of drawers beside the madonnas. She conceals the most important parts of her life, just as he does, so she doesn't have to move forward. Mónica is cool and regal, but not snooty; she's simply elegant with what she has. The little spoon in the sugar bowl and the flowers that match the curtains.

2 0

– What do you want? he says, without lifting his eyes from his book on the table or laying his cup down on the saucer. It's Friday morning, and the three men in shirts are watching Erhard drink his coffee. One is vice police superintendent Bernal.

Bernal slips a sheet of paper on top of Erhard's book. It's a newspaper cutting and impossible to tell its origins; not many of the words are legible, the ink is smudged and the paper worn. Still, Erhard spots the words 'pengepungen' and 'bankpakke'. Strange words that he doesn't instantly recognize.

– What does it say? Bernal asks. – Is that Danish?

– I think so. He would need the rest of the article, which is missing, to understand it, but it appears to be Danish. – Where's it from? he asks, fearing for some reason that it has something to do with Raúl.

– That's not something you need to concern yourself with, says Bernal's colleague, a small man with narrow eyes and an unkempt moustache. He glances around the cafe, where there is only one other person, a dishevelled young man with combed-back hair and screwed-up eyes who seems to have partied all night.

– We need someone who understands Danish.

– So find a tourist guide. There are plenty of those.

– Not as many as there once were. Come on, Jørgensen.

– Tell me what this is all about, then I might help out.

– You owe me a favour after the last time. I could've hauled you off to the station.

– Tell me what this is about, Erhard says, noticing that Bernal suddenly seems more tired-looking. Maybe he's not sleeping enough, maybe he drinks, maybe his kid still has measles.

– Forget him, Bernal, the little man says. He's the resolute type who'd rather arm-wrestle than offer a hand. – The foreigner can't help us. He has too many bad memories, he adds, swiftly downing his espresso, eager to go.

Apparently Bernal had told him about Erhard before they arrived at the cafe. About the case with Federico Molino, whose suitcase was found out near Lajares. With his passport and socks and hair wax and tube of lubricant, which the police so smoothly managed to include in court. They ought to have been happy for Erhard's testimony. But they always seemed to think he knew more than he was telling them. A few officers were bitter. Bernal was the only one who understood that Erhard cultivated his relations to others on the island. He told the truth, but he didn't tell everything. He didn't name Raúl Palabras or the former regional president, Emeraldo or Suárez. It's been more than eight years now. – No thanks, unless you want to arrest me, Erhard says.

Bernal looks at him as if he hopes he'll change his mind. – Say hello to young Palabras, he says.

The two men leave.

The cafe owner is standing stiffly behind the bar, observing them in the wall mirror. He probably doesn't have a licence to sell beer. Many of the city's cafes don't. Then he glances up and calls out to the young man at the back of the cafe. – Goddamn it, Pesce, don't put your greasy hair on my table. Go home and get to bed.

When Erhard walks to his car – parked at the end of the queue on High Street – he sees the officers standing on the corner near Paseo Atlántico. He climbs in his car and continues reading Stendahl's *The Red and the Black*. It's an unwieldy book, strangely incoherent.

He checks the mirrors. No one's around. He pulls the bag from his pocket, removes the finger, and tries prying off the ring. But it doesn't budge. The finger is like a stick marinated in oil; he puts it in the empty slot next to his own ring finger. It's too big, and it's the wrong hand, but it resembles a little finger. The hand looks like a hand again. With a finger where it's supposed to be. He packs it away again. Deep down in his pocket.

He spots the officers saying their goodbyes to one another. Then Bernal saunters over to his taxi. He climbs in.

– Puerto, he says.

Erhard looks at him. – And since we're heading that way anyway, you'll ask me to come to the station?

– Maybe, Bernal says.

– It's not my turn. You see the queue ahead of me?

– Just drive.

Erhard exits the queue, and one of the drivers from Taxinaria shouts at him. Luís. He's always shouting. Big mouth with no teeth. They drive up the high street, across the city, and out onto FV-1. Neither says a word.

– Does this have anything to do with Bill Haji? Erhard asks. – I've told you everything I know.

The policeman grins. – That case is closed. It's history. His sister wasn't happy, to put it mildly.

– And it doesn't have anything to do with the Palabras family?

– Not at all. One of Bernal's boots, crossed over his knee, bounces to the music emerging from an old John Coltrane tape that Erhard's had for more than twenty years. – You were out at Cotillo yourself recently. Haven't you heard the news?

Erhard hasn't read the newspaper for several days. He shakes his head.

– Don't you do anything besides read? Haven't you listened to the news on the radio?

– Not really.

– The short, and true, story is that the car was abandoned out near Cotillo. We don't know why. It ought to have been in Lisbon, but oops, it's here now. Someone stole it, then shipped it here. We don't know who drove it. Since it was standing in water above the bonnet, the motor is dead now of course. The only interesting lead is a newspaper ripped into tatters.

– So what do you want from me?

– You're going to examine the fragments we've got and tell me what they say. It's probably nothing. Maybe they're just pieces of a newspaper, meaningless. Right now I'm trying to understand what happened. Between you and me, I'm not getting a whole lot of support from my bosses on this one. And I'm going a little rogue with this newspaper stuff.

They reach the first roundabout leading out of the city. The sun is stuck between two clouds, like an eye that's been punched.

– Tell me again why you were out on the beach the other day? Bernal asks.

– My friends wanted to watch the lightning.

– Your friends? Raúl Palabras and his girlfriend?

– Yes.

Bernal stares at Erhard, while Erhard gazes ahead at the traffic.

– I haven't read a Danish newspaper in years, Erhard says.

– Just look at the fragments and tell us what they say. That's all I ask.

Both the police and the island's inhabitants call police headquarters in Puerto 'the Palace', because it's located in the ruins of a palace built for the Spanish king at the turn of the twentieth century. Apart from the impressive outer walls and beautiful arches between some smooth columns, however, not much of the royal grandeur remains. The offices, where six or seven men sit sweating behind their computers, resemble that of some building in a sleepy 1960s Copenhagen suburb.

On the way in they pass some metal detectors. Erhard is afraid they'll body-search him and find the bag with the finger in his pocket, but he ends up just following Bernal down the hallway and into a room that resembles a warehouse or a garage. Bernal closes the door behind them and rummages around on a large shelf; he returns with a big, light-brown box, then slips on rubber gloves.

– Shouldn't I wear those too?

– It doesn't matter, Bernal says, glancing momentarily at Erhard's missing finger. He begins to gather the fragments of newspaper from the box. – The bastards left a little surprise for us on the backseat.

– The bastards, Erhard says. He recognizes the box as the one found on the backseat. Even though it was night time and the only light came from a teetering police lamp.

– We don't know how the pieces connect, whether they connect at all, or even if it's worth it for us to sit here putting the puzzle together. Can you read any of it?

Erhard studies the fragments. There are photos, words, some colours. – They must've gotten wet. The sheets are stuck together.

– Yes, Bernal says bitterly. – That's the problem. We can't tell if it's just a newspaper, or if there's a message in it somewhere.

– So what am I supposed to do?

– Read the headlines, the ones in bold. Can you decipher any of that? This one, for example. He points at a large section with a headline and a subhead. It's very strange seeing so much Danish text gathered in one place. – What's it say?

– 'More homeless will die in Copenhagen if the winter is as hard as last year's. A man froze to death.'

– What does that mean?

– I don't know. That it's tough being homeless in a cold country?

Bernal gestures with his hands. – Go on. What about this one?

This fragment is clearer, but it's stuck to another fragment. – 'Fathers have no success with appeals.'

– What does that mean?

– I don't know. That's what it says.

Bernal looks unhappy. – OK, study the fragments. Tell me if anything seems out of the ordinary.

Erhard rummages through the papers, reading them, then stacking the ones he's read in a pile. There's nothing – nothing at all – that captures his attention. They are your typical, not especially interesting articles about Danes and their finances and their children and their institutions and their divorces and their TV programmes. A great deal of what he sees is about the Hell's Angels. Although it's been many years since he last read a Danish newspaper, he doesn't feel it's much different today. He doesn't recognize some of the names, but other than that, it's the usual.

– I don't think there's anything, but I don't know what I'm looking for.

Bernal gets to his feet. – I don't know what you're looking for, either. This is a shitty case.

That last bit he practically whispers. He scoops the fragments in great handfuls and tosses them into the box. A urine stench wafts through the room. From another room, behind the shelves, a small child hiccoughs or whimpers. Bernal doesn't notice.

– I can't help you unless you tell me what I'm looking for. I need to know more.

Bernal considers at length. Erhard guesses that he's weighing his words. How much he's allowed or wishes to say. – Come, he says. – Over here.

They walk around the shelf and into a dark corner. He turns and stops Erhard, who's right behind him. In the darkness Erhard sees only half of Bernal's face. – You don't have a weak stomach, do you?

Erhard shakes his head.

– Do you remember that girl Madeleine?

– Did you find her?

Bernal looks annoyed. – Do you remember her?

Erhard nods.

– Good. We don't want that kind of case here. Not at all. We've done what we can. You need to know that. No one is working at cross purposes here. What happened in Portugal completely destroyed the tourist industry in Praia da Luz, and the police were hung out to dry in the media as a flock of fucking Thomson and Thompsons. The difference here is that no one is missing the child. No crying mothers or fathers, or cute siblings pining for their little brother.

– The child?

Bernal flicks on two wall lamps, then moves to the whiteboard. – The boy, he says, pointing at a photograph.

It's a large black-and-white photograph, probably a colour photo originally, and difficult to look at. But there is no colour now, only gradations of black, maybe brown or some greenish tint. Crossing through it is a big, black square marked by four light-grey cubes that provide the square with depth. In the centre of the square, as though surrounded by an invisible eggshell, is a tiny human being. One hand is up near its head as if to scratch itself, while the other hand is, almost impossibly, wrapped around its back. The child is covered in pale-grey newspaper fragments.

Erhard has to turn away. His eyes slide towards the whiteboard and more photographs with the same horrible scene. Close-up images of the boy's mouth, his eyes – which are closed, sunken in a sickened darkness. Photographs of the car, of the backseat where the box rests between seatbelts as if someone had tried to secure it.

– How old is…? Erhard's mouth is so dry he can hardly speak. – How old is he?

– Three months. Thereabouts.

– Someone must be missing him.

– Unfortunately not. Whenever a case like this arises, it's always worst with the babies. They don't know anyone. They don't have nannies or playmates. They leave behind no colleagues, ex-girlfriends, or empty flats with unpaid rent. If Mum and Dad don't care, then there's no one worry to worry over them.

– Someone must've reported the child missing. On the islands or in Spain?

Bernal goes on: – If you ask me, Mum went out in the waves and drowned herself like some cowardly dog. No one walks out on her child like that, unless something's wrong with her.

– What if something happened to the mother and the father? What if they went for a walk out on the beach and fell and...

– What if they shagged in one of the caves? Problem is, we've scoured the area. With dogs. With helicopters. There's nothing. It's Bill Haji's bloody ring all over again. Gone.

– Someone must have seen the car arrive. What about that guy on the beach? The surfer?

– We've spoken to him twice. He didn't get to Cotillo until the day after the car turned up. Nobody knows anything. Nada. And the car was registered to an importer outside of Lisbon, but the car never arrived; he thought it was on some lorry in Amsterdam two months ago.

– Maybe a car thief stole it with the boy inside?

– Where? In Amsterdam?

Erhard doesn't have an answer.

– The most bizarre thing of all is the odometer. It registered thirty-one miles. Thirty-one.

– What about fingerprints?

– No fingerprints on the wheel, the gearstick, or the front seat. Finding prints is not as easy as some people think. And maybe Mum was wearing gloves? Maybe someone removed all traces? We found prints on the cardboard box, but no one we recognize, and who knows who had the box before the boy was shoved inside it? Someone, in any case, secured the box tightly in the seatbelt. It appears as though it's been shaken around quite a bit, perhaps when they drove the car off the hilltop near the car park. It was on the beach at high tide, but no water gushed in, and no one in Cotillo saw the car when it arrived. If only we'd had some dogs. They've got dogs on Tenerife, but it takes a day and a half to get them over here, and by then it would've been too late.

– What if the mum and dad left the country?

– We've searched all departures. No one has arrived with a child and left without one. The absolute worst part is the autopsy report… Bernal walks over to the photograph of the boy. He points at the region around his eyes, the blackened area. – Lorenzo estimated that the boy was starved to death, two to three days before the car was abandoned on the beach. Before… Before they left him in a cardboard box. The autopsy report also determined that he was around twelve weeks old. When we found him, we all thought he was a newborn, because he was so thin and tiny. We've called all the delivery rooms and doctors on the island, and all young mothers with boys ranging from one month old to five months. One hundred and eighty-seven mothers in all. All the babies were accounted for. We've spoken with a number of fathers, too. We got a few leads, but nothing that took us anywhere.

Erhard can't look at the photograph any more. – How can someone abandon a child? he says.

Bernal looks even more tired now. – In the end, we had to bury him. Yesterday morning. East of Morro Jable, Playa del Matorral. A fucking Bobcat dug a hole the size of a microwave oven. We did it quickly to avoid media attention. We were afraid journalists would come out and see the small coffin. Do you know how creepy that is? I thought of my own 3-year-old boy. There's something all wrong about burying children that small.

– Are you still working on the case?

Bernal gives him a look. – Only because the press has begun writing about it. They've found out there was a dead boy in the car. They don't know anything more than that. The higher-ups don't wish to have another Madeleine on their hands. That's the only thing they say. Bad PR won't help the tourist industry, which is already in the dumps. I shouldn't get you too involved – we've got something. A local angle.

– What does that mean?

Bernal turns his back to Erhard as he speaks. – A local angle. An islander, a suspect.

Erhard doesn't understand. – If you've resolved the case, why am I here? Why are you wasting my time?

– It's not a waste. We need to examine everything. Now we're just more certain. We're barking up the wrong tree with that box. Bernal shakes Erhard's hand. His is the warm hand of someone who spends the bulk of his time in an office. And then he follows Erhard out, down the hallway, and into the dark hall, which is kept cool by the massive stones in the masonry.

– Let me know if there's anything else I can do, Erhard says.

– Will do. Bernal pauses at the heavy oak doors that are difficult to nudge open. Through the small glass in the door he gives Erhard one final glance.

Erhard walks to his car, feeling the evening sun irritatingly insistent against his back. He needs water. He has a bad feeling.

It's one thing to hear about the police's strange methods, their nepotism, corruption, brutality, rape of detainees, and the alcoholism within its ranks – but it's another thing entirely to experience it firsthand. He's met plenty of inebriated policemen, having ferried them home to shrieking girlfriends or sobbing wives, but it's appalling to see a case being evaluated and solved on a policeman's desk.

He finds a warm bottle of water in the boot and sits in the car for some time before starting the engine. How random and harsh is life that a child can be born into such complete neglect. First by its parents, then by the system, and finally in death: a deep, black hole that sucks everything into it. He dreads to think of the outcome of the case. He dreads to think what awaits.

THE WHORE

14 January–21 January

21

When he gets up on Saturday morning, he turns on the radio. He spins the dial from Radio Mucha over to Radio Fuerteventura. He waits for the news as he cautiously removes the finger from the glass in which it spent the night. It appears to have completely stopped decomposing. Holding onto the ends, he wriggles it and tries to free the ring. But it's still jammed tight. He drops the finger into the bag, then slips the bag into his pocket.

He's exhausted, or maybe just angry, after yesterday. Not because of the conversation but because he cannot let go of the image of the boy, the tiny box, the unresolved ending, the local angle – whatever that means.

He drives down to Alapaqa and drinks his morning coffee. Aristide, a fisherman who doesn't usually come to the cafe, is busy with a group of Finnish tourists who've ordered breakfast. Erhard showers and sits on a rock beside the harbour, watching the fishermen discuss who's allowed to fish where as they point across the sea at some buoys lapping on the water. He fills his cup and drives north. He cruises slowly through Corralejo, then onto the country road, and finally out towards Cotillo.

There are very few customers at this time of day. He picks up a young man out near Las Dunas who hails him in an exaggerated way, waving his arms and legs. He has no luggage but needs to go down to Puerto, to the ships, before 8 a.m. So Erhard floors the accelerator in the old Mercedes. The young man goes on and on about a girl he's just said goodbye to, telling Erhard that she's not like other girls. Of course it turns out that he doesn't have any money. His money's on the ship, he says, which is probably a lie. If Erhard lets him go he'll never see any money.

– Give me your business card, I'll give you mine, the young man tells Erhard, handing him a card. – I'll send you the money.

But Erhard doesn't have a card. It's almost eight o'clock now. He doesn't care and tells the man to get going so he can reach his ferry. The man dashes from the taxi and down the street towards the piers. Halfway, he turns and waves, still running.

This episode just reminds Erhard that he needs to ask people like that about a credit card before the fare begins. A confused young man in love.

Driving westward, he lowers the volume on the radio so he can't hear dispatch, which, as always, is thick with rubbish. Discussions about who had picked up the most rides last month, or who has the hottest wife. There's always a lot of complaints from drivers being scolded by the boss because they don't submit their paperwork in a proper fashion, or because they don't drive enough per month, or because the substitute drivers don't tidy up the cars properly following the night shift. Or because someone budged ahead in the airport queue for crying out loud. The girls at dispatch poke fun at them. Lucia teases the drivers who are in the doghouse. In his fourteen years as a cabbie, Erhard hasn't heard one unsolicited peep from the boss or from the auto workshop, not so much as a single admonishment or comment or criticism. He's thorough and methodical in his work. He spends fifteen minutes each day balancing his accounts. Every day he pays 30 per cent to TaxiVentura, 25 per cent in taxes, and 25 per cent to Annette, then leaves the last 20 per cent to himself. On a good day it's enough, on a bad day he barely has enough to eat. But that's the way he likes it; it's what's fair. TaxiVentura receives all of it except for his own cut: they pay the taxes and transfer Annette's money to her bank account at the People's Bank of Denmark once a month. And he keeps the car clean. He's even tried to liven up the atmosphere down at dispatch, suggesting a bookshelf and a break room where people can have a cup of coffee or tea. But it went nowhere. Wait until you're the boss, Barouki says, washing his hands – first without soap, then with soap, and then finally washing them all the way up to his elbows before drying them with napkins. He does that five or six times during the course of a single meeting. He's a friendly man who loves air conditioning. He'd only driven a taxi for a few months before he became a haulier, a fleet operator, and ran his own business for almost ten years before becoming the director of TaxiVentura in 2004. He's good with schedules. Erhard snaps on the radio and waits for the twelve o'clock news to come on, but there's nothing of interest.

He stops at a petrol station and washes his car. Afterward he rinses off the yellow foam, then dries the car with an old rag, polishing it with wax he's gotten from one of the other drivers. He rarely does this. On an island where it's always windy and dusty, it almost seems idiotic to wash and polish your car.

While the wax settles, he reads the last chapter in the new book by Almuz Ameida, the great hope among Spanish crime novelists. He sits in the shade on a bench next to the station. From there he can see the rocks and cliffs on the beach. He can see the sand as it swirls up each time the wind sweeps eastward, like a broom, towards the island. There is always a bunch of cars parked on the flat section of the rocks. Surfers and nudists. Tourists who don't get out of their cars, because of the drifting sand. At this moment he sees a family sitting in a most-likely-rented Seat and staring across the beach. There are no kitesurfers. They are all down at Playa Cualpa. But if one looks hard enough between the rocks one sees several brown, mosslike lumps reclining in inflatable chairs. Usually with a beer close by or small bottles of white wine. It's the island of intoxication. Not like Ibiza or Mallorca or Crete – youthful boozing that's mostly an excuse to have sex. The drinking here is discreet. Outside the few noisy discotheques and roaring cocktail bars with their improvised menus, hundreds of people are quietly crawling from one buzz to the next. Alcohol is cheap, the weather is good, and the calendar empty.

Why not?

He'd sat between those rocks himself once, horny as a bull, during his first seven months on the island. His skin becoming brown and hard. From morning to night he lay with an erection behind a rock, his rest interrupted only by short hikes down to the water. At night he slept under a ledge farther north up the coast. He'd light a fire and eat jellyfish or fish he caught himself. Mostly, he ate the leftovers from family picnics, heels of bread or hunks of sausage. If it got really bad, he walked to the supermarket and bought tins of food. He had money from home. Not much. A backgammon case stuffed with a few thousand euros. But he didn't want to spend the money. For a long time he didn't feel he deserved to spend the money. For a long time he just wanted to be left alone. Without smiling. Without any kind of pleasure. Not even the sunshine or the starlight. He lay quietly, dispassionately observing the sky. But in the end this proved difficult. In the end the small pleasures found him.

The sound of the water trickling through the rocks when the sea was at low tide. Warm bread from the fire. One morning, a large bird sat with a fish in its beak a metre away, dripping water and blinking its huge buttonlike eyes. Sometimes he had company. But only later, after a few months. People who wanted to see him for themselves *el ermitaño*, the man who lived among the rocks. Most of them just gawked at him, standing as far away as possible to watch him clamber about. Others came all the way up to his campfire and offered him food or asked him questions. But he never responded. In those seven months he said nothing. Not even when the two men attacked him with bats and beat him senseless, leaving him lying in the sun like a shelled turtle.

What doesn't kill you makes you angrier, as the saying goes.

He parks his car and crosses the road to the flat section down the slope, steep and covered with chunks of rock. He notices that his left boot is in tatters. He notices his sock through a slit between the sole and the leather. It's been a long time since he's spent money on that sort of thing. He doesn't like to. Just the thought of trying on shoes makes him delay buying them. Maybe he can mend it with a little glue or some duct tape.

The car was parked here, right here.

He walks up and down the slope. It looks like soft sand, but there are actually rocks right beneath the thin layer. It's hard to walk on. Suddenly he's standing in the water, the beach disappearing into it. Tidewater is distinctive across the entire island, but because the sandy bottom is so flat, it seems stronger here. Here, napping girls or some family on a picnic are suddenly surprised by a wave that crashes all the way up the beach and against the first row of rocks.

Erhard thinks about how the car must've gotten down the slope. Was it shoved? What did they want to happen to it? Did they want the car to sink into the sea? Was it supposed to have washed out into the waves and vanished? Why else would they push it down the slope? He's seen some of the youths riding their ATVs down here. Was it a mistake that the car rolled down here? Had the mother somehow disappeared?

Maybe Raúl was right. He'd said that it was probably a car thief having some fun. But Raúl didn't know there'd been a child in the backseat. That made it much worse.

Erhard gazes across the water.

If a person wanted to drown, all they would have to do was walk 100 metres out to the sandbank. The undertow is so strong out there that a body would wash ashore in Lanzarote in two days. He's heard that from his colleagues who discuss Los Tres Papas, who earn their money from dry-cleaning businesses, coat-check services, gambling, and prostitution. Now and then they cut ties with a member or two, and that member washes up on the beach in Lanzarote, disintegrating and tender. Some rumours even have it that Raúl's involved, but Erhard has never seen or heard anything that gives him any reason to believe it. Raúl may not always be a clean-cut kid, but he's no criminal. People say a lot of stuff. Even about Erhard. They say he's driven clients out to Vallebrón, and buried them underneath two metres of rock. At the beginning of the aughts, several bodies were found down there. Beneath rocks on which were carved three small matchstick men.

If the mother was the one who drove the car down the slope, then she must've been wracked with grief and shock. The boy lies dead or dying in a box in the backseat, she's desperate, and maybe she'd drowned herself because there was nothing else she could do. That doesn't explain the car. That it wasn't registered. Or that it was wiped clean of fingerprints. A desperate mother wouldn't clean fingerprints from her car. Besides, a tormented mother would leave behind an excuse, an explanation. To hurt a child is the most unforgivable act – that's how it is in every culture the world over. Even in Catholicism, which otherwise revolves around forgiveness, it's one of the sins one is least likely to forgive. But a mother from these islands would be unable to kill herself and her child without attracting attention. Too many things don't add up. Erhard senses that the beach holds secrets. The car was abandoned here for a reason.

It's like having twenty pieces to a puzzle and not knowing whether the entire puzzle has twenty-one or one thousand pieces.

In the supermarket he sees one of those kinds of boxes the boy was found in. Maybe not the exact same kind. But a simple, brown cardboard box with staples on the bottom along with a narrow slit. He removes the bags of rice and turns the box over.

He stares at the bottom and can almost see the boy, folded up, emaciated, alone. The tiny body clatters around. The little boy with the big eyes. And he sees a pair of hands that either put him in the box or aims to lift him out. Hands that either push him down into the darkness or hold him for the final time. Erhard doesn't understand why it makes him angry, why it makes him so coal-black inside, why he can't simply let it go. There are probably thousands of cardboard boxes across the globe with small children inside; one could no doubt fill an entire warehouse with them all. It's the most brutal thing he's ever seen, and he's convinced someone took the boy there to die, but not the boy's mother or father.

He puts the cardboard box down and buys tinned tuna.

On the way home he examines the finger taped to his hand, which rests on the wheel. It no longer resembles a finger, but a dry, spicy sausage. It looks terrible and it won't fool anyone. Not even himself. Of course not. Of course it doesn't work. He always recognizes the clients who're wearing toupees. Only the most naive among them believe no one notices – everyone else knows it looks like a discoloured broom. But one can hope. One can pretend. He considers sending the finger to Bernal. Anonymously. With a friendly message. He considers burying it. He considers throwing it out the window while he's driving.

Instead he finds a plastic container, one of those kinds used for food storage, with an airtight lid. He stuffs the finger inside a small, transparent baggie and then the container. He removes some books from his shelves and shoves the container in, then returns the books. He makes a note of which ones: *Binario* by Almuz Ameida and *Victim on Third* by Frank Cojote. He retreats a few steps; the bookshelf is now a wall of books, impossible to see that anything's concealed there. Then he gets the tuna fish and eats directly from the tin, sitting on the edge of his chair, listening to the goats.

22

He has a new piano-tuning client on Monday morning.

Sometimes he gets new clients through his existing clients, but most hear about him from one of his fellow taxi drivers. If their conversations during the journey lead in that direction, they sometimes recommend the Hermit, even if they find it strange that he tunes pianos, too. Some time before Christmas, Alvaro – an olive farmer who went bankrupt last year and began driving a taxi – had told him that he'd given a lift to someone who wanted him to call her. The woman lived out in Parque Holandes and owned a Steinway that hadn't been tuned in years.

– Why are you calling me only now? she said, when he rang on Christmas Eve, half in the bag and incapable of selling himself.

It was the beginning of a horrible conversation. Three times she asked him to speak up and to think hard before he named his price. *It's a very expensive piano and there's nothing wrong with it,* she said, and negotiated more stubbornly than anyone he'd ever dealt with. They finally agreed on forty-six euros. Less than half his usual figure. *Get here on the dot,* was the last thing she said to him. *Don't waste my time.*

He's out there now, parked in front of the woman's house, and looking at his clock. It's past the agreed-upon time. But the radio's tuned in to Radio Fuerteventura, and the news has just begun. The biggest news is that there's been progress in discussions concerning salaries at the new casino. *More than fifty employees are now…*

As he's listening, the door of the house opens. A woman stares at Erhard. A pretty woman. She's wearing a white safari outfit, and she has white, maybe light-grey, hair. She waves as if to tell him that he may enter. He ignores her. The newscast has moved on to a segment on the EU, which is trying to help the Spanish economy by guaranteeing the nation's banks, including Sun Bank, Fuerteventura's largest. *Many customers were nervous in January because…*

The woman approaches the car. She looks like a widow. Relaxed, yet wearing high heels and some kind of glistening, flesh-coloured lipstick. When she gets close to him, he sees that her skin is stretched unnaturally tight across her cheekbones. She doesn't seem friendly. At all. Erhard rolls the window down.

Just then, the newscast begins the segment that he's feared.

A twenty-seven year old woman from Puerto del Rosario has confessed to abandoning a baby on the beach last week near Cotillo, where it…

– Señor Piano Tuner.

… of a car. When the car was discovered the baby was dead.

– Señor!

… now cooperating with the police to clarify the details in this unfortunate case. The police are positive that the mother herself is…

The woman's head appears right next to the open window. – I've waited all day.

– Be quiet, Erhard says, turning up volume. – I need to hear this.

… not remanded into custody. A decision in the case and the woman's punish-ment is expected before the end of…

The woman beside the car raises her voice so loud that he can't follow the news. – I have never in all my life experienced such abysmal service. We had an agreement. I asked you to arrive on time.

The news segment is over. The story had sounded exactly as the vice police superintendent had laid it out to him. And as Erhard had feared. The world moves on to other news.

He glances to his left, where the woman glowers at him as if he's about to leap out of the car. His entire nervous system wants to obey her stare, her command, but something holds him back.

– I'm not paying you one cent more than twenty euros. In fact, I should get a free tune-up if this is the way you treat your clients.

Erhard starts the engine.

– Stop, you can't leave. I've waited all day. Her face looks as though it's about to crack.

– There are more important things than your Steinway, Erhard says, before turning the vehicle around and heading towards the Palace.

Bernal is surprised to see him. – Hermit, he says.

– Is this what you meant by a local solution?

– Calm down. What are you talking about? Bernal guides Erhard behind an ordinary shelf with files and boxes stuffed with electric cables.

– This isn't police work, damn it, this is nothing but…

– What? What is it?

– You and I both know that she's not the one.

– And why not?

– Three or four days ago you had nothing, and you were frustrated. But now you've tied it all up in one neat little bow?

– It goes quickly once you have a lead.

– C'mon. You have no licence plate and a car with only thirty-one miles on the odometer? A girl from Puerto my ass.

– Watch your language, Hermit.

– Don't you have any integrity?

Bernal whispers. – I told you we will not survive an unresolved case like this. It's bad PR. We won't let that happen. With the casino and all that.

– The casino? What does that have to do with anything?

– Get out of your cave, mate. The tourist industry is bleeding. If they build the casino on Lanzarote because we're suddenly bad company, then a whole lot of people will lose their jobs.

– So what? You've charged some random mother so that we can have our casino?

– Of course not. We've concluded a nasty case that doesn't have a happy ending.

– And what about the girl?

– She's not a girl, she's a woman, and she knows what she's doing.

– Why did she do it then?

– Does it even matter, since she's confessed?

Maybe it doesn't matter. Maybe it's just Erhard. What the hell does he know about these kinds of things? It's probably rare for all the pieces in a puzzle to fit together. – Where was the newspaper from? Erhard asks abruptly.

Bernal is irritated. – I'm sorry that I brought you into this. It's a terrible case, also for me. But it's over now. Just forget it. We've made an arrangement with her. It was her baby.

– An arrangement?

– Lower your voice. Yes, an arrangement. We've closed the case.

– Isn't that just like Thomson and Thompson? An arrangement that gets exposed? Bernal, what have you done?

– My job. Goddamn it, you don't know what it's like. Bernal is losing his patience. – No one wants these kind of unsolved cases, regardless of how impossible they are to solve. The higher-ups tell us it needs to be closed.

– But why would she do it? Why would she let you do this to her?

– It's a question of arguments, Bernal says, and Erhard knows at once that he means money. – If you've got nothing to lose.

– I don't know whether I should feel bad for her or wish for her death, the dumb girl. Will she wind up in prison?

– First she'll have a hearing before a judge, of course, but we'll make sure she gets off easy, as far as the court's concerned anyway.

She'll get what she needs. More than what she makes in her awful line of work now.

– A whore, in other words? You bought a whore? One of those dumb junkies? It's only a matter of days before she…

– Weren't you the one who called yourself Señor Againsttherules?

Erhard knows many of the island's prostitutes. There are about twenty or thirty girls primarily working the tourists and a few wealthy men. He can easily picture one of them enthusiastically accepting the offer, her hand trembling. She won't need to shag anyone, just pretend that she has, then given birth to a child she's lost. Erhard searches for the finger in his pocket, then remembers that he no longer has it on him. He doesn't get angry often, but he is now, and his ears are burning hot.

Bernal retreats a step. – Don't look at me like that. I'm the only one who tried to solve this case. Trust me. I really thought you could help. One last stab at something. We didn't know whether or not there was some kind of lead in all those newspaper fragments, but there wasn't. They were dead ends.

– But it must mean something that the fragments were in Danish? You've got to follow the leads you find.

– But what does it actually mean? That the father was Danish? That the mother stayed at a hotel where they had Danish newspapers? That there are many Danish tourists here on the island? It doesn't mean shit. They're just newspaper fragments. In a few days the case will be completely over.

Silence. Bernal turns off the light.

– I'm going home, Erhard says.

– Thanks for all your help. Again.

If there was any sarcasm to Bernal's words, it would add insult to injury, but it just seems like Bernal's final attempt at being friendly.

They walk side by side through the office, out of the Palace, and down to the car park.

– I thought policemen became hysterical when little children were involved. That they stayed up all night turning over every stone.

– Trust me, I've stayed up late. Ever since we found him. We've turned over every fucking stone on this island. Sometimes there are shitty cases, and this is one of them. We've got our own lives to lead, too. You think it doesn't haunt me to find a little boy like that? We can't take it personally, for God's sake, every time a child dies. At least now the case will be closed.

– When are you taking it to Armando?

– The hearing is at the end of the week. Friday morning.

They shake hands. Erhard likes Bernal, and that irritates him. – Goodbye Thomson, he says.

He drives out of the city. Heading north. He pushes the tape into the tape deck and John Coltrane begins his version of 'Stella by Starlight'. In the side mirror he sees a plane emerging from a few wispy clouds. The sun's rays make the wings appear as though they're on fire.

23

He drives around without picking up anyone and without replying to dispatch. He listens to the radio, and every time he hears the segment – each time in a shorter or slightly revised version – he hears Bernal's voice instead of the newscaster's. No one wants an unsolved case.

He parks for half an hour out near the new casino. They've blasted the rocks away and levelled the cement, but they still haven't built beyond one storey. The entire city is talking about the venture. The entire island. In the beginning it was just a project to create a few new jobs. But gradually, as ambitions grew, the casino was viewed as a way to save all of Corralejo, the island, and the Canary Islands, creating stability, growth, and happiness. According to Alphonso Suárez, head of the new casino, it's a visionary construction, Corralejo's new beating heart. Erhard is more sceptical. They've discussed the casino since 1999. They've already spent more than 30 million euros, but no one knows on what.

There's no one to be seen. He leans back in his seat, ready to take a nap, but each time the radio announcer starts talking, his thoughts begin to swirl. When the news comes on again, he reports to dispatch that he's taking the rest of the day off, then turns off his sign.

He doesn't drive home.

Instead he takes a route that leads him through Puerto del Rosario's industrial district, with its shedlike pavilions, and the Selos Quarter, where everything seems closed but isn't. He drives past Sport Fuerte's exclusive mansions, and then purposefully around Guisguey. The swingers club here always attracts interesting people. When he sees one of the girls he knows, he brings the car to a halt and offers her a free ride. Several of the girls just laugh at him. But Angelina and Michelle and Bethany, three girls he's driven multiple times, want to head into the city or up to Corralejo.

He asks them if any of the girls has been arrested recently. No, not that they're aware. None of the girls has stopped working or gone on holiday? They haven't noticed. Angelina names a few she hasn't seen in some time, but they've probably just gone home or to Barcelona or taken ill, she thinks. None of them know of a 27-year-old.

He doesn't ask directly, but Bethany coincidentally mentions that she's heard about the boy found down at the beach. People are fucked up, she says. Erhard doesn't say anything.

It's a sad business. Though their lives are similar, the girls work alone, wandering the island in search of customers. Like a small travelling theatre where the production is the world's oldest story, which never ends happily. When they sit in the car, they look like children in costumes. He thinks of Mette and Lene when they got dressed up. The older of the two with her makeup askew and her pale, thin legs sticking out of her mother's slip. He doesn't want to think about them now. Not in this connection. Absolutely not in this connection.

The third time he passes through Guisguey, a city consisting of an abandoned farm, a large house, and a former supermarket turned swingers' club, he sees a new face. She's clearly a junkie and a prostitute, and she's in such wretched condition that Erhard almost doesn't want her in his taxi. But he snaps on his indicator and slows beside her, letting her walk around to the open window. She thinks he's a john, and she gives him a terrible smile, leaning towards him with a practised ease so he might see her breasts in a tattered pink bra.

– I'm not a customer, but I can drive you to Puerto. There's probably more action down there. He expects her to protest. Many of the girls learn to be sceptical about those they accept rides with, but her pupils are mostly vacant, and she climbs in the passenger seat with robotic obedience.

It makes absolutely no sense to ask her about anything. She's practically asleep, and he just drives her to Selos and decides to drop her off on the corner near the restaurant where many of the prostitutes gather to share fags and gossip about their johns. The newscast is on again. This time the segment is shorter, and Erhard guesses that next time the news comes on, there won't be anything about the boy found on the beach.

He turns down Via Juan Carlos, the largest street in the Selos District, and the busiest. He searches for La Costa, which looks like an ordinary lunch restaurant with tables on the pavement. When he sees it, he parks and cautiously nudges the girl.

– Señorita, it's time to get out now.

She glances around. – I don't want to git out, I want to git t' Guisguey.

– That's where we were. You wanted to come downtown, remember?

She gives Erhard an irritated look. – I can't ainymore today.

– Do you have somewhere to go?

– Guisguey. Got a bed there.

She can't be more than twenty-five or so. Her nose is frayed from some substance, and her arms in her sleeveless blouse are discoloured and red, the colour of squid. A battered body. She's one of the unfortunates.

– I'll drive you back, he says.

– Hey, she says and is about to shout at him, but then she falls back in her seat and fumbles in her little purse for a cigarette. Customers aren't allowed to smoke in the car, but he rolls down all four windows and says nothing to her. She lights a cigarette and sucks smoke through the filter.

– Wha' d'ya want? A blowjob?

– No, he says.

She smokes disinterestedly, then ashes so that the flakes swirl around the car.

– W're are we?

– You're on your way to Guisguey. I'm driving you, I'm helping you.

She falls asleep again with the cigarette between her fingers. He takes it from her and tosses it out the window. The trip takes ten or eleven minutes if one drives directly. But he takes the long way to let her rest. She's fidgety in sleep, but her breathing grows deeper and deeper, and soon she sinks down onto the backseat. When they reach Guisguey, he leaves her be; he climbs out of the car, stretches, and crosses the street. The swingers' club still looks like a supermarket with large glass windows and a long, well-lit sign in garish neon. But the windows have been painted red, and the sign now reads *Pleasure World*. It's difficult to find the entrance. He's driven a number of customers out here, but never watched them go inside. It's not his style, this kind of place. It's too businesslike for him, too social. Wandering around with a stiffy among other men who are younger, fitter, and hornier. Sex doesn't need to be love, but it damn well better not be some kind of fish auction.

He walks back to his car. – Guisguey, he tells the girl. – Final stop, Guisguey. It makes him laugh.

She climbs out of the car, her eyes closed, but fumbles around for her purse and her cigarettes. – Thanks. You're an angel, a true angel.

She's so spaced-out that what she's saying should seem like meaningless clichés. And yet there's a sweetness to it that touches Erhard to the core. She stumbles across the street, and he follows her.

– Y' can go home now, taxi'man. I'm 'kay.

He watches her. – Have you heard anything about one of the girls being arrested? Something about a baby?

– What, we can't have kids now? She makes a face as if she's laughing, but no sound emerges.

– Have you heard who it is?

– They didn't arrest her, they bribed her with a thousand euro.

The girl's on her way around the corner of the building.

Erhard goes after her. – Who? Who is it?

– Only because you've been so nice, she says.

He considers getting out his wallet and giving her 100 euros. Not only to get her to talk, but also to help her. And maybe to impress her a little.

– It's Alina, Alinacita, the snobby bitch. She waves two fingers in goodbye and pulls on a doorknob that Erhard hadn't noticed. Then she vanishes inside the building.

24

It's dusk when he gets home.

He looks at the telephone in the corner, but there's no sign that it's rung. He drops his clothes into the laundry basket. He likes to do his laundry on Mondays. He makes dinner in his underwear, eats lamb goulash standing in the doorway, considers getting a beer at Guzman's down Alejandro's Trail, the little grocery that looks like it's about to go belly up and has looked that way for years. But he's got a bottle of red wine and pours himself a glass in a beer mug, then gulps it as if it can quench his thirst.

It's dark now.

He boils water, then washes his clothes and hangs them on the line which runs from the house to a tall flagpole. The darkness presses against him. He shaves. Although he looks too proper when he shaves, like a real grandfather, completely smooth-faced, he still does so a few times each month. He irons a shirt, but it's harder to find trousers; the two pairs that he likes to wear are still drying on the line. He tries on four old, ratty pairs, oil-stained and much too short. In the end he tugs on some shorts. The other cabbies don't like it when he wears shorts. Shorts are for tourists. But he doesn't care. He'll wear whatever the hell he wants, including a pink shirt once in a while. He drinks red wine as he listens to Monk. He removes the finger from the shelf and holds it in the empty slot on his hand. It looks genuine only when he squints. Carefully he returns it to the plastic container, lays the container back on the shelf, then puts the books in place.

Soon the red wine is gone; he hurries to his car, then drives downtown before the alcohol makes him tipsy. A bottle of wine makes him drunk, but at this moment he can't feel it.

He parks in the courtyard behind Oly's Laundromat, where no one ever goes at night. The city's got its own unique tumult, which he loves. A cacophony of music going on and off, people suddenly shouting, piercing machinery turned on in the middle of the night, then dying out as if it's been choked in oil. He walks up the street to Greenbay Jazz bar and onto the little patio. The band for that evening is already on stage, testing its equipment. It's the best time to arrive. The asynchronous horns and drumbeats give him gooseflesh; they've got a particularly experimental quality, as if he's listening to a child's first words. He orders a beer and takes his glass to the back corner of the bar.

Fifteen years ago, this was an exclusive jazz club with expensive drinks and table service. It attracted tourists, but the locals stayed away. Then the place got a new owner who kept the music, lowered the prices, and brought the locals in. The bar still tries to seem sophisticated and exotic, even though the clientele consists primarily of bankrupt directors, tourists with old tourist guides, and prostitutes trying to look like someone's girlfriend.

Two women are seated on a white sofa out on the terrace and three men are up at the bar. It's still early, only 10 p.m.

He always recognizes his customers' faces. There must be something wrong with him. There should be so many faces that he forgets them, that they merge into one. But he remembers them all. He drove one of the women on the sofa six months ago, when she got a flat tyre and had to get to her sister's wedding. The other woman was abandoned once, long ago, on a barren stretch just beyond Corralejo; she told him several times a friend had dropped her off, but Erhard doubted this. She'd stood waving a bouquet of flowers as he drove past on his way downtown. That was maybe four years ago.

The men are locals. He recognizes them without remembering what they do for a living or who they are. He's driven them home a number of times, dangerous, charming drunkards who come here as early as possible to drink red wine, looking like people supposed to meet someone. They don't want to sit at home, and they don't fit in at Luz, the city's shabbiest dive, or the Yellow Rooster, where trash collectors, demolition men, lorry drivers, masons, and taxi drivers fill each other up with cheap liquor and stories from the mainland. The three men just sit there trying to keep their balance on the white barstools, glancing towards the entrance every time new voices appear.

The band puts their instruments down and heads to the bar to wait. One can't quite call them a band. They are four small, thin boys in tight-fitting black jeans and hats and fingerless gloves. One of them orders for the others, and they drink giant beers out of fat bottles. Erhard has never played in a band, but he's always wanted to be in one: to sit in an old car together, to get all the equipment ready on stage, to smoke cigarettes while waiting for the show to begin. Then warm-ups and finally the sets, assuming you manage more than one, and afterward drinking beer and laughing without a care in the world, praising one another for things others hadn't noticed.

Erhard's father had taken him to his piano lessons. The piano instructor in Taastrup was a man with rolled-up sleeves by the name of Marius Tønnesen. His teaching method consisted of sitting in a plush chair and humming over his pupils' attempts at playing the notes, and he didn't comment or instruct, just smoked hand-rolled cigarettes, content, almost cheerful. After nineteen instructional hours, Erhard's father decided to come watch a lesson, and he realized they were not producing the results that he'd hoped; he didn't believe the teacher punished Erhard enough for striking the wrong keys. In the end he went straight up to his son and screamed that Erhard bloody well not pussyfoot around the goddamn keys. After that his father got on Tønnesen's case, asking him to get his ass together, find the belt or something, teach the boy how to practice, because he wasn't going to become a pianist playing cowboys and Indians. Following that day, Erhard's father stopped paying for piano lessons. The next week, when Erhard showed up without money, Tønnesen said that he could have one final lesson, but that was it.

In one way it was his first lesson. Erhard discovered that he played better when he was angry. He suddenly played so energetically that Tønnesen got up from his chair, walked over, and stood observing Erhard's fingers. All ten. My word, boy, he said excitedly, how angry you are at the piano. Erhard pounded every key. When the hour was up he was exhausted; he stood in the entranceway, broken and sweaty, as Tønnesen rummaged around in his office. Erhard was just about to leave when the teacher bounded out. I want you to have this. It was 'Saxophone Colossus' by Rollins from 1956. On the cover, near a gleaming lamp, sat Rollins behind his saxophone.

– Can you play 'You Don't Know What Love Is'? he asks one of the slender boys at the bar. The boys turns. Erhard figures they know it.

– We don't play jazz, the boy says.

– Isn't this a jazz club? When did they start playing anything but jazz at a jazz club?

The boy says they call it new funk.

– Let me guess, Erhard says. – Three-four time, two bass guitars.

– The young crowd likes it.

– Looks that way, Erhard says, glancing around.

– This is just a practice jam. Our last YouTube video has more than 1.3 million views. We're playing Madrid next month.

– It's a long road, my young friend. Erhard inspects the boy's holey jeans. – You can't cheat with music.

– Whatever, Yoda, the lead singer says, laughing in a not-unfriendly way. – Let me guess: You're another misunderstood island genius?

– Is it that obvious?

– You're not exactly a business type.

Erhard smiles. – Neither are you.

– I'm young and irresponsible, you know?

– Yes, I remember how great that was.

– What happened to your hand?

Erhard looks down at his left hand. – Old injury.

– Don't you have kids or grandkids you have to get home to?

– I've not quite reached that stage.

– So now you're here grieving your fate?

– I'm listening to music, unless you've decided to drink your evening away in the back room instead?

– Yeah right.

Erhard turns away and takes a pull of his beer. Talking to young people can be uncomfortable. Halfway into a conversation he feels the bridge between the generations is too long, too winding, ruined. No one else shows up, it's not your typical evening – perhaps there's a football match on the telly. Normally it's pretty crowded by 11.30 p.m. Erhard wonders whether he should just drive home while he's able. Wonders whether he's just wasting his time. Wonders whether she even comes here any more. Wonders whether she comes here on evenings like this one.

The red wine has announced its arrival, but not as he'd expected. He doesn't feel the buzz. It's been a long day, too long.

He stares at one of the musicians' skinny legs, which look like curtain rods covered with black denim. They probably live in a small flat in Puerto, or maybe here in Corralejo. Probably smoke hash and pop pills and whatever else it's called. They probably fuck each other and each other's girlfriends and argue about the rent twice a month. The one wearing the flat cap may be different. He may be from the mainland, Madrid, Valencia. There's something of the student about him, unlike the others. He's unique. Natives call Fuerteventura *Isla Ingenua*, the island of the stupid. From here, you've got to sail for three days or fly for five hours to find a decent university. So when you meet a young man with the ability for self-reflection, you take note. Erhard does anyway. Truth be told, he's got a few half-finished degrees himself, but life has taught him to recognize an intellectual when he sees one. In profile, the boy's nose is enormous. It juts over his mouth and forms a broad arc up to his eyes. He resembles a Greek statue carved in stone.

*

The band get up and return to their equipment. Right as they pass him, one whispers something. It happens so fast, and so quietly, that Erhard doesn't notice at first that anyone has spoken: *Are you into young guys?*

He wants to turn to see who said it. But before he can, he checks himself. He knows that not all voices are spoken out loud. There are just so many hate crimes committed on the island. Locals who pummel homosexual tourists. Muggings out on the sandbanks where German and English men copulate behind dunes – easy targets for a pair of youths with a knife.

More people arrive, many more. Young couples holding hands. Some large groups of men and women enter the bar laughing, dissolving all the tension that Erhard sensed during the past ten minutes. The band plays better and louder the longer they play, but he doesn't glance in their direction.

He finishes his beer and goes outside. He's heard people arriving on the patio, and he walks around the building, underneath the palm trees. He spots Alina along the wall, absorbed in a magazine crowded with images of famous actors. Her attention is surprisingly focused, as if she's reading the articles. She has a pinkish face and the kind of funny little girl's breasts that poke up like cupcakes, but which are mostly pads and wires.

He has driven her here a few times. He has also driven her to some of the toniest addresses on this island. And he's picked her up, early in the morning, after she'd sneaked out the gate of the villa carrying her stilettos. The last time he saw her, she was down on her knees and the President of the Canary Islands had his cock in her mouth. That was a year ago. Raúl had taken him to a party on a boat anchored behind Isla de Lobos; he knew the island's elite, and Erhard had given all the prostitutes a ride at some point. When Erhard searched for the kitchen in the middle of the night, he found her and the president in a small storage room, while on the deck Raúl was beating the president's bodyguard at poker.

She's not pretty. She's naughty in a kind of country-girl way. There's something about her mouth or cheeks too: they sag as if she was once operated on for an overbite. But in relation to the other prostitutes that he's spoken to, she's different. More mature-looking. In better clothes than Erhard recalls. She reminds him of some celebrity from the eighties, but he can't remember which one. She's wearing a dress, a loose, gold-coloured blouse with slits, and cream-coloured sandals. Erhard doesn't know much about fashion, especially ladies' fashion, but he can tell she's more expensive than other prostitutes. When he sits opposite her, she gives him a measured glance that tries to determine Erhard's sexual predilections and his financial wherewithal.

– No thanks, she says.

He laughs then. – I'm not here for that.

– If you want something from me, then you can book me at my website. I'm busy tonight.

– I'm here to talk about the boy, Erhard says, lowering his voice.

– The boy? she says. She looks as though she's on some sort of tranquilizer.

– Yes. You know, the boy you starved to death in a cardboard box.

She abruptly sits up and glares at him.

– My lawyer has advised me not to discuss my son.

Smart girl. She's listened well. My son. Indignant. Maybe she's not as high as she looks. – How much did they pay you? I heard the police gave you 1,000 euros.

She shushes him. – Of course not. That's what I earn on a good Saturday night in December. I don't want the police's money.

– Why did you do it then? He closes her magazine so that she'll look at him.

– It's my son.

– Enough with that. I'm not a journalist or anything.

– You're a cab driver. I remember you.

– For 1,000 euros I'd be the boy's mother, too.

– No, because I am.

She manages to respond with so much conviction in her voice that Erhard's suddenly in doubt. But she doesn't look like a grieving mother. She looks like a happy widow enjoying her night off. She looks like the local angle, as Bernal had called it.

– If I can find you, then so can the press. When they find out that you lied, that the police… He lowers his voice… that the police are paying you to be the mother, it won't be easy for you.

– It's all about presentation, she says, sucking on her straw that's planted in a green mojito-like drink with cucumbers along the rim.

Erhard doesn't know what to say. He'd expected she would regret what she'd done, maybe break down. But she doesn't appear troubled. – They're giving you more than 1,000 euros, he says. – Much more.

She releases her straw. – Whatever the money man says. She grins. – A lady gets tired fucking old men like you.

He pretends not to hear. – Thanks to you, the police are shelving the case. It's not right.

– The boy's dead. The parents don't give a shit about him, you got that? Or they're dead too. That's what the police say.

– They just want the case closed, even if it's unsolved.

– It won't be open very much longer, apparently. Listen, Señor cab driver, I'm not allowed to discuss it. There's nothing to discuss. You're ruining my night. She opens her magazine and returns to her reading.

– Your night? If you're playing the mother role, then you damn well better put more heart into it.

He wants to slap her.

He goes back to the bar and orders a beer, then gulps it, causing foam and liquid to slosh down his neck and onto the opening in his shirt. The music is livelier, and some of the young people have begun to dance. The band seems to love it, but when it comes right down to it, the bar's not a good place for dancing. It's unbearable to watch; only the younger generations can stomach such affectation. They rub up against one other. A girl in a miniskirt thrusts her groin against the bulge in a boy's colourful surfer shorts. An act that's impossible to misunderstand. And it's neither charming nor sexy, just fake and disgusting.

Such a dumb, irritating, gold-digging bitch. Honed and shaped by inbreeding and corruption. After almost thirty years, Erhard has seen his fair share of this kind of thing. Unscrupulous bureaucrats and self-ish citizens.

It's not too late.

He still has time to spoil the police's account of events. He can expose Alina and the police's incompetence. He doesn't give a crap about Bernal and their almost-friendship. If the vice police superintendent is unwilling to find the boy's parents or uncover who was behind his death, then he'll have to pay for his laziness.

He keeps an eye on her. Through the window, he watches her order champagne and read her magazine, behaving like a Señora, the entire time with this self-satisfied smile on her lips, as if she's just about to laugh. A few men approach, but she waves them away. It amazes Erhard. He thought she was here to find work, but maybe she's just here to enjoy a night out that doesn't conclude with some sweaty pig pressed against her little girl's breasts. Now that she's got an unexpected source of income she can allow herself a break. But he can't quite allow her that.

When the concert is over, something unexpected happens.

While two young guys with strange pigtails pack up the equipment, the band falls into a cluster of sofas and light fags probably laced with marijuana. Some young girls approach and get pulled onto their laps. Erhard doesn't quite see who they are before he spots Alina leaning over the lead singer, who's in the process of lifting up her dress to catch a glimpse of her knickers. What strikes Erhard is not so much what's happening as the speed at which it is happening. There's no refinement, none of the usual introductions; it's just full speed ahead. And even though music is blaring through the loudspeakers, their voices travel and it's so intimate in the room that it feels as if Erhard can hear everything. Including Alina's perverted urban snarl right next to the lead singer's ear: *I want to suck your cock, muchacho.* Erhard practically falls off his chair, but turns instead towards the bar before draining his beer. *Not now, not here, in a little bit,* the lead singer whispers. The little shit. Alina hasn't noticed Erhard, even though he's sitting less than four metres away. Either that or she's already forgotten about him. So that he doesn't attract any more attention, he slowly exits the room and goes out onto the street. Although it's a weekday, there's still a little life: a Vespa carrying three young men buzzes past, and two girls in bright dresses are heading to the beach while chatting on their mobiles.

It doesn't seem as though her new income has given her the incentive to change careers. The greedy bitch. She's not worthy of being the boy's mother even in a concocted story. She's the worst kind of whore, the kind who can choose another life but uses her body to take revenge on men – men's stupidity and single-mindedness. See what you do to me? See what I'm subjected to?

Under the streetlight, the guys with the pigtails are almost done packing the equipment in the van, and they arrange with the bassist to drive it all home. *We're going to stay*, he hears the bassist say. Erhard scoots underneath the long leaves of a slender palm tree and waits for a few minutes. Then the band exits the bar. They look different. Their sophisticated attitude has been spent by the concert. Now all that remains is a group of giggly teenage rock stars. And they walk right across the street without noticing the cars forced to brake so as not to hit them, or the van that's still parked under the streetlight because the two men are smoking inside it, or Erhard under the palm leaves, his gaze levelled directly at Alina clutching the lead singer's skinny chest. A young girl clings to another band member's arm. She looks like a young, much-too young, edition of Birte Tove, the Danish soft-porn actress from the 1970s. The group heads up a short driveway and into the Hotel Phenix.

After a few minutes, Erhard follows them inside.

There are only a few people at the hotel bar. A husband and wife drinking white wine, and a man who looks like a salesman staring at a laptop. The bartender waves at Erhard, but Erhard returns to the front desk.

He knows the clerk. An older man by the name of Miguel who has been behind the counter for as long as Erhard can remember. As a taxi driver, one gets to know the hotel employees – if one cares to. A good connection at a hotel might mean more work, more customers, but also better tips. Miguel is the kind of man one remembers. Friendly, always well-coiffed, with soft hands that welcome every man who stops in. Rumour has it that he still lives at home with his 80-year-old mother.

At first Erhard pretends he just happened by. – Busy night, Miguel?

– We're never busy, Señor Jørgensen. Always plenty of time for our guests.

– Have you seen Jean Boulard recently?

This is an internal joke about one of the island's celebrities, who found himself in the gossip column because he danced with Penelope Cruz on the hotel's penthouse terrace.

– I don't discuss the hotel's guests, Miguel says with a thin smile.

– Not even if they break the law?

– We don't have those kind of guests.

– What about the five or six who passed through a few minutes ago?

– Is there a problem, Señor Jørgensen? Did they forget to pay their fare?

Erhard looks at Miguel. – Yes, you could say that.

– How much do they owe you? Shall I put it on their bill?

– I'll take care of it. I'm sure it's just a mistake. What room are they in?

Miguel gives Erhard an uptight look. – Only because it's you.

– You know who I mean? Three young men and two, what can I call them? Women.

– I saw only two young men. They booked the rooms earlier today. Were they accompanied by females?

Miguel doesn't gesture or bat an eye or anything that might suggest he understands that female accompaniment means prostitutes. Erhard doesn't need to embarrass him.

– It'll only take a moment, Erhard says.

– Rooms 221 and 223. Right below the room you had last time you stayed with us.

– Thank you, Miguel. I'll be right back.

Erhard walks around the corner and takes the lift. He's too tired for the stairs.

He hears them already in the corridor. The boy sounds like a hoover, Alina like bagpipes being kicked, but there's no doubt about it: it's her. The sound increases in volume until he's standing at the door of room 221. Erhard doesn't want to run into the other band members, but he knows that at least one of them is busy with the little girl who looks like Birte Tove. It's possible they're both with her. No sounds emerge from 223. Maybe they're all asleep, wasted and high, in a heap.

He raps on the door three times. A not-too-insistent number.

– Go away, he hears the lead singer say.

– Champagne, señor.

– Go away.

– From the record producer who was sat at the bar, señor, Erhard says, hoping the message is interesting enough.

He hears Alina make a noise, then footsteps.

At the moment the lead singer opens the door, Erhard leans all his weight against it, so the skinny lad is plunked in the face at full force and stumbles backwards while reaching for something to hold onto. He doesn't find anything, and so he falls against a chair and a small table, knocking over a picture frame that smashes against the floor. Erhard follows him quickly into the room.

Alina's lying in the centre of the bed, her legs spread, and her arms outstretched towards the headboard, so Erhard has a clear line of sight to her shaven, almost light-brown crotch, a narrow strip of belly, and her beak-shaped breasts. When she recognizes Erhard, she doesn't ball herself up as he expects she would, but puts her arms calmly behind her head and crosses her legs.

The singer tries getting to his feet, but Erhard pushes him against the wall, then the bed. His nose spills blood into his mouth. He's unable to speak. There's an open bottle of whisky on the nightstand. Erhard looks at the label; it's Jack Daniels, but it's not the usual square bottle. Maybe it's a knock-off. The boy sits with his hand pressed to his nose. Erhard takes a swig before pouring some on the boy's face; he writhes in pain but doesn't make a peep. Erhard can't decide whether he's a man or an idiot.

– What the hell are you doing here, Fourfingers?

Erhard stands quietly, waiting for the boy to glance up at him with his bloodshot eyes. – Get your things and leave. Stay away from her. You and your friends, stay far away from her.

– What did I do? I thought… we talked at the bar, the boy says.

– She's the biggest fraud on the island. Once again Alina doesn't react. Erhard expected her to say something, but she's silent, waiting, which makes him nervous.

– What are you talking about? the boy asks.

– Get out of here, now. Now. Erhard considers lifting the bottle to show that he means it, but the boy quickly gathers his things off the floor and leaves the room. A sad sight with his hairy, scrawny buttocks. His back is spotted with acne.

– What are you up to? Alina has an obnoxious smile on her lips, as if she's enjoying all this, as if she's the popular harlot in some John Wayne film. – Is it because you want me all to yourself, you old pig?

– I wouldn't fuck you if you were the last woman on the island, you fraud. He wishes he'd said something harsher, something harder-hitting to knock the smile from her lips. But she's unaffected.

– Sure you would. She grins.

He wants to smash the bottle against her forehead and slam the broken bottle into her childless belly. He wants to destroy her. He suddenly hates her face, her tiny curls, her upward-pointing nipples that she doesn't try to conceal, and her self-assured smile with its twist of grief – a smile Erhard all at once understands cannot be wiped off with violence, humiliation, or hatred. Powerless, he stares at her. He sees the Alina from the village, when she was a teenager, seated in the bus or in the back row at school. A cross-eyed girl in a flowery dress. He envisions her as a little girl kicking stones down the road and chasing some big dog's tail.

– How did you get this way? he asks. The question surprises her. Still smiling, her eyes dart uncertainly. Erhard goes on: – How did you become so indifferent to others? To everything?

– I'm not going to let you ruin my business, she says, and begins to crawl out of bed.

– Stay right there, Erhard says sharply.

She pauses and, for the first time, covers herself with her hands and the bed sheets. – What do you want from me?

– I want you to sit there like the dumb girl you are. Like the sad sack who wishes to make money off a little boy's death.

– What does it matter to you? It has nothing to do with you.

– You can't abandon a child and get away scot-free.

– Listen to me, I didn't abandon anything. I've just…

– I know what you've done.

– Oh yeah, and what are you going to do to me? Report me to the police?

Again this irritating resolve. As though playing the role of child killer amuses her.

But she's right. He doesn't know what he'll do. He thought he could somehow bring her to her senses, but now that he's failed, he doesn't know what to do.

– Whatever the police gave you, I'll double it. It's a shot in the dark, and he hadn't anticipated suggesting it. He hopes that the prostitute out in Guisguey had heard wrong, and that it's less than a thousand euros, so he can afford to pay her around two thousand.

– The police didn't give me anything, she says tiredly.

– You continue to lie.

It amazes him. Why does lying come as easily as drawing breath for some people, while others have such a difficult time of it that they'd rather travel far away? That they'd rather sacrifice everything than lie?

– I'm not lying. I'm not getting one cent from the police.

– But…

– It's not the police.

– What are you talking about?

He recalls Bernal telling him that it was all about having the right enticements. He'd meant money. Erhard was sure of that.

– It's someone else. I don't know who. The police told me a million times that it wasn't them, it was this *majorero*. Someone who wanted the problem dealt with as fast as possible. Stop looking at me like that. I'm telling the truth. That's what they said.

– So how much? Erhard knows the sum is probably ten times greater than 1,000 euros.

– Five thousand a week for every week I spend in jail. And a plane ticket to Madrid if it gets too difficult for me here on the island.

He looks at her. While she was talking, she forgot to cover her breasts, and now she's eating some multi-coloured marshmallows that she'd found in her purse, talking to Erhard as if they were a couple of friends at a bar. He thinks of who she reminds him of. At first he thought it was Beatriz; she has the same kind of hair, just shorter, and the same colour skin and body shape, though Alina is a little chubbier. But it's not Beatriz – it's the singer Kim Wilde. An uglier, shabbier version of Kim Wilde after ten years as a whore. Kim Wilde as the plump girl with a taste for disgusting sweets, drugs, and mojitos.

He takes a long pull from the bottle. – I'll buy you a plane ticket. Maybe give you 1,000 euros.

She scrutinizes Erhard. – Are you stupid?

– That's all I have.

Honesty. He's not sure it impresses her.

– Listen, even if I wanted…

– Tell them you don't want to lie in court. Tell them you've changed your mind.

– What good would that do? It wouldn't help one iota. They'll just find someone else. Someone who'll take my money and a drink at Plaza Mayor.

– Maybe. But they can't keep it up.

– So you'll go to the next girl and the girl after that? You don't have enough money for that.

Erhard is annoyed that it has suddenly become a question of money. But she's right. He doesn't have the money. He barely has enough to give her a thousand. If she actually agrees, and he has to throw a plane ticket in to boot, he doesn't know where he's going to find the money. Not right away, in any case.

– If you really want to bring all this to light, why don't you go to *La Provincia*?

That's the largest newspaper on the island, and Erhard has considered it.

– Because it's a case for the police, not the newspapers. Something terrible happened to that boy. It was a crime. I know it was.

– Did they choke him?

Alina becomes alert. She snatches the bottle from Erhard, drinks.

He can tell by her expression that she hasn't seen the images or heard very much about the boy and how he died. More's the pity that she's willing to accept the blame. – No, they starved him to death. The assholes.

– I can't back out of it, she says.

– What did they tell you?

– It's a *majorero*. He's someone important.

– Did they threaten you?

– No.

– Is he from Los Tres Papas?

– I don't really know. Maybe.

– You haven't accepted the money yet, have you?

She glances around the room. Maybe she's looking for her clothes. Erhard doesn't see her clothes – the black dress or the gold blouse – anywhere.

– You haven't spent any of the money yet?

– I've spent everything that I got so far, she says, gathering up some fabric from the floor, a pair of skimpy knickers.

– How much? How much have you spent?

– Two thousand, maybe more.

He doesn't understand. How does a girl like that spend so much money? – What the hell did you buy, a car?

– Chill out, you're not my grandfather.

– If you've already spent the money… He can't finish the sentence. It makes everything that much more complicated. If she has already accepted the money, the whole thing is at a different level now. She snaps her bra across her chest and spins it around, then lifts the straps over her shoulders. The bra makes her small breasts appear large and inviting. It's an expensive bra. Even Erhard knows that. At least 100, maybe 200 euros. Her golden blouse would run a few hundred euros at the fancy shops in Corralejo, the same with her dress.

– Stop staring at me. I'm not as dumb as you think, she says, before heading to the loo. She switches on the vent fan and it begins to whir.

– You have to pay the money back. You have to…

– What are you thinking? I'm not paying the money back. It's my money, it was given to me.

The sensitivity Erhard noticed a moment ago is once again gone. The businesswoman has awakened. The police picked the right whore. Naive, but not without intelligence. Someone to be dominated, but not manipulated. Ambitious, but not desperate. Though it's not exactly a mystery how the daughter of olive farmers wound up as a prostitute, there's surely more to it than bad grades in school and a rejected job application at the local supermarket. Only a parent can destroy a person this badly. Only an evil parent can make a person so cold, so indifferent, that one will sell oneself in bite-sized chunks garnished with one's soul.

– If I… If I pay you the money that you then pay back, he says. – I can get a few thousand tomorrow morning. When do you go to court? Friday?

– Don't bother. It won't happen. You don't have the money.

– I'm telling you that I'll pay back what you've spent. Then we just need to figure out…

– It's a lot more, she says. Dressed now, she looks different, adult. – Closer to four thousand.

Erhard feels the energy draining from him. All the whisky and other alcohol he'd consumed that evening suddenly rises to his head, making him completely drowsy and sulky. You stupid little girl, he wants to say, but he can't do it. Since it's about money, Erhard can't compete. – Forget it, he says, starting towards the door.

– What are you going to do? she calls after him.

– Find the boy's real mother, he says. He walks out the door and into the hallway, passing the lead singer and one of the other band members, who've stood there listening. Erhard appears so belligerent that the two boys step back when they see him.

He's too drunk to drive, but he does anyway. He ignores everything around him and drives irritated, dirt and stones plinking against the undercarriage, until he gets home. He doesn't make it inside, just sinks into his seat and falls asleep before the engine stops ticking.

25

Sleep. All too uncomplicated. An area untouched by worry.

What's the opposite of sleep? Wakefulness?

Wakefulness – all too complicated. Completely tangled up in irritation and bitter thoughts. He can think of nothing else. Other than the whore and her expensive bra and the boy in the box and the police's wall of files.

He waddles about, unable to sit in one place; his breakfast tastes like cardboard, the air is dusty, and his coffee is lukewarm. Looking at his books, he thinks about Solilla and her secondhand shop where he buys them.

Solilla's around sixty years old, a frail woman who seems too confused and too busy to eat. Her laughter is fake and she organizes everything in her shop according to a system only she understands. Clothes are sorted by the length of the zipper, books according to size – and dog leashes, insect curtains, and pillows by their nickel content. Regardless where one is in the shop, even down in the basement, one hears her muttering to herself, complaining about the weight of a box, the appearance of a plant, the busyness of the shop, or a customer who tries on too many clothes without making a purchase. She doesn't like those customers, but as long as one makes a purchase, as Erhard does, she's both kind and knowledgeable; and as long as one makes a purchase, one is welcome to sit on the sofa outside the shop and talk to her. When it comes to literature, politics, and the history of the islands, she's engaged and chatty. Once a journalist, she worked for many years at C2, the Canary Islands' TV station.

Maybe newspapers or television news are the last chance to find the boy's parents. In any case, he knows that a case like this one will interest Solilla. Not necessarily the boy's story – which she'll probably find too fraught with emotion – but the police's closure of a case through buying a suspect and a confession. Although she's no longer an active journalist, her network of contacts remains intact, and she can probably find an old colleague who'd take up the story.

He gets dressed and drives to Puerto. He parks behind a van, then bounds up the stairwell to the shop, which is in a villa below an enormous tree. In the shadow of the tree there's a sofa and a table surrounded by boxes of books and magazines.

Solilla's down in the basement sorting the shawls. She calls his name without looking up. She's one of the few on the island who tries to pronounce his name the Danish way, and nearly succeeds. Erhart Jørkenzen, she says. Very different from the stuttering Js and soft Ss he's used to.

She appreciates it when you don't waste her time. – I need the name of a good journalist, Erhard says. – Someone who'll write an article on corruption.

– Ha, she says and looks at him. – They're all dead. What's the news?

– The police buying a suspect, a confession that's not legit.

– And?

– And that means that the child murder case is unresolved.

– Child murder? Go on.

– Maybe it's not a murder. Do you remember the boy who was found in a car on the beach recently? Out near Cotillo?

– No, she says.

She sets the box of shawls on a shelf, then gestures for Erhard to follow her. They skirt a customer thumbing through a box of African porn magazines. Solilla has always loved freedom of the press. Also when it comes to pornography. It's one of the things she likes about Erhard. That he's from the country that first legalized pornography.

– They found a car, and on the backseat was a cardboard box with a little boy inside. Dead, of course.

– But not murdered?

– No, probably starved to death. They can't find the parents.

– So?

– So they've found some, if you'll excuse me, dumb prostitute and made her the scapegoat.

– Why? Solilla smiles.

They are on their way up the stairwell now; she's walking ahead of him, and Erhard glares right into the back of her long blue dress.

– The police want to close the case. Because of the tourists, they say.

She grunts as if she understands their reasoning. – What do you want then? What have you got?

– I have the girl who's been paid to take the blame.

– Don't the police have her?

– No, she's walking free, waiting. Her court date is Friday.

– Will she talk to a journalist?

Boom. There it is, a problem. – No, probably not.

– So what exactly would a journalist write?

– He can write an article in advance of the hearing that details how the police plan to charge a girl who wasn't involved in the case.

– Can you prove that the police are going to indict her?

– I've spoken to the policeman who's in charge. I've spoken to the girl.

– Proof, Mr Jørkenzen. Do you have proof? Papers, photographs, you know? Something a journalist can use?

Erhard knows what she means. – No.

– And what does the girl say? What's in it for her, as they say?

– Money. She's one tough bitch, if I may be so blunt.

– OK, so I know a few journalists who aren't completely hopeless, but they'll all say the same thing: The girl won't talk, and the police will obviously deny everything. How am I supposed to substantiate this story?

– How do I know? That's why I wanted to get a journalist involved. You know how to dig up stuff and investigate these kinds of matters.

She smiles again. Flattered. – I'm not getting involved, if that's what you think.

– Trust me, Solilla, there is something fishy going on. It's a shitty case, like the policeman said.

– How much are they paying her?

– The police aren't paying her. That's what's odd about it.

– Then who is?

– Some *majorero*, the girl told me. Five thousand euros for every week she sits in jail.

– That's interesting. Of course, that means that if the police aren't paying for her confession, they can deny everything.

– Listen to yourself, will you? This is a sick and twisted story. It deserves to be publicized.

She hands him a book. – Read it. It's a classic.

He glances at the book. It has a colourful cover with a black silhouette of a man smoking a pipe. *The Adventure of the Speckled Band and Other Stories.* He remembers reading parts of it. Many years ago. He riffles through the pages. Like every other book by Doyle, he never finished it.

– Maybe, he says.

– Diego Navarez. The son of an old friend of mine. He's a journalist now, too. At *La Provincia* here in Puerto. He's critical and bright. If anyone takes this up, it'll be him. But he's not as experienced. Not yet.

He sounds good, Erhard thinks. Young people take a more idealistic view of corruption. – How do I get in touch with him?

– Let me. His father owes me a favour.

– Today?

– *Dios mío*, you're so wound up. I've never seen you like this.

– The hearing is on Friday.

She glances at the clock above the door. – I'll call you in a bit. Wait outside on the sofa. I'll be out when I've spoken to him.

He sits on the sofa underneath the tree and reads Sherlock Holmes. Tries to, anyway. A cat belonging to the property – at which Solilla always throws rocks and bottle caps – sprawls out beside him, swishing its tail across the book.

A short time later, Solilla walks down the stairwell. She hands him a telephone. – You can arrange a meeting with him yourself.

Just as he's about to forget Aaz, he remembers him. He drops him off at Mónica's house and promises to return by 4.30 p.m. at the latest. Then he drives back to Puerto and finds the cafe. And waits. Orders two draught beers, one for himself and one for Diego. The foam settles.

Diego's much too young. He looks like a teenager wearing a shirt that was passed down to him, or which at the very least is not ironed. He sees Erhard and sits down.

– So the mother who's not the mother is getting money to take the fall?

Erhard glances around the cafe, but there's no one else but a few young men playing pinball behind an espalier of plastic flowers. – You've done your homework, Erhard says.

– I read what little's been published to date. Seems like a sad case, but not so unusual. People find little babies here and there. Two similar cases on the islands in 2010. Immature girls who didn't want to rebel against their religious parents, I think. Third-trimester abortions, if you ask me.

– But in this case the police have got a girl, a prostitute pretending to be the mother. They've concocted a lie.

– Why would they do that? I imagine they'd like to solve the case.

– Apparently not. That's what's so crazy. They've stopped doing police work and have found someone to take the fall so they can close the case.

– But why?

– The policeman I spoke to said it's because of the casino. Because they want to build it here on the island and not Lanzarote. A case like this would ruin their plans.

– Interesting. But it doesn't sound likely.

– That's what he said.

– The same one who told you the rest?

Erhard can hear for himself how problematic it sounds. – Yes, he says.

– The police tend not to care so much about that kind of thing. They don't really give a crap about the tourist industry, I think.

– Didn't they get new leadership recently, a new police commissioner?

– Sure.

– And he says he wants to investigate corruption, to follow EU directives.

– Sure.

– Well, there's your story.

Diego smiles. He's a little too cocky, it seems to Erhard. – Yes, that's a good story. Down at the *bodega*. But not in the newspaper. Nothing in that story of yours makes it probable.

– I've just shown you how probable it is.

– But what's the motive?

– That's what you've got to find out.

– My editor will ask me the same thing, I think. And he'll want answers before he lets me use even half an hour researching anything. How much did the police pay the girl to confess? Have you seen any bank receipts or something that can prove it?

– No. But the police aren't paying her. Someone else is. Some guy with a lot of euros in his wallet.

Diego rolls his eyes. – OK.

– OK what?

– That only makes it worse. Who says the whore didn't simply earn the money? Getting mixed up in this will get ugly, very ugly, I think.

Erhard shifts in his seat. The energy he'd felt before Diego arrived is nearly gone now. – But the boy. What about him?

– The harsh truth, Diego says, is that the boy is dead. He wasn't murdered, his whore of a mother probably just forgot about him. It's sad and awful. No one wants to read about that.

Erhard thinks about the car, the thirty-odd miles on the odometer. – But there's more, he says. – The car was stolen in Amsterdam, or somewhere, and suddenly shows up here. There's something peculiar about that.

Diego drains his beer. – OK. Listen, Jørgensen. I like you. But I'm here because my father and Solilla have worked together. I'll keep my eye on this case and see if anything new turns up.

– Something new *has* turned up, Erhard says. – The mother is not the mother. What else do you need for it to be new?

– That's interesting, but the police are doing what they can, I think.

– The hearing is on Friday. If she pleads guilty and is sentenced, the police won't reopen the case any time soon.

– What if I go to the hearing? If there's anything fishy that supports your theory, then I'll be in touch with you. Give me your telephone number.

Erhard gives him his number.

– Don't you have a mobile?

– I don't. You can call dispatch at TaxiVentura if I don't answer at home.

– Say hello to Señora Solilla. Tell her that my father still talks about her. He's still fond of her, I think. In spite of everything. Thanks for the beer.

– I'll do that.

So much for the idealism of youth. He feels like an angry old conspiracy theorist. He orders another beer and watches the dark-skinned boys playing pinball, listening to the strange sounds emerging from the machine.

Just because he doesn't know what to do with himself, he parks in the queue down at Carmen. He tries to read, but the words are meaningless to him. Right before siesta he's told he's got a phone call. He goes into Café Bolaño, whose number he gave dispatch, and awaits the transfer. Is the journalist already calling him? He hears the click of the switch.

– There's a problem, Emanuel Palabras says. Ever dramatic.

It turns out it's only something about the Fazioli.

– It can wait until tomorrow, Erhard says. He and Palabras have a regular appointment every second Thursday of each month.

Palabras doesn't think it can wait.

– I've got something I need to do, Erhard says. – I'll stop by afterward.

He picks up Aaz and drives him back to Santa Marisa.

They don't talk much. Erhard can't think of anything positive to say. So he settles on squeezing the Boy-Man's shoulder in parting.

He parks for an hour down at Carmen. Takes one trip out to Las Dunas with an enthusiastic young couple.

It's not until six o'clock that his irritation and rage simmer down. He drives a family to the airport and enters the terminal to buy a sandwich. It too tastes like cardboard. Cardboard and fresh but flavourless local tomatoes. It's the disgrace of the island: the new growers, who just want to export as many tons as possible, cultivate perfectly round tomatoes in dust-free hothouses. He eats while reading the headlines of the day's newspaper. There's an article in *La Provincia* about the biggest olive farmer on the island, who's now moving to the mainland. He throws the rest of his paper sandwich into the trash and pays the girl at the kiosk with coins.

There's an ad for the Sheraton Beach Golf and Spa Resort under his windscreen wiper. The construction projects begun before the financial crisis are finally being completed and can now fight for tourists' attention, while the unfinished, cancelled hotels stand like monuments to naive investment fever and serve as giant bunk beds for the island's beach bums. Hotel Olympus, Corralejo, is illuminated at night by fire and battery-driven disco balls as loud gangs of youths party inside its concrete shell. Such parties were once a problem, but the authorities have now chosen to look the other way. Where else can the poor wretches go? It's more expensive to provide them with a place. There's no barrier or fence. In January, a young man fell and died. An orphan without a story. Glue in his nose and a body ravaged by alcohol and drugs. The discussion that followed was focused more on the gangs than the dangerous construction sites that have sat abandoned for years. Erhard doesn't mind the unlawful squatters. He's been in that position himself, quaffing homebrews from petrol cans, watching little girls shuck off their clothes and run naked across glowing hot coals.

He glances at his watch and drives north. A visit to Papa Palabras is nothing to look forward to, but today he wants to take his mind off things. And a beautiful piano, a masterpiece of a piano, always has an uplifting effect on him. He hopes so anyway.

26

At the end of Calle Dormidero, the little road loops around a palm tree. At the top of the loop is the entrance to Papa Palabras's enormous property. For some reason the gigantic wrought-iron gate automatically opens every time Erhard arrives. Other visitors have to place a call through the gate telephone. But not Erhard. He drives straight through and parks next to the servants' quarters, located on the west side of the house. Erhard crosses the lawn, knowing that Emanuel is either sitting outside sleeping, head lolling on his belly as if his neck is broken, or he's in his cactus-filled greenhouse asking his servant, a Maasai girl, to prick her finger on the various cacti to determine whether the plants are thriving or in need of water. That's how you know, he has explained. But today, as Erhard skirts a bush and heads up the stairwell towards the terrace, he notices that Emanuel is indeed asleep. Someone rings a bell, and Emanuel wakes with a start, then watches Erhard impatiently, as if he'd been waiting for hours, bored.

– *Noches*, he says, getting to his feet with the Maasai girl's help and going inside. Erhard follows him. Visiting Emanuel is never fun, but he's Erhard's best client. The client he's had the longest, and the only one who pays Erhard a regular salary to tune the piano on the third Thursday of every month. And to be available if something's wrong with the piano. But during the course of fifteen years, Emanuel has only asked for that extra service twice. The second time being today.

The first time Erhard came out for special service, it wasn't the piano that needing tuning, but a son who played pop music. That was when Erhard met Raúl. Erhard examined the piano for twenty seconds, then saw the young man standing in the corner. Erhard inspected the piano again, raised his hammer, scraped a little steel wool against the strings. Then he explained to Emanuel that something was wrong with the piano. It could be fixed, but it would be pricey and take a few months. Palabras, who was a heavy-set man, glared at Erhard, then threw up his hands in the way that Erhard had come to understand meant, *It already has*. The man loved his Fazzi. That much was clear from the outset.

On his way out, Erhard took hold of Raúl. He was a gangly, frivolous person, Erhard sensed. I'll take you to a real teacher, he told him. If he was going to play a Fazioli, then he should play it properly. Erhard used the money he earned fixing the perfectly tuned piano to pay the city's best pianist, the schoolteacher Vivi, who lived in Gornjal. If Erhard happened to be in the area, he picked up Raúl himself and drove him down there. Raúl became a good, if not great, pianist. Whenever his discontent was transferred to the keys, he could play Gershwin and Bernstein with conviction.

Although Emanuel is less imposing that he'd once been, he's still a force. Also from the back when he's wearing his strange cloak – blanket, really – over his shoulder. His gait is shuffling and he breathes in wheezy gasps, as if he's fighting his way through a swamp and not his own mansion towards his sunroom in the opposite wing. The man has built – with the help of his architects and his gardeners – a home that doesn't sound, smell, or feel like anything else on the Canary Islands. The orange clay walls, bamboo fans, patterned columns, and endless rows of lion heads are meant to resemble Africa – that colonized and ravaged continent, suffocated by the obese white man.

That's Erhard's view of it anyway, not part of the romantic tale Emanuel has told him again and again, whenever he wants to say something about his residence, the Maasai girls – who're kept in God knows what room – or the Spanish mother country, so far away, so beloved, so yearned for, and so cursed. Oh, remember back when the Spanish conquered Africa and enjoyed its nature and the simple things in life.

They've reached the piano. Emanuel sits on the bench and plays Abril's 'Coral'. It's the only piece that he ever wishes to play, or even knows how to. Everything else is just noise to him, an unnecessary burden on the piano, unworthy of a Fazzi. Erhard is no Abril expert, but he can tell that Emanuel plays the music well and fiercely and much too fast. There's an imprecision on the E key, not a huge problem – in fact, it's one of those problems that Erhard actually likes, one that he prefers to ignore, because it gives the piano its character. Standing beside the piano, he listens as Palabras wraps up the piece. Emanuel's fingers rise from the keys as if they were a house of cards.

He doesn't say a word, just fixes a firm stare on Erhard: Do you hear that clinking noise? his eyes seem to suggest.

Erhard says he hears something on F, but no clinking on Gb. He tests the chords. He sweeps some dust from the box and lightly polishes the strings.

Emanuel once again plays the entire composition from the beginning. Still Erhard doesn't hear anything. When Emanuel plays the piece for the third time, Erhard walks around the piano and stands on Emanuel's left side. Now he hears a faint rustling sound, like a pinecone rolling across a dry forest floor. But it's not coming from the piano, it's coming from Emanuel himself. He's breathing excitedly, too rapidly. Erhard sees his chest in the slit between the cloak and his unevenly buttoned shirt. 'Coral' is a stimulating composition, and Erhard's certain that if he gazed in the darkness between Emanuel's legs, he would see an erection in his thin trousers. The man's more than eighty years old, no doubt horny as a goat, and incapable of fucking any of his Maasai girls no matter how much he'd like to. But here at the piano he can, for whatever reason, still get it up. But he pays for it with his laboured breathing.

– Do you have a CD player? Erhard asks.

Emanuel looks at him, confused. Of course he doesn't. In this house they have gramophone records and radio. Erhard explains that if he doesn't want to hear the crackle in 'Coral' he needs to do exactly what Erhard says. No questions asked. Emanuel's sitting uneasily on the piano bench. He's not used to doing what others tell him. Finally he throws up his hand.

– I'll be back in an hour to remove that noise. In the meantime, find that girl who takes care of you and ask her to wait in the driveway until I return. Emanuel sizes him up, but says nothing. Erhard heads out to his car.

He drives downtown. As he passes Calle Cervera he searches for Alina, but if she's still working, she's not there now. There's an odour, a mixture of lamb and petrol. He keeps the motor running while he runs into a music shop on the corner of High Street called Bird. They sell mostly jazz and a sampling of modern music, but in the basement they've got a rather pedestrian collection of classical music. Luckily, Abril's 'Coral' is among the most popular piano concertos on the Spanish islands. Erhard even knows of a version produced by Orquesta Sinfónica de Madrid; he nods at the shopkeeper, Antón, then heads directly down the winding stairwell to the basement. They've got two versions of 'Coral', one of which is the Orquesta Sinfónica de Madrid. He also asks Antón to go online and find the sheet music to the concerto 'Allegro' and print it out, with Erhard paying half a euro per sheet. Antón doesn't like doing that. Stupid Internet, he says, standing beside the computer. He'll go out of business soon, he adds, because no one wants to pay for music any more. How am I supposed to compete with the geeks of the world when you can get everything you want for free? Erhard agrees with him in principle, but doesn't know much about how the Internet works. Once he's done in the shop, he drives up the street to Electron and buys a CD player. He doesn't own a CD player, but they have one in the break-room at work. He haggles the price down to thirty euros. When he emerges from the store, he considers getting some roasted shrimp at the small corner kiosk, but watching the man flip the pink shellfish with a newspaper nauseates him. He drives back to Palabras's mansion.

27

She's like a space alien in black leather: sleek, gorgeous, and frightening. And she's standing in the driveway waiting for him, just as he'd asked. He's never spoken to her. Never heard her voice. In fact, he doesn't even know whether she speaks. He explains to her what she needs to do. She listens without blinking. When he asks her if she understands what he's saying, she nods, but it doesn't seem like she does. She doesn't have any questions about Erhard's plan, or any reluctance to carry it out.

– Me to do it with Manny with music, she repeats.

– Right, Erhard says, and considers how funny it is that one of the island's most powerful men is called Manny by a... what is she? A 20-year-old girl.

– Manny can't, he can't, his stick too soft, it makes him angry.

Erhard shakes his head, points at a CD, and shows her with his index finger how Manny's dick will respond. Her eyes gleam with laughter, but she remains silent. It makes her look even more frightening.

– Come with me, he says.

They go inside and find Emanuel where they left him an hour before. He stares unhappily at Erhard's hands, as if he'd expected tools instead of shopping bags.

– What now, Piano Tuner?

Erhard reminds him of his promise to do exactly as he'd asked. The man nods once. Erhard clutches his arm and guides him into the next room, then deposits him on a white leather sofa that's never been touched.

– Sit here and listen to the music while I fix the piano.

Erhard unpacks the CD player, inserts the CD, and presses play. Emanuel lurches at the sound of the first notes, staring distrustfully at the CD player. Erhard nods to the girl, who sits beside Emanuel and pulls up her dress. Emanuel doesn't notice, a combination of astonishment and undefined softness having overtaken his normally livid face. Erhard returns to the piano room.

He sets the 'Allegro' book on the music stand and opens it to page one. He fiddles loudly at the piano, putting in the tuning lever but doing nothing with it. The piano is extraordinarily beautiful, one of the first F308s ever produced at Fazioli's workshop, in 1987. Although Erhard has never played anything on it but chords, he's often dreamed of sneaking into this room when Emanuel wasn't home and hammering on the enormous piano. The sound is much different than other pianos: pure, undisturbed, and better than the best Steinway Erhard has ever tuned. Thanks to the air conditioner, it's housed in the perfect temperature, and it's never in direct sunlight. He can't even begin to describe how ridiculous it is to suspect the piano of making a rustling noise. In all the years that he's visited this mansion, he has never made the piano sound better – only worse. Some clients have called him a wizard because he can touch an instrument for a few minutes with the tuning wrench and make their piano-playing better than it's ever been. They expect him to arrive with modern equipment. Instead he simply listens, then makes their piano sound like a living, breathing creature instead of a robot. The secret isn't to make every tone perfectly pure, but perfectly imperfect. It gives the piano its character, and the right sound. Every piano tuner knows this, but none will ever tell their clients. Throw in mathematics – and forget mathematics. Every client wants the optimum, the correctly harmonized instrument, but in reality that's not what they want.

The music reaches the dramatic intermezzo about three minutes into 'Coral'.

He hears the cigar table being scraped across the floor, then sees the girl's long legs sticking out. There's an odd grunt, probably because she's seated astride Emanuel's lap, riding him like a debt-ridden jockey on the last day of the season. Emanuel's not used to hearing 'Coral' played with strings, and Erhard wonders if he'll develop a new appreciation of Abril. Erhard pours himself a glass of Pedro Ximénez from a bottle resting on a small table next to the piano, then walks out to the little orchid and cactus garden that adjoins the sunroom. The garden, now the domain of butterflies, is covered by a thin net that provides shade during the day and keeps birds and other large pests out. The butterflies are everywhere. They sit on the cacti's sharp spikes like birds on branches, fluttering their wings. Lamps arranged between the plants illuminate the garden, along with a few large floodlights in the ceiling, which almost make it feel like daytime.

Right in front of Erhard is one of those butterflies with bright yellow wings, and he considers how long it's actually been since the last time he saw a yellow butterfly like those they have back home in West Jutland, in Denmark, where his maternal grandfather Claus lived in a squalid little house with a wife who never spoke. Through the door he hears 'Coral' start up again. Emanuel must be getting a second ride. The lucky bastard.

Erhard holds up his index finger, trying to get one of the butterflies to view him as a black cactus. But they know the difference. Of course they do. There are very few butterflies on the island, and he guesses it's because of the wind and the climate. That's why it just seems like another expression of Emanuel's power: to own a surfeit of butterflies. Like his stock of cars, girls, water, flowers, hunting trophies, expensive beef, and Spanish wine. And money. But Emanuel never talks about his money, that's one difference. He refuses to talk about it. If someone mentions money or the fact that Emanuel's wealthy, he becomes cross. On multiple occasions Erhard has heard him call Raúl a cursed Judas, because he asked him for money for some project or to pay off his debts. One time a while back, Emanuel told Erhard that his family hailed from Vallecas, the poorest quarter of Madrid, where all the houses are built with plastic bottles and corrugated cardboard. Maybe he's ashamed of his money – or at the way he earned it?

Erhard thinks about the little boy. And Alina. Emanuel Palabras could finance her little Madrid trip and an extravagant shopping spree as if it were nothing more than purchasing a couple of lottery tickets. Hell, it's cheaper than a few butterflies or a new cactus. He could ask him. He has a special relationship to Emanuel, a relationship that he's never taken advantage of or wished to take advantage of. But maybe it's time to cash in on that goodwill. Send the girl away and teach the police a lesson. Emanuel would like that, Erhard is certain. Like most everyone whose business is balanced on the edge of the law, Palabras takes exquisite pleasure in seeing the police exposed and humiliated. On the other hand, he wouldn't like the story about the boy. Why should Erhard get involved? If he says anything to Palabras, he's got to have a good reason.

28

When the sherry is gone, he heads back inside. 'Coral' is playing for the fourth or fifth time, but after a few minutes, he sees the girl trot down the hallway, her clothes bundled in her arms. Emanuel enters the room and goes directly to his piano. His lower lip is red and puffy, as if he – or the girl – bit it.

– So, have you fixed it?

– I forbid you to play 'Coral' on this piano for three months, Erhard says.

– You're not my doctor. I'll play whatever I wish to play, Emanuel barks angrily, and yet with a smile beneath his beard, as if he knows what Erhard's about to say.

– You've promised to do what I say. Play 'Allegro' for three months, and you will no longer hear the rustling.

He knows what effort this will require of him. For two decades Emanuel has played 'Coral' like a man smoking his favourite cigarette, focused, his sights set on death. Now Erhard's asking him to switch to nicotine patches.

Emanuel sits on the bench staring at the music as if he doesn't understand it, deep in concentration. Erhard suddenly feels warm. What if he doesn't know how to read music? Emanuel usually studies the sheets when he plays 'Coral', but now Erhard wonders if he doesn't read them at all, just pretends to. That's why he's never played anything else; he doesn't know how to play anything else, and doesn't wish to admit it. Can Erhard force the man to admit this or somehow get him to take lessons with Vivi down in Gornjal? She'd probably hate Emanuel, just like she hated Raúl in the beginning – for his wealth – but over time the old man could learn something, and it would out turn out OK. No, it wouldn't. By the end of his lessons, the house in Gornjal would be emptied. Vivi's mynah bird would squawk for an entire night before the neighbours found the pianist dead in a wine cask on the terrace. Her beliefs are diametrically opposed to Emanuel's. She keeps photographs of her godchildren on her walls, and organic tomatoes on the window-sills, and she's no good with money, often forgetting to accept payment for her lessons. But now Emanuel lays his fingers on the keys and strikes the first tones from 'Allegro'. It's a very different sound than 'Coral'. More militant. More ceremonial. Emanuel feels his way through the first sheet. Stares in surprise at the ivory pavement where his fingers march along, as if incapable of understanding how they might produce sounds other than those he knows so well from 'Coral'.

As Erhard expected, the rustle is gone. Palabras is breathing calmly. All he needed was another piece of music. He makes a few mistakes that give the composition a little life. Erhard sees the girl peering in cautiously, she's dressed now, once again the space alien, sealed off, on guard. It occurs to Erhard that there's a new sound in the house. For so many years the house staff, the Maasai girls, and the Greek gardener have only heard the same music repeated on an endless loop. Like a lion circulating in its cage, Emanuel has returned to it in order to arouse himself using all that remained of what had once been a full-fledged fantasy. But with a new sound the house breathes easier. And Emanuel, though he's still too fat and too unhealthy, no longer wheezes. Time for Erhard to leave.

He pours himself another Ximénez without asking for permission, then walks through the house without saying goodbye. That's their custom. Emanuel sits at the piano, and Erhard drains a glass in front of the mansion before tossing it into the small pond.

29

9.30 p.m. He's about to head home. He parks on High Street and begins tabulating his accounts. He's made so many small fares that it takes time to calculate. In a little while he'll go down the street to Cannes, a small sandwich shop. It's not a place he frequents often, but they serve some really terrific and greasy burgers that they squeeze into a wrap.

– Hermit, Isabel says. She's working the late shift at dispatch. The telephone girls never use that name. He didn't even know they were aware of it.

He presses the button. – 4823.

– Hotel Phenix. A fare to the airport.

– The 10.15 Berlin flight?

Silence. – How should I know? All they said was that they needed to get to the airport.

– I'm wrapping up for the day. Can you call someone else?

– They requested you.

– Miguel from the Phenix?

– No, it was a woman. She asked for you. Should I send someone else?

– 4823 confirms.

He lays his paperwork on the backseat and snaps on his indicator light. The fare sounds harmless, but all the same he feels a little uneasy. He wonders if the band he watched recently, or its Arabic lead singer, has plotted revenge.

He drives up to the hotel and toots his horn once. Normally that's not necessary, but if there's a new desk clerk and a guest needs to reach the Berlin flight at quarter past ten, then they have to get going. He waits for three minutes, then cuts the engine and enters the hotel. He doesn't see anyone in the lobby, either on the sofas or at the front desk. He dings the bell, and Miguel emerges from the office.

– Good evening, Señor Jørgensen. Miguel glances around. – How can I assist you?

– Good evening, Miguel. Someone called for me. A woman. One of your colleagues? Someone at the bar maybe?

– I'm the one who orders the taxis.

– But... could a guest have called?

– It's possible, Señor Jørgensen.

– I'm supposed to take someone to the airport.

Miguel checks his watch. – The 10.15 Berlin flight?

– That would be my guess.

– No one has checked out yet. But she can still make it. There's an Englishwoman on the fourth floor. Perhaps she called you. He glances at the key cubbies. – She's not in her room.

– I'll wait in the car, Miguel. Just send her out.

He returns to his car and climbs in. If she doesn't come out in a few minutes, she'll miss her flight. Maybe she doesn't need to catch a plane. Maybe she's going to pick someone up. Or maybe she's going to work.

Suddenly there's a loud squealing on the street, and he raises his arms to protect himself. Then he realizes it's just a big pick-up truck with loud music zooming past, three guys in the truck bed.

He glances in the rearview mirror, and stiffens when he sees Alina. She's in the backseat. Smiling her irritating smile.

– I don't have time for you now. I've got a customer on the way.

– I'm your customer, Fourfingers.

– Get the hell out of my car. He feels his left hand buzzing, as if he can crush her by smashing the mirror.

She laughs. – No way, I need to get to the airport.

– I refuse to drive you. Get out of my car.

– Why? You need money like everyone else.

– I don't drive criminals.

She laughs again. – Since when?

– I don't need your money.

– Just drive, she says. She has this strange ability to manipulate people so that it's easier to do what she says than resist.

He spins around. She's wearing a salmon-coloured suit with a pair of gold-rimmed sunglasses resting on top of her head. It's tacky, and yet it makes her look better than she normally does. – What do you want? There are no more flights today.

– I need a ride to the Palace, you know.

– Isn't that tomorrow?

Laughs again. Apparently it's all very amusing to her. She's plastered. That must be why. She looks plastered anyway. – I guess I'm supposed to sleep there tonight.

– Then why the hell did you call me? There are thirty other cabbies you could've requested. Or the police. They could've picked you up.

But he knows, even as he's talking, that she called him to gloat. To show him that she's doing exactly what she wants to do. No one tells her what to do.

– Because you remind me of my father, she says. – Old, angry, funny.

– The poor man. His daughter's a whore.

– He doesn't give a shit. He's a fucking asshole.

– No parent is like that. Doesn't give a shit, I mean.

Again she laughs.

He begins to drive. He might as well get it over with.

– That's how you do it, Fourfingers.

Mindlessly he drives along Avenida and out towards Las Dunas, while she prattles on about Madrid, shopping, and a friend with forty pairs of shoes. He has to remember to shift gears, and fumbles with the air conditioner to get more cool air in the car.

– I want you to know, she says when they've reached Route 101, that I considered it. I really did. You made me think about it. You know how you weigh things in your head? Should I take the money or should I do what old Fourfingers says? I spoke with Tia, and she was super excited for me to come to Madrid, and so…

– Stop. I don't want to know. I don't want to know why you're doing it. You are… you are so unbelievably selfish that it doesn't…

– Selfish? No I'm not, goddamn you. I've… You have no idea how much shit I've been through. I'm not selfish or bad or…

Now it's Erhard's turn to laugh. – You're just stupid. You're so incredibly stupid that I fear for the future. Because of people like you, I fear for the future.

They fall silent.

– You're so goddamned holier-than-thou, Alina says. – I'm telling you that I considered it. But I can't afford to say no. I can't.

– Shut your mouth.

– I didn't kill that boy. I didn't do anything wrong.

– But thanks to you and your Madrid trip, the police will never find out what happened.

– So what? Why the hell is that my problem? Why is it yours for that matter?

– Because it's a crime. The worst kind. Someone killed a little boy. And it wasn't the parents.

– Not all parents are equally good, you know.

– You don't starve a child to death and abandon it in a cardboard box. No parent would do that.

– Parents do whatever they feel like doing.

– When you have a child you'll be ashamed of yourself…

– What the fuck do you know? Besides, I'm never having children. Understand? Never.

– For your kids' sake, I hope you don't.

He's driving so fast now, over 90 mph, that the car begins to vibrate. He wants to get this over with, he wants her out of the car as quickly as possible. The sun has set, and the landscape on the car's right side is black, the sky above greenish-purple.

He glances at her in the rearview as she peers into her small compact mirror, adjusting her lipstick. It's almost as if she has a date with the entire police station. He imagines her in court. The salmon-coloured suit perfectly underscores the story of the lapsed Catholic. She'll twirl her hair in her finger and apologize. At most she'll get a few months in prison. The officers will flock to her cramped cell and serve her food, and in the evenings they'll fight to sneak a peek into her cell while she crawls underneath the blanket. The worst part is that she's a good choice for the role. She doesn't appear to be hooked on heroin like many of the other girls; she's more mature, and she looks like a mother – her cheeks, her suit, her hair, all of it. She's a good liar too. If she sheds a tear at the preliminary hearing, no journalist will question her. In any case, not unless the real mother or father shows up and gets involved.

She notices him looking at her. She smiles. He turns away.

– The little shit. He probably deserved it.

It takes a moment before he realizes what she'd said. What she means. They're just words. But words can be more malicious than actions. More premeditated, more manipulative, more stripped of humanity. He knows she's watching him in the rearview mirror. To see how angry he'll get. To test whether or not she can get him worked up, as if he were the regional president or any of the horny old men she grabs by the balls and cock-slaps to show who's boss.

It does something to him. In that moment he understands what he must do. How he can jam a wrench in the machinery and make the police work overtime. She's already in his car. No one knows that she's with him. It's getting dark, and soon all the light will be gone.

– Where the hell are you going? she says when he turns right at the roundabout.

30

She resists. She shouts and screams. As soon as he parks the car, she leaps out and begins to run away, but the darkness is too much for her, and she stands frozen long enough that he's able to come around and grab her.

She's strong, clawing at him and punching the air and cursing. But it's nothing to him now. He's made his decision. He shoves her across the garden towards the shed.

– No, no, no, she shrieks, when he pushes her into the shed and slams the door. He's sweating from exertion. Gasping for breath, he retreats a step from the door, afraid he'll get so worked up that he'll enter the cage and pound her senseless. It would be easier for him to beat her when it's dark rather than in daylight when he can see her. It's as though he's captured a she-devil and can put an end to all the world's evil. But then he smells her perfume and hears her whimper like the girl she is, and he knows that the darkness, the night sounds, and the uncertainty will break her by morning. He considers telling her that he'll let her out tomorrow afternoon, but it's too early. He can't be friendly yet.

She cries and curses him. It's a strange mix.

When he goes inside his house, he almost can't hear her. The generator and the wind – which has picked up – drown out her voice. He hopes she won't begin messing with the generator, which is also out in the shed; she can easily destroy it or turn it off, either in anger or to irritate him. Tonight, she's probably scared and confused. She'll simmer down soon. If he's lucky, she'll fall asleep. But early tomorrow morning, when a little light begins to filter through the chinks in the shed, maybe she'll discover the generator and start hacking at it or rip the cables out.

He pours himself a full glass of cognac, then drains it without pleasure or even taste. He doesn't switch on the light, just ambles around the house, unable to get any peace so long as Alina's voice is a perfectly pitched C behind the continual soughing of the wind and her hammering. He even walks to the window and gazes at the shed, purple in the moonlight. There's no movement there, of course, or any sign that a person is inside. Only the sound, like a dog clawing and whining. He tugs off his trousers and shirt and turns on Radio Mucha and night jazz. The John Coltrane Quartet.

Finally, after fifteen or twenty minutes she falls silent. He exits through the kitchen door, walks onto the terrace, and listens through the wind. Laurel's munching on a pair of underwear that have fallen from the clothesline. Erhard rubs him behind the ear, patting his coarse pelt. He's not sure he's made the right decision. In fact he's sure he made the wrong decision. But at least he's done something.

She starts early the next morning. Shouting one moment, crying the next. Judging by the light, the sun has just risen. He hears Laurel walking around outside. The wind has settled a bit. She's managed to shut off the generator – and he hears her just as clearly as if she were seated on his lap. If Erhard had neighbours who lived nearby, who jogged in the hills or visited him to borrow a cup of sugar, he would have a hard time explaining the noise. Clearly someone in need. A frustrated and scared person. A wounded animal. Whimpering and screaming and pounding on the door.

He gets up and walks out. Stands beside the shed.

– Hello, she says. – Hello, Taxi-man?

– I'm not letting you out, no matter how much racket you make.

– Let me out, you psychopath, you fucking psychopath, you motherfucking shit, you… Hello? Are you there?

– Not until the hearing is over, he says.

That makes her cry again. She tries to hide it, but there's something about the sound a woman makes when she cries. You can always tell, even at a distance.

– I'm OK now, she says. – I'll calm down. C'mon, please let me out. We can talk it over. Erhard almost reaches for the lock, but he checks himself. She has foul mood-swings. He must remember to remind himself of that.

– I'll make some breakfast for you. Be quiet and I'll bring you something, he says through the door. He makes it sound as though he'll serve a small tray with fresh melon and tomatoes, cold cuts, bacon, and an omelette. But the truth is, he doesn't really have anything. He rarely eats breakfast and so he stands staring for some time at his cupboards and fridge. He grabs some peaches, olives, and relatively fresh bread. Plus a glass of water.

– Get away from the door, he says, before opening the padlock. He holds out the food, so she doesn't shove the door against his head. He peers inside. She's seated on the ground in the back of the shed, tiredly watching him. Her clothes are wrinkled and filthy, and her arms are browned with dust and dirt, as if she's tried to dig her way through the floor.

He sets the tray down at her feet.

She looks at it disinterestedly. – My smokes, she says. They're in my purse in the car.

He closes the door, locks it, and walks to his car. Pushed underneath the passenger seat is her small purse, which jingles when he pulls it out. There's not much inside. A wallet, a key ring with four keys and a plastic dollar sign, a mobile, and a pack of fags – a brand he doesn't recognize. There's also an entire bag of the coloured marshmallows that she was eating the last time he saw her. He tastes one, but it's too synthetic and sweet for his liking, and he spits it out. He tries the lighter, which catches with a long, eager flame. Why should he be nice to her? He thinks of her almost as a guest on whom he'd like to make a good impression. One cigarette probably isn't too much. Perhaps it'll make everything easier. He lays the purse and her other things inside the shed.

– You promise not to try anything? he says, when he lights a fag for her, and she sucks on it greedily. People and their cigarettes.

– I can report you to the police. You know that, right?

He hadn't thought of that. Not yet. This idea had come to him so swiftly that he hadn't really thought it through. But she's right. If he lets her go in the afternoon, there's no reason for her not to go directly to police headquarters and report him. The only thing he has hindered today is the court hearing, which in all likelihood will only be delayed while they search for the girl. He needs to find out what the police are doing before he lets her go. But she can't sit inside that shed. If she keeps turning off the generator it'll be hard on him, and he can't just hide her like Bill Haji's finger.

He locks the door, and she begins to curse him again. He's got to go to work, in any case, for a few hours. Before he leaves, he shoves her mobile in his pocket and rifles through her wallet. It's stuffed with business cards – probably from all the men she services – and two 50-euro notes. There are also a few photographs, the kind you take in a photo booth. She was probably ten years younger when the photos were taken, but it's Alina all right. Alina and another girl that resembles Alina, the same slightly puffy face, just prettier. They're both wearing black jackets, white shirts, and some kind of bow in their hair. A school uniform, the fashionable kind. And they each have pigtails. Two sisters, the elder sister strong and serious-looking, the younger sister curious-seeming and more naive – her appearance so thoroughly maintained, so puritanical, so held in check by reprimands and maybe religion that it's easy to be confused by the trembling gaze of her defiance, the near hatred, that burns through, especially in one of the images: Alina leaning towards the camera as if to stop the photographer, while her sister, seated on her lap, laughs without laughing, turning her head away from the camera. Of course she was someone else before she became a whore. She was a broken soul long before she took the job that destroyed her body. No one becomes a whore by her own free will. No one. The prostitutes who say otherwise, who say they like it, they are the most hardboiled of all.

He folds up the bills and stuffs them in his pocket. He hides the rest of the wallet's contents behind his books, on the shelf next to the finger. It's not the most original hiding spot if someone were to search for valuables in the house, but for now he can't think of a better place. And anyway, who would look for valuables in such a dump?

When he reaches the road, he parks the car and cuts the engine to listen. Her banging and shouting were so clear up at the house, even after he'd climbed into his car, that he feared they could be heard down here. But the wind, always the wind, erases all sound. Even the wind is difficult to hear; it's just part of the scenery.

Maybe he doesn't need to work, but he needs to think about his situation, and a few hours in the car, on the road, tends to help him whenever he feels this way. He drives around picking up some pedestrians, but at eleven o'clock he parks in the queue at Carmen. He pulls out his book and tries to read, but he can't focus on the pages. He imagines Alina slipping out of the shed and running – naked for some reason – down the road, to Guzman, where she points up the hill and explains how the Hermit, that crazy man, locked her up. He knows that's not likely. She can't get out of the shed. Despite its rickety appearance, the shed is solidly built, the boards are thick, the door has four hinges, and it would take two men with a bolt cutter to break the padlock. Then he imagines a scene in which he comes home and invites her into the kitchen; he grills a fish – for some reason, they eat it together – and sit out back watching the goats and gazing up the hill. He doesn't even like grilled fish.

While he's out grabbing a cup of coffee, he saunters past a taxi, inside of which two men are arguing. One is Pedro Muñoz, who normally drives on weekends, and the other is Alberto, an older cabbie who works a regular Monday to Friday shift. Alberto waves him over to the window.

– Hola, Jørgensen. Tell this young man here, again, why we use a taximeter.

Erhard dips his head forward and peers into the car. Muñoz looks a little trapped.

– What's the problem? Erhard asks.

Whenever there are disagreements, his colleagues come to him. He's earned a reputation for being a fair man of few words.

– The problem is that Alberto doesn't like a little competition, Muñoz says.

– All I'm saying is that you've got to use your taximeter and not give customers any discounts.

– You always tell me that the taximeter is best for the customer, and I get that. But, well, don't you get discounts when you buy new shoes? The price signs are only for tourists.

– It's not just about money, Erhard says.

– We're not shoe salesmen, Alberto says, affronted.

Pedro Muñoz throws up his hands. – Ridiculous. What about regular customers who ask for you? Or some girl who's afraid to walk home alone?

– I know it's against the rules, but why can't Pedro do as he wishes, so long as he settles his accounts? Erhard asks.

– Because it's my car, Alberto says, and I need to pay TaxiVentura along with all the expenses! I can't tell if he's had a bad day or just pocketed all the money. His discounts don't always make it into his accounts.

– Did you cheat? Erhard asks Muñoz, knowing that will push his buttons.

– Of course I haven't! he says, red-faced. – Honest.

– Why would you let him drive your car if you think he's cheating you?

– Because he takes 70 per cent of the cut, Muñoz says on Alberto's behalf.

The men fall silent.

There are two possible outcomes to this. Either they figure it out or Muñoz quits driving for Alberto and officially begins working for TaxiVentura. It's happened before. Alberto would have to work full-time again, at least until he finds someone new to drive nights for chump change. Some drivers still rent out their cars to substitutes; it's a way to finance their cars without working all the time. But it's usually not a good deal for the substitutes. That's why part-time cabbies are on the way out, and the two large taxi companies, TaxiVentura and Taxinaria, have organized all the drivers on the island.

– What if Pedro gets 35 per cent and stops giving discounts? he says to Alberto, offering one last chance to keep his comfy day shifts.

Alberto stares at the photograph taped to the dash. It's a faded old photo of a woman balanced on a ladder picking olives. His wife, or maybe his mother. – OK. But from now on everything goes through the taximeter, he says.

Muñoz appears to be calculating whether it's worth it for him. He simply nods. In a few months' time, he'll probably move on. Erhard doesn't know what the guy wastes his time on during daylight hours, but if he wants to earn real money driving a cab, he'll have to find a better arrangement. The 35 per cent solution only solves the problem here and now, and it helps Alberto as he draws nearer to his retirement.

– And you have to clean up all your coffee cups, Alberto says, handing Muñoz a paper cup.

– Muñoz smiles, takes the cup, and steps out of the car. For a moment he and Erhard walk side by side on the pavement, each carrying a cup. When they come to Erhard's vehicle, Erhard sets his on the roof to open the door.

– Thank you, Muñoz says.

– You're welcome, Pedro.

– It's hard, you know, because he's a nice fellow.

– Alberto's not as friendly as he seems. Just ask some of the others who started with him.

– Why did you help me? I thought you'd help him. You go back a bit, don't you?

An honest boy. Curious. Erhard appreciates that. – Justice, he says. – It's a matter of fairness. Without justice, what have you? What comes around, goes around.

– Kind of a yin and yang thing, huh? Is that what you mean?

– Why do you ask?

Either the lad's smarter than he looks or he doesn't know what he's talking about.

– They say you're a wise man, that you read a lot of books. Muñoz peeks through the passenger window at Erhard's book.

– The blind leading the blind, or whatever people say, Erhard says, getting into his car.

– What?

– Don't believe everything you hear. And come speak with me if you have any more trouble.

Erhard starts his engine and rolls forward in the queue.

During siesta he drives home, suffering from a bad conscience. She's been locked in the dark shed all day long. He listens at the door and calls out for her to step forward. Without waiting for her response, he prepares a few things inside his house, then carries out a long tow chain and hitches it to a metal ring on the side of the house, where the tarpaulin used to be. He drags the chain to the shed and unlocks the door.

It's silent in there. At first all he can see is darkness, the compact kind that swallows virtually all light. But then he sees her face. She was waiting just inside, and has begun sneaking towards the door, trying to slip around Erhard to get outside. He discovers her in the nick of time, forces the door shut with all his might, and slams the padlock closed. She screams in frustration.

– You can't do that, he says.

She doesn't reply, but he hears her punching the wall.

– I want to let you out, but don't try anything. Do you understand? No reply.

– Do you understand?

– Yes! she shouts shrilly.

– Stand against the wall. And stay there. Cautiously he opens up and peers inside, positioning his foot against the door. She's standing against the back wall, hands at her sides. She's been in the shed for only seventeen hours, and yet she looks like a shipwreck. Her hair, once meticulously coiffed, has tumbled loose. Her makeup is smudged and smeared with dirt, and the thighs of her creased, filthy trousers are torn. He steps towards her, and she stares in terror at the chain he holds in his hand.

– I'll let you go soon, he says. – When the police have figured out they've got the wrong person.

She says nothing.

– Did the telephone ring?

She doesn't look at him.

He shakes her. – It's important. Did the telephone ring? He hopes the journalist will call to let him know that he went to the hearing, and that the police will now continue their investigation. Maybe he should've gone to the hearing himself. It was probably open to the public.

He repeats his question, but she stares at the ground.

He shows her the chain. – I thought I'd put this around your ankle, so you can be outside instead.

She shakes her head almost imperceptibly, but he quickly drops to his knees and fastens it to her ankle, securing it. It's clamped tight around the skinniest part of her leg, and will begin to hurt at some point, but it's got to be better than sitting in the dark.

The chain is long enough for her to enter the house. She can use the toilet. She can reach the kitchen and open one of the cupboards, which he's removed the glasses from and stocked with water bottles, biscuits, old cookies. If she's inside, he won't be able to close the main door because the chain will be in the way, but that doesn't matter. No one ever visits anyway.

He shows her around and explains everything. – You can't reach the telephone or the bookshelf, so don't bother trying. You can sit here or sleep.

He points at an old mattress that he's positioned in the corner, near the door. She stares at it disinterestedly, almost in disgust. He'd hoped for gratitude, and he's irritated at himself. It confuses him that he continues to give her chances, acting like she's a guest in his house. Perhaps it's her wretched appearance and round, dirty cheeks that arouse his compassion. She deserves exactly what she's getting, an old mattress and a chain around her ankle. He leaves her alone while he boils water for coffee.

For a long time she just stands there. But finally he hears her plopping down on the mattress, the chain rattling against the floor. He pours coffee and drinks it, sitting in the chair where he can see her feet.

– Don't take pictures of me or anything gross, she says.

– Why would I do that?

– Many men do. Then they post them somewhere on the web without permission.

– I'm not one of your disturbed johns.

– You're just as disturbed. The only difference is that I don't want to fuck you.

– Stop talking like that, Erhard says, and sips his coffee. – I don't know what you're talking about, and I don't care.

She's asleep when he walks past. Once again he feels a certain satisfaction, almost delight, that she's relaxing. Like an exhausted girl in a day-care centre, her arms and legs splaying every which way after a busy day in the playground. He closes the door, though not completely because of the chain.

The Dutch winter holiday began early this year, and suddenly there are two or three flights a day, spitting tourists onto the streets of Corralejo; this means short trips to Las Dunas, the harbour, or the nearby hotel.

After all of Alina's questions, he suddenly notices cameras everywhere. Customers snap photographs through the car window, of each other in the back seat, of him driving. Out near Las Dunas men with a small video camera film the sun, the sand dunes, and goats. Once upon a time, back when he went on holidays with his mum and dad, he would take carefully planned snapshots. With twenty-four or thirty-six pictures on a roll and only two extra rolls in the suitcase, you had to be selective when on holiday. Ten photographs a day. You didn't take unnecessary photos of passing goats or sweaty socks or ordinary meals at ordinary restaurants. You didn't take photographs of people you didn't know or rubbish along the side of the road or a cloudless sky. Photographs were a rare event. Now it's completely different: People snap a surplus of photos; everything is photographed. And it sounds as if there's a place on the Internet where you can develop your photographs. He recalls a girl who photographed her girlfriend with her tongue jammed in a beer bottle outside the discotheque Corralejo Beach in Calle Cervera.

Were photographs taken of the car, of its owner, when they arrived in Cotillo? Images of the boy's mother or father saying farewell through the car window? Images of the car, alone, as the water edges up the beach?

At six o'clock, he turns on the radio and listens to the news. But it's just the international news, nothing local. Maybe the hearing was postponed, maybe the boy's story is no longer newsworthy. He won't reach out to Bernal again, but he wishes he knew a policeman who could fill him in on what happened at the hearing. The courthouse is in a separate wing of the Palace; the executive and judicial branches are so close that one can hear the judge's gavel while standing in police headquarters, quite literally.

For dinner he picks a brown rotisserie chicken that has rotated on a spit most of the day, along with a carton of sliced tomatoes mixed with firm goat cheese. He buys enough for two and hopes Alina will like the food. Things will go much smoother if he keeps her calm, more manageable – more receptive to his point of view. He's heard of the Stockholm Syndrome, but how does it work? How long does it take to go into effect?

Alina knows nothing about the Stockholm Syndrome, and she despises chicken – it tastes like rubber, she says – so she tells him to sod off. She bangs the chain angrily against the floor until he's close to losing his mind, and considers throwing her back in the shed. When he tells her what he's thinking of doing, she calls him a pathetic *extranjero*. He can do whatever he wants with her, she says, spitting and hissing at him, yanking on her chain. Erhard has to get away from her, so he goes outside to feed Laurel and Hardy, who're standing up on the hill licking a rock. It's like being kicked out of his own house, he thinks, hoping that it's only a matter of hours before he can release her. He hardly cares what the police will do to him if she reports him for kidnapping. But he hopes she doesn't. He wishes she'll crawl into a tiny cave and stay put. No more johns, no more drugs.

Listening to her railing inside the house, however, he's not sure how it'll play out.

From the hill, he can see several miles: the mouse-grey water pounding the surf all the way from the West Indies and South America, crashing and ripping against the choppy, jagged coast. As Laurel tries to get at Erhard's belt loops, his little bell dings. Erhard gently scratches the goat behind one of his long, soft ears and gives it a handful of food from a bag.

Back at the house, he finds Alina sitting on the kitchen floor. She has pulled everything out of the cupboard, so honey, rice, and peppers are strewn across the floor. She's worse than a naughty child. Luckily, she couldn't reach the refrigerator. Not that there's much in it. Her salmon-coloured outfit is unrecognizable now, more like a prison uniform.

– If you help me with one thing, I'll let you go.

This seems to discourage her, and Erhard doesn't understand why. It occurs to him that she might feel hopeless, lacking any spark of life. Maybe this lie she was set to tell and her trip to Madrid were all she had left. And now Erhard has snuffed them out.

– You mentioned posting photographs on the Internet. How's that done?

She squints at him. – What do you want?

– To find a photo on the Internet, where would I look?

– Of me?

– No, he says. She probably thinks he's looking for a pornographic image; he doesn't care to know what photographs of Alina he might find. – A photo of the car stranded on the beach in Cotillo. My customers say they find photographs on the Internet, snapshots taken a few days or even hours before, and so I thought maybe I could find some of the boy's mother or father when they first arrived in the car.

– You're still stuck on that, Fourfingers?

– Just tell me where I can find the photographs.

– I can't, she says. – They're all over. Google it or something. She stands, then plops down on the mattress next to the door. Like a tired dog.

– Help me find it and I'll give you your cigarettes.

– Fuck you. You've already ruined my deal. My trip to Madrid is gone.

– I saved you. You would've regretted it the moment you signed your name.

– I regret everything I've done since coming to this cursed fucking island. In fact I regret everything that's happened to me since my mother, may she burn in hell, gave birth to me.

– Help me. Help the boy.

– Are you daft? I don't give a shit about that boy. If I do anything to help you, it's only because I want to get away from here.

– I'll drive you downtown as soon as I've found what I need.

– What if I can't find it? If the photo you're looking for doesn't exist?

– Help me and I'll let you go whether we find it or not.

She studies him at length, then shrugs. Which means yes.

– So how does this work? Erhard asks.

– How should I know? Type it into Google and hit return. She glances around. – Where's the computer?

Erhard stares blankly at her.

– You don't have a computer?

– I don't need one.

– What, you think we'll search on my mobile? That's fucking expensive. Will you pay for it?

He almost says yes, but changes his mind. – If you find the photo I'll remove the chain.

– Get my purse. Where is it?

He doesn't respond, just saunters into the living room and finds her mobile. He hands it to her. – Cotillo Beach. Right around 7 or 8 January.

– I don't have much battery left, less than a quarter.

She pokes around on the device. He stands behind her, so he can watch her. It would be easy for her to call the police or send a message to someone she knows. But she's already found a bunch of photographs, and more emerge as she scrolls down her screen.

She types some more. The date. Images of the beach appear, but nothing that resembles anything from those dates. What he sees are a mix of summer and winter images. You can tell the difference in the sky: white-metallic in the winter, white-yellow in the summer. She shows Erhard a few. One is of the slope, another of the sea as viewed from the beach. Then, a short time later, more surfer photos, two women on a towel, and a man standing up through the sunroof of a rental car. There are a surprising number of photographs, and seeing them appear and disappear makes Erhard's head spin. They are photographs sent through the air and into air. Cables he sort of gets, but not these new smart phones.

Searching takes time, much more than Erhard had anticipated. He thought it would be like using a card index, where one looked up relevant dates. But Alina keeps reminding him that images are everywhere and that the connection is bad. Each image takes a long time to emerge. She tries to explain this to Erhard, but he doesn't comprehend. The sun sets. He prepares instant coffee. While pouring water into a mug, he forgets yet again that she's his hostage, that she's being held against her will. She's not some neighbour's daughter who has stopped by to show him her holiday pictures. He hands her the mug, and she sets it down beside the mattress.

– Maybe there are no photos of the car, he says.

She's brought up another endless thread of irrelevant images: tourist snapshots of beaches, Las Dunas and its unnaturally blue skies, giant mounds of olives at the market in Morro del Jable.

– I don't think so, she says.

– I'll drive you home tomorrow, he says tiredly. He lies down on the sofa.

– You promised you'd drive me home today.

– But you didn't find anything, he says.

– You promised to drive me home as soon as I helped you.

– I only promised to do that if you found something. I'll take you home tomorrow.

She kicks her mug across the floor, splashing coffee onto the stove and a stack of books along one of the lower shelves. He lies still, listening for her movements, but hears only her chain. He's looking forward to getting rid of her, but right now there's something tingly and strange about having her here. Inside the walls of his home. The walls are too thin, the rooms too cramped. He buries his head between the pillows in the sofa and…

– ... Ola, Fourfingers, fetch your car keys.

He wakes up when a pair of shoes and a hat plunk his head.

– I've found something.

She's seated on the kitchen floor, the chain pulled taut, and waving her mobile. It's not yet dawn, but the sky is brown. Before long, the sun will rise above the sea and shine a cone of bright light through the frosted windows.

– I'm almost out of battery, so you need to see this now. Right now.

He listens for dishonesty in her voice. Why did she keep searching after he fell asleep? What if she hasn't found anything at all, but just invented some excuse for him to go over there, tired and unprepared?

When he sets his feet on the floor the usual ache in his back returns, part of his routine morning stiffness. He just needs to get moving – to deal with it. He pushes off from the edge of the sofa and stands. She doesn't seem hostile. Mostly, she seems eager. Her legs are splayed like a little girl playing marbles.

– See. Some surfers from that day. And there's a car.

With her thumb she sweeps the images downward. When she finds what she's looking for, she taps the image and hands her mobile to Erhard.

Though he doesn't show it, he's impressed. Surprised. He didn't think she could help him. Her reaction last night had been expected, predictable. Whores aren't exactly known for their intellectual capacity. But Alina, something tells him, is not like the others.

The image is small, and it's difficult to make out what it is. As usual, it takes a few seconds for his vision to focus. He lifts the mobile up to his face. It's an early morning shot, much like now. The sand is shiny, golden, flat. He sees the VW in the background. That's the one, no doubt about it. It's black and doesn't belong on the beach, a foreign object. And the glaring, dark windows conceal the boy in the box.

Erhard feels a jolt. He's found it. A photo the police don't know about. A clue. There's water along the car's front wheels. Erhard thinks about the boy lying in the back seat. Dead. The photographer wouldn't know at this point. Or ever. He's just taking a photograph.

– There are more images, Alina says. – Someone named MitchFever.

Erhard reads the name on the narrow, black band along the top of the image. The name reminds him of a child with a warm forehead. – How do you bring up a new image?

She flicks the photo with her finger and the image becomes that of a boy's back. He's wearing a wetsuit and carrying a surfboard on his head. Then the screen goes black.

– Shit, shit, shit, Alina says.

31

Her charger's in the flat she rents above the bar in Calle Taoro. But instead of going to get it, Alina suggests that Erhard find a computer. Even better: a computer with high-speed Internet. He doesn't know where to look for one. There's the break-room computer at work, or maybe one of Raúl's, or Ponduel's – Ponduel studied computers. Of course, Ponduel's an asshole. None of these options sound appealing.

– Anyone with Internet access can help you just as well as I can, she says. – Now that I've helped you get started, you have to drive me downtown.

Erhard stands up so fast his head is dizzy. He walks across the room where, because of the chain, she can't reach him. He wants to drive her downtown so she can help him find the image again. But it won't do, taking her to dispatch or up to Raúl's place. How would he explain that? She'd probably try to run, or cry for help.

– I'll get your charger. No computer.

– So drive me home, and I'll help you at my place.

He has the feeling she's got ulterior motives.

– No, you can stay here. I'm sorry.

This makes her angry, but then she holds herself in check.

Before he lets her go, he wants to talk to Diego Navarez or hear on the news that the police are continuing their investigation. But that's something he doesn't dare tell her. He can't bear to hold her hostage.

– I'll give you the money I told you about. Find the images for me, and I'll give you the money.

She laughs that sickening laughter of hers. – How the hell can I trust what you say, Fourfingers, when you change your mind all the time? You've promised me three times now that I could go.

– OK. Honestly, I don't know anything about computers. I need your help.

– I can see that. But I'm not exactly a computer geek. Let me go and I'll find someone who can better help you.

– What does your charger look like?

– Fuck you, she says, spitting at him.

For some reason, he waits in the car for a few minutes before crossing the street. It's so early in the morning that the flats appear drawn and sleepy. Music emerges from La Mar Roja on the corner, which is the sailors' preferred wine bar and always open. An anxious young man with a fag between his lips is seated on a low wall across from the bar, kicking his legs, smoke pouring from his nose as fast as he puts the cigarette to his mouth. He's staring at the bar as if he's going to rob it, another of the city's many current or former drug addicts, so wretched that he can't even earn money selling leather goods or making sand sculptures. Farther down the street, a man sweeps the sidewalk with a stiff broom.

Erhard heads towards the doorway directly to the left of the bar. Above the entrance, there's a large painting of a schooner in the process of being swallowed by a whale. He lets himself in and reviews the names taped on the sea-blue wooden post boxes. He doesn't see her name anywhere, only men's names. Then he spots it on the top floor. Angelina Mariposa. That must be her. He considers taking the stairs, but chooses the lift instead, which is already holding in the lobby.

The key slides right into the lock, and then he's inside, closing the door behind him.

It's very dark. Thick curtains block the sunlight as well as the view, and he draws them back to find his way around. He doesn't know exactly what he's looking for, but he's seen chargers before, so he scans the room for electrical outlets. Although the flat isn't new, it has been remodelled, and everything is square and sharply defined. On a curtained shelf, he finds at least thirty pairs of shoes resting on cheap wooden racks. Pink shoes and black stilettos with thin laces. It makes him laugh. He owns only one pair of shoes himself, and he'll wear them until they fall apart. He quickly locates the charger in the tiny black kitchen; it dangles from an outlet above a table for two. There are two wine glasses on the table, one filled with white wine, along with salmon-coloured nail polish resting on an American magazine. There's no cooktop, just this small table and a black refrigerator. Like him, she's apparently not much of a cook, and he wonders how she gets her meals. Does she go out every night or do men pay for her dinners? He grabs the charger, then studies the black-and-white photo magnet that he finds on the fridge. It's a pretty photo. In it she's raising a champagne glass at the photographer and laughing as though she doesn't have a care in the world. Directly above her cleavage a caption reads: *Good company?*

At the bottom of the photograph: *alinacompania.es.*

Erhard can hardly believe that the woman in the photo – who looks like a film star – is at this very moment chained up in his living room.

While leaving her flat he catches a whiff of something. He follows the scent into the bedroom, a darkened cave with a queen-sized bed underneath a pile of undulating black blankets. The scent is powerful – cinnamon and citrus. Normally, his sense of smell is not great. To his left he spots a wooden wardrobe painted black. He opens it, then runs his hands across the sequined dresses and a few suits of almost transparent fabric. He's often dreamed of walking into a lingerie shop and examining all the pretty fabrics and feeling the thin straps between his fingers, but now that he has the chance, he doesn't really dare. And yet he removes some things from the drawers: a pair of soft white trousers, a t-shirt embossed with large letters, and pink underwear with blue lace that looks like something a child might wear. He bundles them all up inside a pair of Alina's trousers. Then he walks out of her flat, slamming the door behind him.

He waits for a lorry to pass before crossing the street to his car.

– Erhard!

He turns, but he already knows who it is. It's one of the few who pronounce his name so that it nearly sounds Danish.

Raúl Palabras waves to a man heading in the opposite direction, then trots across the street. He looks relaxed, his shirt unbuttoned, his sleeves rolled up, and his hair meticulously combed.

– I was in the bar and saw you come out. What are you doing here so early?

– What are you doing? Going home without Bea?

– Pesce and I had too many beers. She went home, Raúl says, taking one of Erhard's hands and touching Erhard's elbow with the other, as if he were about to swing him around. It's Raúl's style. – Would you drive me home?

Erhard doesn't see how he could say no. He doesn't have a reason to say no. Besides, he's heading in that direction. – I can drop you off, he says. I've got to earn my living somehow, I guess.

– Oh, yes. Money.

They look at each other.

– What have you got there? Raúl asks, staring at the clothes and the charger.

– Just a few things I needed to pick up for one of my customers.

Raúl grins. – Oh, Old Man. You're getting mixed up in something, aren't you? I can see it in your eyes.

– Sod off, Erhard says, opening his door and climbing in. Raúl dashes around the car and hops into the passenger seat. They drive. Erhard manages to toss the clothes in the backseat, so that Raúl doesn't notice they are girls' clothes. There's no way he could explain it to him now. No, he's not ready to tell Raúl what happened.

They head down one-way streets, and Raúl tells him how busy he is and that he's sick and tired of people not doing what they're told. Erhard laughs at his stories. They arrive at Raúl's flat.

– Come on up, Raúl says. – Let's have a Sunrise and watch the sunrise.

– The sun came up long ago, Raúl.

– Then a Bloody Mary. Come on. I need you, *Hermano*.

Something he says when he's most desperate.

– What, to get plastered? You should go up and sleep with your beautiful girl. She's probably worried about you.

– No she's not. That's the problem. She hates me.

– Shut up, Erhard says. He doesn't believe that at all.

– Bloody hell, Erhard, she's going to leave me.

– Did she tell you that?

– No, not exactly. But she doesn't love me like she used to. I just know it. Come with me. She's crazy about you, you're like her favourite uncle or something. We'll wake her up with Bloodys and breakfast.

It's Saturday. He won't be able to work this morning. Maybe tonight. He can go home to Alina afterward. She's not going anywhere. – OK. One Bloody Mary.

He wants to drive into Raúl's car park beneath his building, but it's being renovated, Raúl says, and he doesn't think there'll be a spot. Instead they park at the abandoned construction zone near HiperDino, then amble down the street towards the harbour and Raúl's flat. Lying on the street next to the building's entrance is Crazy Enrique, sleeping with his baseball bat. Raúl shushes Erhard as they edge past him and go up the broad stairwell. For some reason Erhard glances down the street right as they enter, and he sees the same anxious man who'd sat on the wall opposite the bar. It must be a coincidence. This flat borders the busiest section of town, and maybe the man just walked down here to sell or buy something or sleep on the beach.

– What did you say you were doing at La Mar Roja? Raúl asks.

– Do you remember the incident with the car on the beach? The night of the storm?

– The car theft? Raúl says, his back to Erhard. – Yeah, is there anything new? I heard they found the mother.

– That's what they say. But they're lying.

Raúl pauses. – Who? The paper-pushers?

That's Raúl's word for the police.

– Yes. All they did was find a prostitute who's got nothing at all to do with it. And someone paid her to confess.

– What makes you think that?

– I've done some investigating.

– Playing Colombo now, are you?

Raúl unlocks the door of his flat, and they enter. From the entrance-way one can see through the French doors and into the living room.

Beatriz is sleeping in front of the TV. On the screen are some black dancers, a motorcycle, and a man dressed as a dog. She stretches lazily and reaches for Raúl, pulling him into a kiss. When she asks where he went off to, Raúl gently closes her eyes and tells her she shouldn't get pissed.

– But I wasn't that pissed, she says, laughing as she squeezes Erhard's arm.

– Come, Raúl says. – We're going to have some Bloodys.

– Oh no, Beatriz groans. But she follows them up to the rooftop terrace anyway. The stairwell is located around the corner of the balcony. Narrow and rickety, it clings to the house and climbs up to the already scorching private terrace, which is furnished with an outdoor sofa, an African-inspired coffee table, a pair of wicker chairs with thick pillows, and a small worktop with a fridge and a sink under a large umbrella. Beatriz plops tiredly into the sofa and crawls beneath a thin blanket.

– Erhard's playing amateur detective, Raúl says. – Remember the car down at the beach?

Raúl walks over to the little prep counter and begins removing items from the fridge. White liquor, juice, fresh lemon. The kinds of things that are always available at Raúl's place.

– Throwing away kids like that isn't normal behaviour, Erhard says.

– I can't stand it, Beatriz says.

Raúl laughs. – Even an old dog has a good nose. Isn't that what people say?

He squeezes the lemon over the glass, squirting juice into the air.

– Who says that? Beatriz says, laughing.

– Here I was thinking that the Hermit was just living in his own little world of piano tuning, alcohol, and cab driving.

Erhard laughs because Raúl has never called him the Hermit. Then he tells them about the box filled with newspaper fragments. His curiosity piqued, Raúl asks if the police found any DNA or fingerprints. Like you see on television. Erhard explains what Bernal told him. That finding DNA is not as easy as one would think. Beatriz is mostly interested in the little boy. About whether he'll get a proper burial. Can't they find the mother? she wants to know. Raúl thinks it was just a horrible accident: a car thief finds a child on the backseat – oops! – and so he leaves the car on the beach and hurries away.

– You'll see, Raúl says. – In the end, they'll discover that the prostitute was the mother.

– No, Erhard says. – I've talked to her. It's not her.

Silence.

– What did you say? Beatriz says.

Erhard tells them how the police have charged the wrong person.

– She's lying, Raúl says.

– No, I've pressed her on it. It's not her.

– That's crazy, Beatriz says.

– Did you see her downtown? Raúl wants to know, his back still turned to Erhard. He hammers the pestle which he's used to crush celery and lemon and spices against the edge of the sink. The scent is tangy.

Erhard glances cautiously at Beatriz. – She's over at my place. Hiding. She's told me everything and is ready to tell her story. But she's afraid of the police.

– Erhard, Beatriz says excitedly. – Wow.

Raúl hands them each a bright red drink with a large spoon poking up from the liquid. He loves to eat the mashed celery stalk after he's drunk half the glass. – I've made it extra spicy for you, *Hermano*.

Erhard accepts the drink from Raúl and notices the thick film of pepper on top.

– Thanks, he says, sucking vodka through the straw. Strong vodka.

– But isn't that an awful mess to get dragged into? Raúl asks.

– The press won't write about it, Erhard says, wiping his mouth with the back of his hand. – I've already spoken to a journalist. But maybe something will happen now that I've got the girl.

– *Got?* What do you mean by that? Beatriz asks.

– Now that she's hiding at my place.

– Doesn't she want to leave the island? Get away from the police? Raúl asks. – Maybe we can help her do that.

Beatriz gives Raúl a sceptical look, because Raúl usually isn't eager to lend a helping hand. Maybe it's more than scepticism. Maybe Raúl's right that she's leaving him. To Erhard, it sounded like there was a hint of irritation or even contempt in her voice. She has complained about all of Raúl's female friends before, his toadies and ass-kissers, girls and women from every social class who want a piece of the rebellious rich man's son's colourful life.

– Right now she's helping me find the boy's parents. We need a computer, actually. Do you have one we can borrow?

It almost feels normal to talk to someone about this.

– I can't do without mine, unfortunately, Raúl says. He raises his glass and clinks with Erhard's. – Always good to see your old mug.

They drink. Beatriz sips, then makes a face. Raúl sucks his drink until it begins to slurp. Erhard follows suit, but hardly tastes the tomato for all the vodka, pepper, mashed celery, and Tabasco sauce.

– What about my computer? Beatriz asks Raúl. – I'm not using it.

– How will you check your email? Or update the website?

– There's not a lot going on right now. Or for a while, you know.

She yawns, and Erhard can see the fillings in her teeth.

– What about the boutique? Raúl asks her.

She shrugs.

– Forget it, Erhard says. – We'll figure something out.

– Sorry, but I'm knackered. Standing, Beatriz suddenly seems spent. – Goodnight, my sweet, she says to Erhard, while running her hand across Raúl's arm. Erhard watches her go, but says nothing.

On the rooftop directly across from them, an elderly woman has begun hanging clothes. Soaked, heavy jerseys that tug on the line until it begins pulling down the antenna the line is attached to. Football jerseys for an entire team and then some. It reminds Erhard of Aaz, who loves football.

– You probably won't be able to use that computer, Raúl says.

– Well, I don't know anything about computers anyway. The girl asked for one. So we can see the images better, I imagine. She found a photograph of the car on the beach in Cotillo. Before the police had arrived, I mean.

Raúl takes the glass from Erhard and mixes another drink. – What does it show? When was it taken?

– We'll need to have a closer look when I return.

Erhard looks forward to driving Alina home, getting that over with. No matter how little he thinks of her, a twisted girl with a taste for shoes, and no matter how important he thinks the case is, it seems wrong to hold her hostage. He considers asking Raúl for a small, temporary loan so he can send Alina to Madrid with a few thousand euros in her pocket. Maybe later. Tomorrow.

– Don't forget to have fun, Raúl says, handing Erhard a second drink, similar to the first. – Salud.

– Salud, Erhard says. – For the life of me, I just can't understand how anyone could do it. Throw a small child, an innocent boy, into a cardboard box and starve him to death.

– I once heard a wise man say, 'You need a brain to get a driver's licence, but you don't need a heart to have kids.' A bitch like that is no mother. She's a heartless, pathetic person only concerned with her own wellbeing.

– But it's not the prostitute. I'm convinced of that. She says one of the island's wealthiest men is paying her to confess, and that the police are playing along to avoid having an unresolved case on their hands.

– A wealthy man, eh? Who else could that be but my father? Raúl laughs. – Cheers.

– Cheers.

They drink.

– Speaking of your father, have you heard that I've gotten him to play something other than 'Coral'?

Raúl grew up with his father's 'Coral' obsession and, after the death of Emanuel's second wife, Safín, he heard his father play the piece on an endless loop, morning, evening, and night. She died in 1999. Raúl was in his mid twenties then, living in the annex across the garden.

– Hell yeah. Baya called. She thinks you're a genius. He's apparently a changed man, suddenly involved in his business again. He's even writing his last will and testament. There goes 100 million.

Raúl laughs.

– Hmm. Erhard hadn't considered such consequences. His head is cloudy, and he doesn't know how to respond.

– Wonder if he'll leave a few pennies to his only son. But what the hell, it's just money, right? I don't even know if I want anything from that old asshole. Cheers.

A typical Raúl conversation – always full of scorn at his father's wealth. Though, at the same time, he happily accepts his money, doing nothing to earn any for himself.

– Cheers, Erhard says. He has to sit down so that he doesn't tumble over the railing and fall off the roof.

He feels dizzy, a sensation that begins in his legs and creeps up his body. As if his body's asleep while his thoughts remain awake. Dazed, but awake. Raúl's trying to get him pissed, he figures, but that's nothing new. That's what he does. Raúl has only two modes of being: Either he drinks until he collapses, or he doesn't drink at all. There's no such thing as a one-beer lunch or a little Irish coffee after dinner. Just like when they played poker. Raúl would play along steadily, scheming, so miserly that he would only win or lose small sums of money until he was the last player standing. Or he would teeter on the edge of ruin from the very beginning and go all-in by the end of each hand. Without a doubt, it was what made Raúl fun to be around. But it was also what made it exhausting for Beatriz. It was always either Sunday or Friday in Raúl's world.

– Lie down on the sofa, Raúl says. – You can sleep here.

Erhard mumbles a thank you. He tries to say something about Alina. How she's alone, I have to get home to her. She's waiting for me. I've promised her. But Raúl sweeps a soft hand across Erhard's face, closing his eyes. Easy now, easy, Erhard hears above the din of the teeming street. A lorry, squeezed into a narrow alley, honks its horn. A child on the harbour-front calls out for his brother. A much-too-large baby hand nudges Erhard's head down onto the sofa pillows.

THE CORPSE

22 January–28 January

32

– Are you ready for Virgin del Carmen's arrival?

A loud voice down on the street cuts through Erhard's sleep. He sits upright on the sofa and glances around the empty terrace. He recognizes that sound. It's coming from a loudspeaker on the roof of an old Mazda that's cruising the streets advertising the festival on 23 February.

– Sign up for our events and help give our city and its tourists the island's best party.

To judge by the brightness of the sun, it's past noon. The sun is a hot glowing ball in the middle of the sky, and all shadows have been pushed aside. The morning's drinks are still on the table, stained a dark red, with dried-up lemons on the rims of the glasses. Beatriz and Raúl must still be asleep, since they didn't wake him up.

He gets to his feet and spots the washerwoman on the other roof staring at him. He waves at her, but she scurries through a door and leaves an empty clothesline. He pulls a Perrier from the fridge and unscrews the cap. He gulps it down, then descends the narrow stairwell to the balcony. The balcony door is open, the curtain fluttering.

He walks into the kitchen and the living room, then returns to the balcony as if they might have appeared while he was inside. He turns around and goes back to the living room, then the dining room – a room he's never set foot in – and onward to the office, which seems unused, and finally to the bedroom, where he pushes open the door with his foot. He pretty much expects to see Raúl on top of her or fucking her from behind, her breasts dangling free, Raúl angry and excitable as a donkey. But no. As if they'd been in a hurry to leave, the bed is unmade.

He calls out for Raúl several times. Each time it sounds more and more bleak, as if someone's clipping his speech, or as if the walls somehow swallow the sound. Raú. Ra. R.

In the entranceway, he opens a small chest of drawers and rummages around inside. He searches for paper and a pen to scribble a note for when they return, probably very soon. He steps on something that's sticking out from under the chest of drawers, a set of keys to a Mercedes along with some house keys – Raúl's. He must have dropped them. Maybe someone drove him. Just as he bends down to pick up the keys, he hears a sound coming from the office. He hasn't heard it before. If he heard that sound at home, he would know exactly what it was: the goats rubbing against the wall of the house when it's raining or too windy. But here, in a three-year-old building thirty metres above the sea, you would hardly expect to find any goats or rats or other animals clawing or scratching so loudly. Perhaps a seagull has gotten into the flat looking for French fries or deep-fried shrimp or something else it's developed a taste for down at the harbour. Cautiously, he enters the office: a dark space that's in stark contrast to the style of the rest of the flat. It has Emanuel Palabras's stamp all over it – a mahogany desk, reclining leather chair, two leaf-shaped shields wrapped in colourful skins. The sound has ceased, but must have come from the large, built-in wardrobe. One of the wardrobe's doors is pushed a little to the side, leaving a black slit running from floor to ceiling like a colourless block.

Erhard shoves the door aside. Inside, the shelves have fallen down. Clothes and boxes filled with CDs and computer cables are piled up.

Every second or third month Raúl binges on whatever he can get his hands on. He doesn't plan it that way; it's how his mind operates. Just when everything's going well between him and Beatriz, and him and the world, he shits on it all and starts taking whatever the pushers in

Calle Mirage give him. Erhard has picked him up several times strung out some place, causing trouble at a party, or in his wretchedness just needing some company. But it's not Raúl he sees at the bottom of the wardrobe, underneath the clothes and the shelves. It's Beatriz's hair, an ear, a large orange earring.

He removes the clothes and the shelves, then lifts her out of the wardrobe and carries her into the bedroom, where he lays her on the bed. She doesn't look heavy, but she's not easy to carry. His back aches, but he doesn't have time to worry about that now.

– What happened? Where's Raúl? Where the hell is that idiot?

She doesn't respond, of course. There's blood on her nose and mouth and down the front of her blouse, and she has a horrible gash on her lip. Most of the blood appears to be coming from a deep wound below her hairline. She's just staring at the ceiling, slowly blinking her eyes and breathing in wheezy gasps. The telephone is on the nightstand right beside Beatriz. He calmly punches 112 and hears someone answer. Then he looks at Beatriz.

She's staring directly into Erhard's eyes. There's something about her expression. It's not pain or confusion or death. At first he believes that she's dead, that her pupils are completely dilated because she has slipped life and found peace, but then he sees that her gaze is more insistent, almost commanding. Her pupils are tense from exertion.

You mustn't tell them. For Raúl's sake. Let me go.

– What? he says. On the other end of the line, Emergency Services repeats their questions, but Erhard doesn't hear them. Beatriz closes her eyes and goes quiet. She's somewhere far, far away.

Emergency Services keeps asking Erhard what has happened, and where he is located. It's a man's voice, friendly. Erhard removes the telephone from his ear and presses the red button, ending the call.

Her words – and he's certain they are her words – turn everything upside down. *Help me. Let me go.* What the hell does that mean? The words reverberate and then seem to vanish into nothingness. And why didn't she wish him to call an ambulance? Why was it for Raúl's sake? Was there something she didn't want him to get mixed up in?

Raúl may be an arse in many ways, but Erhard has never seen him physically harm Beatriz. That's not the kind of relationship they have. It's not like him, either. Or Beatriz. It's what makes her so modern, so lovely, so irritatingly unobtainable: her independence, pride, and strength. Whatever occurred in the flat, it wasn't an accident or an ordinary domestic dispute. Something very bad happened.

He checks Beatriz again. As part of his job, he has learned first aid and has kept his certificate up to date for years. He lowers his head to her chest and watches it rise and fall. He tilts her head back slightly, so she can breathe easier.

His eyes wander from her mouth to her throat and down, down. Her bloodied robe is wide open, revealing her breasts and hairy vulva behind cotton knickers that appear rather cheap. He quickly cinches her robe and wraps her up in the bed sheet she's lying on.

He walks through all the rooms again, now searching for clues. Blood, overturned objects, feet sticking out from under the sofa, disembodied limbs. He notices nothing out of the ordinary. But some of the desk drawers in the office aren't fully closed, and the bed appears messier than usual. And why is the bread knife in the middle of the kitchen table? It's as though someone got it out to use it, then left it there.

Help me. Let me go.

He goes to the kitchen and cracks open a Dos Equis, gulping it down greedily. He pulls his notebook from his pocket. Although he has no system, he knows exactly where he'll find the number. One evening in Puerto he wrote Michel Faliando's name and telephone number with a blunt-tipped pencil. He doesn't remember why he wrote it down. But Faliando is a member of the City Council – and, he remembers, a doctor.

He grabs the wall telephone.

First he tries Raúl. But his call goes immediately to voicemail. He doesn't leave a message. He redials and gets the same response.

Then he calls the doctor.

– Michel Faliando? This is Erhard Jørgensen, Raúl Palabras's friend. He doesn't have the energy to explain, but it's the only way. – Do you recall that we met at an event once in Puerto?

Erhard explains that Beatriz has been hurt. She's hit her head, badly, and requires immediate medical attention.

– No, unfortunately I can't ask anyone else, Erhard says. – It's complicated.

Silence on the other end of the line.

– It's Emanuel Palabras's daughter-in-law, Erhard says, trying to get some leverage.

Continued silence.

– Is she unconscious? the doctor asks.

– She's breathing.

– Are there drugs involved?

– No, Erhard says automatically.

– Is she a diabetic?

– No, I don't think so.

– Irregular breathing? Wheezing?

– Yeah, a little, maybe.

– Is she lying on her back or in the recovery position?

– On her back, Erhard says.

Silence.

The doctor says he can be there in two hours. Erhard doesn't know what to say, so he just thanks him.

Two hours. Hopefully she'll survive for that long. He'll do everything in his power to make sure she does. He'll take care of her and feed her with a spoon and hold her head and…

And then he remembers Alina.

The drive to Majanicho takes fourteen minutes. And the entire time he's certain that the whore despises him. She has now sat chained up for nearly a day, with no food for more than sixteen hours. Unless she's managed to find something in the one cupboard she can reach. He steels himself to tell her what has happened, but he's not sure whether or not he should tell her anything about Raúl Palabras or Beatriz. He'll just say he was in a terrible car accident. Hell, his shirt is soaked with blood.

At least he's got the charger with him. The bundle of clothes, under-wear, and charger are all on the passenger seat.

He knows he needs to release her today.

He quickly parks the car, leaps out, and hurries inside. She's not on the mattress or in the kitchen. He glances warily around each corner, ready for her to jump him or throw something at his head. It makes sense that she would.

– Alina?

He peers in the shed. Empty.

Then he remembers the chain. He inspects the ground and the floor inside the house, searching for it, but it's nowhere to be found. Maybe she succeeded in breaking it and getting loose? But how far might she have gotten? And where is the rest of the chain? Cautiously he walks around the corner of the house and looks up at the metal ring the chain is fastened to. The ring is still there, but the chain's not dangling down the wall as he would have expected if she'd pried it off her foot. Instead it runs in a taut line straight up the house before disappearing on the roof.

Erhard turns towards the hill. Half-expecting to see her walking barefooted across the rocks. But she's not up there. Just wind and dust.

She must be on the roof. Erhard keeps the ladder around back, but now it's lying at a ten-degree angle away from the house. She must have brought it over here. When she got up on the roof, she'd either pushed the ladder or accidentally knocked it over.

He positions the ladder against the house and begins to climb.

If she's hiding up there, he should have seen her as he drove in. But maybe she's lying down, fatigued by the blazing sun. Maybe napping, ready to attack him as soon as he peeks over the edge.

The rooftop is a hotchpotch of various materials: plastic, corrugated cardboard, a tarpaulin drawn over a sheet of plywood, and chunks of rocks in the 1.5- to 2-stone range that are supposed to hold it all together against the wind. He peers over the roof's edge.

It's empty.

His gaze follows the taut chain running from the metal ring to the opposite side of the house, where it plunges over the roof between two large rocks.

She's thrown the chain over the house, he thinks. To confuse him. So she'll have time to get away. That confirms what he'd suspected – also when he visited her flat. She's smart. Maybe smarter than Erhard. He doesn't feel like crawling across the roof. He's not even sure it can support his weight. On his way down the ladder, he curses to himself. Then he hustles around the house to verify the broken chain.

He scans the countryside, hoping to see her trotting away. But he sees nothing. Not even the goats. The bleached sun is three-fifths of the way across the horizon. The rocks are scorching hot. Any living thing in direct sunlight would be fried.

What he sees when he turns the corner of the house makes him gag, because the girl's face has gone. The chain is just short enough that she's hanging with her foot against the wall, her hip and femur torn from their sockets, and yet long enough that her head and arms touch the ground, resting in a red pool of blood. When he nudges her with his foot, the corpse swings to one side and reveals her face. A swarm of irritating flies buzz away. Alina's face is in fact gone, her round cheeks replaced by something that resembles grilled cheese. He raises his hand to his mouth and turns away in disgust.

Maybe she was planning to attack Erhard, but stumbled over the rocks and fell to her death. Maybe she leaped off the roof on her own – to put an end to her misery or to break the chain. He can hardly stomach the thought. He'd not intended for this to happen. Not at all. Hell, he'd almost begun to like her.

She couldn't have been hanging there long. The blood's not even dry. Erhard recalls the wild dogs that helped themselves to Bill Haji.

The police won't care for the true version of events. He knows what Bernal will think. He won't believe Erhard's story; he'll think that Erhart kidnapped the whore, blackmailed her, and threw her off the roof. Witnesses have seen Erhard in her flat, and his fingerprints are all over that place.

He needs to reconsider. He needs to think and think hard.

He puts on a pair of work gloves and pulls out the tarpaulin, spreading it beneath Alina before cutting the chain with the bolt clippers. She tumbles onto the tarpaulin. A couple teeth, or what look like teeth, dislodge from her mouth along with a fresh gout of blood. He wraps her up and drags her into the shed. He shovels the dark-red soil into a bucket and spreads it across the stones five hundred metres from the house. With the backside of the shovel, he scrapes gravel over the pool of blood, then pours a few litres of water on the spot, so the gravel appears less arranged. Inside the house, he scrubs every surface Alina has touched, first with a wet rag and then a dry. The time is 2.20 p.m. He has forty minutes until the doctor shows up at Raúl's place.

As if he's been flying in an airplane, he feels nauseated, and he pours cognac in a coffee mug, then drinks it standing in front of the house and staring down the trail. There are no sirens, no blinking police cars. Nothing. If he'd just let the girl go when she'd begged him. Now he's got a dead woman whose body he somehow has to dispose of, an unconscious woman he has to hide, and a friend who has gone missing. At some point, people will start looking for all three. He doesn't know how long he can keep things under wraps. If he's caught, he'll have a hard time explaining himself. No matter how he spins his story, it looks bad.

It almost makes him laugh. But it's not funny. If they find Bill Haji's finger on the shelf, too, then it'll look even worse. The Hermit. That twisted old geezer out near Majanicho.

Majorero. The word hangs in the air, then fades. He stares at the girl's ruined face, mouth, nose, and lips like a red slab.

He goes inside and brings out the finger. It looks like a liquorice stick, the kind he used to eat as a child. The ring is still stuck tight, but it would come off if he broke the finger. No longer can he wear it as if it were a new finger. Which annoys him. Because it was a real treat for him to prop it in the empty slot on his hand, no matter how out-of-place and miscoloured it appeared to be. He recalls the afternoon that he drove several people, who all gave it no more than a passing glance, because it appeared to be nothing more than a sprained finger. They didn't figure the taxi driver was riding around with a dead man's digit, so they'd probably guessed he'd had an accident. Even though the finger looked different than the others, thinner and darker; some might have even thought it resembled a ring finger where the pinky should be. But no one stared at it or grew suspicious. They accepted the most logical explanation and overlooked any indications pointing to the opposite.

What if? he thinks, returning the finger to its container and hiding it behind the books once again. When she was alive, he'd tried to hide Alina just like he had Bill Haji's finger. But he doesn't dare bury her out here. The dogs would smell her at a distance. Besides, the ground is solid, and a really strong man would have to dig for at least a day. Maybe he could rent a Bobcat or an excavator, or bribe a sexton to throw her into some other person's grave. He could also drive her to the coast. There's a vast ocean to heave her into.

The doctor will arrive in thirty minutes. He considers postponing the appointment, but he doesn't want to put Beatriz's life in greater jeopardy. She should have already had medical attention. On the other hand, he doesn't want Alina lying here in the shed if he needs to go anywhere with the doctor or do something else. His only alternative, no matter how foolish it might sound, is to put Alina in the car and figure out what to do with her later. After the doctor has gone. It's a bigger risk, but he doesn't dare do anything else.

He doesn't have any more time to consider alternatives.

He puts on a pair of gardening gloves and carefully places Alina's body in the boot. He wraps the tarpaulin up in an elastic cord, keeping her snug. Then he drives back downtown. There's the usual Saturday traffic. He gives Muñoz and some colleagues parked at the giant HiperDino supermarket a quick wave. He continues down Calle del Muelle.

By the time he noses down the ramp to the private car park under the building, only eight minutes remain until the doctor arrives. Although a construction crew is in the process of removing columns and laying more parking spaces, no one is currently working; the basement is empty and dark. A plastic sheet covers much of the small basement. Wheelbarrows, buckets with congealed cement, shovels, and a few strange orange machines that look like steam locomotives are scattered about. He parks next to the lift and cuts the engine, then glances around. It wouldn't surprise him to find security cameras down here. He gets out of his car. Wind whips down the ramp and around the corners. He locates the camera on the ceiling, just to the left of the lift, but the plastic sheet is blocking it, so Erhard remains out sight. He presses the red UP button.

He realizes that he still has Raúl's keys in his pocket. The silver-grey Mercedes 500 SL is parked a short distance away. He backs his own car beside the Mercedes, arranging the boots of the two vehicles against one another. He checks for cameras, and doesn't see one on this side of the lift. They might be located behind some large boards that are leaning against the wall, but this side of the basement is not under surveillance. He unlocks Raúl's car and quickly transfers Alina's body to Raúl's boot, which appears to have never been used.

Afterward, he parks his own car crosswise in a handicapped spot, then hustles to the stairwell that leads up to the sixth floor.

When he reaches the flat, the doctor's already at the door. Irritated at having to wait.

– *Buenas*, Erhard says.

– Someone let me in the front door, the doctor says.

– I'm sorry. I had to run an errand.

The doctor gives Erhard a concerned look. – You should probably sit down for a bit.

Erhard shakes his head as he unlocks the door. – I just need some water.

The doctor goes directly inside and glances around. – I've been here before.

– This way, Erhard says.

– Where did you find her? The office?

– Yes.

Erhard opens the bedroom door. Beatriz is lying in the same position as when he'd left. The doctor has brought an ordinary shoulder bag, the kind used for laptop computers. He quickly fits his stethoscope to his ears and listens. With a small penlight he illuminates her dark eyes. He runs his knuckles across her cervical vertebrae, right below her gold necklace and its amethyst eye, which stares into the air. He pinches her cheek too. For a moment Erhard thinks she'd dead. He holds his breath.

The doctor continues to examine Beatriz. – How did she strike her head?

Erhard describes how he found her.

– Water, the doctor says suddenly. – Lukewarm water.

Erhard fetches a bowl and a dry towel in the kitchen.

The terrible-looking gash that progresses from her hairline and up underneath her hair is messy and red. The doctor dabs her with the towel, then inspects her throat, shoulders, ribs, belly, and thighs. Erhard feels as though he should turn away, but he can't help but follow the doctor's brown fingers gliding across Beatriz's body.

The doctor turns to Erhard. – I need to ask. May I be honest?

– Of course.

– The Palabrases aren't exactly your average family.

– What are you trying to say?

The doctor nods at Beatriz. – Someone did this to her.

– Did what?

– A contusion. Someone pushed her and gave her a blow to the top of her head. A very powerful one at that. It's a miracle she's still alive.

– Can she talk? I thought I heard her speak earlier.

– Not likely. This appears to be acute swelling with possible brain damage. Moderate to severe head trauma. She's comatose.

– What does that mean?

– That she's suffered a brain injury. She's lucky that she was operated on a few years ago. Someone bored into her cranium. He lifts her hair to show him something, but Erhard turns away. – See these holes. They're bleeding, but they've reduced the pressure from the blow. Anyone else would be dead right now after being struck with such brute force.

– What if she was pushed or something fell on her head, an accident?

– It's possible. If she ran into a barbell weighing four stone.

Erhard doesn't recall having seen any barbells on the floor next to the collapsed wardrobe. Or anything heavy for that matter. It was stuffed mostly with folders, cardboard boxes filled with photographs, and wooden shelves.

The doctor lets go of Beatriz's hair, and it falls across the darkened punctures, concealing them again. – Someone hit her with a blunt object, possibly a baseball bat, that doesn't leave any evidence. This appears to be an assault committed in rage.

– So you think it's... You mean to say it's...

He can't bring himself to utter the words. Even though he'd come to the same conclusion, he just can't believe it.

– Who else could've done it? I've known the Palabrases for many years. Raúl's quite the party. I don't think he's mean-spirited, but he's known for his benders and his outbursts.

– No, it's not possible. I can't believe that. He loves her.

The doctor makes an involuntary cluck with his throat. – I'm sorry, but love has many faces, and they're not always of your Romeo-and-Juliet variety.

Erhard tries to recall what Raúl said last night about their relationship.

– What's going to happen to her now? Why won't she wake up?

– She has swelling in her skull. And the pressure has increased so much that the blood-flow to her brain has ceased. She needs to be taken to the neurological centre in Puerto and put on a respirator as quickly as possible.

– Will she wake up then? Will she be normal? Erhard asks the first questions that come to mind.

– Maybe. Maybe in a few hours. Or days from now, weeks. But she needs to be on a respirator now. That's the important thing.

– Are there any painkillers for her or medicine?

– She needs time.

– What about... you know?

– He will have to face his punishment.

The doctor gathers his things and leaves. But before he goes, he pauses in the doorway. – Take her to the hospital. Now. Call if there's anything I can do. By the grace of God.

That last is a salutation Erhard can't stand, but it's meant kindly enough. Yet it sounds definitive and gloomy.

Erhard heads straight to the cupboard and pours himself whatever he can find. A white rum. He gulps it and returns to the bedroom, sitting down beside Beatriz. Cautiously, as if each movement could cause the blood vessels in her head to burst like soap bubbles, he peels back one of her eyelids with his thumb. Her pupil is nearly as wide as her eyeball, but it's still a pretty eye. Like a glass ball with neat patterns. He releases her eyelid and it glides shut. The gravity of the body is enough to make you cry. Her mind. Knocked out of her with one blow. If Raúl's responsible, it is unforgivable. He knows Raúl did it, but the implications are too much for him now. Right now he can only focus on saving the body before him.

He picks up the telephone, then hears the voice again.

Help me. Let me go.

He looks down at Beatriz, but this time her eyes are closed, and he knows he's imagining the voice. It's not real.

Help me. Let me go. What do the words mean? Let her die? Get her away from Raúl?

– Beatriz, he says out loud, his voice choking up uncontrollably.

Take care of me.

He calls her name again. He wants to shake her, but doesn't dare touch her. – I need to call, he says, dropping his hand to the telephone.

Por favor.

That last makes him cry. He doesn't recall when he last cried or even felt pain like this. He feels uncertainty, and he feels grief due to her condition, but most of all uncertainty. Is he imagining it? Or is it really her voice that he hears? It sounds like her. It sounds exactly like Beatriz. The same rusty voice, almost whispering, pleading. He lets go of the telephone and cries into her bathrobe, into her naked breast.

33

– Can you get me a respirator?

 – I told you she needs to go to…

 – I know, but I'm not going to do that. You'll have to call. And report me.

Silence.

 – Can you get me a respirator?

 – Yes, the doctor says simply.

 – How fast?

 – An hour. Maybe sooner.

Erhard glances at the clock radio on Raúl's side of the bed. – Meet me at 9 Via Majanicho at six o'clock. The little house at the end of a long path.

 – After Guzman?

 – Just before Guzman.

 – Are you moving her out there?

 – Yes, it's peaceful there.

 – Are you sure? Is he really worth it?

 – No, but she is, Erhard says and hangs up.

As he was talking to the doctor, an idea formed in his mind.

How might he hide Beatriz and keep her alive, so that no one searches for her? How can he hide Alina's body, so that no one finds it? Maybe the answers are the same.

The two women have the same hair colour and are approximately the same size. Alina's a little chubbier than Beatriz and has slightly larger breasts, but not everyone notices such things. Beatriz has no family here on the island, or anywhere else for that matter, so there's no one to confirm her identity besides Erhard and possibly a few casual acquaintances whom Erhard doesn't know. What he does know is that she has no close relations. She has often complained about that lack of intimacy. Someone to talk to. Every Tuesday or something she assists one of Raúl's friend's daughters, who runs a boutique down on High

Street. But that's only so the daughter can take a day off, not because they're friends.

And Alina. Like any whore on the island, no one will miss her. A few johns will call in vain. A pimp somewhere, maybe in Guisguey, will lose a little income. But no doubt he'll think she went home to the mainland.

No one will miss them. And no one will link the two women.

But he's all alone in this plan of his. He can't involve the doctor any more than is necessary. Keeping Beatriz alive and out of the searchlights is one thing, but it's quite another to rid himself of a body. The kind doctor wouldn't go along with that. Erhard will have to take care of that himself.

Under the sink he finds the kind of rubber gloves people use to clean. He grabs a red blanket from Raúl's sofa and takes the lift to the car park. The lift is narrow, fitting at most two people. Erhard rarely uses it, because it's usually too slow, and Raúl never uses it but trots down the stairs so fast that Erhard can't keep up. Right now the lift is the only real choice. He sticks a wedge in the door, keeping it from going anywhere.

He stares into the boot of Raúl's Mercedes. At the strangely lifeless pupa. The easiest thing to do would be to drive her down to the harbour and heave her into the sea, or over to the construction site and toss her into one of the chutes. There are security cameras down there, too, probably.

He quickly wraps the tarpaulin – with Alina inside – within the red blanket. It doesn't look completely natural, but it's not as suspicious as the tarpaulin, where the whore's shoulder and hands are visible though the translucent fabric. Then he scoops her up and returns to the lift; the bundle is heavy and it takes him some time. In the lift he squeezes her tightly so she doesn't slide out, and barely manages to push the button. The door closes. His back aches from the load, and he's forced to brace her against the wall in order not to drop her. He keeps his eye on the numbers, −1, 0, 1, 2. Between each storey Erhard fears the lift will stop. Third. Fourth.

Fifth. The door opens. He can't hold her any more. His back can't bear her weight. He drops her on the floor, then drags her to the flat and hauls her inside. He listens briefly in the entranceway, hears nothing. He slams the door and tugs her cautiously into the office and behind the desk. Blood has dripped onto the tarpaulin, but he unfolds it and pours the blood into a bowl from the kitchen. Using scissors, he cuts Alina out of her ripped tights. Because of her broken ankle, they're impossible to remove. He removes two necklaces and a bracelet. Though he can't wear gloves to do this fiddly job, it doesn't matter. He throws the jewellery in the rubbish bin. It's hard to look at the whore's face; not all the blood has congealed yet.

Alina's lying in her underclothes. Apart from her face and her ankle that's poking out to the side, her body resembles a mannequin, an advertisement for cheap lingerie.

He walks into the bedroom. Before he touches Beatriz, he listens. Listens to her breathing; it's rhythmic, but with a faint wheezing, like a plastic bag filling and emptying. He hears the air passing through her nostrils, soughing through her nose hairs. But he can't hear any words. On the one hand, he'd like to hear the words again, but on the other, they make him nervous and uncomfortable. As he watches, he notices a hint of a scar above her mouth, as if she's been operated on for a cleft lip. He's never noticed that before. But it looks so healed and natural that it's almost a joy to see.

He carefully removes her arm from her robe and pulls the robe off underneath her back. He takes off her thick athletic socks, too, which probably belong to Raúl; they're splattered with blood. And the pendant. He tilts her head slightly to the side; it's hard to see just what he's doing, but his fingers are familiar with this kind of jewellery, and finally he manages to open the tiny lock and remove the necklace. As he walks back to the office, he notices Beatriz's fantastic nails. The one on her middle finger is dangling loose, revealing a pale, cracked nail underneath. He needs to remove them all. If he's to turn Alina into Beatriz, those nails will have to be part of the ensemble. He twists the loose nail free, then begins to remove the others. They're firmly attached, but he's able to wriggle them off. Only the thumbnail requires a strenuous effort.

In the bathroom he finds a special glue that looks just right for the job, and he affixes the nails on Alina's fingers. One by one. Calm, thorough. He has never glued nails, but it reminds him of the model airplanes he used to build as a kid. After a few minutes, the nails are all fastened. Alina's thumbs are a little too big for Beatriz's nails, but the rest fit quite nicely.

He arranges Beatriz on the passenger seat so that she looks like a sleeping customer. With pillows and a blanket, she's packed in so tight that she won't slump or slide to the floor. He drives slowly through the city and around Majanicho; he doesn't dare take Alejandro's Trail, which is too uneven and bumpy. It'll take an extra ten minutes, but he still has time.

He carries her into the living room and swaddles her in a blanket that he's shaken free of dust and crumbs.

At 6.15 p.m. he hears the doctor's car and goes out to greet him and to help bring in the equipment, which isn't much more than a mouthpiece connected to a small machine by a thin tube. The doctor fastens it to Beatriz's mouth, then pulls an elastic band around her head. The device is already on, and Erhard sees Beatriz's abdomen heaving unnaturally, like bagpipes. The doctor explains that she needs to hyperventilate to create rapid circulation in the damaged regions of her brain. Erhard just watches her belly rise and fall underneath the all-too-large t-shirt. The respirator inflates. It blinks and glows.

Afterward, the doctor gives her a thorough examination and takes her blood pressure. At last he affixes a catheter to collect her urine in a bag, then instructs Erhard to change the bag as soon as it's more than two-thirds full.

– If we can't bring her out of this coma in two or three days, we'll need to insert intravenous nourishment, the doctor says. It's important that Erhard keep an eye on her; it's important that he call as soon as the machine beeps or something happens. – If she's going to be here, you'll need to be vigilant. The doctor acts peevish to make it clear that he disagrees with Erhard's plan.

Erhard glances nervously at the wall outlets, which throw sparks. He'll need more power from the generator, and he'll need to buy a new one, especially if more devices will be added. The doctor rejects Erhard's offer of a beer, then walks out to his car, promising not to tell anyone.

Erhard watches Beatriz for the next hour and a half. It occurs to him that the two women have already exchanged places. Alina's story ends right in the place she'd always striven for. Beatriz's story concludes right where – perhaps – she feared it would. He considers building a partition in the living room so that she can have her own room, then decides that if she's still here in a week, he will do that. Maybe he could construct a private loft? It would be easy to take care of her that way, and easy to check the devices.

He latches the backdoor, then puts an extra padlock on the front door. Something about the episode with Alina makes him worry that someone will pay him a visit. It's a Saturday afternoon, and probably no one will stop by, but still.

He drives out to Tindaya.

The island is so small that he knows every nook and cranny. And he knows where Lorenzo Pérez-Lúñigo lives: a large yellow house that's passed through five generations of doctors. Lorenzo married into the house via Adela, Dr Agosto's eldest daughter. Together they have four adult sons, and a stable of horses in the fields behind their house. He parks on a small private road that skirts the grounds. Then he strolls around and up to the house, which is quiet, sealed off. When Adela opens the door, she seems ill.

– We didn't order a cab today, she says.

– Happy New Year. I need to speak with Lorenzo.

– He's no longer practising.

– I know.

– One moment, she says, closing the door.

Five minutes later Lorenzo opens it.

– Yes, he says, perceptibly startled when he recognizes Erhard.

– I need to speak with you. Alone.

Lorenzo scrutinizes Erhard, possibly considering what will happen if he says no. Then he steps outside and follows Erhard.

They walk onto the street. There are never any cars here, but the neighbours sometimes peer through their shutters. Erhard guides him up the narrow road where the car is parked.

– How can I help you, Señor Jørgensen? the doctor says with a kind of affected highbrow manner that doesn't match his typically vulgar style.

– Let me be blunt. I've kept quiet about your little secrets for more than ten years.

– *Dios mío.* What secrets are you referring to?

Erhard gives him a look, but Lorenzo doesn't notice, so Erhard has to explain: – All those times you showed up plastered at car accidents, or that incident down at the shipyard, when your blood-alcohol level was far above what it should've been.

– That wasn't unlawful. I rode in a taxi.

– But it's not good form, so far as I'm aware. And there's probably a good reason you once gave me a 100-euro tip.

– Are you complaining about tips now?

– Only when they're a type of payoff.

– It was never a payoff.

– What about the time I found you out near Molino?

Lorenzo stares at Erhard in alarm. He doesn't like to hear any mention of that episode. The doctor had crashed his car in the ditch early one morning, and he'd stood by the side of the road six miles from the closest village. On the backseat of his car was the naked body of an elderly person. Before Lorenzo called the mechanic to request a tow, he wanted Erhard to drive him and the body back to the Department of Forensic Medicine at the hospital in Puerto. It wasn't the first time that Erhard had dealt with a body. But Lorenzo's arrogance – as if it were part of Erhard's job description to haul corpses – had made Erhard obstinate and sceptical, even though Lorenzo gave him a handsome tip. In the end, Bernal had saved Lorenzo from a police report. Though it probably would've been dismissed anyway, it would have ignited devastating rumours in the circles where Lorenzo Pérez-Lúñigo most wishes to be regarded as a respectable and brilliant official of the highest sort. Possessing a corpse in some godforsaken part of the island would've been awfully difficult to explain, and it would've called to mind some very unfortunate images. Lorenzo had understood that.

– What do you want? Why do you come here with this?

– Do we agree that you owe me a favour?

Lorenzo stares unhappily at Erhard. – I thought I'd already demonstrated my gratitude. So what do you want, Señor Jørgensen?

– I want to bring peace to a good friend.

– I can't do that. I'm not a murderer.

– Lower your voice, Lorenzo. Nobody's killing anyone. You just need to dispose of a body and pass it along quickly to the mortician, that's all.

Lorenzo glances around. – What do you mean?

– Sometime in the next day, Beatrizia Colini's body will be delivered to you for your examination. You need to report that her death was the result of a fall down a stairwell. You can note other small things, but you have to conclude that Beatrizia Colini died following an unfortunate tumble in which she struck her head.

– What have you done, Señor Jørgensen?

– I haven't done anything. I'm just making sure that my friend Beatrizia's reputation remains intact, and that the Palabras family isn't involved unnecessarily in her death.

As soon as Erhard utters the name Palabras, Lorenzo flinches as if he's bitten a lime. It was exactly the effect Erhard was hoping for.

– Lorenzo! Adela calls from the door.

– Do we have an agreement? Erhard asks.

– Can I trust that you will never visit me like this again?

– If you do this, I will never come here again.

Lorenzo turns and walks back to the house. – Coming, Adela, he says in a baritone voice.

When the door front door closes, Erhard climbs in his car and collapses in the seat. Only now does he realize how nervous he has been during the entire conversation. He starts the engine and heads back towards the city.

*

As soon as there's some shade on the balcony, he carries Alina to the rooftop terrace. Halfway up the stairs he lets her slide headfirst out of the tarpaulin. He turns her around and lays her head on a pillow, so that he doesn't have to look at her face. Rigor mortis has begun to set in. Erhard wipes the blood from the tarpaulin and the wooden balcony floor.

Erhard is unsettled and indecisive, pacing between the balcony and the bedroom. He drinks the expensive coffee. The sun is red, and he gazes across the city and the beach at the kite surfers out near the Dunes. The city noise below makes him sad. Children shout when they leap off a buoy down in the harbour. One of the city's many impatient lorry drivers honks as he squeezes his load of cucumbers or beer into some narrow alley. Erhard has always loved the city. This city. God only knows how much he hates other cities, particularly Copenhagen; no other city is so hyper-regulated and boxy with tower blocks as Copenhagen. But Corralejo is incomparably unique, marked by aridity, an excessive desire to please, and a population of inbreds. It's just the place for Erhard. A provincial hole with long opening hours, a little city with a big city's attractions. But even if he had the money, he's not sure if he'd choose to live here. The noise, the smell, the nightlife, the bars, the friendly women, and city living as a whole – it would be the end of him. It has always been a pleasure to visit Raúl, to sit on the terrace with two attractive friends and enjoy the moment. Now he wishes, most of all, to go back to last summer, when they went to a fish restaurant near Morro Jable. That evening when they sat together in the car and laughed at the thunder.

He calls Raúl's number again. But he knows that he won't answer. So he dials 112 and requests an ambulance.

Then he waits on the street for it to arrive. The paramedics need to carry the stretcher up the stairs. As they climb, Erhard tells them how he found her, and how he kept his eye on her. His nerves are calmed when one of the paramedics seems unconcerned. As if picking up dead women is an everyday event.

When the paramedics see her, they sit down and wait for the police and the doctor who'll perform the post-mortem to arrive. Although

Erhard has predicted this, it still makes him uncomfortable. He prepares coffee in the kitchen so they won't notice his trembling hands. Five minutes later the doorbell chimes and he hopes it's Bernal, whom he knows. But it turns out to be a young policeman, a tall, Arabic-looking man who might very well be a troublemaker. Erhard states his full name, but the officer just introduces himself as Hassib, then asks Erhard to tell him what happened. When Erhard tries to explain, Hassib doesn't pay attention. Instead he stares at his mobile. Behind the policeman, a young, short-haired doctor in a suit enters the flat. The new health inspector.

– The wealthy and their fucking lifestyles, Hassib says, watching the inspector as he pulls back the plastic sheet they've covered Alina with. He examines her without touching her; he photographs her, close up and from a distance, then rolls her over and repeats the procedure. He also takes photos of the stairwell. He sees a tooth on the floor and photographs that, too.

Erhard observes everything while he drinks his coffee. The officer speaks with the doctor briefly and in a hushed voice, then they strap Alina to the stretcher and begin carrying her downstairs. The inspector asks Erhard for the name of Beatriz's doctor, but Erhard doesn't know. Ask Emanuel Palabras, he finally says. The inspector thanks him and hands Erhard his business card, which is printed on cheap paper, before he exits the room, his mobile phone stuck to his ear. Hassib walks around the flat, circling Erhard until at last he's standing beside him in the kitchen.

– So when did you find her?

– Around eleven o'clock. We'd gone out and had a few drinks, and I slept here. When I woke up, I found her. Then…

– Eleven o'clock? Why didn't you call earlier?

– She cried out in ways I didn't understand, so I thought she was just hurt. When she was better, I was going to drive her to the emergency room.

– Emergency room? That woman is a mess.

– I thought she'd get better.

– But she's dead, don't you get it? Someone may have pushed her. Since Raúl Palabras hasn't turned up yet, he might be our man.

– It's not him. He would never do that to her. It must've been an accident.

– Where did you say he went?

– I didn't say. I don't know where he is. I've called him, but he doesn't answer.

– If you know where he is, you need to tell me now. If we don't get any more information, we'll have to charge you.

They would do something like that, Erhard thinks. Take the first and best suspect. – All I did was sleep here, he says.

– If you talk to your friend, tell him he's better off turning himself in.

Erhard doesn't know what to say. He plucks a sour grape from a bunch on the table.

– Where did you say you slept?

– I didn't say. In the bedroom, Erhard says, pointing.

To his amazement, the policeman strides through the living room and into the bedroom, then snaps on the light and looks around. – Where did Palabras sleep?

– I don't know. I was pissed. We sat up on the terrace this morning drinking Bloody Marys and talking. I got really tired and pissed and wanted to go home, but they asked me to sleep down here. So I did. When I woke up, Raúl was gone and…

Erhard notices that the policeman is not writing anything down. He's investigating the crime scene because that's what he's supposed to do, but he doesn't actually care.

– How much did she drink? The girlfriend.

– Not much, I don't think. We woke her up when we arrived, and she came out to the terrace with us. But she was tired and yawned the whole time.

Erhard's surprised at how well he's lying. All he has to do is recall the events of the morning and alter them slightly.

– How long have they lived together?

– Eight or ten years, maybe. Eight.

– They were happy together?

– Yes. He was crazy about her. And vice versa.

Erhard considers the words she'd uttered: *Help me. Let me go.* Do they mean anything? Are they just something Erhard imagined? He hopes not. Now that he's set everything into motion so that he can hide Beatriz. To save her from someone who wishes to do her harm. It can't be Raúl.

– But why did you sleep down here? asks the policeman. He rounds the bed and opens the wardrobe.

– How should I know? Hospitality, I guess. That's the way Raúl is.

– Where did they sleep?

The policeman riffles through Raúl's collection of suits.

– Maybe on the sofa. Or up on the terrace.

– Have you ever witnessed Raúl Palabras abusing Beatrizia Colini?

– Abusing?

– You know, hitting her? Slapping her around?

– Never.

The policeman goes to the living room. On the way he peers through the half-open door into the office. – What did you say was in here?

– The office. They never use that room.

The policeman switches on the office lights, and a twinge of misgiving runs through Erhard: Did he remember to clean up in there? For some reason, he hadn't thought the police would spend any time searching inside the flat if the body was discovered on the balcony.

Hassib walks around the desk and strokes the closed laptop. – Whose is this?

– I don't know. Maybe Raúl's?

– I'll take it with me, the policeman says. He picks up the computer and the attached cord.

– What's going to happen now? Erhard follows the police officer into the living room and onto the balcony. The red stains on the stairwell and the woodwork are still there. – What will happen to her? Will she be taken to forensics now?

– We have to find her family. Do you know where they live?

– She doesn't have any family here on the island. Maybe on Gran Canaria.

– Girlfriends? Ex-boyfriends?

– Not as far as I'm aware. It was always just Raúl.

– Work?

– A few days a week. Down at the boutique on Señora del Carmen. The one with the elephant. She'd just started.

– Does she have a mobile anywhere?

– I've looked, but I haven't found it.

– Let's give Señor Pérez-Lúñigo some peace and quiet to find out what happened to your friend. Anyway, we'll seal off the flat. What is your name and address? We'll need to speak with you again, I'm sure. He unwraps a long white stick of chewing gum and folds the stick three times before popping it into his mouth. – And we've got to find that bastard Raúl Palabras.

34

He's hardly able to breathe until they've gone. He stands listening, his ear pressed to the door, as the paramedics and the police officer chat all the way to the lift. He hears the lift rattling down the shaft.

The corridor falls silent. Sitting at the dining table, he stares at the front door, anticipating the policeman's return. But he doesn't return.

Evening comes. He loves the evening. Aromas swirl up from the street: cinnamon, caramel, urine, sea.

He has to save Beatriz. When she opens her eyes, when she wakes up in a few days, she can tell him what happened. Maybe she can tell him where Raúl is. Erhard can save both of his friends. Suddenly Emanuel Palabras comes to mind. Maybe Raúl called him? Or maybe Raúl's at his place? He decides to drive home and give him a call. It's time for a Lumumba.

The house is darker than usual.

Knowing that Alina died at his house, right around the corner where the field begins, makes everything feel unsafe and barren. More than ever.

He checks the generator and snaps on the light, then brings pillows from the sofa and a dining room chair into the bedroom and sits watching Beatriz's body fill with air, empty, and fill again. The rattle of the wind, a tug and pull, hypnotic and exhausting.

But he doesn't sleep. He sits rigidly, like a night watchman, and listens to Beatriz's inhalations, thinking of Raúl the entire time, that he's dead, and thinking of the little slit in the blanket through which he can insert his hand and feel her vagina. It's terribly wrong of him, but even now, after having been unconscious for more than twelve hours, she still smells of juice and cinnamon and warm raisins. Just because there are no other women in his life. If there were, his sexual fantasies wouldn't be about Beatriz. He tries to imagine Emanuel's Maasai girl and her little ass, which he could see through her sheer dress. But he can't. She's too much and not enough. What the hell does he know about women? It's been so long since he's had one. There have been women in his life, brief encounters, mostly with the prostitutes he could afford. But he has always picked the older models, so that it wasn't too embarrassing or strange for either one of them. Not to mention to give them a little business. The young ones have enough work. Those his own age just hang about reading magazines or eating yoghurt. Twice he's picked the same woman, a Spaniard by the name of Afrodita. That wasn't her real name, of course, but that's what she called herself. She was a rather uninteresting woman who might've been mistaken for a cashier at a souvenir stand. The first time was at a place called La Mouscita in Puerto – which is now a pizza joint – and he'd actually pointed at another woman, a more exotic-looking mulatto; but the manager had misunderstood Erhard, and Afrodita almost appeared grateful when she was nudged forward. He didn't have the heart to correct the mistake. Besides, it turned out, she had a strange but pleasurable fellatio technique which Erhard could feel the effects of for weeks afterward. The second time, he'd planned in advance to go right after the mulatto, but she wasn't there; she might have been out sick or had the day off to attend her little brother's wedding. During the hesitation that followed, he made eye contact with Afrodita, and he felt that he owed her another round for old time's sake. He asked her to focus on sucking him off. He enjoyed her talents, but more importantly, he wouldn't have to watch her remove her clothes. Not because he didn't like her body, but because the first time she'd been so meticulous about removing and folding her clothes. He'd guessed that she'd once worked at a clothing shop, not a souvenir stand; it took such a dreadfully long time. So much time, in fact, that he lost interest in sex and didn't get aroused again until she began to breathe warmly on his penis. Afrodita on her knees like a cleaning woman. Afrodita scouring the bottom of a boat. Afrodita diving among turtles. Afrodita talking to him under the water, bubbles pouring from her, downward, between the rocks where she gathers oysters.

Erhard wakes up every half-hour. He listens to Beatriz's breathing, listens to the device. And every time his eyes scroll down to that dark slit that fits perfectly with his hand. Drowsy and horny, he turns back to his pillows. The night seems endless.

3 5

The hills lie in shadow, and the sky is as yellow as an egg-yolk.

He's standing among the rocks watching the goats trot towards him one after the other. Laurel's little bell jangles each time he plants his front hooves on the ground.

Emanuel Palabras had been strangely detached on the telephone. He hadn't seen Raúl for weeks, he said. When Erhard told him that Beatriz was dead and that Raúl was missing, he said Raúl was his mother's child. Then he laughed as though he were sitting in a sauna shooting the breeze. Erhard has always felt oddly connected to Palabras. Two men out of step with modern times. A generation with a strong work ethic and a rawness towards life. One shouldn't get mixed up in things one doesn't understand, Palabras said several times, his pent-up irritation at his son on full display. In the end Erhard had to change the subject: *How's it going with 'Coral'?* Palabras just grunted and ended the call.

He herds the goats back to the house and feeds them. When he scatters the food the pellets clatter against the stones, and he watches the animals sniff at each one before licking them up with their grey tongues. He returns the ladder to its proper place on the other side of the house. Not so far from where he'd found Alina. It amazes him that she'd carried the ladder around the house before she'd crawled up on the roof. Why not just climb up on the same side?

The most important thing right now is to ensure peace and quiet for Beatriz. And to get a new generator, a better, more reliable one. Maybe one of those kinds that turns on and off automatically at night when he goes to bed. He's wanted one of those for a long time, he's just never had the money. Of course, it also wasn't a necessity until now. If it costs less than 1,000 euros, he can buy one. The appliance shop won't open till the morning.

He goes inside and eats a bowl of corn porridge, keeping an eye on Beatriz and the small drainage bag while listening to the radio. He finds his book and plops into his plush recliner with its worn fabric and its clawed-up armrest, a result of the previous owner's cat. He reads a few lines in the story about the speckled band. 'The least sound would be fatal to our plans,' Holmes says, growing still. Two women die in the story. It's ironic that Solilla's book recommendation has become relevant these past few days. In some way, the red thread leads him to the boy in the cardboard box. Though he can't quite see how, he can't help but think that it's all connected.

Did someone beat up Beatriz and do away with Raúl? Someone who frightened Alina so badly that she jumped off the roof? What did it have to do with the boy? Did someone see Raúl and Beatriz out near Cotillo that night of the lightning, and guess they were involved? Raúl and Beatriz weren't celebrities, but when they entered a room or a restaurant, heads turned. They were memorable. And everyone knew the name Palabras. People whispered it at the farmer's market and said it aloud at the Yellow Rooster – when the men had had enough to drink.

He hasn't gotten anywhere with that image Alina found on her mobile. The image from the beach, the car parked at the water's edge. He caught only a brief glimpse. She had her phone when he left to get her charger. That was the last time he saw Alina alive. The mobile must be somewhere nearby. He lies down on the floor and peers under the shelf and the chair. He lifts the mattress in the hallway. At last he spots it on the coat rack, balanced there as if someone had set it down to put on a jacket, then forgot all about it. He presses the buttons, but it's still dead. He can't remember what he did with the charger. It seems like several days ago, weeks even.

Why must everything be so bloody difficult? If he's ever going to find something on that mobile, he needs some assistance. He thinks about Jorge Ponduel, whom he'd prefer to avoid. He's a hot-tempered *majorero* whose worst day of life came when the goat-cheese producer Quesotierro dropped its sponsorship of UD Fuerteventura, the island's only good football team. Ponduel loves electronics of all kinds and likes to discuss loudspeakers, monitors, and strange devices that can hoover by themselves, items which he has bought or wishes to buy. And he likes to complain about old equipment that's either broken or just Japanese crap. As far as Erhard recalls, Ponduel works the morning shift Monday to Friday.

Erhard doesn't usually drive his cab on Sunday afternoons. But he's restless – and anyway, he needs the hours. Before he leaves, he pulls the curtains closed and turns off the light. Only the respirator lamps reveal her silhouette. In the darkness she looks like someone transforming into a corpse. If Raúl's the one who beat her up, then he can go to hell. If Raúl is innocent, he'll thank Erhard one day for having saved her life.

36

There's a new salesman in the appliance shop. A stylish Turkish guy with a fashionable goatee. Immediately he begins discussing something he calls the fuel economy. And sound investment-strategy. He shows Erhard a catalogue with photos of big blue generators.

For Erhard, the conversation is one of those that too quickly moves away from its starting point. The man is clever, but all he does is make Erhard feel stupid. He'd thought he could go home with a new generator today; he'd thought he could get it all taken care of in fifteen minutes. But he's already been staring at this expensive catalogue for thirty minutes, and he's none the wiser. Except that he's now aware that his current generator is a kind of miracle; it came with the house and has only been repaired four times. Erhard has just about had it with all this sales chatter. He needs fresh air.

– Up to 100 kilowatts, and it's all controlled by this remote control, the salesman says.

His name is Jorge, according to his badge.

– It seems a tad too fancy, too big, so…

– You said you'd like it more automated.

– Yes, but not… not like that. I'll come back another day. Is your boss here tomorrow?

– My boss? You mean Christiano? No, he's not here any more. I'm the new owner. What's the problem?

– I just want a generator that's better than the one I've got. Not some fine, pretty machine with all these bells and whistles.

– How much do you have?

– What do you mean?

– Money. How much do you want to spend?

It's a very direct question, and Erhard has never heard anything like it. Young people. They do whatever the hell they want.

– That's none of your concern.

– If you want to know how much you can get for your money, it's easier if you give me an idea.

Erhard sees the time above the door of the shop. It's almost eleven o'clock. – I have around 1,000 euros.

Jorge claps the catalogue shut, possibly insulted but not defeated. – OK. You know what we'll do? We'll go out here.

He exits the shop and starts towards the courtyard. Erhard follows him. He stops beside a broad door and removes some cardboard that covers up appliances on pallets.

– Here, you can have this generator for fifteen hundred.

Erhard sees a colourful, welded-up apparatus with a big tank and what looks like a black suitcase fashioned to a radiator.

– Forty to fifty kilowatts on a good day and at least twenty years of loyal service on an Atlantic fishing vessel. Not good as new, but damn well better than most of the things you can get for fifteen hundred or two thousand euros.

It looks older than the one Erhard already has, but his produces, at most, only twenty-five kilowatts and has only three power outlets. This one has six.

– Can you add a power switch with a timer? Erhard asks.

– Yes, Jorge says without blinking. – For 2,000 euros you can have a timer.

– Seventeen.

– Nineteen.

– OK. But I want it delivered to my house today.

– Will you be paying cash?

– I have one thousand.

– You'll get it as soon as you pay the entire amount.

– Your old boss let me pay in instalments.

– He's not here any more, the smartass says.

Which is a problem for Erhard. He needs more power in order to leave Beatriz all day. Right now there's enough for only four hours on one tank-full, at most. That means he has to drive home and fill it with diesel in the middle of his workday.

– If you want to sell this old scrap metal, you'll have to accept the thousand euros today and deliver it to my house today. Then I'll return with the rest of the money, the eight hundred euros, later this week.

But that's not how it turns out. Erhard can have it for 1,850 euros, excluding delivery. Twenty-two hundred euros in all. In exchange, the salesman promises to wait a week before selling the generator to anyone else.

He drives slowly down Atalaya and then Primo de Rivera, and finally Milagrosa. A customer practically leaps onto his taxi when he turns a corner, but he points at the *Not in Service* sign. He circles the block, then heads down Calle Nuestra Señora del Carmen.

Erhard is searching for Ponduel, but he can't find him anywhere. He pulls up alongside Alberto, who's reading a newspaper in his car, and rolls down his window.

– Morning, Alberto.

Alberto lowers his newspaper and says hello.

– How's your arrangement with Muñoz going?

– Good, Señor *Extranjero*, Alberto says.

That means it's going well, perhaps really well. Because of the arrangement, Alberto is now actually making money. Erhard pretends not to hear *extranjero*, which is the term natives use to put non-natives in their place. – Have you seen Ponduel?

Alberto looks down the street and points over his shoulder with his thumb. – Try number 62.

– Isn't he working today?

– There's nothing to do. There's a strike in London, Berlin, Madrid. No flights until tomorrow.

Erhard parks opposite number 62. An electronics shop. The owner is a well-known figure – an Irishman who loves poker and beer.

There's no one in the shop. Erhard heads into the backroom through the beaded curtains. He's never been in the backroom before, having declined the invitation to play numerous times. The door to the rear courtyard is open. The owner, Cormac, is telling a story about doing business with the Chinese. With his index fingers he's tugging the skin around his eyes upward. When he sees Erhard, he lowers his hands. – Hermit! he says excitedly.

Ponduel just gawks at Erhard, annoyed. As if he were a little boy unhappy about being picked up by his father. Erhard shakes Cormac's hand.

– Ponduel, you're the one I'm looking for.

– That figures, Cormac says, laughing. Probably already pissed.

– What do you want? Ponduel asks.

Erhard had forgotten just how unfriendly Ponduel actually is. Not a bad person, just unfriendly. Does he really want this man's help? he wonders. They might have to spend several hours together, but he can't think of another alternative.

– I need your smart head, Ponduel.

– As far as I can recall, you're not the type to ask for help.

– But I am now. I need someone who knows computers.

– Oh yes, this man is a genius with a computer, Cormac says, handing Erhard a beer.

Ponduel seems reluctant. – What is it? I don't do that kind of thing any more. There are teenagers who know more than I do. Ask one of them.

– This is different. I need to find something on the Internet.

– Hell, I could do that, Cormac says.

– What? Ponduel asks.

– A photograph.

Cormac erupts in laughter. – Oh, we know what you mean, he guffaws.

Erhard doesn't know what's so funny.

– What kind of photo? I need more than that.

Erhard's afraid it's going to become complicated now. – I don't know.

– Where was it taken? Who took it?

– I don't know.

– So it's like finding a needle in a haystack.

– I know it exists. I've seen it on a mobile phone. But I can't find it any more.

– Forget it, Ponduel says, gulping the last foam-filled swallow of his beer.

– I'll pay you. Just let your taximeter run while you help me.

– Eager, are we? Cormac says, ambling out to the shop when a customer arrives.

– What's the image of?

– I'll tell you if you help me.

– Tell me. I can't help you unless you tell me.

– It's a photograph taken at Cotillo Beach, and it shows something very important. I found it with a friend, but she's dead now. I would like to find it again.

– Who's dead? Cormac says, returning.

Erhard hasn't thought this through properly. Cormac doesn't seem like the type of person you discuss this kind of thing with. It could get around quickly. – A lady friend, he says simply. – She fell down a stairwell.

– Where's the mobile phone? Ponduel asks.

– I thought we could use a computer. The screen's bigger.

– Where's the computer?

Erhard stares at the floor. Ponduel snorts.

– You can always buy one here, Cormac says.

– So you need to get your hands on a computer and you need help? Cormac laughs again.

Erhard's sick of the tone. Why is everyone always just looking out for themselves? Why doesn't anyone just want to help, without asking for anything in return?

– Forget it, he says. – I wanted to ask you. I don't know anyone else who knows about computers. I don't know any teenagers.

Cormac stands. – Ask Luisa Glades.

– Who's she?

– She teaches at the IT school in Puerto. She lives here in town. Or her mother does, anyway. They say she's very smart. She bought her computer here a month ago and even put it together herself.

– She sounds expensive. I don't need an expert, just someone who can find an image.

– You can always ask her. Maybe she can teach you something. I don't have her number, but you can find it easily enough.

Erhard pauses. – Glades?

– Yes, the hairdresser, the one down in Acorzado.

– Does she have two daughters?

– No. A daughter and a son. And the daughter's called Luisa.

– And if you want all the juicy details, Cormac's the man you need, Ponduel says, chuckling.

– Yes, gentlemen. I'm the ears, the eyes, and the travelling switchboard of Fuerteventura. Electronics can make even great men gossip like parrots.

This is a phrase Cormac utters now and then.

Her name is not Luisa Glades, it's Luisa Muelas, but he doesn't tell the two men that. Erhard recalls standing, horny and pathetic, outside the girl's door in Calle Palangre. Inside she might have been sleeping naked on a red leather sofa with a champagne bottle between her long legs, while the fireworks boomed over Isla de Lobos and Bill Haji's finger was in his pocket. Now it turns out she's a computer expert.

Ponduel begins to deal the cards.

– Watch your fortune, Erhard says, exiting the courtyard and walking through the overheated shop past all the beeping machines.

Erhard musters his courage before going up the stairs to the salon. Three schoolchildren are getting haircuts. They're sitting still, lollipops in their mouths. He turns away from the photograph of the daughter that's hanging on the wall.

Petra is friendliness itself, asking to write his name immediately in the appointment book. But no, he's not here to reserve a time. Perhaps another day.

He doesn't even say computer and Luisa before Petra begins to brag about her daughter, and how busy she is. It's only temporary, Petra promises. She's getting married soon.

– Oh, I see. Well, congratulations.

– Let me call for you, Petra says, punching the buttons on the salon's cordless telephone.

They chat for five minutes before Petra tells her daughter about her good customer who needs help, that intelligent older man I've told you about, the one from Norway.

The conversation embarrasses him.

She turns to Erhard: – Where do you live? Out in Majanicho, right?

– No, Calle Muelle. Fifth floor. It says Palabras on the door.

Petra repeats the information for her daughter's benefit. – And when can you do it? she asks him.

– Whenever. He thinks of Beatriz. – Tomorrow after siesta.

– Luisa says Wednesday around 8 p.m.

Erhard simply nods.

Petra hangs up. – Shouldn't we schedule a haircut since you're here?

There is an American couple staying at the hotel in Las Dunas.

She complains about the wind. – You could have told me when we booked the vacation, she says.

The man tries to explain how he didn't know. – It looked great in the photographs!

– You can't see the wind in a photograph, the wife protests. – You've got to do some research.

He drives home straight before siesta. He shops at Super HiperDino and buys some bread, cheap cheese, and a newspaper, which he reads from front to back after checking up on Beatriz, her pulse, her pupils; he shifts her position and massages her arms and thighs to get the blood flowing. He listens for her breathing, putting his ear next to her mouth. But she makes no sound. All that he hears is the huff of the respirator. He knows her body, it seems to him, as well as any woman he's ever been with or loved.

There's something extraordinary about being with an unconscious person. The normal rules of intimacy do not apply. He scrubs her with a wash cloth. Carefully. He watches her belly rise and fall, and he recalls sitting beside her on the beach or the rooftop terrace. When she exhales, her breath is gentle and billowing, alarmingly light. Her face seems paler, too. He finds the telephone and calls Michel Faliando, the doctor. A day has passed. There's been no change or improvement. Michel asks Erhard various questions: Has she moved? Has she…? and so forth. Erhard repeats the same response for each question: no. Her pulse is stable, around sixty-one beats per minute, and the respirator's working properly. For the first time, he hears uncertainty in the doctor's voice. If there's no improvement in the next forty-eight hours, Erhard will need to take her to the hospital. At most, she can survive three or four days without food or liquids.

Lying on the sofa, she's visible to anyone who might open the front door. He's tried to move the sofa, but it doesn't help. It unnerves him. Besides, he needs something to do, so he starts building a bed in the pantry, the lowest-lying room and also the room with the highest ceiling. If he builds the bed on the shelf and encloses it, she can lie up there unnoticed even to someone standing in the pantry. At the same time, he can easily keep an eye on her condition by standing on a crate. There's even an outlet at the very top, so the respirator can be positioned right next to the mattress.

It's hard work, but he loses track of time. He saws old laths and screws them into place. He carries some old boards in from the shed, balances them first on top of the shelf and then the laths. One of the boards is too wide, and he's forced to hack off the corners so that he can wedge it through the door and up under the ceiling. When the boards are in place, he finds an extension cord and arranges a small lamp along the wall. He hauls the mattress on which Alina had lain up to the bed and seals it with yet another broad lath, which he screws in place.

When the sun snips the hills in two, he drinks another glass of cognac from a wine glass and listens to Gillespie on Radio Mucha. During the news report, there's no mention of the boy. Everyone on the island has happily forgotten about him.

– But not me, he tells Beatriz.

Now comes the hardest part. The worst part.

First he carries the respirator up to the bed and plugs it in; it hisses like a sick cat. Then he lifts her onto his shoulder while holding the catheter and drainage bag, and he bears her out of the room. One step at a time. He climbs onto a crate and then a chair, and he rolls her cautiously over the lath and onto the mattress, before nudging her carefully towards the wall, away from the edge and into the corner, illuminated only by the faint bulb in the small reading lamp. He affixes the drainage bag on a lower shelf. He attempts to figure out how to turn down the beeping respirator, but is afraid to mess with anything he doesn't understand.

He puts everything back in the pantry: tins, old loops of twine, bottles of cooking oil and vinegar. He throws nothing out, even the stuff that's past date. Finally the room resembles a pantry again. An unappealing pantry, but the illusion remains intact.

Next he checks the generator and fills it with diesel, hoping it'll be one of the last times he'll have to do so. He makes himself a plate of cheese and eats, gazing out the window at the road. The daylight is fading, and the dusty ground is getting darker and darker.

The police arrive at nine o'clock.

He'd figured they would come earlier.

A single officer, his silhouette in the black car, headlights bouncing over potholes. It's Bernal. He can almost recognize the sound of his cowboy boots. Erhard lets him knock a few times before he opens the door.

– Hermit.

– Bernal.

Erhard doesn't invite him in. Not right away.

– What is it with you?

– What do you mean?

– Bill Haji. The boy on the beach. Keeping company with Beatriz Colini, who's now dead, and Raúl Palabras, who's now vanished without a trace.

– It's a small island.

– A small world if you ask me.

– You know me. I had nothing to do with her death.

Which is true, Erhard thinks.

– I know, but we've toyed with the idea. For now you're not a suspect.

– They are my two best friends. I would never dream of…

– Were.

– What?

– *Were* your two best friends. Past tense.

– Raúl Palabras might still be alive.

– Do you know where he is?

– No. I told the other officer the same thing.

– Why would he hurt his girlfriend?

– He didn't hurt her. She must've fallen. Raúl would never hurt her.

– Are we talking about the same Raúl Palabras who was twice charged with assault?

– He would never touch Beatriz. Not like that.

– Hassib wrote in his report that you spent an hour with her before she died. What were you doing?

– Trying to save her.

– How?

– By helping her, arranging her comfortably and talking to her.

– For an hour?

– A doctor came.

– Who?

– Does it even matter? He came and said there was nothing to be done. He left right after she died.

– He's a witness. He's a doctor. We need to speak with him.

– He was there as a friend of Beatriz's. I don't care to tell you who.

– I can arrest you and find the doctor myself.

– I know.

– When did you find her?

Erhard repeats the story he told Hassib.

– Eleven o'clock? You're sure? Bernal asks.

– Yes. After I found her and made her comfortable, I went up to the rooftop terrace to look for Raúl. A woman on one of the other roofs saw me. She can confirm the time.

– Did Beatriz say anything?

– She mumbled something. She said Raúl's name.

– Did she tell you what happened?

– She said she'd fallen.

– On the stairs?

– Yes, that's what it looked like.

– Lorenzo says that both her ankles were broken, and that her face was a complete mess. That's quite an atypical fall, if you ask me.

– How should I know? That's how I found her.

Bernal gazes down the path as the goats trot towards the house.

– What's with the horn?

– That's how it looked when I got him.

– Let me in for a beer, Hermit. We need to talk about this.

Erhard had feared this would happen. But he doesn't see how he can refuse. – I'm on my way to bed, he says.

– No you're not. You're staying up all night, the policeman says, stepping past Erhard and into the house.

Erhard fetches two lukewarm beers from the pantry. He glances briefly up at the bed, but he can't see or hear Beatriz. He switches off the light and hands one of the beers to Bernal.

– You've rearranged, Bernal says.

Erhard looks around the room. What is it that he sees? – You mean the sofa?

The sofa he'd moved for Beatriz.

– Possibly. The room is different. He turns and looks at Erhard. – I have something important to tell you.

Pause. Silence. Too much silence.

– Raúl Palabras has fled the country.

– Have you found him?

Erhard feels a strange form of relief that Raúl is still alive, followed by anger that he's fled from his crime. From his girlfriend.

– We have a photo of him at the airport. According to the passenger list, it was taken just before he boarded a plane.

– To where?

– I can't tell you that.

– Spain?

– No.

– If it was taken before ten o'clock, there are only three possibilities: Casablanca, London, and Madrid.

– We'll get our hands on him. As soon as he sets foot on one of the islands.

– I hope so, Erhard says, and nearly means it.

– OK, listen up, Bernal says. – If there's anything, anything at all, that you're not telling us, you need to fess up now. My colleague Hassib thinks you're lying, that you're hiding something. He wanted to bring you in, but I vouched for you. Bernal eyes Erhard as if it's a question. – You need to tell me if there's something we should know.

– I can repeat what I've already said, if you wish. I haven't killed anyone, if that's what you think.

Bernal grins as if he can't imagine Erhard killing anyone and yet that's exactly what he was thinking. – The girl falls down and dies, and Raúl flees the country. It can hardly be a coincidence.

– All I can tell you is that I found Beatriz. And that Raúl was gone.

– That's what I'm saying. You're clean. Hassib says you're fucking with us. Those are his words, not mine. But you're all right. He rises from his chair. – Beatriz Colini had a cousin and an aunt in Madrid. They can't come to her service, or maybe they didn't have the money to pay for tickets. If you wish to come, you'll be one of the few. It's tomorrow at five o'clock. Out near Alto Blanco.

– Why there?

– On the request of Emanuel Palabras. He's paying for the service.

– Will he be there?

– I don't think so. Thanks for the beer, Bernal says, setting it on the table. He hasn't touched it. When he reaches the door, he turns: – One last thing. If you're still wondering about that case with the boy, then, well, we didn't get any further. The case is still open, but no one's working on it.

– I thought you were going to close it with a false confession.

– She's vanished. That's what her kind does. She probably got cold feet. And we haven't heard from our local sponsor, so you can rest easy again.

– You still haven't found the mother.

– The earth keeps spinning, Hermit. New crimes are committed that need to be solved, and you're sure keeping us busy.

Bernal walks out the door. Into the brown darkness of night.

37

On Tuesday he drives from early morning to late, much too late. When he gets home, he's absolutely whipped. Tired and out of sorts. He's only had two breaks all day, each time to fill diesel in the generator, check on Beatriz, and grab a bite to eat. During the course of the day, he's come to realize that earning 1,200 euros quickly is next to impossible so long as he's obligated to share half of his earnings with TaxiVentura. When the day is over, he can only put 128 euros aside. It'll take him several weeks to earn the money for the generator. Goddamned generator.

Standing on a crate in the pantry and listening to Beatriz, he sees the small, transparent mouthpiece covering her mouth steam up. She says nothing. She's begun to smell a little, but he doesn't dare shift her around or roll her over. Too exhausted to remove his clothes, he falls asleep on the sofa, stiff, inhuman.

He's driving along a tall dike between reality and a little village bathed in sunlight, where people are walking in and out of restaurants. He hears footfalls outside the house and knows that he's dreaming when he sees the body of a young woman slicked from head to toe with cooking grease from a pan, and he can't quite make himself believe it's all in his imagination. Someone jolts him with electricity.

But they're just leg cramps followed by a stinging pain, as if someone has warmed his veins up to ninety degrees Celsius. Before he can question what the dream meant, he clambers to his feet and hurries out.

The wind is strong today, and it rips at the car. The downtown streets are quiet. For several hours, he's parked in the queue on High Street.

It hardly matters. It doesn't do any good. And, in truth, he can't stomach talking to anyone. Around ten o'clock, a man tries to barter a trip to Puerto for his family. Erhard accepts the man's offer, but it's all for naught. The man and his wife argue, then drag their daughter with them into a cafe. He tries to read Doyle, but he can't.

At noon he snaps on his turn signal and exits the queue, heading to Café Miza.

There's no one there. The place tends to be filled with students, young tourists who've found the place in their Lonely Planet guidebooks where it is named one of the top-five cafes with a scenic view. When he enters, Miza has the music turned up and is busy cleaning the coffee machine. She's surprised to see him at this time of day. Even with young people there's a certain unwillingness to change routines, Erhard notices, so he chooses to drink his coffee in the cafe instead of the car, as he usually does. As she scours the large machine, humming along with the music, Miza glances at him from time to time. She asks Erhard how his work is going.

– Fine, he says.

He gazes out at the sea. Nothing changes. Not a cloud in the sky. Just the hypnotic flow of waves crashing against the shore at knee height, rising, and then slipping across the rocks only to dissipate against the cliffs. The sky is clear. The invisible winds wash everything away. Everything is pure blue. Everything is white. Like last year. And the year before that. It's not as poetic as it sounds.

The telephone rings. Miza puts down her rag and goes to the kitchen to answer. As she listens to the caller, she switches on her computer screen and punches a few keys. Someone must be making a reservation. – We look forward to seeing you, Miza concludes, clicking around on the keyboard. She's in her mid forties and seems like a natural on the computer.

Erhard scans the beach and the road, then stands. – I've been coming here for, what, five years?

Miza laughs. – More like ten.

– You've never asked me about anything but my work until today.

– No. Your personal life is none of my business.

– You're a good person, Erhard says.

– Thank you, Señor Jørgensen. She reassembles the coffee machine and brews a pot of coffee. – We try.

He looks at the computer. It would probably only take her ten minutes to find the images, but it would take him several hours, days, to find them himself. There's no reason to bother Petra's daughter with this; she's a computer expert, she would just laugh at him and think he's even more old-fashioned than he appears. But asking Miza would be easy; she has been his acquaintance for many years, maybe even his friend. Even if they've mostly just exchanged pleasantries about the weather, coffee, football, and fishermen.

Miza's face knots in concern. – What's wrong?

– I'm trying to find a photograph.

She glances around as if he might've lost it in the cafe. – I haven't seen anything here, if that's what you mean.

He looks at her. – I'll find it.

She laughs. Although her husband seems pretty stiff, she's got a good sense of humour. – Aren't you working today?

He nods.

He drives to Alto Blanco. Takes a bouquet of white roses with him. They cost seventeen euros. Flown over from the mainland. He parks on the gravel lot and walks up the long stairway, which feels as if it's going downward. The hilltop offers a flat, white landscape, but also a knockout view. The dust of a prehistoric volcano has settled permanently over the spot, so everything is white as though sprinkled with flour all the way to the sea. A little church made of black slate stands in the centre of the hill. Rock-solid and inviting, it's the church for the island's elite. They like the colours and the view, which transform wedding photographs into perfume advertisements. There's even a flagstone area for camera tripods, ten square metres, where the paparazzi can smoke cigarettes as they wait for the bride and groom and their celebrity friends to exit the church.

He's never been inside. He pauses at the wide door and peers in, but it's dark, and he approaches only after he hears some voices within. He's early.

Inside, the shape is that of an octagon, practically ascetic. Ten raw wooden benches in the centre face a granite table. Above the table, a window is cut in the shape of a cross, self-illuminating and heartrendingly simple. Standing on the left side of the church, a choir of young boys wearing ugly yellow trainers below their black vestments silently button each other's sleeves. Meanwhile, the priest is talking to a man in a black suit, who hurries out a side door when Erhard enters. One person is already seated up front, the girl who runs the boutique where Beatriz worked. She's dressed in her smartest city outfit: a little hat with a veil and sunglasses, an ensemble befitting a rock star's widow.

A few other girls soon arrive, clearly friends of the boutique, but no one Erhard recognizes. Affected by the atmosphere and the light and the choir, which has begun to sing, they greet each other politely. They're all dapperly dressed, but one of the girls is wearing a very short skirt, which she tugs down. On the table, the altar, is an egg-shaped urn. The service is typically held before the cremation and with an open casket, but they chose not to do that here, so the ceremony will take place around the urn.

Now that he's noticed the urn, it occupies the entire room.

Alina.

Because it's actually her, of course. He hasn't given her a thought since he switched her with Beatriz. Now he recalls that evening he saw her at the nightclub, the night she wound up in bed with that lead singer. How she lay there, her legs spread, and spoke to Erhard like the old fool he is. Completely indifferent and dumb and lewd all at once, so that all he could do was to fantasize about having his way with her, even if his entire nervous system screamed that she was a wretched harpy from whom he needed to keep his distance. Insolent, that's the word for her.

Now she's dead. He's the only one who truly knows whose ashes are in that urn. Even though it wasn't his fault, she was in his custody when she died. And it's by his hands that her death has concealed Beatriz's survival. Undoubtedly, there would be other kinds of people in the church had this been Alina's real funeral. Maybe it would be packed with the girls from Guisguey, or maybe it would be empty. She probably wouldn't have been buried, perhaps not even cremated, but thrown into a grave scooped out by a Bobcat, just like the boy. Because no one knew Alina. Because no one would pay to see a whore laid to rest. So in a way, Alina got a taste of life in first class, what she'd always dreamed of. Sitting in the back row, he feels the entire building whirl. At the same time, the bells begin their rhythmic pealing.

Why the hell did she go up on the roof? What possessed her to climb up there? If she was so desperate, why didn't she use all her energy to attack Erhard when he returned like she'd done the day before? When he left her she'd been angry, and yet they'd been working on a project together, and she'd asked him to get her charger. Why would she choose to jump from the roof?

Right when the bells stop chiming, the door bursts open, and Emanuel Palabras and a bizarre troupe of servants enter, filling the benches on the left side of the church. They're all dressed in black except for Palabras, who looks like a parrot in a green and blue suit and a white narrow-brimmed fedora. It's the first time Erhard has seen Emanuel beyond his property, and just as all the rumours would have it, he's not alone. With him are men, including his guards and even his gardener, Abril, and his Maasai girls, all of whom serve as buffers between the real world and Palabras. All conversation goes through them.

The priest is standing with his back to the assembly, but when he turns towards the pews, he seems surprised by the sudden spike in attendance. He raises his hands in a friendly gesture of greeting. Then begins. In that moment, Erhard has never felt so powerful a need to hear something meaningful, something eloquent about life and death, about the porousness of humanity, about the eternal search for meaning and familiar faces, about the longing for connectedness and loving hands, about the little person that just wants to be loved and feel the warmth of a mother's lips behind her ear, about the hot, throbbing limbs that long to be held and licked, about the many hours one waits and waits and waits before one dies and dies. And the priest opens his mouth and recites from the Bible, a long passage about a golden calf, a story that Erhard remembers as a drawing in a children's book he once had with a tattered spine. An angel walks in front of us, the priest says, then asks it to guide Beatrizia Aurelia Colini. The choir sings. Erhard's gaze shifts from the cross above the table with the egg-shaped urn to the grey floor, and he doesn't look up until the bells once again chime and the priest is on his way towards the open door. The man in the suit walks behind him, a church servant, holding the urn in his white-gloved hands. The entire assemblage follows them. First Palabras and his retinue, then the shop manager and the girls, and finally Erhard. Hassib, the policeman, is standing near the exit; he's in uniform and he's studying Erhard's face. Or at least that's how it feels. Erhard greets him with a nod and walks past him, into the now pale light outside. The priest and the church servant continue along a path that veers around the back of the church and down the hill, until they come to a plateau and a place with flower pots filled with sprays of fresh red flowers. The procession halts next to a slate-grey wall with metal containers inscribed with white letters. The mausoleum. It's regarded by many on the island as one of the most exclusive places to end one's days. But despite the flowerpots with lilies and roses, despite the nameplates with silhouettes of the deceased and small angels, Erhard still thinks the mausoleum looks like an ordinary row of PO boxes.

The egg-shaped urn is placed in one of the containers, and before the lid is sealed, the priest says a few words in Latin and blesses the parishioners. This is followed by a moment's silence, and the sea is all that can be heard. The breath of the waves. The high point of the service, Erhard thinks; finally, the painful point about the incontrovertibility of existence: our finiteness against the sea that roars on. Life as acts we can practise but once.

They head back to their cars.

The last thing he needs right now is to feel mortal. Or to meet the policeman's eyes. He hustles until his knees ache, getting ahead of the boutique girls and up to the car park. But when he reaches his vehicle, one of the men from Palabras's flock catches up to him. Señor Palabras would like to speak with him. Would Erhard please come with him? The man points at a gigantic Mercedes in the middle of the car park. Erhard follows him and waits a few minutes in the backseat. The interior is of beige leather with plenty of legroom, so much so that Erhard can't touch the front seat with his feet, even when he stretches. Then Emanuel Palabras climbs in, along with two skinny Maasai girls. Charles, one of the guards, sits in the passenger seat. His right foot is in a cast.

– A sad day, Emanuel Palabras says.

– Yes, Erhard says.

– I can't say I knew her, unfortunately. My son wasn't one to show her off.

Erhard doesn't understand that. In his experience, Raúl was proud of Beatriz. Maybe it was his father's company Raúl didn't seek out. He says nothing.

– I believe he'd grown tired of her, Palabras goes on.

– We've just come from her funeral, Erhard says. – Shouldn't we let that sink in?

Emanuel Palabras grins. – Do you think time will change anything?

– If you have an opinion about their relationship, maybe today's not the best day to share it. Respect the dead.

– Respect, yes. But not dishonesty. Dishonesty does no one any good.

– What are you trying to say?

– Don't be offended, Piano Tuner. I'm the one who paid for this funeral. I won't bring shame upon this girl. I'm just trying to understand my foolish son. Why has he acted this way?

– So you've heard that he left the country?

– Yes, my friends with the police like to talk.

My friends. It didn't sound so nice coming from a man like Palabras.

– And you probably think he was the one who killed her? Just like all your police friends do?

– They don't seem to think so any more. Thanks in part to you.

That's news to Erhard. – Good, he says simply.

– I've explained to them that there's no one in our family even capable of removing a dummy from a baby's mouth. We're lambs in God's great game.

That's probably carrying it a little too far. As far as Erhard's aware, both Emanuel and Raúl have beaten up a fair share of people, more than an entire football team's worth.

– God only knows, Erhard says, feeling Palabras's eyes on him.

– But no more chatter about that. How are you doing?

Every alarm bell goes off in Erhard's head. Emanuel Palabras has never asked him such a question.

– In spite of today's funeral, my good friend's disappearance, and an unfortunate decline in tourism and pianos on the island, I'd say it's going swimmingly.

– Tourism? When the hell did that begin to concern you?

– It's macroeconomics. When the tourists go elsewhere and the local economy goes bust, it means fewer taxi rides.

– You continually surprise me, Piano Tuner. I like it when people see the big picture. My son wasn't that strong on such practical matters, but he certainly understood people. I may have been the one to discover you, but he was the one who saw your potential.

Now the alarm bells ring even louder. Compliments aren't free when Palabras is doling them out. An offer is imminent.

– I've been here the entire time, Erhard says. Long before you discovered anything at all.

– You just suddenly appeared. Like a sea god from the water.

It sounds so stupid that Erhard laughs. Palabras laughs too, as do the two Maasai girls, even though they probably don't understand a word of it. Or maybe they understand everything. It's impossible to read their faces.

Erhard moves to open the door.

– Hey, Emanuel says, raising his hand. – Are you leaving?

– Are we done here?

– When do we meet again?

– The first Thursday of the month. As always.

– We should see each other more often.

– Why? Erhard smiles, but he asks the question in earnest.

– Look at us. We have much in common.

– Age and a weakness for expensive pianos are probably the only things we have in common.

– *Au contraire.* We're cut of the same cloth.

Erhard doesn't quite see it that way. – What is it you want?

– I want to hire you.

– To do what?

– You're smart. I'm sure we can figure something out.

– I have a job. Two jobs.

Three if one counts taking care of Beatriz, he thinks, but he doesn't say that out loud.

– But you can use the money, no?

– I manage.

– There will be other benefits.

Erhard regards Palabras intently. He doesn't understand what he means by 'other benefits'.

– I manage.

– The offer stands, says Palabras.

Erhard gets out and the car speeds off. There's no one left in the car park but him. The wind swirls up motes of white dust.

38

Twice he wakes to the sound of a motor, but apart from the pumping of the respirator, he hears nothing. Just the insistent howl of the wind soughing across the stones, and the rustling of the goats alongside the house. Maybe they can't find their food and are searching for shelter to rest. Erhard gets up and goes outside naked to wash himself at the big washbasin in the courtyard.

The light is on its way across the island. Behind his woodpile, he finds a pair of underwear and jeans that the wind blew off the clothes-line. He pulls them on, then gobbles raw bacon on crisp-bread. Radio Mucha's playing Coleman Hawkins's version of 'Out of Nowhere'. A 1937 recording from Paris.

He repositions Beatriz, checks her catheter, and tells her what's in store for the day. It's a Wednesday. He's always a little livelier on Wednesdays.

At precisely 10:15 a.m., he picks up Aaz, who's already waiting with his backpack at the front door of the institution; he climbs in without a word. Erhard lets him roll down the window and stick his hand out, like a seagull against the wind. There's something deeply moving about this, and it causes Erhard to drive slowly and cautiously.

So, Erhard, how's it going?

– Like shit, Erhard replies. He knows Aaz likes it when he swears.

Don't tell me you're busy. I know that you don't do anything but read your boring books and drive me around every Wednesday.

– Aaz, you hick, you know I'd prefer to drive you every day.

You're doing well?

– I'm busy, Erhard says, nudging Aaz. – But not with work. Beatriz is hurt. I need to take care of her.

She's Raúl's girlfriend?

– Was, Aaz. She was Raúl's girlfriend. He took off, vanished.

Something must've happened to him. If he knew Beatriz was hurt, he would come back. He loves her.

– You've got a lot to learn about love, Aaz.

But why would he try to hurt Bea? He loves her. It couldn't have been him.

– For the same reason a mother stuffs her child inside a cardboard box and abandons him in a car on a beach. Because sometimes we'd rather destroy everything around us than change ourselves.

No, no. That's not right. If you love someone, if you have ever looked another person in the eyes, then you can't hurt them.

– People are strange. Trust me, Aaz. I've driven a taxi for many years. I've been alive a long time, and I've seen the worst side of humanity.

My mother loves me. She loves me so much that she gave me to Santa Marisa so I would have a better life, even though she wanted to hold onto me.

– Your mother's unusual. So are you.

No one abandons a child.

– You're wrong, Aaz. But if we're lucky, Raúl will turn up, after having screwed around with some female singer or gone on some drinking binge in Dakar. That's how he is.

They drive through the town of Lorques which has a petrol station. Aaz glances at Erhard, as if he doesn't like the silence.

– I'm supposed to meet the hairdresser's daughter. Luisa.

She's too young for you. In the photograph at the salon she looks like someone my age. Aaz grins, but only with his eyes.

– Just because we're separated by a few years doesn't mean we can't meet up. She's just going to help me with a computer issue I have.

You know everything about pianos, but nothing about computers.

– One can't be good at everything, Aaz. You'll have to come with me to the beach soon.

Liana won't allow it.

– I know that. I've talked to your mum. She needs to write Liana a note, which I will give to her. We'll go out and watch the kite surfers with their huge kites. You like them from a distance, but wait until you see them out on the water. Where I come from, children love to play in the leaves that fall from the trees in the autumn. The leaves fall like butterflies, and kids try to catch them.

Can I catch the kites on the beach?

– No, not really. But you can watch them swirl about. Just like the leaves from the trees.

The leaves don't fall from the trees here.

– No. But we've got the sun.

He follows Aaz inside, and Mónica lets him use the telephone in the kitchen. He calls the doctor. He hears them playing the piano in the living room and whispers into the receiver. He stands at the kitchen door gazing out at Mónica's rear garden, which resembles a typical English garden with roses and bushes, a small bench, and a bird cage with a pair of canaries.

The doctor is busy and sounds irritated, but promises to swing by in the evening. A policeman called his wife last night asking for him.

– She knows nothing. But I'm supposed to call him back today. What do I tell him?

– I've told them that a doctor examined Beatriz while she was alive, but that she's dead now.

– She's dead? The line crackles.

– No. But that's what the police think. And they need to continue thinking that.

– I don't understand.

– Don't call them. If they call you, you only examined her when she was alive and dying. That's it. We'll talk more tonight.

Erhard sits down and watches them at the piano. Aaz is so tall that his mother looks like a little girl sitting beside her father. In his mind he thinks of her as an old woman, but it occurs to him that she's probably the same age as himself. But she's not his type. Or rather: Erhard isn't hers. She may no longer be wealthy, and she may have sealed herself off in her lonely world, but he's got the feeling that she has lived a life of culture, and she's more sophisticated and distinguished than anyone he's met on the island. She has these eyes that penetrate everyone as though she once, long ago, used up all her energy and just can't do it any longer. It's not that she's unkind or cynical, just tired: tired after a stretch of arduous longing. She's almost – almost – like Erhard, just a little happier, a warmer human being. Maybe it's because she's a woman, and women have always seemed more willing to love and be loved than men.

A small TV rests on a crocheted doily, and the local news is on. Mónica has turned the volume down. There's a feature about the casino. Now something's wrong with the environmental-approval paperwork. Critics reference the oil spill that happened in 2009, when a large cruise ship with a casino on board ran aground near Puerto and flushed 5,000 litres of oil into the water just beyond the harbour. Seagulls and fish were smothered in oil, and the entire area had to be cleaned up – while facing sharp criticism from a Spanish delegation from Greenpeace that had sailed out to meet them. It would be much different with a casino on land, of course, but casino operations on the Grand Canary islands at the beginning of the aughts prompted several suits due to the horrible working conditions for custodial staff and croupiers – and illegal rubbish disposal. On the television, Regional President del Fico and one of the island's heavy-weight entrepreneurs are walking around the harbour as it appeared a few months ago. Back then it was basically just rocks, kelp, and old rowboats. In the background, a fisherman is fixing his net, which is all tangled up. Then they show images from the harbour: white yachts and a champagne bottle floating in the water.

Erhard rises to turn off the television. But Mónica comes over and changes the channel to a children's programme featuring a turtle and a fish talking underwater. They aren't really underwater; they're hand puppets performing against a painted backdrop.

– I don't want him watching the news. He doesn't need to do that, she says.

Then she prepares strong Italian coffee. Erhard says nothing, but returns to his chair and lets her pour him a cup. Her arms look old, but he can see the strap of her black bra on her brown-skinned shoulder. He glances over at the computer on the desk.

– Do you know how to use one of those?

– I love it.

This surprises him.

– I've never learned how to use one.

– It's like using a typewriter. Just easier.

– I never learned how to use a typewriter, either. I know everything about pianos, but nothing about computers.

She smiles falsely. – Does it even matter? You manage without one.

– I might as well just say it. I have a problem, Erhard says.

– Excuse me, Mónica whispers, as if Aaz isn't allowed to hear. – What do you mean?

– I need to find a photograph on the Internet.

– Are you asking for my help?

– If I could've, I would've done it myself.

– But are you asking me to help you?

She makes it sound as if he's asked something else entirely.

– Yes, he says.

– Why do men have such a hard time asking for help?

He watches her sit at the computer and strike a few keys. She glances up, then turns to him. – So are you going to help me or not? he asks.

She points at the seat beside her as if it's a piano bench they will share. He gets up and sits beside her. He can feel her hip against his. He describes what Alina found. An image from Cotillo. Taken by some surfers.

She clicks on a page and quickly finds a bunch of images. Hundreds, thousands flowing down the screen. – Do you recognize any of them?

– No, he says. What he sees are images of tourists, all similar. – The photograph was taken around New Year's Day, a few days afterward, maybe a week? He tries counting backward. – 5 January?

– Such pretty photographs of our little island, she says.

She may be right. The sun, the waves, the young men and women. But he's only interested in one photo.

– I've never been out there, Mónica says.

– That one, can I see that one? He points.

– It's not easy getting out there. And it's much too hot.

But it's not the right photograph. It's not even from Cotillo.

– The photographer's name, Erhard says. But he can't remember the name. It had something to do with a child.

– A name would help, she says, her hovering hands prepared to type. He's surprised at how natural all this seems to her. All these women and their computers.

– Did you take a computer class?

– No. I had a friend, and we wrote emails. That got me started. But today I use it for everything. Mostly to listen to music, or read up about Aaz's illness, and succulents. They're a kind of plant, a cactus, she goes on to explain when she sees the confusion on Erhard's face.

He can't recall the photographer's name. He's about to say Mix. It's something that sounds like Mix. And something to do with a child. Fever. – Fevermix, he says.

– I'm afraid I don't quite understand.

– MitchFever! That's what it was.

– How do you spell that?

He spells it for her. He remembers now. The name was written inside a little box on the image. A child with a fever.

She keys in the name. That changes the search. Now there are fewer photographs. At the top of the screen, he sees the image of a girl lying in her bed, shirtless, and he senses Mónica's discomfort. She glances at Aaz and scrolls down the page. – What is it we're looking for here? she whispers. – Is it something naughty?

– No.

He's just as startled as she is.

– You promise?

– Yes. Just keep doing what you're doing, I'll look for the photo.

The beach. Some boys in wet suits. Feet in the sand. More photos of the girl. In a chair, at a bar, wearing a hat, kissing a girl. Mónica shifts uncomfortably. She's more prudish about these matters than Erhard had thought.

– There! That one.

Mónica clicks on the image, enlarging it instantly.

It's the same image. Just better. Closer. Clearer.

– It looks as though the website is called Magicseaweed. And the photograph is called 01062011_42, she says, writing the number down on a notepad beside the computer. – So you'll remember. The photo is in a folder called heather_weekend. She points at the screen. – From 6 January. Does that sound right?

The photograph: The VW is parked on the beach. The sand is rather dry, greyish. There's water up around the front wheels. And behind the window: the boy, his dark eyes.

– Is there a way to see more images like this without losing this one?

– Yes, now that we've found it, we can find it again without any trouble. Tell me, what is it you're looking for?

– The car.

Mónica clicks on something and another image pops up.

It's the same angle. Down on the corner where the surfers always sunbathe. The date reads 5 January. The photo is called newyear_cotillo. Someone named Carlos III Santierrez posted it online. The beach is empty.

– So it's in the first image, but not this one. Can I see the other one again?

She pulls up the first image.

It seems to convey the same mood as the one Erhard saw at police headquarters. The car's black windows seem to merge right with his soul. As if the darkness is continually expanding and he'll eventually be able to stick his hand through it to pull the boy, unharmed, out into reality.

– What is it with the image? The car?

– Does it say where he lives, Mitchfever?

– I doubt it. It's probably just some funny name he came up with. That's what many people do. Use another name. She types MitchFever into a narrow field and a list pops up.

In one way he's happy that he doesn't need to figure out how everything works. It would require too much effort on his part, much more than it took him to learn how to play instruments or understand music. And why would he need to? When this is over, it might be another several years before he'll need to find something else. Still, when he sees what one can do with a computer, how easy it is to find information and images and news, he has the urge to discover what's going on in Denmark, maybe even find photos of his family. Perhaps Annette and the girls, if he could figure it out.

– I think it's a young lady, Mónica says. She clicks on some text. A new page shows a tiny image of a girl who looks like a boy, with short, dyed hair and large glasses. – It appears as though she lives here on the island. Down near Marabu. I can't find her address, but many of the photographs were taken down there.

– How do I find her address?

– You could drive down to Marabu and show her photograph to some of the locals. Surely they know her. She sure knows how to attract attention.

– She's just a child, Erhard says, staring at a photograph she's taken of herself in the mirror. Her wetsuit is pulled down around her waist, and one arm covers her breasts.

– A confused little girl, Mónica says.

– Shouldn't she be living at home with Mum and Dad?

– I hope she is.

– Not judging by these pictures.

– Look. The images all have numbers, Mónica says, pointing at the screen. This one's called 11122010_107. And the next one's 11122010_144.

– What does that mean?

– It means that some photos haven't been posted online. Maybe there's something she doesn't want to show her mum and dad, or someone else.

– And the photographs from Cotillo?

Mónica returns to the photos from Cotillo. She toggles back and forth between the images. – Yes, she says. Here's image number 43. The next one is number 01062011_48. Four images are missing.

Erhard drives Aaz home.

Aaz's hand is sticking out the window. Just like the trip down here, Aaz is happy, easygoing. He keeps smiling, looking about as if everything's lovely, even though he's completely walled off from the world. He's never been to the movie theatre in Puerto or down to the corner to buy an ice cream with five scoops.

Normally Erhard keeps the conversation going, but now he doesn't know what to say. Your mother's a nice lady, he wants to say, but why has he never said that before?

It doesn't usually bother Erhard, but he notices that Aaz shows no sign that he's just said farewell to his mother, whom he won't see for another week. And it calls to mind the thought he has every time he tries to understand why he drives Aaz each Wednesday, for free, when the boy – who except for a few smiles deep in his eyes – shows no sign of recognition or happiness. On the one hand Erhard drives him out of pure love, but on the other hand, it's because of the selfish, distant hope that Aaz will one day say thank you. Thank you for taking the trouble. Thank you for talking to me.

He's touched that Mónica helped him, even if she wound up thinking Erhard was after something other than the car: the girl photographer. He wanted to say, What the hell are you talking about, woman? But he didn't want to seem ungrateful. She could be my own daughter, he wanted to say. The girl was quite a bit younger than his youngest, Mette, who is over thirty now, but it wasn't that far-fetched. He could see why she would think that. He'd stared too long at the photo the girl had taken of herself in the mirror, and maybe also at a photo from the beach in Morro, where she lay on a blanket without a stitch of clothing on. He'd never visited a nudist beach, and the sight of the girl had completely taken his breath away, even if he couldn't really see anything. It wasn't his fault. Mónica reacted as though he shouldn't feel that kind of desire any more. As if he ought to have given up on his sex life years ago. But desire didn't seep from one's body the nearer one came to seventy. On the contrary, he could almost say. Sometimes, all his years of inactivity caused him to tingle with an abstract arousal at gouges in the tabletop or goat nipples, or things that resembled things that resembled things he once had access to, closed country now, accessible only via the narrow gate of his memory. His shame overwhelmed him. If he'd felt any lust staring at those photographs, it was gone now.

At Santa Marisa Erhard says goodbye, but Aaz says nothing. Just walks through the broad front door. He doesn't turn around, and doesn't wave.

The doctor stands on the crate examining Beatriz. – You can't keep her here, he says, rocking her slightly so he can get his hand underneath her. – She needs to see a neurologist in Puerto. She's dehydrated, and her stool is dry.

That's where the strange smell is from, Erhard guesses. Like a pottery workshop. He can't bear to watch. Instead, he rummages around in the kitchen. – Can't you do something?

The doctor looks unhappy. – You can't keep…

– A miracle can occur just as easily here as at a hospital.

– I'm not talking about miracles. I'm talking about equipment. If she has intracranial bleeding that isn't treated.

– Either she stays here and survives, or she goes to a hospital and dies, Erhard says, sounding more confident than he feels.

The doctor removes a plastic tube from his kit and steps up on the crate again. – Did you turn off the respirator at any point?

– No, not at all.

But there was the time he turned the respirator off to move her, and also that one night that he didn't manage to fill the generator with diesel. For a few minutes there was no current, and the respirator whistled. But he got it started again, and she was still alive. He needs another 950 euros to purchase the new generator.

– It's a little difficult up here, the doctor says. – I'm sorry that I'm not sedating you, Beacita. He jabs a long nail into her neck, then the plastic tube. It looks unpleasant. Erhard can't bear to watch. – How much has she urinated? the doctor asks to keep Erhard's mind occupied.

– I don't know. Two or three bags.

Shortly afterward, the doctor steps off the crate and hangs a large bag with some white mixture on a nail. He taps it and liquid begins to flow down the tube into Beatriz's nose. Then he stands in the doorway.

– Have the police contacted you again? Erhard asks.

– No, not yet.

– Tell them everything, just like it was. That you found her unconscious, that you examined her but could tell her injuries were too great. She died while you were there, and I'd told you I would contact the police because I'd been in the flat.

– I'm not allowed to do that. I must report deaths.

– You were there as a friend, as a favour to me.

– I could lose my licence.

– But you won't.

– They'll consider it neglect.

– Tell them I threatened you.

– How?

– I told you that it would be your fault if Raúl got off scot-free.

– What do you mean?

– You could tell it was an accident, but that I was beside myself, and certain that Raúl had done it.

– But didn't you say it was an accident…

– Yes, but if the police need to know why you didn't do anything.

– I'm not sure about this, the doctor says.

– Maybe they won't call you again. Her funeral was yesterday.

– What? How?

Erhard doesn't want to explain. – Let's just say they're convinced that Beatrizia Colini is dead.

– What about her? He points at the pantry.

– She doesn't exist. She's free.

The doctor stares at him. At first he's frustrated, squinting, then he softens, relaxes. – I think I understand, he says. – But you need to… She needs glucose. He points at the white bag. – And you need to turn her. She's on her right side now. Tomorrow you'll need to roll her onto her back, and then her left side the day after that. If we're lucky, we can help her just as well here as they can in Puerto.

– It'll be no trouble for me to reposition her.

– I'll get you more glucose. Without attracting too much attention. And some more bags for her faeces.

Doctors can make anything sound ordinary.

– Thanks, Erhard says. He has trouble saying that word, but he owes him as much for all that he's done.

The doctor simply nods as he packs his kit with all his equipment.

– Have you ever… have you ever heard the dead speak? Heard their voices after they died?

– Personally? No.

The doctor scrutinizes Erhard.

– How then?

– I've heard of couples who claim they've heard their spouse speak following their death.

– You believe them?

– I believe they've heard it, yes. But not that they'd actually heard a voice.

This annoys Erhard. – What do you think they heard then?

– I don't know. It's their imagination. A hope. A kind of phantom conversation. Pain over something left unsaid. Did Beatriz say something to you?

– She said something when she was still conscious. Before you got there. She told me that I should help her.

– And so you have.

– Yes.

– I still don't understand why the police believe she's dead.

– That's my secret.

– What about when Raúl returns? He may be charged with murder.

Yes, Erhard thinks. – He won't return, he says. – And if he does, that's his problem. I don't think Raúl hurt her on purpose; it was his behaviour, his lifestyle, that did it. He'll have to explain what happened.

– And if he's convicted?

– You said it yourself at one point. He'll have to accept his punishment. And I'll have to tell the authorities what I know. I'll have to take it as it comes.

The doctor circles back to the beginning. – I could lose my licence.

– Not if you tell the truth, and only lie about everything that has happened since I brought her out here.

– My wife is worried. She's afraid of Los Tres Papas.

This surprises Erhard. – They're just a group of boys in oversized jackets. With padding in their sleeves.

– I thought you were with them. That you were some kind of gangster.

Erhard laughs, but it's not actually funny.

– We thought you would threaten me or kill me.

– Why the hell did you come out here then?

– My wife didn't want me to, either. But what can I do? I can't leave the island. I can't run from my problems.

Suddenly he seems less bureaucratic and more alive, even though Erhard still doesn't like his sand-coloured tie, his sand-coloured shirt, his sand-coloured slacks, or his sand-coloured face. – Why do you think that about me?

– It's no secret. Everyone knows.

– Knows what?

The doctor doesn't wish to say. He claps his kit shut. – I'll see you in a few days. I'll come out and examine her again. If she shows no improvement soon, she's as good as dead and the lie will be true after all.

He starts towards the door. Erhard notices Alina's mobile lying on top of the box next to the door.

– What does everyone know?

– That Raúl Palabras works for Los Tres Papas.

There's still some workday remaining, and he feels the need to earn some cash. He tells dispatch that he's available and listens for a call to head south. He drives down 101 and FV-2. He gets a one-way trip from Puerto to Pájara, but otherwise it's just an ordinary Wednesday evening, warm and rather dull, interrupted only by the radio announcer's observations about football matches in Spain. Historically, the entire island has rooted for Madrid, but in the last few years, young people have begun to side with Barcelona, which is evident from the cheers, snatches of song, and cussing on the radio. Erhard doesn't care about any of it. He laughs at them. He's never played football. Not even in school. He had crooked feet, he was told, and for many years he thought his condition would worsen if he ran around too much. Maybe it was just something his father said. His father thought football was for yokels, a loser's sport, he sometimes said. Look at all those filthy boys playing football because they don't know how to use their heads or their hands. They don't even care to learn a sensible trade.

He approaches Risco del Gato, which lies right where the sun is setting; the town's skyline is practically burned away by the strong sun. He sees the sign pointing towards Morro, and turns up the FV-2, but chooses instead to drive around Risco del Gato on the dusty north country road. On his left side he sees, for a long time, Zenon's olive grove, the pride of the island. The only business with several hundred employees – at least until a few years ago. There's no one in the fields today. Or in the courtyard visible through the fence and between the two giant buildings that face the road.

Erhard tries to recall what the photographer girl looked like. When he left his house, he didn't think it'd be very difficult to recall her face, but the farther he drives the more it seems to be supplanted by other things: the woman with the shopping bags, a little boy swinging on a playground outside of Risco del Gato, a painting on a wall, the olive trees with their soft leaves. Now he remembers only words like 'short', 'white', 'glasses'. He hopes it's enough, he hopes things work out on their own once he arrives in Marabu.

Not until he sees the dashboard clock, a digital affair with green numbers, change to 7:02 does he recalls his meeting with Luisa, the hairdresser's daughter, who is now fifty minutes away by car. Erhard has no telephone. Nor does he have her number for that matter.

There's nothing to be done about it now. He doesn't even remove his foot from the gas pedal. *C'est la vie.* He didn't need her help any more, anyway; he'd solved his problem without her. He notices his own severity. Of course he's embarrassed that the girl will ring the buzzer and wonder why no one answers. If he could, he'd call Petra at once and explain the situation to her, and she could then relate it to her daughter when she got the chance. He had pictured Luisa wearing a red snug-fitting blouse, he had imagined the scent of her hair or the sound of her hoarse voice as she explained to him how computers function.

To hell with it. There's probably a reason that he's forgotten her, and their appointment. He's been busy with Beatriz, Aaz, the doctor, the boy. He owes Luisa an apology, maybe he'll buy her a box of chocolates for her trouble. He'll drive past a supermarket on his way home and, if he has the time, deliver the chocolates to Petra's tomorrow morning.

He approaches the coast.

The beach is dark and small, and the water is relatively calm though there is a good breeze. He sees a few windsurfers and kitesurfers on the edge of the horizon. Now and then they streak through the sunlight like birds. Gravel plinks against the undercarriage. He drives until he spots a place on the beach where several people are seated beneath an umbrella under the shade of a small wooden kiosk, one of those places where you can rent kitesurfing equipment or buy ice cream. He gets out of his car and crosses the hot sand. He scrutinizes the faces he sees. Although there are people of all ages, a few of them are girls and boys the same age as MitchFever. Erhard walks around the kiosk and spots a woman his own age selling coffee and ice cream inside. He buys a cup of coffee that tastes of chlorine, and drinks it while watching a group of young people lying on blankets and towels, arms and legs all mixed up. Next to them are surfboards and duffels. Somewhere in the distance music plays.

The woman in the kiosk asks him if he's going out today. By 'out' she means on the waves. Erhard shakes his head.

– I'm looking for a girl with short blonde hair. She looks like a boy.

The woman laughs. They all look like boys, she tells him.

– She's with a group of young boys and a Spanish girl with long black hair.

The woman laughs again and points out that Erhard could be talking about anyone. Look around, she suggests. Just as Erhard's about to repeat his question, it occurs to him that she doesn't wish to help him. She doesn't wish to get mixed up in anything. These are her customers, and she doesn't want to ruin her business.

– I'm not a policeman if that's what you think. I'm just… a cab driver.

The woman grins and scrubs the countertop with a rag. Erhard gazes across the beach. He thanks her for the coffee and starts towards a group of youths. Most of them are asleep. One of the boys is awake, and he's watching the waves. Erhard speaks to him briefly. He's a shy but friendly guy. But he doesn't seem to like adults or even talking to them. He doesn't know a girl with short blonde hair. But he says the name MitchFever sounds like that American girl who often surfs with some older guys. Erhard gets him to point him in the right direction, then he starts to go. – Hey, the boy calls out, you can't walk there, it's a couple of miles on the other side of Marabu, close to Morro Jable. Erhard heads back to his car.

39

On the beach he waits for five surfers. One is skinny, feminine in appearance, could easily pass for a girl. It's impossible to tell from here. He's sitting on the sand, his toes buried in the moist layer just below the surface. Erhard recalls that time he'd waited for Raúl on the beach up near the Dunes. It was a Friday evening, they were both pissed, and Raúl wanted to surf before they went to a party. The water trickled over the shore, then retreated. He fell asleep, and when he awoke, the sun had gone down and the sky was aglow with stars and he could see Raúl riding the darkened waves.

One of the surfers lowers his sail and carries his board up to the beach. He's a hundred metres away, but he's walking in his direction, Erhard thinks, because the surfers' duffels are lying between some rocks, and their car is parked along the road. Erhard stays put, not getting to his feet until the surfer is right beside him. He explains what he's looking for, a girl with short hair, an American. The surfer studies Erhard, then asks if he's her father. Erhard laughs. He wonders whether or not it'd be advantageous to say yes, he is, but decides that, judging by the way the surfer asked the question, the father isn't a popular person in the girl's life. He's heard she's a good photographer, Erhard explains, and he wants to speak with her about an assignment. This catches the man off guard. He begins to remove his wetsuit, and his bathing trunks, and figures Erhard is talking about January, an American, a fucking good surfer. She lives down near Morro Jable, but works at a beach bar in Marabu called Great Reef. He doesn't know her, but everyone's heard of her. Erhard asks why. Because she's a little wildcat, if you know what I mean, the surfer says, disappearing into a large towel.

Erhard drives back to Marabu. This time down to the city beach, where he parks behind a supermarket that abuts the water. He has never been down here. In his many years as a cabbie, he has never driven anyone to this place, and he doubts that he can find the beach bar the surfer mentioned. But when he reaches the sand, he discovers how impossible the bar is to overlook; it's the only building on the beach, and there's a huge metal sign on the flat roof with the bar's name etched on a surfboard. Bleached deckchairs are arranged on the sand, but no one's outside. A handful of people stand inside the dark room leaning against a bamboo bar. They're all surfers except for the one farthest away, whom Erhard recognizes as one of the island's sand sculptors, a black man. But Erhard's eyes roam immediately to the girl behind the bar. Her hair is blonde, and not exactly short, but close enough.

He approaches the bar and glances down at a bucket containing bottles of cold San Miguel beer. He opens one bottle and chugs half of it before setting it on the bar. The men don't stop talking.

The girl is seated on the floor, and she's busy filling a cabinet with Cokes. Erhard looks down and gets a glimpse of her fine-skinned, youthful white neck. He turns away. She stands up and puffs on a fag that was resting in an ashtray on the stereo system.

– MitchFever, Erhard says.

The girl spins towards him, startled, and it occurs to Erhard that there's a great deal of mistrust and fear within the surfer community. As if they all expect to be sent home to their beds.

– Don't worry, I just like your photographs, Erhard says in English, and quickly senses that this only makes her more uncomfortable. He swigs from his beer, giving her time to respond. She says nothing.

– I'd like to buy two of your photographs, he says, switching to Spanish. How does 100 euros sound?

– Photographs? What do you mean?

It sounds as if she doesn't even know the word.

– The ones you took of local beaches. I saw a couple from Cotillo Beach that I really like.

– Oh, those, the girl says, approaching the bar. – On my blog?

– No, on the Internet, Erhard says, as if he's always finding stuff he likes on the Internet. – I'm interested in Cotillo Beach.

– Are you some kind of journalist?

– No, I'm a cab driver. My name is Erhard.

The girl relaxes. – January, she says.

– How'd you come up with the name MitchFever? Is that some sort of artist's name?

– Not exactly. It's a long story. Let's just say that's what I call myself on my blog. Why do you want those pics of Cotillo?

– Just interested in them, is all.

The girl smiles and lights a new fag. Several of the surfers have left. Only two remain.

– I'm not really a photographer, you know.

– Do you have more photographs from Cotillo Beach? That aren't on the Internet?

– Yeah, a few. I always take a ton, then can't be bothered to upload them all. My connection is really slow.

– I see. Do you have any from the 6 or 7 January?

The girl eyes Erhard. Suspicious again. – Why?

– Do you recall the beach on 6 January?

– No. Was that the day I hurt my leg?

– I don't know.

– Then I definitely don't remember. My mother says I have the memory of a cat. Pretty bad.

– There was a car on the beach, a Volkswagen.

– So what?

– Did you take any photos of it?

– As if I could remember. She laughs. Almost indignant.

Erhard drains his beer. The two surfers are absorbed in watching something on one of their mobile phones. The girl lights another fag and rests her foot on an old beer crate. She's pretty in an old-fashioned way, but her fine skin and features are almost ruined by too much exposure to the sun and alcohol.

– Listen, he says, I need to find out what happened to a little boy who lay dead for several days in that car. As far as I know you're the only one who photographed the car before the police found it two days later. The picture was called… Erhard begins. Then he fishes out the little note that Mónica wrote for him. It was called 01062011_42.

– You some kind of detective?

– No, I'm a cab driver.

The girls pours a glass of tomato juice for one of the surfers and drops in a couple lemon wedges. She returns to Erhard. – I don't remember the numbers. I've got loads of pics from that beach, I think, and maybe I recall one with a car, but… I'll look when I get home.

– When?

– Tonight. I get off work just on the other side of midnight. I'll check my hard drive. That's where I keep my photos. I'll call you if I find anything interesting.

– I don't have a telephone. Can you meet me after you've searched your photos? I'll just sit in my cab waiting.

She gives him a strange look. Maybe she still believes he's an odd duck trying to lure her into something. But then she nods.

In the end, Erhard buys a sandwich from a nearby shop and waits at one of the tables in the bar. For three hours he gazes out at the water and reads his book, while she smokes a pack of cigarettes and watches television, switching between a football match and a snooker game. She wipes down the counter a few times.

Shortly after midnight he drives her home.

He enjoyed waiting for her. Sitting patiently and watching her clean up. Walking beside her to his car and asking if she'd had a good day. She lives on the roof of an old furniture shop in Morro Jable, where the owner has built a shack that is visible by the light of powerful street-lamps. An old stairwell leads to the roof, and Erhard follows her, but stays outside her shack, which seems small and intimidating.

She's inside for a long time. He counts the minutes because he knows he needs to get home and fill the generator with diesel. He pictures January's place filled with bottles, surfing gear, rickety shelves with Lonely Planet books, and maybe those vampire books that young girls always seem to be reading when they're in his taxi, books they pick up in the airport probably.

The door opens, and the girl exits with her camera. She explains that she needs to click through hundreds of photos to get back to 6 January.

Erhard watches while she scrolls through photographs of the beach, the bar, the surfer boys, and the same girlfriend over and over. She lives a colourful but monotonous life. All the photos could've been taken on the same day.

Finally she reaches the photos from Cotillo.

Erhard can tell right away. The light is very peculiar there. Unfiltered. Nearly blue. At first they breeze past a bunch of images of her friends surfing. Then they're on land. He spots the car in the background of a photo showing her girlfriend wrapped up in one of the boy's arms. Erhard takes the camera from her and goes through every shot, many of which he hasn't seen. At one point January seems to have been chasing her girlfriend around the car and snapped, perhaps by accident, two photos.

One is of the car's doors – the left rear passenger door – along with the handle and the lower part of a window.

The second photo was taken at a more directly downward angle, so that one can see the car's left rear tyre. There's a bright streak underneath the petrol cap. As if the water reached this level or the waves lapped against the side of the vehicle.

There are no more pictures of the car. Only those two that Erhard has already seen on the Internet. The rest of the series shows the youths arriving at the beach and getting ready to surf, January wearing a hat. In one image taken with an outstretched arm: the girl herself.

The next day he buys a box of chocolates, but he forgets to take it to the hairdresser's because two businessmen climb in his cab and they've got to hurry to the ferry, and it's Thursday, which means the doctor is bringing fresh supplies before siesta: an IV, a catheter, and some bags of what he calls glucose mix. The doctor shows Erhard how to take care of the bags that provide her with liquids and sustenance, and how to drain and clean the little container that collects urine and faeces. When the apparatus is plugged in, the light in the room flickers. He needs to fill the tank with diesel more often, the doctor says, and Erhard wants to yell at him, but instead sends him kindly on his way.

He earns 103 euros on Friday, only 42 on Saturday. On Saturday he sees something white sticking out of the mail box near the side of the road; it looks like a flag, but it's his post. Just the very word: post. It's been months since he last received mail, and this is a large envelope with no return address. But he knows who it's from. The photographs are printed on ordinary paper, and the quality's not great. But it's good enough for him to see the car, its nicks. He's thought about those nicks. He hangs the two photographs up on the fridge and lays the envelope on top.

What he really wants to do is take Sunday off, buy a couple bottles at Guzman's, and drink them inside, under a blanket, sweaty and feverish. But he can't afford to take a day off or get pissed. He might as well just turn off the respirator if he does that. He's got to come up with the money. So on Sunday he drives until almost nine o'clock, earning a measly seventy-eight euros, then empties the half-empty bottles from the pantry into one earth-coloured cocktail. He toasts Beatriz, but what he'd really like to do is shake her, shake her awake, shake her to death. The responsibility is too enormous. He can't do it. He can't do it.

THE FLAT

29 January–6 February

40

– Wake up, Piano Tuner.

He recognizes the voice. But it lacks its usual tone and depth.

– That's it, Piano Tuner.

Emanuel Palabras.

Outside his own space, in completely unaccustomed, unsuitable surroundings. Erhard isn't embarrassed, more like disappointed, that Papa Palabras would enter a dump like this. He's brought one of his young Maasai girls along, not the extraterrestrial but another younger, more emaciated version – the kind that Palabras favours. Standing behind her, near the door, is Charles, the brawn with his leg in a cast and propped up by crutches. An accident while painting, Palabras has explained, even though Charles doesn't look like the painter type.

Erhard glances towards the pantry, but the door is almost completely closed, and none of the guests seem to find the room interesting. He pulls the blanket over his cock, visible through the slit. A reddish-grey bird. Emanuel sees it and evidently thinks it's hysterical, but he says nothing.

– How about that? Erhard says. – Señor Palabras out exploring the real Fuerte. Welcome to the dregs.

– You're no more the dregs than I am, Emanuel says, searching for a place to sit. – You're a busker among the kings. You lack for nothing, you could live in a proper home if you wished, but you choose this… this hideaway.

– Get to the point, Palabras. Why are you here?

– I'm a man consumed by grief. My daughter-in-law is dead, and my son will soon be too.

– Has something happened?

Emanuel waves his hand. – A matter of time. Meanwhile, there's no one to care for me. I need people whom I can trust. And now two of them are gone. You're all I have left, Piano Tuner.

Characteristically melodramatic, but Erhard has the sense something's coming.

– What about Charles and the girl?

– I need you, Piano Tuner. For Raúl's sake. Emanuel sits opposite the sofa. On the coffee table. – I need a man in my business. Now that Raúl's gone, there's no one to steer the ship. No eyes to navigate.

Erhard doesn't understand what Palabras is driving at. – What do you mean?

– You know the profession inside and out. You even have a nose for business, I'm aware. Rumour has it you're the best taxi driver on the island.

That rumour had escaped Erhard's attention. – Do you mean Taxinaria?

– You won't need to drive any more. All you'll have to do is tell me what's happening on the ground. Maybe keep people in line.

– So Raúl wasn't just on the board of directors? You own Taxinaria?

Emanuel Palabras glowers at him as if he's an idiot. – What else but his father's money qualifies my dumb boy to join the board of directors? But now I'm looking for a man who knows the business, someone who can think for himself.

Charles is now right beside the pantry, leaning against a section of bare wall. Erhard doesn't like him standing there, but doesn't know how to get him to move elsewhere.

– I can't work for Taxinaria, Erhard says. – That would be disloyal.

– Rubbish. No more communist camaraderie chatter. Of course you can. We are the future, you should join us.

– I can't just take over Raúl's job like that. It's undignified. What would you need me for over there? I'm an old man, closer to retirement than a promotion. Why should I work for you?

– To help me. That's what I'm telling you. You and I, we understand each other, and I'll pay you handsomely. There, that's the short answer.

Erhard doesn't take the bait. – You can't just buy people, he says, staring directly at Palabras.

– I'm not buying anyone, I'm rewarding those who see opportunity. C'mon, Piano Tuner. Are you planning to spend the rest of your days here? *Here?*

He repeats the word 'here' to underscore just how absurd the thought is.

The idea of ending his days here doesn't frighten Erhard. Probably because he's accepted it. But when Palabras puts it that way, it doesn't sound attractive. – I'll manage, he says.

Palabras goes on without listening. – You can even move into his flat until it's sold. Get away from this place for a few months.

Erhard rises to his feet and gets dressed, his back to his guests. He pulls on his jeans and no underwear, which he can't find now and doesn't care to search for.

Emanuel Palabras starts from the beginning. – I hear you're looking for a new diesel generator.

Erhard stands stock-still. Sees the MitchFever photographs stuck to the fridge. – Yes, he says and nonchalantly flips the photographs over. – Who told you that?

– Small villages talk, as they say.

– Do you own the electronics shop?

Palabras owns so many things, one can never be certain.

– No. Thank god. Too trifling for me. But one hears things. They also said you were looking for a girl down near Morro Jable.

Erhard's a little alarmed that people have been talking about him. He's usually too uninteresting for that kind of thing. Why now?

– Isn't that right, Piano Tuner? Is she some whore you just had to have?

Palabras's typical reasoning. – No, she was a sensible young woman, who… Just as he's about to say, *Who takes good photographs*, something causes him to change his story. – Owed me some money for a taxi ride. I got my money, and that's that.

Palabras scrutinizes him. Then he nods. – You're not just some old dog, you're also a stingy old dog. He laughs. – Just don't run around wasting your time, and keep everyone happy. Drive your taxi, tune my piano, take care of yourself.

It sounds like a threat of some kind, though Erhard can't say why.

– What is that beeping noise? Charles suddenly says, nudging the pantry door open with his crutch. He stares into the darkness at the shelves of coffee and tinned soup. The cords with the IV and the catheter are concealed behind the shelves and run above the door, invisible unless one enters the room and closes the door. Since there's no light in the pantry, Charles won't do that. – It's coming from in here, he adds.

Erhard knows what it is. It's the sound the respirator makes when she hyperventilates. It could mean that she just peed. But he can't go out there now.

– It's just a temperature gauge signalling that it's too warm in there. It's better if we close the door.

Just before Charles steps into the pantry, Erhard manages to shut the door. He tries to make it seem natural by continuing on to the refrigerator and taking a quick, desultory peek inside. It has been days since he last went shopping. He hasn't had any desire to spend money on food. He sees January's envelope on top of the fridge and pushes it further in, so that it doesn't stick out so much.

– Thanks for the offer, Palabras, he says, trying to redirect conversation. – But Raúl's not dead. He might return tomorrow from his little drinking binge in Dubai. So I don't want his job or his flat. *But I will take care of his girlfriend*, he thinks. Then he continues: – I'm not going to stop driving a taxi just because you've had some great idea. *You're not going to tell me what I will and will not do.* – And anyway, I don't know what I would do at Taxinaria if I'm not driving a taxi.

A moment passes, then Emanuel Palabras begins to laugh. – Fine. If you think my impossible son will return. One can always hope, and may the gods have mercy on him, but until then, his business, which is my business, needs to be kept afloat. It's not a company run by robots, a factory that just spits out product. It's people-based, you understand; it requires one's presence.

Emanuel follows Erhard around the house and then outside, while Erhard brushes his teeth and finds a t-shirt and feeds the goats. For a moment, the two men stand side by side watching the grey goats leap around the rocks. Charles has followed the two men out, and now he laughs at Laurel, the one with only a single horn. The Maasai girl brushes her hand through the pelt of the smaller of the two goats, Hardy, who usually isn't very cuddly when he eats.

Emanuel explains how important it is to land the right person in Raúl's position. – I was the one who gave him the company when he turned twenty-four. Back then it was a simple business without any competition. That was precisely thirteen years and four months ago. He needed to have something to do. But he's never really been interested in it. He came to the office mostly when it rained.

– I'll consider it, Erhard says, without meaning it, when they're once again seated at the little kitchen table with a cup of instant coffee each.

– Raúl probably told you about his work? Palabras asks.

– We didn't talk about it, but I'm sure he had his reasons for that.

– Wasn't he the one who got you your job way back when?

– In a way.

Raúl had found a poster somewhere in the city: Good Drivers Wanted. When they went downtown one evening, he'd pulled the poster from his pocket and tossed it at Erhard. That was at the beginning of their friendship, before Beatriz entered the picture, and they would get pissed together. Erhard had applied for the job, and was hired immediately. This was in 1998, and they needed full-time drivers. Erhard drove for a man called Roberto. A few years later Roberto joined up with three other cabbies and formed TaxiVentura. Erhard continued to drive for Roberto until Roberto's death a few years ago. After that he kept driving for TaxiVentura.

Emanuel Palabras discusses Taxinaria's finances, which worsened after TaxiVentura signed a contract with the airport three years earlier.

But Erhard's not listening. He knows all about the conflict because of the many arguments the drivers had down in the queue, but he doesn't want to hear any more about it. – You haven't made it easy for us, Palabras concludes, as if it is Erhard's singlehanded efforts that have saved TaxiVentura. – But now it's time for you to join the good guys.

– I'll think about it, Erhard says, wondering how he might say no.

– Think good and hard, Papa Palabras says.

His three visitors ride off in Emanuel's boxy white 1972 Mercedes 60, the girl driving. She can barely see over the steering wheel.

41

He hurries to the pantry to check on Beatriz and the equipment. The drainage bag, which is small and difficult to remove from the container, is filled with urine, even though he'd emptied it the night before. Maybe the glucose has begun to take effect. He rolls her onto her side and fills the generator with diesel.

Afterward he turns on Radio Mucha and studies January's photos, jotting questions on the back of the envelope. In one column he writes questions that he can answer himself; in the other he writes questions only the police can answer. He tries to shift questions from one column to the other. His hand trembles, and his penmanship is uneven.

How high was the water at Cotillo Beach at night during the period between Wednesday, 4 January and Saturday, 7 January? When the car had stood on the beach for at least one day?

Who saw the car arrive? In parentheses: No one. He recalls Bernal telling him that. No one saw the car arrive.

Was there an onshore wind?

Who sails along the coast, and how close do they sail? Could they have seen something?

How do new vehicles arrive on the island?

Why Danish newspapers?

He has the feeling that the newspapers are a dead end, not worth wasting his time on. The newspapers were what the boy happened to be wrapped in, that's all. Nothing more. Who reads Danish newspapers here anyway? Many of the tourists – including the Danes – arrive on the island with English newspapers tucked beneath their arms or, at most, *Jyllands-Posten* or *Politiken.* There was a time when Danish newspapers were delivered to some of the hotels, but no longer; people use computers to read their news now. At the end of the nineties he subscribed to *BT.* It was sent to him once a week, arriving seven days late, stiff and crumpled from the night dew and the harsh morning sun. He subscribed to follow the football scores. That was back when you could still be a B1903 fan. He read every article and imagined the matches while pretending to hear Svend Gehr's voice, even though he probably never announced those kinds of matches or was on TV any more. He still remembered the players: John Beck Steensen, Martin Løvbjerg, Kim, 'Gold Paw' Petersen. But when they merged all the Copenhagen clubs into one super club, all the magic disappeared. He maintained his subscription for another six months, then cancelled it, and never held another Danish newspaper in his hand until he went to the police station with Bernal and rummaged in the box with the newspaper fragments.

As a subscriber, he'd had his name and address stamped on the back of the newspaper. Even though his house number wasn't included, it always reached him. He underlines the question about the newspaper and writes: *Where did it come from?*

To answer that question, he needs to get hold of the newspaper fragments. It's illegal, but wouldn't necessarily be all that difficult. He knows where the box is.

His shirt with TaxiVentura's logo on the breast pocket is still in a laundry sack at the bottom of a wardrobe. He smoothes it a little and pulls it over his head without buttoning it. It smells strange, worn, although he hasn't put it on for seven or eight years, since that time Barouki wanted to make everyone look more professional and take up the fight with Taxinaria in earnest. He gets a cardboard box and packs it with tins and other items to give it weight. Then he closes the box, wraps it in heavy-duty tape, and writes the address on a yellow Post-it note. He then scribbles a second note with the address of the local police in Morro Jable. He shoves the second note in his pocket along with the role of tape.

He takes the back roads down to Puerto. No one follows him. No Mercedes, no Palabras and company. Still, he makes a wide pass around the Palace and waits to turn into the car park until he's the only car on the roundabout. He parks just around the corner from the entrance.

The atmosphere is that of coffee klatsch for the island's grumpy residents. In the reception area, there's a woman with a small dog, a married couple and their son, two women who appear to be together, and a man with a large suitcase. The floor is littered with papers and forms that blow off one of the shelves every time the door opens; in the centre of the room is a large, dry potted plant. Erhard walks over to the metal detector, hands his box to the guard, and points at the logo on his shirt. The guard glances at the address and lays the box on the other side of the detector. Erhard passes through the detector, picks up his box, and heads down the corridor as if he's done this many times. The guard doesn't even watch him go. An older man in overalls who's drinking water from a tap in the hallway gives him a disinterested glance.

He passes the open office space where all the officers sit. But no one's there at the moment. The room is empty. Perhaps they're in a meeting, or they've gone down to the harbour, a three-minute walk from here, where Antonio the deaf man serves the best Spanish omelettes one can find for breakfast.

Erhard continues to the storage room, where Bernal brought him last time. It's dark in there, and he snaps on a large wall switch. The fluorescent tubes click and hum. He starts at the big shelf where he saw the cardboard box; he'd expected to find it where he had seen it before, but it's not there. There are other boxes, small bags filled with clothes, stacks of paper wrapped in elastic bands. The shelf is four metres high and five or six metres wide. He walks around it and finds three other shelves. They are organized following some method that's incomprehensible to Erhard, probably by case number, but all Erhard is looking for is the box. He could use more light or a torch; he has to poke his head across every shelf. He inspects shelf number two and is halfway through number three when he hears voices and footfalls out in the office. Then laughter as if from a funny film or a strip show. The policemen have returned to their desks.

Through the shelves he can see people walking around in the hallway. The man in overalls is washing the floors in front of the storage room door, so there's no one out there at the moment besides him.

Erhard picks up his pace, his eyes darting faster over the shelves. He pauses only when he sees square shapes: cases, cardboard boxes. The police seem to use a standard box, with the docket for the case number on one side. Although those boxes are smaller than the one he's looking for, each time he sees one at a distance he thinks he's found the right one. He turns around and begins investigating shelf number four when he finds the one he's searching for on the lowest shelf. Written across it is the word *Archivados*. It looks like an ordinary box packed with porcelain, but he recognizes it instantly.

He sits down and pulls out the box to analyse its contents. But it's impossible to see anything in such bad light. He'd like to carry it to the table near the door, but he hears some men talking either at the door or in the storage room near the first shelf. If they spot him they'll wonder what he's doing. There's no lid on the box, and no flaps that he can fold out. He grabs some paper from one of the other shelves and wraps it around the box. From his pocket he withdraws the yellow note with the address of Morro Jable's small police headquarters and affixes it. The paper doesn't stick, but it doesn't matter. He just needs to get out of here, fast.

He hurries past two men now seated at the table, and out into the corridor before they can say anything. He doesn't look up, but heads straight towards the exit. The entire office is now a bustle of activity, and people rush past him. There's even a voice that sounds like Bernal in the back of the room. A group of five people on their way through the metal detectors. He hopes to exit while the guard is occupied and doesn't notice. The coast is clear on his right.

– Señor Jørgensen?

Hassib, the police officer he met in Raúl's flat, is standing in the doorway of a small, well-lit room with great big copy machines. – Hello again, Erhard says, not slowing.

– What are you doing here? Hassib calls after him.

– I'm delivering a package on behalf of your colleagues, Erhard says, passing through the metal detector without glancing back. Just as he's about to shove the door open with his shoulder, he feels a hand holding him back.

– Who sends packages by taxi?

Hassib has set down his coffee and is looking at the box in Erhard's hands.

– How should I know? I'm just doing what I'm told. Erhard nods at the yellow note. – Morro Jable headquarters, he reads.

– Jable? Hassib studies the note closely. – What's the rush?

– You can drive it out there if you want to, Erhard says, holding out the box. – I don't need the forty-five euros.

The young Arab's eyes are bleary, with dark bags beneath them. He glares at the box as if he's considering something. Then he shakes his head and retreats a step. – I'm not done with you, he says. Then he turns and leaves.

Erhard pushes the door open and hustles to his car.

42

At home he empties the box on the table. Because of the draught that always breezes through the house, the newspaper fragments flutter like ashes in a bonfire. The smell of urine is nearly gone, but not quite. He sorts the fragments, tossing those with clear images or text back into the box. Then he arranges the rest in orderly rows, studying them one by one.

He uses a magnifying glass. He's thorough, lifting each little fragment and examining both sides before returning the fragment to the box. Once he's checked the first rows, he arranges new rows. He's never considered how much empty space there is in a newspaper. After he's gone through half, he counts all the blank fragments. Seventy-seven white or newspaper-coloured. Fifty-one black or grey. Thirty red. Five green. Four blue. Two purple.

Then he takes a lunch break. Sits on the stool eating a heel of stale bread.

He hasn't deliberated on Papa Palabras's offer yet. Which is to say: He hasn't made a decision yet. On the one hand, the offer is interesting; on the other, it's inappropriate and completely wrongheaded. Palabras knows Erhard has zero experience running such an operation. He knows that Erhard would have difficulty – if he doesn't find it impossible – being the boss of people who've been his competitors these past few years. With a couple of them, he wouldn't mind demonstrating that he can do better without them – Pauli Barouki for one – and he's already begun to consider the improvements he might implement. One could do a lot for the drivers: improve the situation at dispatch and with the taximeters, get better coffee in the break-room. But it's too early to think about these things.

Right now he's mainly curious as to why Palabras is so eager to bring Erhard aboard. There's no simple answer. The charitable answer is that he wants to maintain control of the business, and now that Raúl is gone, Erhard is the closest thing to a right-hand man who knows something about operating a taxi company. The practical answer is that Palabras wishes to delay any decision regarding Raúl's business until it's clear just what happened to him. The cynical answer is that Emanuel Palabras wishes to assert his influence on his son's company, even in a future where someone like Marcelis Asasuna probably will aim to increase his role in the company. In reality, Erhard really wishes to say no thanks and continue his life as usual. There's something about the offer that seems strange, even if he can't precisely say what.

He finds scribbled on one of the fragments, in faint ink, *rick 2310*. He examines the fragment carefully under the magnifying glass. Someone traced it repeatedly, so that it pierced the paper.

He sets the fragment aside and inspects a new row, not looking at the contents of the newspaper, only the forms, colours, structures. He knows exactly what he's searching for; he's seen it a number of times without thinking about it. If the newspaper was sent to the island from Denmark, then someone in Denmark would've stamped the recipient's name. A name and an address in grey, blocky type. It may have worn off some, or it may be illegible, but nevertheless it would've been added after the newspaper had been printed, all the way up at the top of the front page so the mailman would have been able to read the address even when carrying the newspaper in a stack of letters. Finally after almost three hours, and after laying down a forth row of newspaper fragments, he finds it. Part of it, at least. The address is incomplete, consisting only of a name, road, and house number. The name of the city is missing.

Café Rústica, c/o Søren Hollisen, 49 Calle Centauro.

It doesn't ring any bells. In thirteen years as a taxi driver he has never heard of Calle Centauro. Or a cafe by that name. He goes out to his car and calls dispatch. Two minutes later he gets a response. There's no Calle Centauro. Not here on the island, the girl adds.

Maybe *Politiken* wrote the wrong address. If only he could find the name of the city. He continues to rummage through the pile of fragments. Evening falls, then night. He takes a short break and checks on Beatriz, making sure her IV is stable and giving her the right dosage. Her body is absorbing sustenance. Though his hands are cold, he feels her body, warm and pulsating.

He makes it all the way through the pile of fragments, but doesn't find a city name. He considers starting over again from the beginning. But something tells him that the fragment he's looking for isn't there. He has been thorough. A thousand fragments might be missing. If he gathered every single one of them, laying each one together like puzzle pieces, then maybe he would see the holes here and there and know that the fragment with the city name is one of the missing pieces. But he can't do it any more. He'll have to find Calle Centauro another way.

On Tuesday morning he doesn't drive to Alapaqa but to Tuineje. To Mónica's. He has never visited her without Aaz. It's a big step. He parks at the side of the road to gather his courage, but instead grabs his notebook and dashes over the road to the payphone.

– This is Erhard Jørgensen. May I swing by?

– It's only eight o'clock. Quarter after eight, Mónica says.

– It's important.

– Does it have anything to do with Aaz?

She sounds afraid.

It hadn't occurred to him that she would think of Aaz. – Not at all, everything's OK. It's about the computer, like last time.

She's relieved. – Can't it wait?

– I'm parked down the road. I'm calling from a payphone.

Pause. It annoys Erhard a little how long it takes her to respond.

– Give me ten minutes to eat my breakfast.

He waits in the car, then walks to her house fifteen minutes later. Before he reaches the door, she opens it and leaves it ajar, so he can enter. She has apparently cleaned up. Papers are neatly stacked, and a dishrag dangles from a little cord above the sink. She's wearing a red dress with small, glistening sequins. It looks like something one wears to tango. Erhard doesn't tango.

– You're a cab driver. Don't you know every address on the island? she asks when he explains what he's looking for. The computer is on, and she sits at her desk. – Didn't you say something about learning how to use a computer?

– Someday, maybe, Erhard says, though he can't picture ever doing so.

– What was the place called again?

He spells the cafe's name as well as the name of the street.

– It's on the east coast, Mónica says, zooming out. – Oops. I forgot to write Fuerteventura. Just as she's about to tap the keys, she zooms out again. – Wait, it's on Tenerife. Does that sound right?

– Is there a cafe nearby?

– Let's see. She points at an aerial photograph, taken right above the little waterfront city. Some text is written across the map, and Erhard spots the name of the street. – Café Rústica. Was that it?

– It's on Tenerife?

– Yes, in Santa Maria del Mar, just south of Santa Cruz.

– And there's no Calle Centauro here on this island?

– No, not as far as I can tell. She stands up. – Would you like a cup of coffee since you're already here?

– Can we find one more thing first?

She returns to her seat.

He shows her the fragment with the pen's scratch-marks: rick 2310. – Maybe they're digits from a telephone number?

He gives up trying to follow what she's doing on the computer. Instead he watches her fingers deftly manoeuvre across the keyboard. She obviously plays the piano.

There's no one called Rick with those digits in his telephone number. Not on Gran Canaria either. No one's called Rick, for that matter. But plenty of Ricardos, Richards, Rickos, Rickys, and Rickis, of course. There's no connection. She also searches for the name Søren Hollisen and finds a Søren Holdesen Jensen, an engineer from Farum, Denmark – but no Hollisen anywhere close to the Canary Islands. She tells Erhard that you can't always count on the Internet to find answers. Not every-thing is online. If a person doesn't want to be found, he won't be found on the Internet, either.

Then she prepares coffee.

Erhard studies the map again. Sees the cafe's name in small white letters across the aerial photograph. For some reason it seems right.

It must be the place, even if there's one 'a' too many or too few in the name. Mónica cleans up the kitchen and he tells her loudly about the newspaper fragments, and how he'd put them together to locate the address. He wishes he could tell her what it means. About the boy in the box. But he can't do that. Not yet. He drinks his coffee. It's strong and bitter. As he watches her wipe coffee grounds from the kitchen counter, he notices her nice round ass behind all the sequins.

He heads home to fill the generator, then drives to the garage to hoover the car and wash the doors and panels. Normally he cleans his car every other week, but it needs a scrubbing: all the black surfaces on the seats and the steering column are grey with dust. The auto workshop has a special brush that blasts water through the seat cushions and sucks it out again, removing grime and stains. He also gives the boot a thorough scouring. You never know who might look in there.

After his conversation with Emanuel Palabras, he's curious to see things with fresh eyes. He'll stop by the office, maybe run into Pauli Barouki and tell him that he bloody well better take care of those damn forms. And the carwash in front of the office which Erhard never uses because it's always too crowded. White foam runs into the drain, which is plugged with disintegrating cardboard.

But now he can take his ideas to Taxinaria and push some of them through. From colleagues who've changed sides, he knows that they have the same problems. He could be the man of the day, the man of the month, with all of his ideas. Raúl, that asshole, used to just laugh at Erhard's angry outbursts. Who knows whether he implemented any of his ideas at Taxinaria. According to rumours he'd heard, they'd purchased more sponges for their wash centre and a new smart-board for the duty roster. The only thing Erhard has ever managed to get Barouki to agree to was a bookshelf for a lending library. Erhard had installed the shelf himself and donated the first books. Of course, Erhard was the only one who ever used the shelf. In the end, Erhard removed his books and took them back home.

When he's done cleaning his car, he parks on the other side of the fence and enters the gate. He waves a quick hello to Gustavo, the brand-new driver, as well as Sebastiano, who works for Taxinaria.

Maybe Erhard was right all along that Pauli Barouki didn't like him. Perhaps because Pauli knew that he was friends with the Palabrases. It seemed as though he treated Erhard differently than the others. Like that time with the lockers. Each driver was given a little locker to store his coats, a change of clothes, or personal property. At one point they were reassigned lockers to accommodate the new drivers. Erhard's was moved into the corner, squeezed up against the electrical box. Which meant his locker wasn't even half the size of the others. Earlier, that locker had been given only to substitutes and part-time drivers. Erhard complained, but Barouki simply retorted that, unfortunately, there was nothing he could do for him, and that Erhard shouldn't expect special treatment just because he had friends in high places. At the time, he'd thought Barouki meant his reputation in the company, where Erhard served as a kind of confessor for several of the most frustrated drivers. But maybe he'd meant something else entirely.

Erhard walks through the workshop, down the corridor, and up the stairs. On this floor are three small rooms clustered around a small terrace, where the sun blazes down on a cactus surrounded by rocks. He heads directly into the office. Pauli Barouki is washing his face in the sink he had installed. He's lanky and grey-skinned.

– Hermit, he says, without glancing up.

– I just want you to know that I never realized until now that Emanuel Palabras owns Taxinaria.

Barouki laughs. This surprises Erhard. – Well, well.

– Is that why you gave me that tiny locker? I asked you to reconsider. It wasn't fair.

Barouki's smile vanishes. – Save your idealism. You got that locker because you got the bookshelf. It's that embarrassingly simple. You can't get everything you wish for.

– You still don't get the idea behind that shelf.

– Seems no one does. Barouki washes his faces again, then removes a towel from a small basket underneath the sink. He sits down and pats his face dry, his hands, his arms. – I haven't treated you differently because you're friends with Raúl or old man Palabras. I am many things, but I'm not unfair.

– Then why don't we have the new whiteboard for duty rosters? We've discussed it for years.

– Will you pay for it? No. If everyone chips in ten euros, we can talk about it. Or forego your salary for two weeks and we can buy one.

– Maybe I should move on. Maybe Taxinaria's not as stingy with its money. In the thirteen years that I've worked here, this company hasn't spent so much as a hundred euros on its employees. We painted the break-room ourselves, and the chairs are Gonzo's, for Christ's sake.

– You got the lockers when you asked for them.

– That was more than ten years ago.

– C'mon. I wasn't even here ten years ago. I've helped change a lot of things in my time. I helped you get that new dispatch console. You know that.

– That was years ago, and anyway it was just an investment in your equipment. Besides, the drivers weren't exactly clamouring for that new console.

– Look around you, Hermit, you're not in wonderful *Danimarca* any more. Every one of us, this entire country, is deep in debt. Mainlanders don't come here if they owe the banks money. The entire island lacks tourists and we don't have the funds to pamper drivers, even if we wished to.

– Enough with all that financial-crisis rubbish. You could have done something long ago. You seem to be doing all right lounging around on your manicured lawn up on the hill.

– Careful what you say, Hermit. You're no *majorero*. Don't you forget that.

– I'm just telling you to do something. If you don't care to listen to me, then listen to Anphil. He's a *majorero*, and he lives and breathes for this place. And what have you done for him? Nothing. I've gotten a job offer from Taxinaria, and I'm going to accept it.

Barouki is washing himself again, his back to Erhard. – We do all we can, Hermit. Don't overplay your hand. I've been hearing that young Palabras is now counting pennies on the bottom of the ocean. Those aren't the kind of people you want to fool around with any more than you need. He turns to Erhard now. – Did you forget how we help you each month with your little money-transfer to your ex-wife? It's actually quite difficult to transfer money. Our accountant tells me all the time how much of a mess it is, but we do it anyway. Why? Because I promised to help you. It's called loyalty.

– You think I can't get others to help with that?

Erhard glances down at the empty table. There's not a single paper, newspaper, computer, or telephone. It appears as though the table has just been moved into the room He spins on his heels and leaves before

Barouki says anything more. Everything happened so fast, but maybe it's for the best.

On the way out he says hello to Anphil, who's lying underneath Ponduel's Lexus. Ponduel's sitting out front with one of Taxinaria's drivers, who has stopped in for coffee. The difference between the two companies is negligible, yet they behave like two rival football clubs.

Ponduel's normally not very chatty, but when Erhard asks him how he's doing, he complains about the auto workshop. He doesn't think the Greek – that's what he calls Anphil – should be the sole mechanic responsible for thirty drivers while freelancing for Taxinaria at the same time he does rush jobs on Marcelis's wife's Mazda. Erhard listens for a moment, but knows that Ponduel can keep on like this for a long time. So he heads back to his cab, accompanied by the driver from Taxinaria. He's in his mid thirties, or maybe he's forty, with coarse skin. The son of a driver who was killed in a horrible accident the year before during the Maria Festival.

Erhard taps his arm before the Taxinaria driver climbs into his car.

– How do you like it over there? Working there.

The man gives Erhard a friendly look. He's of the new generation which doesn't want to get mixed up in all the competition, gossip, and idiocy of years past.

– Just like here, I'd imagine.

– Have you ever met Raúl Palabras?

– I've only seen him twice.

– Hmm. Did you know that Emanuel Palabras owns Taxinaria?

– *Quién sabe.* Marcelis is the one who calls all the shots.

– What's he like? Is he as strict as they say?

The man smiles. – More or less. He yelled at me once. You don't want to experience that twice.

– What happened?

– I complained about some moving boxes that have been in the break-room since last summer. Only five people can sit in that itty-bitty space. The secretary was thrown out of her boyfriend's house or something, and she hasn't found a place to live. So she sleeps on the sofa at the temp's place, Loulou's, and she keeps the rest of her things in eleven boxes stacked against the walls.

Erhard laughs. – Why hasn't Marcelis asked her to remove them?

– You know. She's a secretary. He makes a suggestive gesture.

– Isn't Marcelis married?

The man stares at Erhard as if he's stupid. – Between you and me, I'm saving up to start my own company. After three more years of driving I can go independent. I'm not going to sit in some taxi for the rest of my life like my father.

– Good for you, Erhard says. Though, in truth, he doesn't believe there's room enough for three taxi companies on the island. It's hard enough with two. – Good chatting with you. Maybe I'll see you around.

Erhard drives down Calle Nuestra Señora del Carmen and parks at the back of the queue to get a few customers, when dispatch rings and tells him that he's got a phone call. He walks into Café Bolaño and waits by the telephone. Maybe it's Barouki. He picks it up on the first ring. He hears the line click over.

– We don't want you here, Hermit.

– Who is this?

– Marcelis Osasuna, motherfucker. Marcelis practically screams into the receiver. Erhard has only met the man a few times, but everyone knows him. And he's known for his use of English obscenities.

– What makes you think I want to work for you?

– Why do you think, *Extranjero*? Palabras might own me, but he doesn't decide everything.

Sebastiano must've told him. – All I did was ask the boy what it was like to work at your place.

– What fucking boy?

– Forget it. But I haven't given Emanuel Palabras my answer yet.

– Rumour has it you're lashing the whip over at Ventura. Don't come over here and whip me. I'll give it right back to you.

– Does Palabras know you're calling me?

Silence. – Of course not. And if you tell him you're finished.

– So many threats, Erhard says, even though he didn't mean to say it out loud.

– I can keep 'em coming. I've fought tooth and nail for this company. You're on your way into the lion's den, *Extranjero*.

Erhard hears Marcelis ruffle through some papers.

– You might be tight with the Palabrases, but you're not coming over here and taking over.

– Who says I want to?

– What do you want then?

– I want to consider it for a few days, and then I'll let Emanuel Palabras know.

– You think very carefully, Hermit.

Marcelis hangs up.

For a moment Erhard stands with the black plastic receiver in his hand, then he finally hangs it up, staring at the wall. One of the posters taped next to the payphone is an ad for one of the many private boats that sail to Lanzarote, Tenerife, Gran Canaria – even a little ferry that sails to Hierro of all godforsaken places. He studies the photograph of the captain, or anyway someone wearing a captain's hat, who's toasting with some passengers in the ship's bar. Erhard makes a decision. During the next few hours he won't think about his future, as a driver or anything else. He will go to Morro Jable and sail to Santa Cruz. Then he remembers Beatriz and the bloody generator. There's only one person who can take care of her while he's gone.

He retrieves his notebook from the car. He inserts a quarter in the telephone and punches the doctor's number.

43

The trip makes him restless.

There's something strange about leaving the island, the sandy ground under his feet. Apart from short forays to the pile of rocks that is Isla de

Lobos with Raúl and Beatriz once in 2008, this is only the third time he has left Fuerteventura. He's been to Lanzarote twice, once to pick up his Mercedes. That was in 1999.

He sits on the sundeck under the blinding sun for a long time. Ten hours with nothing to do. Afraid to fall asleep, he doesn't drink any alcohol. He makes a game of shaking small peanuts from a sticky bag and tossing them into his mouth.

The captain isn't nearly as friendly as he looks in the photograph. He's grumpy and incoherent. Chain-smokes at the railing and stares down in the water as if he wishes to throw himself into the ship's wake. Erhard converses with him several times, but is interrupted when tourists want to snap photographs with him. The captain salutes and poses for these photos; he has nothing to do with the ship's navigation, of course, but is a kind of steward whose job is to radiate a captain's authority – though he doesn't quite succeed. It is the kind of thing that always amused Raúl. Big shots in decline. Beaten down. Raúl loved getting politicians, policemen and civil servants pissed, then humiliating them with idiotic tomfoolery, watching them blush when a female bartender offered them tequila in a glass squeezed between her breasts. He loved to steal their hats and pick at their ties like a coquettish stripper, stick bills down their snug-fitting trousers, or send them double vodkas with umbrellas. One time he grabbed a man by his collar simply because he'd dressed his son in a sailor suit. Just because of that.

How could Raúl have turned his fist against Beatriz? It's logical enough to believe that's what happened, and yet he can't believe it. He doesn't want to believe his friend is capable. He doesn't want to believe he could misjudge someone's character. What is he to make of the words Beatriz had somehow said? *Help me. Let me go.*

It frustrates him that his thoughts about Raúl are mixed. Not pure, not simply loving or angry. Maybe what he feels is what a father feels for his prodigal son: reproachful, damned, grief-filled. He enters the little bar on the sundeck where the captain stood in the photograph on the poster. Buys the last bag of peanuts. Afternoon arrives, then

evening; sea birds – some long black creatures with square beaks –
squawk in the wind that whistles above the boat. The ship approaches
land.

He stands at the stern.

Tenerife across the water.

Many years have passed since the last time he was here. When he
arrived on the islands and was searching for a place to stay, he'd spent
some days at a cheap hotel near a beach. As the boat skips on the waves
towards the white harbour, he sees the island with new eyes. The island
appears taller and redder than Fuerteventura, and it's impressive. Far
more attractive than the island he's chosen to live on. He thinks of his
mother, who always loved Copenhagen whenever they drove around
Tivoli Amusement Park, but feared and hated the city if one of her
children were out of her sight for just two minutes, or when they waited
at the Central Station for Erhard's father to arrive on a train, and a
homeless man would ask Erhard's brother Thorkild if he had a light.
Living your life in a state between destructive hatred and deep-seated
love is exhausting.

He gazes across the water at the island. Every time the boat sinks into
the valley of a wave, the island appears larger and more solid.

Calle Centauro is a sad-looking place. A beige road in a business district.
But the cafe is white and large, actually more of a discotheque than a
cafe. There's a massive room, constructed around a small atrium with
palm trees that jut through a hole in the roof. Erhard sits at a table
underneath one of the palms and scans the handwritten menu. Not
something he sees very often. Even the dinkiest and shabbiest wine and
cocktail bars in Corralejo have lively menus with flamingos and headlines in alternating font colours. This menu is grey and brown, scrawled
in cursive with fat circles above the 'i's.

The owner must be a woman. There are flowers in small vases,
something he can't recall seeing anywhere in Fuerteventura. Everything
is nice and clean and newly painted; all the waitresses seem busy and
happy. One of them, a heavy-set girl wearing a tight white peasant

blouse, reaches up to light a candle in a candlestick set in an old-fashioned wagon wheel. Then she approaches Erhard. She's almost too nice, asking him whether he's on holiday. He nods and she stands ready with her little notepad.

She tells him about nearby sites that he should visit, though not on Saturdays, because there are too many people on Saturdays, and not after nightfall, because the Tunisians are there, and not around noon when the sun is strongest. He asks whether she's from California, and she is. She laughs, tells him she's impressed, then asks him where he's from. He tells her. She says that several of the girls are from Fuerteventura, too, then goes on to say that she lives just above the restaurant, in a flat where the girls can stay if they have just moved here, as long as they work off the rent. She'd like to be a manager some day, she says, if she can learn how. He orders a Mai Tai. He can see the girl's cleavage over the rim of his menu. Before she walks off, he asks if she knows Søren Hollisen. She hesitates. She has heard the name, she thinks, but she doesn't know him. Then she heads back behind the bar, where she talks to another waitress, a fierce-looking girl with her combed-back hair in a ponytail. As if Erhard's some rich grandfather who might dole out some pocket money, the California girl eyes Erhard while she speaks. The ponytail girl drinks from a bottle, unimpressed.

He counts his money and finds he has just enough for a couple of drinks and a meal, but not to spend the night. He'll have to sleep on the beach, which he's done before. It's easy enough if he's pissed. Maybe it'll be the last time he'll ever need to.

The notion that his luck is about to change doesn't stick; it slips through his fingers like sand. He doesn't dare believe it. For nearly twenty years, misfortune has followed him; he has made poor decisions and lived the wrong kind of life and met the wrong people at the wrong times. Usually he feels, and even says, that his timing has been ten years off. First ten years too early. Married while still a teenager – that says it all. While the last twenty years have been ten years too late. Too late to do anything about his music, to meet a nice woman, to lean back and enjoy life as one does at his age in Denmark and as so many of his Danish contemporaries here on holiday do. And suddenly, emerging out of his wretchedness, in the middle of all that's going on with Raúl and Beatriz and the dead boy, he sees an opportunity that he needs to grasp. No matter how difficult or foolish it might turn out to be. The opportunity to become something else, to be someone. Maybe he'll be able to purchase one of the houses above the city. With a garden. He can sit reading in an air-conditioned office or take a walk down to the workshop to speak with Anphil, or he can host meetings and offer his guests a dram of whisky.

He hasn't told Emanuel Palabras anything about this.

In the morning, before he left his house, he called Palabras and mentioned the episode with Barouki, and Marcelis's phone call. He didn't repeat everything that Marcelis had said, but he did say that Marcelis seemed unhappy with Erhard's potential role.

All bark and no bite, Emanuel had said. Raúl had his share of confrontations with Marcelis too. Welcome to the company, he added.

The last thing he said: *Say yes and I'll give you a salary worthy of a director.* Which sounded good at that point, but Erhard considers his title now. What did Raúl actually do for the company? If Erhard assumes Raúl's job, does that also mean that Erhard should keep a low profile and stay out of daily operations? He wants to make a difference; if he can't, he can always quit. Nobody owns him.

But he's tempted by thoughts of skipping his generator idea and getting Beatriz to a private hospital in Puerto, maybe inviting Aaz and his mother to his place for coffee.

Ponytail girl is the one who brings his Mai Tai, setting it on a saucer. He pays sixteen euros and lays four in her hand. It's a decent tip, and yet she stares at the coins with no change of expression. He asks her if she knows Søren. Her gaze is sharp. Maybe she's mostly into girls, he thinks. She glares at him as if she thinks men are pretty much a waste of time.

– What do you want to know?

– Søren Hollisen, do you know him? Perhaps he's a customer?

– I know who he is. Everyone here knows.

– How do you know him?

– I don't *know* him. It's impossible to know him.

– But you've met him.

– Met, she says, making air quotes with her fingers.

– Are you from this island?

– Fuerteventura.

– Oh, Erhard says. But he isn't interested in small talk with this girl. – Does anyone here know him better than you?

– Ellen.

– Who is Ellen?

– The owner, a Brit. She's out in the back. But she's leaving soon.

Erhard thanks her, then sips his Mai Tai. It's too sweet. Too much syrup, not enough lime. But it's got plenty of rich, dark rum. He eats the embellishment, a pineapple and orange. While he chews the pineapple, a woman in a light-blue shirt and black trouser-suit sits down at his table. She looks like a man, but one with long hair gathered up in a bun and a mouth so tight and narrow that it resembles a line drawn with a Sharpie.

– Friend or foe? she asks with a distinct Irish accent.

Erhard says nothing, just looks at her.

– You're looking for Søren Hollyson. She pronounces it Soren – Are you a friend or foe?

– Neither.

– What has he done this time?

– As far as I know, he hasn't done anything.

– Why are you looking for him then? I'm guessing it's not because you're attracted to him?

There's something sly about the way she questions him. It feels like more of an interrogation than when Hassib asked him questions.

– Maybe I'll tell him myself.

– Go ahead, but you'll have to travel to Dakar. Has it got anything to do with money?

– Maybe, Erhard says, to confuse her a bit.

– He has nothing to do with this place any more. We've done everything we can to get back on our feet again after the mess he left behind. We don't want to get mixed up in anything.

– Easy now, easy, Miss…

– Blythe-Patrick. Ellen.

– OK, Ellen. I don't know Søren at all.

– Are you with the Danish police?

– No. I'm from Denmark, it's true, but I haven't been back in many years. I live in Fuerteventura.

– Well, I haven't seen him in months, perhaps a year. But I've heard he's in Dakar.

– I may not even need to talk to him. Maybe you can help me?

She straightens in the chair and glances around the cafe, as if she's nervous someone will hear them. But there's no one around. On a sofa in the back of the room sits a couple, so clearly pissed that they're practically asleep. – I don't want to get mixed up in Søren's shit.

– I'm not mixing you up in anything, Erhard says. He draws the small baggie from his pocket with the slip of paper inside. – Do you recall if the cafe ever had a subscription to a Danish newspaper? Sometime last year?

The woman glances down at the paper and grins. – Yes. I do. I do, because no one ever read it. *Politiken*, it was. She butchers the pronunciation as *pollyticken*. – It just sat there. Turned out that we never got Danish visitors. And the Norwegians and Swedes apparently don't give a toss about Danish newspapers.

– When did you subscribe?

– I don't know. A year ago? One day it just stopped coming. Søren started the subscription, but no one knew how to cancel it, so we just chucked all the newspapers into the rubbish bin.

– Have any of your colleagues suddenly vanished in the last three months?

– Vanished, no. But a few have them have gone home. To England, Spain, Holland, or wherever it is they're from.

– Do you know any young girls who've gotten pregnant and had an abortion?

– You Danes aren't afraid of stepping on people's toes, are you? She laughs. – But I like that, as long as you don't scare my girls.

– I'm trying to help someone I know find his girlfriend. She was last seen here with this newspaper.

She leans across the table and lowers her voice. – If you're looking for girls in the 18- to 30-year-old range who forget to insist on condoms, then you've come to the right place. There are all sorts of girls like that here, in every stage of pregnancy, even the skinny ones that you don't notice are pregnant until they retch on the floor of the bar. Islanders may be Catholics, but their daughters aren't exactly nuns. The clinic down in Santa Cruz makes a pretty penny. This is a party island. The men don't care, and the girls are too stupid. It's as simple as that. Is she Danish?

Erhard had always imagined the mother was Danish, because the child had been swaddled inside a Danish newspaper, but now he's not sure. He recalls the images he's seen of the boy. – Possibly. She's light-skinned.

– A friend's girlfriend, you say? You don't know much, do you?

– Did someone take the newspapers home? Maybe a Danish girl, a customer here?

– Well, on any given day except Sundays, more than 1,500 people party here until the sun rises. Could one of them have taken the newspaper home? It's hard to say. I know that we mostly just threw them out. We got tired of them.

– So when did you stop receiving the newspapers?

– In October. Maybe November.

– What did you do with them? Where did you throw them out?

The woman scrutinizes Erhard as if he doesn't understand something. – In the rubbish bin, of course.

– May I see?

– Sure, just walk around the building. Have fun.

Erhard looks at her as he gets to his feet. – There's too much syrup in your Mai Tai. Don't put so much in or use more fresh lime.

44

He doesn't care to rummage through the rubbish bins. It was just something he came up with to irritate her. Why would he? What would he search for? What good would it do him to see where they threw a bunch of newspapers months ago? So he walks up and down the street and finally into a bar that's broadcasting horse races on its many televisions.

At around eleven o'clock he eats a ham sandwich and drinks the cheapest beer on the menu. He doesn't speak to anyone. He practises being the director: crossing his legs and looking dignified, smiling a little, and waving at the waiter – a small man with a waist apron underneath a pair of man-boobs. Erhard orders another beer. A woman sits at the bar, and he dreams of impressing her in conversation. He knows his newfound confidence is only because he's on Tenerife. At home he wouldn't puff himself up like this. At home he would've already gone home. The woman, who's at least twenty years younger, is seated with her back to him, but he can see her spine through her thin yellow dress. She doesn't even glance in his direction, but seems mostly interested in writing something on her mobile phone.

After he's eaten, he goes down the hill to find the beach and a place to sleep. He's tired, wiped out. He brought an extra beer from the bar. Café Rústica, just as the woman had said it would be, is packed. People are hanging from the windows and sitting on the patio as the music thumps and vibrates. The nightlife vibe is different here than on Fuerteventura. There's a different kind of abandon, as if young people here are wealthier and more willing – which is probably true. He walks slowly past the cafe and pauses on the path leading around the building. He can see and smell the rubbish bins, which by the light of the streetlamps resemble parked tanks. A couple is making out intensely around the corner. Erhard coughs loudly so that they know he's there, then saunters past them and down the alley. On his right is the cafe, a high wall lacking windows. Around thirty metres ahead, a yellow square forms an open door from the kitchen to the alley. On his left, a tall fence encloses what appears to be a container terminal. Erhard spots movement, and a posse of soft, mewling cats scuttle between his legs. In the darkness they're all blue. The stench is powerful. Not from the cats, but the overflowing rubbish bin. Cinched rubbish bags are poking up from underneath the lid. He starts towards the open door, through which he hears rap music. A young man, a Moroccan dishwasher wearing yellow rubber gloves, strolls outside smoking a cigarette. The light from the doorway illuminates the fence and a row of wicker baskets, bottles, cardboard, and rotten fruit that smells sweet and hot. Erhard stands quietly until the dishwasher discovers him and nods. A young man like that doesn't dare speak. Besides, it's not illegal for Erhard to be here.

– Newspapers? Erhard asks, nodding at the rubbish bin. The man, who doesn't seem to understand him, just nods again. – Are there newspapers here?

Erhard points at the bin.

– No, you put newspapers over there. They have to go in the container for recycling.

Erhard returns to the tall black container that he'd passed earlier. He peers inside it. It's nearly filled with Spanish and English newspapers. He pulls out a few. They are from yesterday, Tuesday, Sunday.

– What do you need them for? the dishwasher asks. If you need them for sleeping, then you can borrow a blanket from me. It's going to be cold tonight.

Just as Erhard's about to respond, he sees a broad hole in the fence next to the newspaper container.

– What's in there? Only containers?

The dishwasher has lit another cigarette and now sits on a folding chair beside the door.

– Storage, freight, import/export, furniture, antiquities. Anything that fits inside a container. They get angry when people go through there, but they won't put up a new fence.

– Why would anyone go that way? Is it a shortcut?

– People host huge parties in the waterfront houses sometimes, and it only takes five minutes to get down there if you go that way. Otherwise you have to walk around, and that takes maybe fifteen.

– Do you have a torch? Erhard asks. But he doesn't wait for a response before stepping through the hole in the fence.

He gets all the way through the container terminal without noticing anything particularly interesting. Partly because the area is dark, lit up only by some old streetlamps with tyres around their foundations, and partly because there's nothing particularly remarkable. The dishwasher was right. Many of the containers are sealed with heavy-duty padlocks. There's all sorts of stuff in the open containers. Boxes and bubble-wrapped items, or things packaged in glass cases or foam. Some containers hold steel and old bicycles. Down near the driveway, one hundred metres before the guardhouse and the barrier that blocks entry to the terminal, stand several refrigerator containers, a couple of RVs and small trucks, and what appears to be construction materials for a house. He passes the guard, who's watching a Sylvester Stallone film, and continues to the beach. There he sits next to a bonfire with a sand sculptor and his dog.

The two men share the beer Erhard has brought, and they give the dog a slurp from a metal tray. The heat, the bonfire light, and the sound of the sculptor's voice tires him out. The man talks about Lanzarote in the 1980s, when Moroccan fishermen filled their boats with people and knowingly crashed their cutters against the coast so they would have to be saved and brought to land. Erhard thinks he's met this man before and wonders if he's that well-known businessman who was convicted of fraud. Then he falls asleep. He wakes briefly when the sculptor lays some old towels, coats, and blankets over him, but otherwise sleeps. The sun rises. The sculptor must have packed his things and headed to the beach with his dog early; Erhard sees their footprints in the sand when he wakes around eight o'clock. He sits for a long time staring at the water.

45

He's back on Fuerteventura after lunchtime. He finds his car parked alone in the small car park next to the harbour. A seagull's on the roof. He shoos it off and drives northward, wondering how he'll avoid screwing everything up. It's up to him now; he can't resort to his old methods of problem-solving.

He arrives fifteen or twenty minutes late, and he spots Aaz standing at the door of Santa Marisa's, along with Liana, one of the nuns. He steers the car up alongside them and Aaz climbs in. The nun lowers her head to the window and taps on the glass with her thin finger.

– It's very upsetting to him. You need to be punctual. He doesn't like to wait.

– I'd arranged with Mónica that I would pick him up at 3.15 today.

– It's bad enough that you changed the appointment. He knows how to tell time, you know.

– I know that, sister.

Each time Erhard talks with the nuns, they say something that makes him feel like an idiot.

– But the worst of it is that you're fifteen minutes late. It's 3.30.

– I'm sorry. He hates these kinds of petty arguments. He hadn't planned to be late, after all. It just happened.

– I'll let his mother know you're running late. She's probably worried.

– Thanks, Erhard says. He prefers that Mónica not be told.

They leave Corralejo and head through Las Dunas. Erhard sprays washer fluid on the windscreen. Aaz likes that, laughing as if everything were normal. He holds absolutely no grudges and it's liberating to be around him.

– I've been over the water. To Tenerife.

Oh, what were you doing there?

– Trying to find the mother, you know, of that little boy.

You learn anything?

– I don't know. Maybe.

What does it look like over there? Is there sand and rocks like here?

– There are green palms, just like they have at Santa Marisa. Cliffs rise from the water. And the wealthiest residents build their houses along those cliffs. There was a beach with white reclining chairs, where men rake the sand in the evening, and a small bay where I sat with an old friend and watched the sea turn black, and we talked about you.

Aaz glances at Erhard. The boy understands everything.

– Some day you can go with me on the boat and cross the water to the big island. When Liana isn't so angry any more. Maybe your mother will want to come along.

Erhard wishes to tell him about Emanuel's job offer. About the better days ahead. But he's suddenly afraid it'll only confuse Aaz and make him nervous if he says too much about such changes. He needs to consider what he says before he speaks.

When they drive through Antigua, they laugh at a man chasing a hat caught in the wind.

He'd like to let Aaz walk in by himself, but Mónica is standing outside, waiting. Erhard gets out of the car with Aaz and nods apologetically at Mónica, trying to absorb the worst. Aaz brushes past Mónica and into the house.

– Did Liana call?

– What happened?

– I was just delayed.

– I don't know what you've gotten yourself tangled up in, but I hope it doesn't mean that Aaz can no longer count on you.

– I'm not tangled up in anything.

– It's OK if you call me and ask me to change the time like you did yesterday, but don't start forgetting your commitments and arriving late and…

– I'm not tangled up in anything.

– You show up here early in the morning, then suddenly you're going on a trip. Something is going on.

– It won't affect Aaz in any way.

– You won't be late again?

– I promise.

His promises are piling up, he thinks.

– Did it have something to do with that address I found for you?

– Yes.

– Is it something illegal?

Erhard laughs.

She repeats her question.

– No. It's… it's… something good. I'm looking for someone.

– The girl in the photograph?

– No. She just helped me with something, he says. It would be foolish to involve Mónica in this, he thinks. But in reality he's afraid to tell her what he's up to in case he doesn't find the mother. – I'm just looking for an old friend who's gone missing.

– Hmm, she says, dubious. – Who?

– Raúl Palabras, he says, because he can't think of anyone else.

– Is he your friend?

– Yes.

She stares at him at length, and he suddenly feels old. As if she's judging him for the first time, really *seeing* him and his wrinkled face. – It doesn't matter what you do and who your friends are. As long as you don't let my son down. As long as you don't do it again. Tears well in her eyes.

He wants to lay his hand on her shoulder. But she's already on her way back into her house.

– I was going to invite you to an early dinner, she says, but I guess that doesn't matter any more. Just be here at eight o'clock.

It's the first time she's ever given him an order like that.

He doesn't even care to defend himself. There's no way he can eat dinner with them. The doctor was at his house the night before and then again this morning, but it's time Erhard went home and filled the generator with diesel. He slumps back to his car.

He hasn't argued with a woman in seventeen years. Not since Annette. In a way, it's familiar and exhilarating, but still trite and annoying. Like playing Ludo with different rules. There are no established truths and nothing to refer to, only a feeling that everything they'd discussed had nothing at all to do with what their conversation was actually about. He wants to drive off and never return.

Or he wants to do precisely what he'd promised her. What he'd promised Aaz.

A bloody maelstrom of emotions and thoughts swirls in his head.

46

As he's filling the generator with diesel, he hears the telephone ring inside the house. A rare event. Since he hasn't even filled half the tank, he ignores the call.

After he goes inside, empties the drainage bag, and affixes a new one, the telephone rings again. He can't just drop the bag he's holding. He studies Beatriz, and can't shake the feeling that he's let her down. Several days have passed since he last stood at her bedside and spoke to her. He doesn't know what to say, so he just stands there growing tired as the machine regulates her shallow breaths.

The phone rings a third time. He glowers at the green plastic device and lifts it reluctantly.

– Where have you been? Emanuel Palabras blurts out.

– South.

– I've talked to Marcelis.

– Did you fire him?

– Easy, my friend. I'm just telling you what I've done. Now that the air has been cleared, we can put the shop in order.

– I haven't accepted your offer yet.

– But you will.

This irritates Erhard. He has a strange feeling this is how things will play out: Papa Palabras will dictate how they do their work. But he won't let his irritation control him.

– Yes, he says.

– Good, my friend. Good.

Erhard wants to know more about the business and its finances. Wants to look through the company's books. Palabras doesn't understand why – it's not something Raúl ever cared about – and he thinks it's a waste of Erhard's time. Raúl has been gone for more than ten days, and before that he was derelict in his duties, so Erhard needs to get down to business.

– What do you expect me to do?

– Keep an eye on the lazy drivers, sign some good contracts. You'll have to figure it out.

– I have some experience with accounts, from the old days.

Silence.

– You never cease to amaze me, Piano Tuner.

– I'll need a thorough review of the finances if I'm going to work with Marcelis.

– Surely the man can set aside a few hours to take you through it? During a nice lunch, Emanuel adds, then shifts topics. – I want you to move into Raúl's flat. I'll pay the rent. You can live there until we sell the place in a few months, when the market's better. By then you'll have saved up some money and can buy your own. They say the housing market will improve this year.

Erhard doesn't know what to think. – What about Raúl? What if he returns?

– Don't say his name again.

– He's your son, Palabras.

– He's dead.

– Nobody knows that for sure. The police say he left the island, but you know him. He might be in Dakar, or Madrid for that matter. It's only been, what, eleven days? He's been gone for a month before.

– He's dead. The flat needs to be cleared, and all his shit hauled away.

Erhard can't tell whether Palabras knows for certain Raúl is dead or has simply made a decision. – Can't you just pack it all up and store it?

– Why are you defending him?

Erhard stares into the darkness of the pantry. – How did he die?

– He took his own life after bringing shame to his father.

That doesn't sound like Raúl, Erhard thinks. He wouldn't kill himself or regret doing anything against his father. – How do you know?

– Why do you keep digging around in something that doesn't involve you, Piano Tuner? I'm telling you, I don't want to hear anything more about him.

– I can't move into his flat with all of his things, it's too strange. What about all his papers and cookbooks? And his collection of eighties records and photos and wine?

– I don't want to hear anything more about him. Drink the bloody wine and throw the rest out. Get someone to take the shit away. Do whatever you wish. Move in if you want. If you prefer your *majorero* cave out in Majanicho, fine. As long as you're presentable and punctual at work. And don't be stingy when you go out to eat with clients.

– I'll think about it, Erhard says. He already has the key to the flat. But he doesn't tell Palabras. He doesn't say that he'll happily trade the cave for the flat. Moving into the flat would make everything easier. Beatriz could return to her own things, and get a nice bed, and he wouldn't have to run around keeping an eye on the generator. If Raúl doesn't return any time soon, or if he really is dead, it doesn't make Erhard a bad person if he lives a good life for a few months. Just until Beatriz is doing better, and he has the money to buy something else. Something worthy of a director.

– Seize your opportunity, Piano Tuner. I'll arrange a meeting with Marcelis. If you have any problems with him, call me.

Palabras hangs up.

Erhard pours himself a glass of wine, then goes out and pulls some trousers, underwear, and towels from the washing machine. They've been sitting in the machine for too long, and now they smell. He hangs the clothes on one of the lines. Laurel's munching on a piece of fabric that appears to have come from one of Erhard's shirts. This happens every now and then. The clothes blow off the line, vanish, and the zipper or buttons turn up in the goats' shit. He fills a cup with feed and scatters the pellets on the ground; the goat shuffles away from the clothesline and over to his food. Erhard hopes it'll attract Hardy, who might be close by, perhaps resting behind a large rock, but he doesn't see a trace of him.

He thinks about Bill Haji and the wild dogs.

Could the wild dogs be getting more desperate for something to eat? Could they capture and devour a goat? Maybe if it was injured or stuck between two rocks. He glances at the ground where someone has dug into the hard soil – one of the goats? Everything happens for a reason. There's a story behind everything. Just as the car on the beach and the cardboard box and the newspapers have a story, a series of actions, regardless of how incomprehensible they might seem.

A mother abandons her child only if there's a reason, an underlying pressure. She's not evil or selfish. Maybe *because* she's a good person, so realistic about herself and her situation that she wants to spare the child from the pain of growing up. It's a crime, yes, but one committed out of love, out of an altruistic consideration for the child's welfare. The most probable reason the boy was left in the box is that his mother drowned herself after having parked the car down on the beach. Perhaps she was at Rústica, grabbed some random newspaper, and stuffed it into her purse. He's not sure how the newspaper is connected, but he's sure there is a connection.

He drives for a few hours, then picks up Aaz at precisely eight o'clock. Mónica says nothing. She seems to study Erhard's face slyly, so he won't look her into her eyes.

– She thinks I'm an idiot, doesn't she?

You were late, that's all.

– She doesn't think I'm an awful person?

She's too proper to tell anyone that.

– That's the problem. She's too proper. Does she have any faults or irritating habits you can't see?

She likes wet kisses.

– That's what mothers do when they kiss their kids.

She's not a good cook. She burns the sancochado and the fish tastes awful.

Erhard laughs. – I can't even make sancochado. I've never tried.

I haven't either.

– What else? What does she like to do?

She likes to take care of her weird plants. Succulents, oleanders, birds of paradise. She talks to them and waters them with a little green canister that looks like an oil tin. She can revive a dead plant. I've seen it with my own eyes. A dry stem became a large red flower. It's like in the nuns' Bible. She can wake the dead with her fingers.

– She's a special lady, no doubt. And so is Sister Liana. Look, she's waiting for us.

Sister Liana says nothing, but shoos Aaz through the gate like a stray goat.

He packs his best clothes. He counts his underwear and scoops up the white ones without holes, then packs his CDs and six books he hasn't read. It takes some time to choose among them. He packs everything into a single cardboard box along with the cigar box of photos. He empties the fridge. Standing in the doorway staring up the hill, he toasts Laurel and listens to the wind and the roof, which continues to bang.

Finally he fills the boot with the IV, the catheter, and the respirator, then hurries to carry Beatriz to the car. He lays her across the backseat, underneath a blanket. He shuts off the electricity and unplugs the generator in the shed. It grows dark and quiet. Almost as if the house, originally a shepherd's dwelling, wasn't here. The cattle rancher lived on the other side of the mountain with his family, and he let his cattle roam freely. But the goats always came over to this side of the mountain, the less windy side, and so the cattle rancher built this house for his son who took care of the goats. When cattle prices fell at the beginning of the eighties, and the huge farm was sold at auction to a real-estate company, the new owners decided to rent out the shepherd's house for a price that attracted the worst kinds of people. The goats came with the place, but the new renters were unable to care for them. Erhard knows nothing about tending goats, but he likes these two creatures, and he feels the need to take care of them even though he's moving downtown.

He scatters a few handfuls of feed around the house so they won't have to search too hard. He calls out for them a few times, but that has never worked.

He settles Beatriz in her own bed and he sleeps under a blanket on the sofa. He sleeps the sleep of the guilty, waking with a bad conscience – as if he's forgotten something important. He peers around in the brown darkness of the flat and wonders about the sounds emerging from the building: lift, water spigot, voices.

While the sun is on its way up, he drinks the last of the instant coffee. It's an expensive brand, Zebrezá, which makes the coffee completely brown and foamy. It's clear they've hired someone to clean the flat, but still he runs a cloth across shelves, tables, and doors. He empties drawers and washes them, sorts everything, then puts it all back. He washes blankets and Raúl's bed linen. When it comes to cleaning, he's self-taught and feels unstructured and ineffective. Since he's lived on the island, he's never had others clean for him or watched others tidy up. He throws out everything in the cupboards. Afterward, he fills the cupboards again with items he buys at HiperDino.

He eats lunch with Beatriz. Her face is no longer thrilling or meaningful, now seemingly just sculptural elements on a light-brown background. So delicately fastened that they might rustle apart at any time. Cautiously he removes the respirator's mouthpiece, then pours a little water on his index finger and runs it gently across her lips. He doesn't hear the words every time, but he has heard them a few times when he's sitting quietly beside her. When he gets used to the wheezes emerging from the respirator and adopts the same rhythm as her. He needs them, the words. To hear them again. To know what he's doing and why. To understand himself and feel less alone. He traces his fingers across her lips, follows each little curve, balancing on the cusp of the mouth's darkness. The index finger which at the slightest mistake slips into the crevice, the woman's most fascinating orifice. The only place where the contents conquer the form. Annette had an average mouth, he discovered after many years of not knowing why she always seemed so ordinary. She was a nice-looking woman in many ways. She had long, straight hair, which had gradually turned silver. Many of his friends envied him for her breasts, which appeared larger than they really were. But her lips, her mouth: over the years he took them personally. It was his job to make her smile. Yet for each day that he failed, he knew it would only grow harder and harder. Not until he left her did he begin to blame her mother, her family, her social standing. There was so much scepticism and frustration in the family that the four sisters – Annette was the youngest – seldom smiled. As if there were no muscles in their faces.

But Beatriz had had the most incredible smile. She was one of those kinds of women who'd achieved everything with her smile. The little girl who gets to sit in front on the scooter, the big girl who gets her first job, the grown woman who decides which man she will drive crazy.

Help me. Let me go. The words are so faint that it makes no sense to call them words, just tiny signals in the noise of the respirator. He calls for her, he whispers to her, he feels the heat from her ears. What should I do, Beatriz? What do you want? Her body seems to respond. Her chest rises, a force having taken hold of her, and her face begins to quiver. Then the catheter makes a noise and a greenish liquid oozes into the drainage bag. All at once he is struck by her state of immense vulnerability, and he affixes the respirator's mouthpiece in place and carefully rolls her onto her other side. She speaks, but he's the only one who hears, and he's the only one who can help her now. Normally he wouldn't want this kind of responsibility or this kind of role, but no one else can do it. There's no one to complain, no one to reproach him. Only himself. Only his own insistent voice.

He returns to his cleaning with a kind of angry energy. He finds Radio Mucha on Raúl's nice stereo and hoovers the flat to the sound of loud music. When he reaches the entrance way, he sees a letter leaning against a vase on the chest of drawers. Someone was in the flat. It's from Emanuel Palabras.

Marcelis's office, Monday, 1 p.m.

It occurs to him how powerful Emanuel Palabras actually is. He actually managed to make Marcelis schedule a meeting with him. Erhard feels a tickling sensation of delight that's succeeded by reluctance to spend time with Marcelis, being forced to ask him questions and to learn from him. Marcelis won't be open and communicative; he'll brush Erhard off. He'll presume that Erhard doesn't understand business economics or leadership or anything but driving a taxi. Marcelis has never been a chauffeur, and he's probably never even driven a cab. He got things under control at Servicio Canarias, a messenger service known for its expensive prices and unreliable messengers, but Erhard doesn't know what Marcelis did there, or what he got under control.

Standing in the entrance way, it also occurs to him that many others might have keys to the flat. He needs to think more aggressively, be more distrustful, and expect the worst if he wishes to maintain control. He empties the drawers and lays all the keys from a little box on top of the commode, then adds the keys to Raúl's car and flat. All in all, there are two keys to the flat, three unknown keys, and the car keys. After trying both keys in the door, he goes to the study and scavenges the shelf, looking for a thin blue and white telephone book. He riffles through to L, and selects the only locksmith in the city. A man called Saragó. He punches the number and schedules him for Friday at 8 a.m.

He studies Raúl's car keys. In some way, it seems more transgressive to take over his car than his flat. The car was one of Raúl's favourite things. He loved its buttons and its white leather interior and its hum when he drove on FV-1. Taking over the car means pushing Raúl definitively out of the way. But at the same time, Erhard knows why he finds it so difficult. Growing up in his family, he was told that one must earn the good things in life; but in reality, no one ever deserved anything good. It was well known that happiness wasn't capricious; it was ridiculous. Though his father had toiled and toiled without asking for handouts or assistance, he ended his days filled with spite, and dementia, mean without knowing why, determinedly and repeatedly insisting that he never had anything handed to him. But what's wrong with having something handed to you, really? What's wrong with gathering up the crumbs that life throws at you? Why not take hold of the good things in life like some kind of drunken busker, regardless of whether one really earned them or not? Now it's Erhard's turn to enjoy the spoils of life, even if he hasn't earned them.

In the afternoon he drives to dispatch. He's never been good at endings, the gentle transitions or gradual shifts. He's not crazy about change, but if it has to be, then it has to be. No reason to camouflage an ugly conclusion. No reason for friendly gestures and kind words. A goodbye is a goodbye.

But that doesn't make it any easier. Or painless. Leaving Annette and the girls was dreadful. But it was a simple, sharp break – very clear. He didn't beat around the bush with prevarications, excuses, and nightly calls. He didn't ask for understanding or forgiveness. One day he followed Mette to school and stood on the stairwell watching her walk down the corridor, the next day he was gone. So even though he's been part of this company for many years, it ends here, now, today. There is paperwork and stuff to do with the Merc which he leases from TaxiVentura, but he doesn't wish to explain himself or give a speech while raising a dram. Already when he parks in front of the workshop, people are giving him funny looks. They know, he presumes, though he doesn't care. He hoovers the car, pounds the floor mats against the grate, washes and dries the panels, washes the headlights and windows, polishes the wheel rims. He empties the glove box and tosses everything in the rubbish bin, and removes the little necklace that dangles from the rearview mirror. He leaves the keys on the table with Anphil, then goes inside. The company's only female driver, Felia, a no-nonsense woman, is standing at her locker organizing her receipts when he enters. He heads to the corner and begins stuffing the few things he owns into a plastic bag. As soon as he has gathered his things, he leaves.

Dispatch is located on the outskirts of Corralejo, and on the way back he follows a long, gloomy road. When he reaches the end of it, he bumps across a ditch and wends through an overgrown construction site. Cats sit on top of rusty barrels.

He's travelled this road many times, thousands, but he's never really noticed the containers. But now he does. Just like on Tenerife, they're behind a crumpled chain-link fence in an area with greyish-brown asphalt and weeds that poke up through tyres and cracks. He slips through a gap in the fence and drives among the closest containers.

Someone transports the giant containers here. No one sees them do it, apparently; they're just there, sealed up in once place and opened in another. At night they sail into port stacked on rusty blue super-tankers. In the morning they're lifted onto lorries that haul them onto land and deposit them here on these asphalt fields. The contents are emptied, distributed. The invisible consumer-machine, well-oiled and smooth and insentient. Erhard now recalls what he saw on Tenerife: A container with an old VW. He only saw part of it; in the available light, he could just make out the characteristic headlights. Where do the cars come from? And how are they transported? Erhard doesn't know. He's never considered where the island's cars actually come from. Barcelona? He runs his hand along the rough sides of a container and gazes into the darkness inside. It's darker than dark. It could easily hold a car.

There's something about that car. It's reasonable to assume that someone drove it from Puerto, then abandoned it on the beach. The distance from Puerto to Cotillo is around thirty miles, if one drives over Corralejo. It ought to be in Lisbon. The plates were missing.

Facts:

An unknown mother.

A dead boy.

Newspaper fragments from Tenerife.

A stolen vehicle from Amsterdam?

The beach in Cotillo. At low tide.

The most likely scenario is that the mother went with her son from Tenerife to Fuerteventura, maybe in a fishing boat or a private boat or one of the big yachts. Something happens, the boy dies, and the mother wraps him in newspaper from a cafe she's visited. In Puerto she gets her hands on a stolen car, removes the licence plates, and tries to drive into the water with her already dead child. But the car gets stuck in the sand, and the mother walks out in the sea and drowns herself, leaving the boy's body in the box on the backseat.

That matches the police's investigation. Erhard's latest discovery of the newspaper on Tenerife, and the fact that the car had stood in high water – as it shows in the girl's photographs from the beach that day – also supports that explanation. And yet, as he stares at a cat running through the container terminal and into a dry bush, he's convinced it's something else. Something else entirely.

He studies the container door, the locking mechanism. It locks in place by jamming an arm-length rod downward: this drives a bar in the lower and upper halves of the door into a hole in the hull of the container. Erhard tries the lock a few times. It seems solid and simple. He knows this kind of mechanism from his work; they have an old trailer that locks the same way. With that one the rod goes the other way; it has to be jammed upward instead, which means that the door sometimes opens by itself if one hasn't shoved the rod all the way up and fastened it with a bar or padlock. But here, gravity ensures that the rod doesn't loosen. He moves on to another open container, then a third. None have the exact same locking mechanism.

Erhard doesn't quite know what it means. He continues between the containers and then onto an expansive zone with construction equipment, stacks of plywood. It's almost five o'clock. He has nothing to do before he meets with Marcelis in three days. For the first time in fifteen years he's free of dispatch. Downtown, with nothing in his pockets, other than Emanuel Palabras's promises.

The islands' tomatoes look like clenched fists. The skins are like apple peel, the juice like egg-white. He picks one at a time. In the bottom left corner of the box he finds three good ones, and one that may be a little too ripe, but smells strange, salty. Three will do. Then he fishes a square chunk of African goat cheese out of a bucket filled with vinegar. He pays with tips from the previous day, from what might have been his final taxi ride – not a memorable event. A solicitor of some kind. Erhard had been more concerned that he picked up Aaz on time.

Just then he sees Cormac. Since it's siesta, he's sitting on the stairwell smoking and gazing curiously at Erhard, who is approaching with his purchases.

– On the way up? Cormac asks.

– In a bit. Just need to get my shopping done.

– On the way up the food chain, I mean.

Cormac grins so that it's impossible not to see where he's missing teeth in the back of his mouth.

– An old dog can enjoy his last days, Erhard says, exaggerating on purpose.

– The good drivers say you've earned it.

– Do they? Erhard's more surprised than he sounds. – And what do the mean ones say?

Cormac looks at him as he sucks his slender cigarette. The smoke rises as if from his hair. – Ponduel, that devilish bastard, says you've brown-nosed your way to the job.

In other words kissed a wealthy man's ass, Erhard thinks.

– That's because he doesn't know what a bad kisser I am.

Cormac laughs. – Others say you're sniffing around doing police work. But one hears a lot of things in an electronics shop.

– Who says that?

Erhard wants to keep his surprise hidden, but he's not completely successful.

– My dear wife heard it from one of the girls down at the harbour. That you're looking for a dead boy's mother.

Erhard laughs tensely and turns away for the first time. He doesn't know how to deal with a telltale. Should he deny the story, knowing full well that it might make Cormac even more curious? Or should he play along and confirm the rumour? There's only one answer: to not care, to laugh it off. But before he says anything, Cormac changes the subject.

– Did you ever get in touch with the hairdresser's daughter? The computer expert?

– It wasn't important.

– You were looking for a photograph?

– I found another way.

– Oh well, Cormac says, seemingly satisfied.

Erhard has an idea. – Do you know anything about my new colleague, Marcelis Osasuna?

Cormac begins to roll another cigarette. – The union-buster? he says without looking up. – If you're not friends with him, I'd tread carefully.

– I don't know anything about that.

– Remember the Servicio Canarias strike?

Erhard shakes his head.

– The lorry drivers struck a deal after refusing to work for eleven days, because they wanted a fired colleague rehired. Your man Osasuna stopped the negotiations without getting the guy his job back.

– So he wasn't the director?

– Maybe he was the assistant director or something fine like that? And there was that issue with the rubbish dump.

Erhard remembers that one. Some locals had opposed Taxinaria's plans to use the construction site west of dispatch for reserve car parts and tyres. A woman who lived behind the area had, for many years, tried to gain permission to use the area to build a playground for the neigh-bourhood children and to have all the construction materials removed in order to create a garden. But the county continued to delay the deci-sion, and then all of a sudden her application was rejected. – What did he have to do with that?

– The parrots all said that it was Señor Osasuna who'd caused the county to support business interests, if you know what I mean.

The rumours on the island were tiresome, but sometimes there was truth to them. He might as well play along. – Did the parrots say any-thing about Osasuna's wife?

– Probably a little.

It's clear that Cormac hadn't heard this one before.

Erhard tosses out a handful of titbits. – Something about the wife not liking Fuerteventura so they only see each other on the weekends? And he has a close relationship to his secretary, who has moved into the office?

– Something like that.

– He's only human, Erhard says.

– Aren't we all?

Erhard picks up his bags. – Have to get home now. *Buenas.*

– *Buenas.*

He cuts the tomatoes and cheese into small slices, then eats at Beatriz's bedside. On Saturday morning, the locksmith arrives and curses and groans for two hours, but finally manages to exchange the lock for a powerful three-point lock and gives Erhard three keys that cannot be duplicated. Erhard affixes one of the keys to his keychain and hides another in a glass of sardines in the fridge. The third key he tapes underneath the hall stairwell. In case the doctor or someone needs to come check on Beatriz.

He opens a bottle of champagne and blasts the cork over the balcony. He passes the entire weekend shifting from the telly to the terrace to Beatriz's bedside. He remains in a state of constant buzz, barefooted. He shaves his face in the bathroom with its many lamps. Saturday, he spends a lot of time finding a football channel on the large flat-screen. There's a receiver under the telly which needs to be set at 23. As soon as he does so, the sports channel appears. He leaves the television on and listens to the commentators argue as he prepares food and organizes Raúl's CD collection. He doesn't throw anything out, but stacks what he doesn't like and shoves it all into a little cabinet under the stereo. During siesta, he sleeps for half an hour beside Beatriz, and Saturday night he also crawls in under the blankets next to her, falling asleep to the plopping sound of the catheter.

The doctor stops by on Sunday. He examines Beatriz, then says he doesn't believe Erhard knows how to take care of her. He stands on the balcony polishing his sunglasses, speaking in a subdued voice. She's not properly washed and now has bedsores on her left side. Get someone to help you at the very least, the doctor suggests, but Erhard refuses. He doesn't want anyone else involved. His brief meeting with Cormac reminded him how quickly stories circulate. He's certain the doctor will keep his mouth shut, but only because he's in a moral bind and doesn't care to admit it to anyone.

The doctor strongly recommends that she be transferred to the hospital. It is unlikely that she'll awaken. She appears to have had a severe swelling of the brain, which has decreased some, but not completely. He doesn't use the words brain-dead, but Erhard can tell that's what he means. She might be suffering silently, Michel says. But Erhard thinks he's just being a coward.

– I take full responsibility for her, Erhard says. – She's not going anywhere. She has to stay here. If she's brain-dead, then she's brain-dead. A hospital can't change that. If she's suffering, I'll give her some painkillers. You can get them for me. If she ever wakes up, if she ever emerges from this state, she'll do so here.

The doctor seems to accept Erhard's position. He would like to continue to check in on her, but he doesn't want to guarantee anything. Erhard shows him where he hid the key underneath the stairwell. Afterward they drink beer in front of the telly, watching golf being played at some lush course in Spain. The doctor likes golf.

47

He stands quietly at the door for a moment. Even though it leads into the reception area, he sees Marcelis's name on the door. Just as he's about to grab the knob, the door swings open.

– It's Jørgensen, Ana says loudly, stepping aside to allow Erhard to enter. – Ana Lorenzo, administrative assistant. She offers her hand, which is cold as ice. Behind her, the entire office is a mess.

– You're too fucking early, Marcelis shouts from his desk. Erhard reminds himself to act like Marcelis's equal. Don't blink, don't flee, don't get tongue-tied.

– I'm right on time, Erhard says. He wants to ask what has happened, but doesn't want to seem too curious. He fears the two of them have just had a good shag on the secretary's desk, scattering papers and folders onto the floor. But he can tell by the open filing cabinet and the way Marcelis is running around his office lifting stacks of paper that something else is going on.

– What did the accountant say?

– I didn't call him. But he couldn't have been the one here on Friday, Ana says.

– Go call the bloody accountant. Maybe he stopped in.

Ana's just about to say something, but gives up and instead dials the number. Erhard sidles past her and into Marcelis's office. He's busy emptying the archives while cursing out the janitors, the accountants, Ana, and anyone who moves things out of place.

– Are you ready? Erhard says, pressing forward purposefully.

– Fuck no, I'm not ready. Someone removed all my account files, all the shit I was supposed to show you.

– You want to meet another day?

– Just wait until we've heard from the accountant. It was probably him. Ana?

Ana enters. – Alquizola hasn't been here since September.

– What about the janitors? Marcelis asks. – They're always moving my shit around so that I can't find anything.

– We've cut the janitorial service on the weekends. They're only here on Thursday and Monday afternoons.

Silence.

– What about your stupid moving boxes? When are you planning on moving all your shit? They've been here for, what, five months now? The files are probably in one of them.

Ana hurries out of the office. Marcelis sinks into a chair. Erhard doesn't know what to do. – I'm sure they'll turn up, he says.

– Welcome, Marcelis says mirthlessly. – Good way to begin.

– There are copies, right? Don't you always make copies?

– Yes, but they're also fucking gone. There are two files. The original papers and the copies. I don't understand it.

– I thought people put those kinds of things on computers nowadays.

– That's what I fucking thought too, but that fuckface José Alquizola, our accountant, doesn't use computers. He does everything by hand. I hope he drops dead.

Ana stands in the doorway. Erhard hopes she'll announce that she's found the files. – I've searched all of my boxes and they're not in there.

– I know, my dear. That was just something I said.

Marcelis removes some papers from a chair so Erhard can sit down.

– I'll stand.

– Are you planning to stand in your new office, too? I'm getting it ready for you next door.

Raúl's office. It could only be his. Erhard has that strange feeling one gets when something completely wrong is about to happen. As if his entire body is shielding itself from becoming the kind of boss that he's made fun of for decades.

– Office? he says.

– Now that you've got his car, you damn well can't impersonate a director in the break-room. You need an office. Or would you like to sit in here with me? Marcelis closes his door. – As long as you don't get any funny ideas about having additional privileges any time soon, if you know what I mean?

– I don't know what you mean.

Marcelis points to reception. – It's not exactly a secret, I'm aware. Even my wife probably knows. So don't even think about using it against me.

Erhard had considered doing something along those lines, but then decided not to pursue it.

– Palabras said you don't know anything about running a business.

– I'm just a taxi driver, Erhard says, though he actually understands a great deal more than he lets on. He wants to hear Marcelis's explanations, to know whether or not he's being honest about the most important aspects of the business and its finances. – I'd like you to explain everything.

Marcelis stares at Erhard sceptically. – It's not rocket science, it's not even very interesting. But OK. If we're going to do it today, then we won't be able to use the budget and actual figures. I'll just explain how we manage our accounts when the drivers bring us their books and that kind of *Business for Dummies* bullshit.

Marcelis raises the lid of a flat cabinet, revealing a whiteboard. He draws a house and some arrows with money, then adds some boxes and arrows back and forth as he explains how it all works. Ana enters with espressos and some pastries filled with red jelly. Erhard learns that the rumour is true: some drivers get a cut of sixty percent, while others only make forty percent. At TaxiVentura Erhard had himself earned seventy percent for the past six years. He could have earned more if he'd negotiated better. But Erhard found Barouki difficult to talk to, and he wasn't comfortable negotiating and didn't want to ask for anything. Now he sits there watching Marcelis explain Taxinaria's finances, and how it influences liquidity, how the late delivery of drivers' books requires financing at the start of each month, and how they've tried to sell their garage and maybe rent TaxiVentura's. And it occurs to Erhard then that he'll never drive a taxi again. This is where he will sit from now on. In a chair. Alongside Marcelis and others like him. Participating in meetings. Talking. Making decisions. Even though he hopes Raúl will somehow return one day, sunburnt and gaunt after months bingeing on drugs, he feels the thrilling winds of real change. It makes him dizzy. He wants to hold on to something. He asks for something to drink.

– We don't drink until after five o'clock, Marcelis says, without glancing at Erhard. As if he'd been waiting to say just that.

48

This is his first longish drive in the silver-grey Mercedes. He would exchange this vehicle with his old car anytime, but the ride is phenomenal. The car glides so quietly through Las Dunas that he can practically hear the kitesurfers.

He orders a black coffee at Miza's place, then sits at the table flipping one of the business cards Marcelis had printed for him in his hand – apparently to amuse himself. A temporary one, Marcelis said. You'll get proper ones on proper paper, of course. The temporary business cards were printed on thin paper with Taxinaria's blue and gold logo in the corner and his own name and title, Chief Operating Officer, in cursive underneath. He shows it to Miza, who congratulates him and lays homemade almond cookies on his saucer. Erhard doesn't quite know what the title means.

He's surprised at how easygoing Marcelis was. Maybe Marcelis thinks they're on the same team now. Erhard recalls that time Lars Bo Römer jumped from B1909 to Aarhus GF and was booed every time he played in Copenhagen. Can a person change his affiliation just like that? During Marcelis's review, Erhard felt like an infiltrator behind enemy lines – whose assignment was to flush out Marcelis. He listened carefully for holes, vagueness, hesitation, evasiveness, and any attempt to turn Erhard's lack of experience into a reason for simplistic explanations. But Marcelis had been, despite the confusion surrounding the missing files, surprisingly thorough, even though he obviously couldn't dive deeply into every detail in a single afternoon. Afterward they'd gone into Erhard's new office, which Marcelis had had fitted out with some furniture and wall paintings.

– I had the aquarium removed, Marcelis said. – That was Raúl's. And the bar in the corner. He was a little too fond of whisky, if you ask me. Is that your kind of thing, too? Are you also into the finer things?

Erhard shook his head and peered out the window at the courtyard below, where two drivers stood talking. Two new faces among the many Erhard had yet to meet. Behind the courtyard he could see the red mountaintop rising into the sky. Yet another cloudless day.

– What will I actually be doing here? Erhard asked.

Marcelis looked at Erhard and began to laugh. – Good question, he said, picking up the business cards that lay on the table, handing them to Erhard, and explaining that he could start passing them out left and right. – Figure out what you can, and do as much of it as possible. But maybe you can begin by figuring out what we do with the cars. We've just scrapped a cab, and we need to buy a few new ones. We've got an agreement in place with an importer, but I don't know if it's the best deal for us. You know what's required, so maybe it's a good assignment for you. I'll send you some emails detailing our current agreement.

He'd pointed at a large, square computer monitor that covered most of the desk. It wasn't the right time to ask, *How do I read emails?* Afterward, Erhard guardedly asked Ana what he should do, and she printed out some papers for him: summaries of car prices and payment conditions. On the top sheet was the name of a car importer.

He walks down to the water. There's no beach at Alapaqa. Only a series of feeble piers running from the breakwater to the fishermen's two- or three-man cutters and racks of nets. The fish are hanging out to dry, and some dogs bark at a big seagull perched on a drying board.

An importer of cars. He thinks about the car on the beach in Cotillo. Last seen in Amsterdam. Could one register a stolen vehicle here on the islands? Or was that why it didn't have licence plates?

The police certainly knew all the importers, and had sent them inquiries. No doubt there was a vehicle identification number. He imagines containers like the two he'd investigated. A young man breaks in, steals a car, and pays the guard to look the other way. It seems improbable that the theft wouldn't be discovered, or that the car wouldn't be missed, but not impossible. There's a saying on the islands: Paperwork makes busy men tired. There's something to that. No one on the Canary Islands likes to file reports, registrations, or contracts. A car might vanish in a stack of paperwork. A lot happens on the islands, including strange, inexplicable things.

He returns to the now slightly dusty Mercedes parked in the little car park behind Miza's cafe. There are two things he'd like to do. One is to find the car from the beach. Right now it's in police custody in a lot near the Palace. The other is to stop by Casa Negra, the only restaurant on the island that serves African food. As he drives down the narrow road leading through Alapaqa to the high street, he thinks about Casa Negra's extra spicy fish dish with rice. The restaurant is in a shitty location right near the airport's runway, so the table shakes and all the diners sit frozen in place every time a plane comes in for a landing. He'd prefer doing the latter before the former, because he's starving, but decides to head towards the Palace to get that over with.

He drives past the gate that leads up to the Palace's entrance and car park, then all the way round the building. The driveway ends in a stony field. He turns the car round and returns the way he came, this time going south around the Palace. He spots a bunch of parking spaces and abandoned cars, but all the driveways lead to similar businesses, like Retail Invest, Joint Markets, Northeast Invest. There are foreign names and rental companies occupying grey buildings behind grey fences dividing the grey landscape. Then he sees a warehouse at the end of a short road, a hangarlike facility behind a tall fence; the police's shield hangs on a wide gate. Erhard swings the car round, parks, and walks up to the fence. To the left of the gate, on the other side of the fence, is an empty folding chair. A CCTV camera is mounted there on one of the poles above the chair. He stares into its black lens and sees the lot's reflection. A moment later, an unseen door opens in the warehouse and a policewoman approaches him.

– What is your business here? she says from a distance.

– I'm looking for a car, a Volkswagen.

– What is your business? This is police property.

– I'm looking for a car that's gone missing.

– I'll have to ask you to direct your inquiry to the police station. She points in the direction of the Palace. – Remember to ask for an inspection form called RO-19.

Judging by her expression, she has uttered that sentence many times. She has an irregular face, tilting slightly to the left, as if she has had tooth pain or migraines for a very long time. There's also something forced about the way she lets her hair fall over her eyes. Maybe she's trying to cover up some ugly brown welts or something. She's the service-oriented type, who has probably fed a bunch of rug-rats since she was seventeen and still irons her three ex-husbands' shirts.

– Maybe you can help me, Erhard says, stepping right up to the fence. – My company is looking for a car that was never registered, but just disappeared. It would mean a lot to me.

– She studies his business card, which he holds up to the fence.

– Unfortunately you'll need an RO-19.

He takes a chance. – I know it's in there. I would just like to see it, that's all. A blue Volkswagen Passat.

– I would like to help you, but I can't.

– Give me two minutes, that's all I'm asking.

– I'm afraid I can't help you, she says a little hesitantly.

She would've already gone back inside if she was going to stand her ground. But he needs to use soft arguments. – Señorita… Vasquez. He sees the name written on her badge. – A little boy was found dead in the backseat of this car. I'm trying to locate his mother, and I need to see the car.

The woman now removes her sunglasses and rubs her eyes, scrutinizing Erhard. He must look like an innocent old man, because she quickly puts the glasses back on and whispers, –I'll check the computer to see if we have a Passat.

To let him in, she'll have to press a large button located on an electrical box a few metres from the fence. She eyes Erhard.

– Why is a taxi company searching for her? Isn't that a police matter?

Erhard doesn't have a good response. – Unfortunately, Señorita, your colleagues are too busy with other cases. Only a few of us worry about dead kids.

It's not an answer to her question, and it's risky. If she doesn't have children of her own, she'll sniff out his manipulation. But if she has children, then she'll push the button.

She loses her focus for a moment. – What happened to the boy?

– The Cotillo case?

– Oh, yeah. I've heard of that.

He tries to nudge her. – Can you believe she abandoned him in a cardboard box?

She regards Erhard at length. Then she pushes the button. – You have to promise you won't touch the vehicle. It's the only thing I request.

– I just need to see it. I'll stand a few metres away and just look.

– Everything in here is evidence.

The gate begins to creak open.

– Here, take my card. And you have me on film, of course. Erhard points at the camera. – I won't touch anything, and I'm not trying to destroy a case.

– I'll give you three minutes, Señor. I'll go with you.

As soon as he's inside, she presses the button again, and the gate closes.

The facility is dark. A few faint lamps light up as Erhard and the woman walk among the rows of cars, motorcycles, boxes of junk, and strange objects wrapped in plastic. Everything divided into numbered units. Only one out of every eight units or so houses a car. Or the remains of a car. He sees flattened vehicles, charred delivery vans, a roofless bus.

They walk in silence. The place reminds him of a mortuary. A war mortuary with dead soldiers. Every item has a story. A fate. A police report. They pass a huge cage, its door swung open, the kind that can hold a tiger or a bear. A motorcycle sidecar without a motorcycle. A chest freezer. He wants to ask the woman where all the things come from. What are their stories? But he knows she won't answer. And he'd rather save his questions for later. They pass a row of cars, some dark blue and one a Volkswagen. Erhard just shakes his head, it's not the right one. He needs to stroll around without the tall woman nipping at his heels. He pauses before a row of peculiar items, twisted and unrecognizable in the darkness. The woman's torch sweeps swiftly over them: an exercise bike, a fountain, a bar stool. It's almost funny. A kind of grotesque children's game, in which one must remember everything one has seen. But his smile quickly fades. In reality, it's all just row after row of worthless stuff that, at the end of the month, will be hauled to the dump north of the city.

– You've got many fine things here. Are you responsible for all of it?

She seems uncertain whether or not he's being ironic. – You could say that. Me and Levi, our carrier, and a few night watchmen.

Erhard tries to think of something with which to praise her without sounding phony. People like her love that kind of thing. – Most people would probably turn on more lights, he says, but you manage with just your torch. You must have guts, Señorita Vasquez. You're a rare breed.

That last part was a bit over the top and didn't sound like a compliment, but the guard didn't seem to notice.

– I'm just doing my job, she says, flashing her torch on another car, a Seat.

Erhard shakes his head, and they continue down through the centre of the hall.

– Well, thank you for your help anyway.

– It's nothing. When was it confiscated?

The girl's photograph from Cotillo Beach was taken on 6 January.

– About a month ago, he says. It's hard to believe.

– Then we should've gone…

Before she completes her sentence, he sees the car and stops. Dark-blue, but black in the darkness. A 2011 model.

– May I borrow that? he says, meaning the torch.

She shines the light on him. – But don't touch it. She hands him the torch as if it were an axe.

Erhard approaches the car. He runs the torch over the body, bottom up, searching for sand marks along its sides, and peers through the windows into the backseat as if the box with the boy was still inside. Then he walks around the car and squats next to the bumper. The guard stands beneath the lamps and is just about to say something, but Erhard makes sure to keep his distance. He studies the bumper. He keeps the torch light trained on it, scanning from left to right, and before long begins to see movement in the lacquered, shiny surface. He lets his eyes roam back the other way now, slower this time. He's certain he'll find a mark, a dent. When the guard steps back a couple paces, Erhard quickly slides his fingers across the rear of the car. Smooth as only a factory-new car can be. A fact that surprises him. He stands and walks around the car.

– Two minutes, Señor.

– OK.

Erhard squats next to the front bumper. It's just as shiny and smooth as the rear bumper. He focuses on the minutest details, but the guard — now standing a couple of yards behind him — puts him on edge, and his eyes dart this way and that, unable to locate what he's looking for. Inch by inch he inspects the bumper's natural curves, created by some computer somewhere in Volkswagen's design department. Perfectly executed and perfectly painted. He sees nothing out of the ordinary.

– Time's up, Señor. I'm sorry, but…

Erhard gets to his feet, and the guard begins to guide him back towards the door. Swiftly he spins and runs the pads of his fingers across the bumper. The guard turns and yells at him, but he's half-concealed in darkness and can now feel, in the very centre of the bumper, a level bump, a directional shift that didn't come from the factory. It's a 20-centimetre-wide area, which can only have been made by something large and heavy. That's why he didn't see it before; it was too big for him to see it. He'd been searching for something minute, but he was looking at the wrong scale. Erhard turns towards the woman and raises his hands.

– I'm sorry. I just had to feel it.

She has brought her telephone nearly to her ear, as if she's called someone, but she hasn't said a word. She looks at the telephone, then presses a button and clips the phone back on her belt. – I told you not to touch anything. You better come with me.

She's not simply irritated, but also hurt, as if he's disappointed her personally. She nudges him towards the door. Behind them, the lights snap off.

– I'm sorry, he says over his shoulder.

– I don't think you are.

– You won't get in trouble. No one knows I'm even here.

– Yes, I will.

– I just needed to see the car. For the boy's sake.

– Stop nattering about that boy. That's just a story you invented to trick me. They've reached the door, and now head outside. The light is strong, but the air is sweet. – I need to ask you to leave, Señor, she says, as if he's not already on his way, and she buzzes him out the gate. Erhard wants to thank her one last time, but before he can say anything, she's turned her back on him and retreated inside the hangar.

He returns to his car and drives to Casa Negra. He orders the spicy codfish and a tall glass of beer, even though he's told himself that he's not allowed to drink any more today. While he waits, he jots down every possible scenario on a napkin: The car was stolen in Amsterdam and later from a container terminal. The car was stolen in Amsterdam and sold to the mother or father here on the island. The car was… He can't bring himself to write this one down. The car was stolen in Amsterdam, fell out of a container on the open sea, and somehow washed ashore here on Fuerteventura.

49

Already in the lift he hears something. Music and choppy voices all the way up through the shaft. When he passes the fourth floor, he thinks it must be Raúl. So he's returned home after all. So he's just been on one of his drinking binges with his friends, stuffing drugs into every orifice, under the radar, outside of Daddy's reach and far away from everyone who loves him, so that no one could try to bring him back. So he's returned to a life in almost total overhaul. So he's home again. He's found Beatriz, and he'll ask Erhard who was cremated and poured into an urn in Alto Blanco. The game is over. In the best-case scenario it's back to Majanicho for him.

Then he remembers the new set of keys. The noise must be coming not from his flat, but the corridor. The doors of the lift open. There are twenty or twenty-five people standing in the hallway. It's the classic crowd one finds in any bar, just dressed in finer clothes, ties, and gold necklaces instead of ragged tattoos on their ankles. He searches for Raúl's eyes, bloodshot after weeks of drinking and random sex. He searches for his friend's face. But as he scans the crowd, it occurs to him that his friend isn't among them. He will never be here. They are hired men and women, no one you know or like. They are little more than sandwich boards, rented to fill space. A pair of Maasai girls stand together against the wall, waiting as if for a big blowout sale. None among the crows seems to know who Erhard is, or even care to find out. He cuts through the throng and towards the door, next to which, preoccupied with a Maasai girl – the nearly coal-coloured doll – stands Emanuel Palabras.

– Piano Tuner, he says loudly, hurrying to pour a glass of champagne that he hands to Erhard.

– What are we celebrating?

– Your first day of work.

– I would hardly call it a day's work.

– Get used to it. You're the director now. You've no need to tally up your hours any longer.

– So you thought you'd bring over some whores and homeless people in suits.

– Speak nicely about my ladies of the night. They hear you. Besides, it's hardly your flat, but mine. Even if you've changed the lock.

– I thought you said the flat gave you the creeps.

– If I tell you to party with the best girls and boys on the island that money can buy, then that's what you should do.

There's something in the tone that sickens Erhard. It makes him feel bought and paid for. The man he's visited and helped for many years, and whom he almost viewed as a friend, is in reality a calculating businessman. But he cannot muster the strength to tackle it now.

– If we're going to party like this, we'll do it on the rooftop terrace, not in the flat. I don't want to see a single one of your little friends down here, or you, Señor Palabras, unless it's to go home or to use the loo. Agreed?

– You've accustomed yourself to this fine station rather quickly, Palabras says. – But we'll be good, of course, won't we ladies and gentlemen?

Everyone nods their assent.

Erhard keys open the door and steps inside the flat, snapping on the light. He stands blocking the hallway to the bedroom and watches the group march into the living room, then out on the balcony, and finally up onto the rooftop terrace led by Palabras and the hobbling Charles. One of the girls kicks off her high heels, and one of the men opens another bottle of champagne.

He checks on Beatriz and locks the bedroom door before taking a glass of champagne and heading up to the terrace. One of the perfumed girls tries to sit on his lap and wrap an arm around him, but he pushes her gently away. Palabras talks about celebrating his victories and grieving his losses. It's the lot of the mediocre man to let his days merge into one grey lump, he says. One should drink champagne any chance one gets. It's the only civilized thing to do, Palabras roars across the terrace.

They rearrange the furniture and empty the bar. Erhard already feels as though these are his things, and it irritates him how they're making themselves at home. They even brought a small transistor radio, and they are playing a little too much electronica, a little too much canned music.

– You owe me a key, Emanuel Palabras says behind two girls. He sounds almost like Raúl when he's drunk.

Erhard grins. He doesn't know what to say.

– It's my property, Piano Tuner.

– Then move into the flat below me.

– I'd hoped you'd be inclined to be a little friendlier.

– I'm inclined to have a little peace and quiet. Thanks for the party, but I prefer my home being mine, not a nightclub.

– So you won't give me a key? Charles, say something to him.

But Charles does nothing. One of the girls is sitting on his lap like a ventriloquist's dummy, drinking red wine.

– It's my flat.

– But I need to know that this is my home. I don't like you coming and going. It's not about you, it's about… *Hmm, what is it about? It's about feeling secure, safe, somewhere.*

Palabras continues: – I can request the locksmith make an extra key. He does what I tell him.

– I wish there were others besides me to keep you in check.

Emmanuel Palabras throws his hands up as if it's all poppycock. Erhard wonders if he'll ever feel at home in this flat, or whether it'll always be in a kind of no-man's land. Maybe a home is defined as a place where one can be alone, by oneself, in the singular. And the elder Palabras feels that he can come and go whenever it pleases him. He raises his glass to Palabras and chugs the expensive – no doubt several hundred euros – champagne in one gulp, which he knows irritates Palabras. The night is full of shooting stars, or at least he read that it would be in the newspaper. He hasn't seen any himself, but maybe that's because his eyes are mostly closed.

By two in the morning, Palabras resembles one of his wooden masks. His face appears softened from exhaustion. It occurs to Erhard that he himself must look just as tired. The Maasai girls have shuffled over to the bar and are drinking champagne, talking softly, incomprehensibly, in their own language, while the young men sit on the balcony stairs smoking. Charles helps Palabras out of his chair and brushes crisps from his jacket. Erhard almost feels tenderness for him. Charles thanks Erhard, then commands the Maasai girls and the men to clean up and carry the glasses down to the kitchen. As they leave, Palabras just raises his arm in farewell before he follows the others.

It's as if they were never even there. It wouldn't surprise him if he went down to the kitchen and found everything in its right place. But the atmosphere has shifted. It's a Monday night, and all is quiet. Not good in Corralejo. It's the sound of unemployment. Of a dearth of tourists. He gets to his feet to trundle off to bed. There's a large wet stain on his trousers. Right on his crotch. As if someone poured a drink on him.

The next day he decides to go to work. On the street, he pauses at Silón's shop to admire a black briefcase. It's one of those with a simple code-lock mechanism, which opens with a click. He lays his book, pillbox, and a long baguette into the case and snaps it shut. Silón asks for thirty euros, but Erhard gets it for twelve. Leaving his things inside the case, he walks to the Mercedes. He beeps the car open, climbs in, and drops the briefcase on the passenger seat. If Annette could see him now. She wouldn't believe it. She would think he was heading to a costume party. She would think he was someone else.

Taxinaria's offices are modern and colourful and resemble those built in the new part of Puerto. He has to punch in a code to enter, but luckily one of the girls from the service – which is what they call their dispatch – is on her way into the office at the same time. He walks down a long corridor next to a travelator, past a few quiet offices and the break-room, which is dark. He tries to buy a cup of coffee from the vending machine in the hall, but can't get it to work. He pulls a bottled water from the refrigerator and sits down to read the previous day's newspaper, which lies on his desk.

Shortly after eight o'clock, someone begins to putter in reception. He stares through the slit in the door, watching Ana organize her things on the table and touch the soil on the plant in the windowsill. A somewhat sad-looking girl – probably Lene's age, mid thirties – dressed in over-sized trainers. Erhard doesn't like to see women in trainers, and he can't imagine Lene wearing them. Last time he saw her, she was wearing huge winter boots from Bilka, the Danish big-box chain where Annette bought most of the things for the children. She is a girl who's used to being abandoned, used to cleaning up after others, used to people around her exploding, breaking down, talking to her meanly, talking badly about her, groping her – without ever complaining. She's a girl who can survive anything, but will never be happy. He hopes he's wrong.

– *Buenas*, he says softly.

– *Buenas*, she says, her back to him as if she already knew he was there.

– Do you know anything about cars?

She turns to face him. – Should I?

She thinks it's a trick question.

– I don't know anything about them, he says. – I just drive them.

She smiles apprehensively. – I don't know much, either.

– The papers you printed for me yesterday. Marcelis says I should evaluate some cars for us to purchase. But I'd like to see some old contracts and do a comparison.

– They're on the drive. On the computer, she adds when he stares at her dumbly. – Would you like me to print them out for you?

– That would be very helpful.

In that moment he sees all the years of irritation and frustration, not pronounced in her eyes but more in a wrinkle forming between them, a wrinkle that has registered all the inept, idiotic, incompetent, and irresponsible men who have made her life miserable. Then the wrinkle smoothes out, and she bends over her desk and looks at her computer. – I'll bring it in, she says. Her helpfulness is practised, and apparently not just reserved for the boss she's shagging.

While he waits, he pulls his book from his briefcase. It's one of the books he brought with him when he moved into the new flat. He chose it because the cover showed an image of a black telephone on a wooden floor. The story's about a female otologist who is recruited to join a team of experts who are tasked with capturing an international terrorist. The culprit, described as a computer genius, has made a machine that rings up people and kills them with an ultrasonic sound. Ultratone. Hence the title. Erhard knows the plot only because he's read the back of the book. He's still reading the first chapter, where we meet the doctor at a conference as she's reviving an old fling with an investment expert from New York City. He reads a passage several times. In it the doctor waits, hot and horny, at her lover's hotel room, until she calls the front-desk clerk and discovers that he has checked out. He's gone. It's a ridiculous novel. Erhard knows that. But he thinks about the doctor, the emptiness she feels in a strange place, and it almost makes him weep.

He manages to sit up in his chair just before Ana enters with the papers and walks him through them, pointing with a pen that's wet with spit because she'd had it in her mouth. Cute. After she has left, he studies the papers disinterestedly. He has nothing to add. It occurs to him that the Volkswagen Passat is a more popular vehicle than he'd previously thought. Through the years, Taxinaria has owned more than fifteen Passats, which had their heyday shortly after 2000.

He walks with Ana to the lunch room. Though everyone apparently eats in the same room, the drivers have their own area behind a row of potted plants, while the others – management, Ana, the sales staff, and the telephone girls – sit closest to the kitchen. At TaxiVentura he'd often heard the drivers go on about the girls and the bosses who were too hoity-toity to sit with the likes of them, but now it occurs to Erhard that it might create problems bringing the two together in an ostensibly equal space, since there is a deep cleft between those who labour in an office for thirty-five hours a week and those who drive a taxi seventy hours a week. With an inverse salary distribution.

He eats pan-seared potatoes and lamb skewers. One of the advantages of working here is that he doesn't need to bring his own lunch. Meals are prepared in the restaurant, Muñoz, next door and carried over on large trays. It's nothing special, but it's much better than what he could ever make. He doesn't talk to anyone. Ana's absorbed in conversation with some of the women whose names and voices he'd heard on those occasions when, out of curiosity, he'd switched over to Taxinaria's frequency. They're discussing the drivers who suddenly turn up in the office bearing flowers or chocolate and making wild gestures, because they've sat far too long in their taxis listening to the bickering and the commentary, and they've fallen in love with the soft voices on the radio.

So did Erhard once. It was many years ago. Michela was her name. The way she talked, every driver thought she was speaking directly to him. For weeks he considered how to go about it, how he would approach her. The problem was, there were few valid reasons for a driver to enter the office. In the end he decided he would wait for her to get off work, then drive her home. That was convenient and offered the least amount of risk. But the day before he was to carry out his plan, he'd learned that all the other drivers – even Luís – had the same thought in mind. Suddenly the idea seemed silly and uninspired, and he felt a kind of disgust at his own desperation. Since then, he's seen the pattern emerge time and again. The drivers are bored, lonely souls, and the girls have refined their voices for years, developing a poisonous instrument as compensation for the immoderate bodies they conceal behind garish dresses. At Taxinaria too, the two girls with the most passionate voices are decidedly plump, while the other three – including the Tunisian, Alissa – have coarse, horse-like features that make them appear big-boned. They talk over one another about their husbands and boyfriends, their dogs, and a new film that was screened on the wall of a house down near the harbour. Ana listens and laughs guardedly as if she's never heard of anything like it.

He heads back to the office. He has no interest in reading the novel about the telephone terrorist. He picks up the car paperwork again. It's a print-out from a dealer's website. At the bottom of the last page he sees a name and telephone number. He lifts the telephone and dials the number. If he's lucky, he can reach him before siesta.

– Autovenga, good afternoon.

– Hello. I'm calling from Taxinaria. My name is Erhard Jørgensen. May I speak to Gilberto Peyón?

– Speaking. New or used?

– Hardly ever used.

– I'm not sure I follow.

Erhard can tell that Gilberto needs to warm up a little before he begins asking him for favours. – The best you have, he says. – I'm the new director here and I'm looking to purchase a few new cars.

Erhard hopes the office door is closed.

– Where did you say you were calling from?

The line crackles.

Erhard starts from the beginning, and this time the man is livelier.

– It would be a pleasure to supply you again. I don't mean to offend, but I thought our partnership was over?

– Why? Erhard asks.

– Palabras said he could get others to supply him with cheaper vehicles.

– Emanuel?

– Raúl. But I've heard that he's dead.

– Don't believe everything you hear.

The car dealer laughs. Confused. – That's true.

– I'm looking for the best of the best, Erhard says. He guesses that the dealer is the ambitious type: the eager salesman who in four years hopes to run his own dealership.

– Let's cut a deal.

– But first, Erhard says. The line clicks as if the salesman received a shock through the phone. – I need some information about a particular vehicle. A vehicle that was ordered... for a colleague.

– With us?

– I don't think so. But I wondered if you might look it up somewhere and see what has been ordered? My old colleague was the one who ordered it. He was a bit sloppy. I hope you're not as sloppy.

– No, we're not.

– Good. It's a blue Volkswagen Passat from 2010, 2011, or 2012.

– From Spain?

– Maybe, but via Amsterdam.

– When was it ordered?

– I don't know.

– Under what name?

– I don't know.

The line goes quiet. – A Passat, you say?

– Yes.

– One moment.

A long silence.

– Hello. There have been no Passat orders to the island since the end of 2010. No Volkswagens at all, in fact.

– How many other companies import Volkswagens to the island?

– There's Bruno Tullo out near Vallebrón, but I don't think he sells any more. In fact, I think he's dead.

– OK. Then let me ask you: How might a Passat stolen in Amsterdam, without plates and with thirty miles on the odometer, now be parked in Cotillo?

– I don't know. That kind of thing... we don't do that kind of thing.

– No, I hope not. But how would one do that?

– There have been cases of stolen vehicles here on the island, but they are rare. They're hard to hide. Everything needs to go through Puerto. Through Ruiz.

– Ruiz?

– The customs officer here in Puerto. Trust me, he doesn't let any cars slip past him. Ruiz has earned his fair share on each and every car that drives on the island.

– So, theoretically, one could convince Ruiz to allow a car onto the island, even if it's stolen?

– Theoretically, yes. But not if you knew Ruiz. He may be an idiot, but if I may say so, he's a stickler for Spanish law. If he found out there was a car on the island without his approval, he would find the person who brought it here and force him to pay the duty. He's not someone you try to cheat.

– How do I find him?

– He's at the harbour. At Customs.

Erhard jots this down. – Listen, if you do me a favour and get in touch with Ruiz and ask him if knows anything about a dark-blue Passat that was brought to the island in the last three months, then I'd be more than happy to strike a deal with you. Two cars on the expensive side.

The salesmen sounds more upbeat, but also uneasy. – I'm happy to hear that, Señor Jørgensen. But Ruiz is not so easy to get in touch with. He doesn't like taking phone calls.

– Then stop by his office. The harbour can't be more than a few miles from where you work.

When the conversation is over, Erhard is dripping with sweat. Every muscle in his body quivers tensely, ready to snap. He slumps over his desk. All he wants now is for Ana to fetch him a glass of water.

He spends the afternoon on a walk. On the street he bumps into a few of the drivers having a cigarette, and one who's filling in a cross-word puzzle on his telephone. He talks to them briefly. Mostly he listens, twice adding that he hopes his many years behind the wheel can help make life better for the drivers and also for Taxinaria. They seem to like the idea, but aren't as excited as he'd hoped. We'll see, the man who was doing the crossword puzzle says, before heading back to his car.

Time passes incredibly slowly.

It's not even siesta yet, and he feels more tired than he's ever been following a fourteen-hour shift. Maybe his body can't tolerate office work. Maybe it can't tolerate the absence of a cold beer or a warm whisky. He ends up sprawled across the broad windowsill with a cup of coffee, reading the terrorist novel. The otologist is off to meet England's prime minister in a secret bunker on the Isle of Man. Before dinner, she changes into a fancy gown and spends more than one page describing her appearance in the mirror. *The gown highlighted my thighs and all those years I spent on the Stepmaster in the living room. My breasts were as inviting as any woman's could be after giving birth to two children and without plastic surgery – with only a little padding in the beige-coloured top from Victoria's Secret.* The book was written for another time, another gender, another universe, and Erhard feels like a visitor, a slimy little Peeping Tom. Just as he's about to throw the book away, Ana knocks on the door with a message from Gilberto.

– He asked me to tell you that Ruiz doesn't know the vehicle in question. She gives him a quizzical look.

– Thank you, Ana, Erhard says, then has to come up with an excuse. – It's something to do with the new cars. He helped me find the right one.

She nods and closes the door on her way out.

He throws the book in the rubbish bin. The image of the otologist in her bra is hard to let go of.

THE CARGO SHIP

7 February–17 February

50

Erhard figured that Aaz would somehow notice the new car. But the Boy-Man's sitting rigidly in his seat, as usual, and they make it all the way to Las Dunas before he rolls the window down, and something in his movements seems to register that it's a new car, a new way to roll down the window.

So you finally got a new car.

– Do you like it?

Better than the old one.

– The old one was OK.

The old one was terrible, its suspension hurt my butt.

– Watch the language, young man.

You have to admit that this one is better. The air conditioning is better. It sounds better. It smells better.

– It's nice, I admit.

What do you think about taking over Raúl's job and his car?

– Don't you think I deserve it?

One doesn't always get what one deserves.

– If Raúl returns, I'll just say thanks for letting me borrow your car and go back to my old job, my old house.

What if he doesn't return? Then you'll be trapped in that mind-numbing job.

– It's better than sitting in an old Mercedes every day, on the same dusty road, earning a salary that can't even support an old man and his two goats.

You've never complained.

– Trust me, Aaz, it hasn't been fun. Why can't a man have a taste of the good life after many years…

What if Raúl comes back? Will you be able to return to your old life? After driving the new car, living in a luxury flat, drinking expensive wine with the upper crust, and playing doctor with his girlfriend? You can't.

– He threw his life away, don't you agree? What I've done is pick up all the pieces. I can always, always, return to my old life. The Mercer was never mine, so I'll never see it again, but the house is only locked up as if I'm on holiday.

So you'll just say, 'Thanks for letting me use your flat and car and luxurious life', then go back to Laurel and Hardy?

– I've lived on this island for nearly twenty years, and during that time not a damn thing has changed. Now that an opportunity has presented itself, are you telling me not to take it?

Will you stop driving me?

– No. It's my favourite thing to do every week, driving an overgrown boy who talks my ear off. Why do you think I've got myself such a fine car?

Will we have time to drive out to see the kites on the beach?

– Yes, Aaz. Someday I'll get a note from your mum, and then we can go see the kites. You can sit on the beach and drink warm tea, while I try to stand on one of the surfboards. It'll be quite the sight.

Mónica is standing outside the house today, as if she has been expecting them for some time. She has prepared omelettes, which Aaz loves. They sizzle warmly on the plates. Cautiously she asks Erhard if he wishes to come in. It doesn't feel like a matter of course. She slices off triangular chunks of omelette and serves them with rosemary. As they eat, they listen to the canaries in the garden. He tells Mónica the news.

At first she's indignant, and practically laughs at him. She knows the Palabrases and isn't crazy about them. She shifts in her seat, picking at the little vase of flowers from the garden which rests in the centre of the table. She thinks Erhard's trying to back out of their agreement, but he assures her that he'll continue to drive Aaz every Wednesday. Hopefully he'll even have time to take him to the beach now and then. Or maybe the flea market in Gran Tarajal. Mónica quietly tines small hunks of egg with her fork.

After the meal, she turns on the telly and lets Aaz sit in the plush chair to watch the programme with the turtle and the fish who run an underwater grocery.

Erhard helps clean up the kitchen. He rinses a plate and sets a jar of sun-dried tomatoes back in the fridge. There's something private about gazing into the fridge. He doesn't inspect the shelves, but gazes straight ahead as he sets the jar on the lowest shelf. He can't bear the thought of seeing Mónica's little weaknesses: the jam, coconut macaroons in a little bag, or tinned pickles.

– We need to leave in half an hour, he tells Aaz.

– As long as this doesn't happen every time, Mónica says. – I'd hoped he could stay for dinner.

He's arranged to stop by Autovenga and check out two vehicles. He'd figured he could drive Aaz back before then.

– Then I'll have to return later, he says.

But it has no mitigating effect on her.

– Forget it, she says. She's standing at a small mirror in the corner, near the refrigerator, and applying lipstick. – I release you from your duties. We'll manage without your help. We've done it before.

Erhard doesn't know how to respond. But he's certain she means to wound him. She doesn't realize that he's not helping for Aaz's sake or hers; he's helping for his own. But it sounds all wrong, selfish.

– I've already made sure that I'm available every Wednesday morning so that I can drive him, Erhard says.

But the truth is he hasn't told anyone what he does on Wednesday mornings, and he won't ask for permission like some kind of teenager, especially not from Marcelis. When he left the office, he told Ana that he was going to meet with Autovenga. Which is true, but he didn't say anything about giving someone a free taxi ride. He can damn well do whatever he pleases.

Mónica brews coffee in the Italian kettle. He drinks it as he watches television, while she goes out in the garden.

– Come visit me on Saturday, he tells her when she says goodbye to Aaz through the rolled-down window. The words just come blurting out of him. Maybe the result of guilt, maybe something else, but so what? He doesn't know what he would do with Beatriz, but perhaps he could just lock the door, like he did when Emanuel stopped by.

Mónica doesn't seem to understand, but also doesn't seem hostile to the idea, either. At most reluctant.

– To thank you for letting me drive your son and for your help with the computer. He imagines Aaz saying, *C'mon, Mum, let's do it.* On one hand, he hopes she'll say no, that she'll reject his invitation. But on the other, he would like to see Aaz. And her. Under different circumstances. He would like to show her that he has something to offer. – If there's a football match, Aaz can watch it on my widescreen telly.

– Is that wise? she asks. Predictably.

– Maybe not. If Barça loses, he'll probably smash the entire flat.

She flashes a faint smile.

– Are you sure about this?

Her doubt seems so deep-seated, so heart-wrenching. He has heard the question his entire life, and he has often asked himself the same thing. He has to turn away before he can respond. – Yes, he says simply. He can't emphasize it enough, and yet he has nothing else to add.

She glances at Aaz, who stares straight ahead through the windscreen as if they're rolling across an interesting landscape. – Then we'll be there.

All he manages to do is give her a smile before she retreats from the window, and says: – Pick us up at noon.

He thought it was difficult to stop drinking. But it's nothing compared to the feeling of stress and confusion that fills him every day when Ana tries to go over his daily assignments with him. There's a management meeting, a board of directors meeting, a monthly meeting, a coffee meeting, a personnel meeting, and above all else: customer meetings. A number of meetings with business clients who wish to be wined and dined before they choose a taxi company.

Ana explains that they can hold the meetings in his office at the little round table with its ergonomic chairs, or down at Restaurant Muñoz, where they've installed bullfighting posters and bottles of sherry in a backroom. He doesn't know anything about these kinds of meetings. He's concerned that he'll need to use proper manners and speak business jargon. He's concerned they will view him as some lousy driver who's bitten off more than he can chew and take him for a ride in negotiations. Nervous, he goes to the bathroom several times at Muñoz before the first meeting with the deputy manager of the Gran Hotel & Spa Atlantis.

But he turns out to be just a young man in a jean jacket. Luckily their sancocho is edible after hours of simmering and lots of pepper. Erhard spills hot sauce on his shirt and tries to remove it with the napkin, which only makes it worse. The deputy manager just thinks it's funny; he seems uneasy, pushing his stew around with his spoon, talking non-stop. He used to work at McDonald's, it turns out, and he doesn't know how long he can stand living on the island. He glances at his mobile phone, as if he expects a call of utmost importance, and orders a beer. Erhard orders one for himself, thinking to hell with Marcelis and his rules.

Erhard knows the Gran Hotel, has often driven customers to and fro. The driveway runs uphill, so a person has to walk up a long, steep stairwell to reach the hotel. Many of the drivers don't want to schlep the luggage up to the foyer, and Erhard's usually knackered after helping an American with four or five suitcases. There's nothing the hotel can do about it, the deputy manager explains. We don't have the time to pick up suitcases for all our guests, and besides, the porter is no spring chicken; he's worked at the hotel for twenty years and all he cares to do is open doors, collect tips, and look for celebrities. We can't fire him. He's somebody's uncle's sister's husband.

– What if our drivers carry up the luggage? Erhard says.

– We've had that arrangement. The young drivers don't care to do it. They're busy. And the old ones, no offence, they aren't capable. Like Alberto.

– If I can get the drivers to do it, do we have a deal?

– TaxiVentura can get there in seven minutes. I've been told that Taxinaria can do it in six.

Erhard knows this is a lie. Gran Hotel & Spa Atlantis is remote. There's no development nearby, just a few ordinary stretches of beach. It's a question of luck, getting to the hotel in seven minutes. From Puerto north, where the taxis park outside the theatres, it takes a minimum of eleven minutes to reach the hotel. – We can be there within thirteen minutes.

The deputy manager laughs. He tosses out a few of the hotel's catchphrases. How they are customer-oriented, how they do their best to go beyond the customer's expectations, training their personnel's customer-service intelligence. But all that depends on pushing more than 3,000 guests a month, on average, through the machine, and during the summer that figure rises to 8,000. He makes it sound like a mincer. – We can't afford to let them wait for thirteen minutes.

Now it's Erhard's turn to laugh. – Make them a good cup of coffee for four euros while they wait. Let them relax.

The deputy manager hadn't considered that. Instead he says: What do *you* think about your offer?

– I think it's realistic. I think the person who told you we can do it in under eleven minutes is irresponsible.

– It was Marcelis Osasuna last year when I sat with him in this very restaurant. Ate the same sancocho. If nothing else, you're persistent.

– I'm not Marcelis. But Marcelis doesn't know anything about driving a taxi. Marcelis knows how to run a business, Erhard says. And Marcelis knows how to send me to meetings like this one. – I can't get the taxis there any faster, but I can give you a realistic offer that you can count on, and ensure that our drivers help your guests with their luggage.

The deputy manager says nothing, but raises his glass as he studies Erhard. – Excuse my impertinence, but where the hell did they dig you up?

– Cotillo Beach, Erhard says simply. The deputy manager laughs. It's an infectious laughter. Erhard can't help joining in.

Soon the bored head waiter returns with half-melted bowls of ice-cream with tinned peaches.

– A few years ago, the deputy manager says, poking around in the dessert, – this was the peak of Fuerteventura's gastronomical capacity. Sad-looking, unserious, tinned food. The sancocho was average, but this is a joke, a disgrace. We need to do better if we're going to survive as a tourist destination. Do you know how many bad reviews this place has on TripAdvisor? More than ninety. Ninety people have spent time writing negative reviews about this shithole restaurant, because they've sat here and stuck their spoons into an absurdly disgusting bowl of ice cream that costs four and a half euros. That's what we're up against. Every time someone fucks something up here on the island, a flag is raised on the Internet to the delight and benefit of anyone who wants to avoid a four-hour flight just to be treated like an idiot.

Erhard knows what the man means; he's heard about instant Internet reviews, but he has a hard time believing it. On the other hand, Alina and Mónica found images rather swiftly on the Internet that were only a few days old. Everything moves so bloody fast now. One would hardly believe that anyone had enough time to post images online, but some don't seem to do anything else.

– You don't understand a word of what I'm saying, do you? the deputy manager says.

– No, Erhard says. No reason to explain himself.

The deputy manager laughs again. – Fantastic. You look like a wasted drunkard three days before his retirement, and we're sitting here at one of the island's shittiest restaurants. Still, you've given me hope, or what passes for hope, that we can still work together and earn some good money. You can pass that on to your boss.

– He's not my boss. I belong to no one.

The deputy manager's smile vanishes. – OK, he says. The vanilla ice cream melts while they drain their beers.

*

After that he begins to enjoy the meetings. He still feels awkward around his former colleagues. Sitting and drinking and eating doesn't feel like work, but the meetings go well. He gets Ana to reserve a table at Miza's instead, and even though the food is a salad or a sandwich, it's better than Muñoz. The view is better too, and Erhard feels more at home. He wins five contracts before he gets his first taste of defeat. The female head of sales, the so-called Customer Experience Officer, from the Oasis Park Zoo doesn't like the fishermen's city of Alapaqa and seems uncomfortable. She says she would rather sign a pact with someone who knows the island and respects its culture. He tries to explain to her that he does indeed know the island, but she notes that neither Osasuna nor Erhard are from Fuerteventura. And besides, Osasuna has a reputation for being disloyal. In the end it sounds as though she has talked to Barouki or already received a good offer, and Erhard is forced to give up. Miza, who overheard the conversation, rests a hand on Erhard's shoulder when she strolls past him.

At the office, he sees flashes of the same hostility.

One morning he meets Marcelis out in the hallway and says hello. – Señor Castilla, I presume, Marcelis practically shouts. Erhard already knows what's coming next. Castilla is the main character in *El Comisario*, the most popular Spanish detective series, which airs every Thursday. Erhard has watched a few episodes at the cafe. – You are well aware that you are contractually obligated not to work a second job. I don't go around building houses in my spare time.

He knows exactly what Marcelis is driving at, but he steers it in another direction. – Palabras gave me permission to continue with some clients on the side.

– I'm not referring to your piano tuning. I mean your detective work.

– I don't have detective work.

– You know what I'm talking about, Jørgensen. Apparently, people are talking about it. Ana brought it to my attention.

It takes Erhard by surprise. She hasn't said a word about it. – It's nothing, he says. – It's like putting a jigsaw puzzle together. It's just something I spend a little time thinking about. Nothing more. It's not a second job.

– Well, stop assembling your puzzle. Just do your job.

Erhard is unable to muster a reply before Marcelis stomps off in the direction he came from. He considers speaking to Emanuel and asking him to put Marcelis in his place, but he knows that, since he has to work with Marcelis, that's not a good solution. Besides, Palabras would probably say the same: Do your job, forget about your little exploration.

Those who don't know him very well, like young Mijael and Gustavo, easily accept that he's the new director without giving it a second thought, but Luís sends him dirty looks and stops talking whenever Erhard marches down the corridor with his vending-machine coffee. One afternoon, Erhard sits down in the break-room to talk with the drivers who stop in during siesta. At first they don't say much, but before long they forget that Erhard is one of the directors, and they begin to complain as usual – about the system and their hours. Erhard simply listens, then heads to his office and jots down some of what they said. He doesn't tell them anything about it, he doesn't make promises, but he would like to improve everything they mentioned. He has begun to understand why management can't satisfy the drivers' wishes, but he thinks that he might be able to show the drivers that management does indeed care about them and their frustrations. That they would like to change some things – if there's enough money to do so. Marcelis isn't against improvements. Erhard has learned that much in the past few weeks. But Marcelis is mostly interested in getting more vehicles on the street, not spoiling the drivers with coffee machines and massages. The lack of tourists and the rising prices of petrol haven't made things any easier.

On those days when he stays in his office, he listens to Radio Mucha on a little transistor radio and riffles through files of contracts and agreements, examining old accounts to understand how they spend their money and how much they spend. Ana or Marcelis has put a globe on one of the filing cabinets, as if the company has an international reach. He spins it and peers at the tiny speck in the middle of the sea that is

Fuerteventura, and the almost-as-tiny speck above Germany that is Denmark. And when there's nothing left on his schedule, he sits on the toilet and reads.

51

Saturday morning he wakes on the sofa before sunrise. Still wearing the same clothes as the night before. Maybe it's the light that woke him, the blue-violet light, the thinnest fissure between the dark sky and the sea. He thinks of Raúl. Becoming Raúl. As if the dream he'd just had was all about being Raúl. As if he has just been Raúl and now can't shake the feeling. He doesn't wish to be Raúl. He doesn't wish to live like him. He would like to be Raúl's age, would like to enjoy his effortlessness, his unconcerned waltz through life. He would like to experience Beatriz's gaze, the way she looked at Raúl whenever he told a story or philosophized about the sea or commented on some wine.

But he doesn't want to be Raúl whenever she looks at him in fear. Like just before, in the dream, when Beatriz was lying naked underneath him, screaming as he beat and raped her. One of her brown breasts jiggled while, for some reason, the other stood firm. Her screams sounded like a rope swiftly lashed around a post, a screechy, dry trill. He is Raúl, his arms are Raúl's hairy arms, so hairy that you can't even see his skin beneath fists bashing her from either side, like a piñata, while he fucks her. She cries out, No! Crying and praying to Santa Maria. Erhard can't remember if she's Catholic. No, she never went to church; he never saw her anywhere near one. She's not reciting Santa Maria, she's repeating the lyrics from one of those pop songs Raúl loved: 'Only When You Leave, I Need to Love You'. She stops talking. She falls silent. She lies still beneath him. He counts his arms, and there are more of them. Up to eight or nine flapping in front of him. Then Beatriz disappears.

He almost can't bring himself to go into the bedroom to check on her. The body that's lying in that bed is so different from the one he's just touched in his dream that it's both a relief and a grief. In the dream, she was a broken soul trapped in a pure sex machine; in reality, she's nothing more than a distressed soul trapped in a broken body. Without turning on the light and seeing her face, he changes her drainage bag and rolls her over in the dark. He doesn't care to see her eyes, the glossy dull buttons, and doesn't care to see the atrophied muscles of her cheeks.

He goes for a walk down to the beach. It's the best time of the day to be reminded how the town used to be. The seagulls eye the cafes' stacked tables, a married couple is having a row on a bench underneath a blooming tree, a young man rakes the sand and then arranges reclining chairs in a straight row. And of course there are fishermen out along the coast, lonely and inept silhouettes, always early to rise so they can do something that resembles work and can get sloshed with a good conscience before lunch. He watches one of the boats chugging into the harbour. If it were a car, one might say it was lurching, but he supposes wind and currents take their toll – just as when the wind out near the Dunes lashes against vehicles and practically sweeps them off the road. Changing direction, he heads towards the harbour. This is also the best time of the day to speak to anyone who knows how the tide and the sea push around large objects.

He sees the boat winding round the breakwater and dock among a couple of empty fishing cutters. Working in silence, the men leap about, and one of them fastens the dock lines to the cleats. Erhard studies them to figure out which one is the captain or even the most experienced sailor. It must be the one with the scarf around his neck, or maybe the one wearing bright orange overalls. He picks the one with the scarf, who's standing on the breakwater now and rinsing out some grey tote boxes.

– Who's the captain of your ship?
– Who's asking? the man says, without looking at Erhard.
– A curious soul.
– There aren't many of those at six o'clock in the morning.
– But it's almost 7.30 now. Are you the captain?

The man chuckles and points at the boat, where a young man stands jotting a note in the little cockpit.

Since the other man's farther away, and the motor's still running, Erhard has to shout. – I have a question for the captain!

A moment passes before the sound reaches the man in the cockpit, and he glances at Erhard. His face is reddish-brown, and his eyes are white, as though bleached of colour by the sun. Erhard recognizes him. Not because he knows him, but because the man grew up near the harbour in Corralejo; he's one of the kids who sold fish on the street and who used to run around naked on the rocks, showing crabs to the tourists, one of those who cries when the flotilla with the Virgin is sent to sea, because his own father died out there, and because he too will die out there one day. A young fisherman of the old school, a child of the island if ever there was one.

The man hops down from the cockpit and offers Erhard his hand. – Polo, he says. The other side of the man's face, Erhard sees, is flattened as if it was once injured by a blunt object. Erhard introduces himself.

– I have a question to whichever one of you has the most experience on the sea, Erhard says, and glances around expecting one of the others to look up.

– Ask me, Polo says.

Erhard doesn't quite know how to formulate his question without making the men laugh. – In all the years you've sailed, you have probably seen a little bit of everything. But I'm just a landlubber who randomly ended up on this island, and I don't know anything about conditions on the sea.

Polo stares at him.

– And I was wondering, well… what's the strangest thing you've seen floating around out there? I've read in the newspaper that there's a massive island of plastic west of Hawaii. Have you ever seen anything strange floating around?

The man studies Erhard as if trying to figure out why Erhard wants to know. – You mean dead people? Like that rich guy's kid they was lookin' for las' week?

Erhard flinches when he realizes what the man means. – No, I wasn't talking about him. But did you see him or find anything?

– Nope. I told the police that very thing when they ast'd. We've not seen a thing. Trust me, we don't want dead people or whatnot in our nets. Bad for bus'ness, it is.

– What about other things? Like houses? Things from last year's tsunami? Cars?

– We've seen the oddest things, haven't we? The other men grumble at this. – But nothing we write down or remember. The sea has lotsa secrets and we learn lotsa stuff all the time, but when we're out there, we're fishermen, not shipwreck-hunters.

– But many things float, right? Not just boats, rafts, and pieces of wood?

Polo shrugs. – Sure.

– Take a car, for example, that somehow ended up in the water. Can't it float a few miles or sea miles or whatever...?

Polo laughs. He seems to know that this was Erhard's question the entire time.

– But it's possible, right? Erhard says.

– Never seen it. Nope, never seen it.

Erhard glances around at the others, to see if one is itching to tell him something different.

Polo says, – My uncle, who fish'd down near Morro many years 'go, collided with a lorry that lay right below the surface of the water. Twas impossible to see, my uncle said. Wasn't many who believed him, but he could get real ornery if you told him you didn't. He said he could remember the Transo Viajes logo because it was vis'ble jus' above the water. When he rammed the lorry, it sank and my uncle had to repair his boat. It was a 'spensive fix. The insurance wouldn' cover it. They didn't believe 'im. The other men on Polo's boat laugh at the story, which they've probably heard many times. Polo eyes Erhard. – So maybe cars float. Who knows?

Erhard watches them work their tote boxes a little while longer, arranging them on a handcart so that they're ready to roll towards the car park. He nods a thank you to Polo and starts back towards the harbour. On the opposite side of the basin, Polo calls after him.

– Let me know if you discover anything. My uncle's dead, but it'll give the fam'ly a little piece a mind to know he'd been telling the truth back when.

Polo makes a sign of the cross. Erhard understands what that means.

The fishermen's scepticism causes Erhard to believe he's right. Walking along the harbour, staring at his feet, he fears it may just be his old reckless rebelliousness, which doesn't like to be corrected, and certainly not by authority figures. If they tell him the car can't have washed ashore, then he's all the more certain that the car washed ashore – and didn't roll down the cliff. He walks all the way out to the Hotel Olympus, the foundering construction project that echoes with drunkards and dogs. When one stands on the plateau which was to hold a lavish swimming pool, one can see across the city and the white line of houses, interrupted only by the fishing museum's green facade with its gigantic octopus spinning round in the sunlight.

On the way home he buys some bread and some thinly sliced ham at HiperDino. He sets the table. He brings out a bottle of red wine, Raúl's, then puts it back again. It's probably ridiculously expensive. He doesn't even know if Mónica likes wine.

He changes Beatriz's clothes. She has two jogging suits that he switches between. The first time it was bizarre, and kind of thrilling, but now it's like changing an overgrown, sleeping baby. Difficult. There's the hint of a wound where the respirator covers the mouth, so he removes the respirator when he's in the bedroom and her breathing seems calm, normal. He turns off the device and wraps the mouthpiece and the cord in a knot and hangs it on the rack. Michel had suggested that she could survive a day or two without the respirator. He leaves one light on, but locks the door on his way out.

Then he showers and gets dressed, though he leaves his shirt off to shave. With his electric razor set on the closest shave, it hums and stutters, and soon his skin is blue-white and smooth – as smooth as it can get anyway with his wrinkled cheeks and strangely baggy jowls. He doesn't like his face clean-shaven, actually, doesn't like *himself* that way, but he's certain that Mónica prefers him shaved. He resembles what he is: an old man with tired eyes.

He leaves to pick them up. At first, he feels like picking up Aaz before Mónica. Both for conversation's sake and because he thinks the atmosphere might be a little awkward if it's only him and Mónica in the car. She's not just any old customer. But right before he makes the turn onto the road leading around the mountain and up to the Santa Marisa Home, he changes his mind and heads towards Tuineje.

At her house, he honks once. She comes running and hops in the car as if it's raining. She shakes her hair and sets her purse between her legs, and he notices her dress and high heels. She's wearing tights, too, which you don't see very often on the island due to the heat and the sand. Mónica is different, he knows, but sometimes she seems stranger in her surroundings than he does.

She seems surprised that Aaz isn't in the car.

– So he doesn't have to drive all the way out here, he says, though they both know that Aaz loves the drive. The farther the better.

They drive through Antigua past the glass factory with its two characteristic chimneys. He's given many people rides, but driving her in a car without a taximeter feels like something new entirely. There's no static from dispatch, and the Mercedes is silent and precise. It would be a good time to tell her about the boy in the cardboard box. He owes her that much, really, after she helped him find the photos from the beach. And the cafe. Maybe she won't want to know. Maybe she'll think the police should handle it. He can't decide whether to tell her about it.

– Do you always talk this much when you drive a taxi? she says after a few moments of silence.

Erhard laughs.

– I like the silent types, she says. – I used to think that Aaz couldn't talk at all, but he can. Did you know that? He's talked in his sleep quite a bit or he's suddenly shouted at the TV if the turtle doesn't do what it's supposed to do. His voice is deep, you might call it bassy. He used to talk all the time. To me and the birds and to people who stopped by. But then one day, he just stopped.

Erhard glances in her direction.

– Maybe it was something he saw or heard. One morning, I simply woke with him crying at my side. This was before he went to live at Santa Marisa. He was five years old. He cried and cried, but without tears. Without a sound. I consoled him as usual. I ruffled his hair and hummed to him. And after that, no more. After that he hasn't said a word. I've tried to get him to… But he won't. Maybe he can't. Maybe it's become too difficult for him.

Erhard considers whether he should tell Mónica that he talks to Aaz. That he's somehow talked to Aaz every week for months.

They reach the base of the steep street that leads up past Santa Marisa. Erhard can feel Mónica's eyes on him. Aaz stands at the front gate with his duffel, gazing blankly ahead. When the car drives in front of him, Aaz stares at Mónica in the passenger seat, and she quickly moves to the backseat.

Mónica is impressed by the flat. As he'd hoped. She claps her hands, walking around the living room touching everything as if they're art objects. She glides a finger across the collection of books – it's Raúl's, but Erhard has added a number of his own titles. He explains that Raúl's things are in storage in the bedroom, and that's why the door is locked. She accepts this without question, then goes out to the terrace to gaze down at the street. She shouts to Erhard in the kitchen, saying that she's never been this high up before. Erhard doesn't quite understand what she means, but guesses that she's never been in a tall building before. Aaz spends half an hour in the bathroom. While Erhard prepares their sandwiches, Aaz plops in front of the widescreen TV and switches between four or five children's channels. Erhard didn't know there were so many channels. But the turtle's not on. It only airs at 12.30 p.m. on weekdays and only on TV Canaria.

When the food is arranged on the terrace table, Aaz won't shut off the TV, so Mónica moves the food, drinks, and cutlery to the coffee

table, where she and Erhard can sit on the sofa while Aaz lies on the
floor with a bowl of calamari. His giant body makes the entire room
seem smaller. She tries to speak, but her words are drowned out by
the puppet voices on the telly, and Erhard zones out of the conversation – about the personnel at Santa Marisa, which doesn't permit
Sunday visits, and about the rooms there. The residents sleep in bunk
beds, often four in one room, and only the noisiest among them get
their own room, and none of the rooms have a window that opens.
At night there is a great deal of whispering, and one would think the
place had ghosts, just as people have been saying for years. Aaz ought
to sleep with an adult who'll hold his hand. Instead, some sort of night
watchman sits in the room keeping an eye on them, following them to
the toilet if they make it in time. Although Erhard only half-listens,
he feels queasy at what he does hear. He leaves his ham in the bread
and eats his tomato.

They clear the table together. Just like at Mónica's place, but this
time in the big kitchen, where neither one of them knows where things
should go.

– I've heard you're playing detective.

– What? he says, glancing at Aaz in the other room.

– They're talking about you. Since there's only *one* Hermit on the
island, you know, and they say the Hermit's doing police work.

– Who are 'they'?

– People. The mothers of the island. They're all married to someone
who knows someone who has heard about the boy they found on the
beach.

– I've asked a few questions. I'm not playing detective.

– Everyone hopes you find the mother, but...

– I'm not searching for any mother. It's more like a mystery I'm
hoping to solve, like a crossword puzzle or one of those Chinese number
puzzles you see in the newspapers.

– Why don't you just buy a newspaper?

– No one abandons a child without a reason. Something must have
happened to the mother.

– Some do. Some people just run away from their problems when they become too difficult.

– What's your point?

– Maybe the mother's not worth finding. Maybe she deserved to drown or be killed.

– Is that what people are saying?

– I'm just saying that if the police have closed the case, perhaps you shouldn't think you can solve it on your own.

– You're afraid something's going to happen to Aaz, aren't you?

– Certain people might come after you. Aaz is very fond of you, you know that, right?

– What are you telling me?

– I'm not telling you anything. I'm just concerned for Aaz's safety.

– It doesn't have anything to do with Los Tres Papas, if that's what you're worried about. This is about a child, not some shipment of pot.

– You know what things are like here on the island.

There's a knock on the door. Erhard looks at Mónica as if she knows who it is. Whoever it is, they've gotten past the buzzer. As long as it's not Emmanuel Palabras. That would be dreadful timing. In the entryway he listens through the door. He hears something in the corridor, a faint rustling. He opens the door.

– Hiiiii, a short-haired brunette says as if they know each other. She's one of those Spanish beauties, semi-blonde, who wishes to be a Marilyn Monroe blonde, but gives up because it's expensive and difficult to dye her hair all the time; she's wearing a red halter-top, cowboy skirt, opaque stockings, and black knee-high boots with ten-centimetre heels. – I'm your new downstairs neighbour, she says.

Erhard has never seen her before. If he had, he would've remembered. – Hello.

– I'd like to invite you to my place for a glass of wine and lunch so we can get acquainted.

– I'm new myself here, he says. Erhard realizes that if this is how he's supposed to introduce himself to his neighbours, he's not been showing good manners.

– That's OK. That's why I'm inviting you.

– Me?

– Yes. Just a little wine. Totally innocent.

And suddenly she doesn't seem the least bit innocent. In fact, he's suddenly aware of her Russian accent and her sexiness, and he's just to about to slam the door in her face before Mónica sees her. – Can't right now. I have guests, unfortunately.

– Another time, he hears her say as he closes the door. To his great vexation, he's completely erect. It normally takes some effort, but right now it irritates him. He forces it back under the waistband of his underwear. What the hell was that all about?

– Downstairs neighbour? Mónica says. She apparently heard the entire conversation.

– Yes, my new neighbour.

– You could have invited her in.

– No thanks. She looked like a prostitute drumming up new johns.

– So what? It wouldn't be the first prostitute you've met, would it? Mónica's searching for a reaction from him.

– Aaz would blush in shame over such a girl, he says. – Trust me, he wouldn't have been able to watch much football if I'd let her in.

Mónica stares at Erhard, then laughs. A laugh rising from the pit of her belly. She stands next to Erhard and lays her hands on his upper arm. He gazes directly into her tired, worn face. Like his own.

– Just relax, he says. – I'm not a policeman. Being the director of a taxi company is enough for me.

Her face softens. A little.

Erhard goes into the living room and changes the channel over Aaz's protests. The football match hasn't begun yet, and Erhard's already tired. Still, he decides to bring out the expensive red wine after all.

– No, no, Mónica protests. – Please don't.

As if he's about to remove all her clothes in front of her son.

He pours the wine, and Mónica sips it, walking from the sofa to the terrace, discussing the potted plants which have dried out. Erhard hadn't noticed until now. Finally she sits on the opposite end of the sofa. She doesn't spread out like Erhard, but sits stiffly, her legs pressed together as if she's in pain or needs to pee.

The funny thing about watching football with Aaz in the room is that he cheers every time Barcelona has the ball. He throws his arms into the air, urging them to hustle down the pitch. As if to say: *The goal's open! And so are four players you can pass the ball to!* Barcelona wins the match 2–0.

Afterward he drives them home. Mónica follows Aaz inside. She disappears through the gate and gives Erhard a look requesting that he not leave her there. As if he would. He notices that three of the letters in the Santa Marisa Home's sign are worn out or completely rubbed off so that it now reads Santa Mar Home.

Mónica returns and climbs in the car. Saying goodbye to her son has made her sad. He tries to imagine what it's like to leave an oversized adult son here. Maybe she's plagued by a bad conscience. Maybe she feels grief for the child she never had.

They drive south in silence. The sun is setting. The island's unique light, filtered through dust and sea-mist – a greenish tint that wedges between heaven and ocean so that you feel as though you're floating – causes them both to sit motionless in their seats. The road feels much too short, and now they've almost arrived. Erhard turns into Mónica's driveway. The car crunches over the gravel and they park in front of the house. He wishes he could start the day over and be in a better mood. He feels the urge to tell her about the dream. To explain to her why he's been so withdrawn. But he can't. It has nothing to do with his dream, either. That's just the way he is; he can't change.

– I've had a good day, she says. – Because Aaz had a good day, I can tell.

– They won of course. He likes that.

– And the calamari.

– Right, that too.

Mónica smiles. – That was the first time Aaz and I have eaten out.

Erhard glances down. He hadn't thought of that. – I've never had visitors. So it works out for all of us.

– But now you have your neighbour to invite over.

– I can't afford that, he says, trying to turn it into another joke.

– Were you nervous?

– About today? No.

– I was. I didn't sleep last night. I lay there wondering if Aaz would have one of his fits during the meal. Or if he would ruin your carpet. He pees on everything sometimes.

– So do I.

– Thank you for listening today, she says, climbing out of the car.

– You were honest. You said what you were thinking.

She stands with the door open, and he can't see her face. – You're a good man, Erhard. It's the first time she's said his given name, and it sounds like Jerrar. – Don't forget that. Even if you don't find that boy's mother. But I don't have room for a man in my life. I can't. Because of Aaz, you understand. She turns and starts towards the house.

What he understands is that she's putting an end to something that hadn't even begun.

52

He hopes to find Marcelis in his office to discuss with him the two cars he's chosen. Osasuna's name is already on the contract, and he's the one who'll have to sign.

Erhard hasn't seen him since their brief conversation in the corridor a week earlier. But the door is closed. Ana's in there with him, and he can hear them whispering in subdued voices. Erhard stands quietly, listening. As soon as they begin talking business again, he'll enter. First he hears a sound like the shuffling of furniture, then a grinding noise, like paper being shredded. Something heavy slides down the other side of the door, and it occurs to Erhard that what he'd heard was Marcelis moaning. They're having a morning shag.

He returns his book to his briefcase and walks through the building as if he has a meeting to attend.

*

The car dealer is eating his lunch.

– Go ahead, Erhard says, seating himself at the small table in the dealership's cafeteria.

– We're not supposed to allow customers in here.

– That's OK.

Gilberto looks around the room. There's a dollop of mayonnaise in the corner of his mouth from his sandwich.

– I'm here because I need you to do me a favour.

– Um, Gilberto says, his mouth full of food.

– You need to change the contract so that I can sign instead of Osasuna. He points at the name on the contract.

– I can't. You know that, Gilberto says, sucking air through his teeth.

– Are you telling me that Osasuna's name is on every one of our cars? Erhard doesn't know if it's true or not, but the expression on Gilberto's face suggests he's right. – Which means that the day he quits he can take them with him. In theory.

– No, that's not true. He'll have to…

– What do you think Emanuel Palabras would say?

Gilberto looks confused at first. Then a kind of panic appears in his eyes. – But I can't change the contracts. I wasn't the one who prepared them. You'll need to speak with my boss.

– But what do you think Emanuel Palabras would say?

Gilberto throws down his sandwich. – I can't change the contracts. That's just how it is, Palabras or not.

Erhard knows that the man can't change the contract, of course, and he glances down at the table as if he's considering something. – Then maybe you can help me with another matter?

Gilberto seems reluctant.

– Who ships the cars between islands and to the continent?

– What do you mean? Individuals? Businesses?

– Who's responsible? Is it a big company or a bunch of small ones? Where do your cars come from?

Gilberto sits up in his chair. – Why do you ask?

– I just want to understand the vehicle-import business, that's all.

– Does it have anything to do with the boy?

Erhard is no longer surprised that people have heard of his interest in the boy's parents. And yet he hadn't expected to run into the gossip here, at a car dealership in Puerto. – Why do you think that?

– Because… because my wife told me that some crazy Norwegian is trying to find the boy's mother. All the women on my street are talking about it.

– And now you think it's me?

Gilberto stares at the tabletop. – How should I know? You're the only Norwegian I've met.

– And you're right. I'm the one.

The car salesman seems relieved. – I'd like to help you, so it's not that. It's good that you're trying to find the mother; she shouldn't get off scot-free. It's just that…

There are always two interpretations of the story, Erhard has noticed: either the mother is a criminal who killed her son, or the mother and son were the victims of a crime. He doesn't know which one he believes. He hopes it's somewhere in the middle. The real story will emerge one day, and he'll have to accept it.

– So, Gilberto, who ships the cars?

– To the island? Importaciones Juan y Juan.

– And when you include the other islands and the continent?

– I don't know. There are a number of import companies.

– Can you find out?

– Maybe. Right now?

– If you can.

With difficulty, Gilberto gets to his feet. Erhard follows him from the cafeteria and across the courtyard, where they walk past a few cars that have been stripped of doors and tyres. – Interested in old wrecks? Gilberto asks when he sees Erhard staring. – Something you can fix up?

– How much? Erhard asks, not because he would know how to fix any of these cars, but because he could buy one for the workshop.

– Those? One hundred euros. The one over there, fifty.

– What's wrong with it? It looks to be in better shape than the others.

– Some moron put a lawnmower engine in it. If you have a son, he would probably enjoy it.

– No thanks.

They pass through the auto workshop where the mechanic who'd earlier brought Erhard to the cafeteria now sits smoking a cigar, and then enter the display floor. Gilberto waves the smoke away from his nose. – We're a little behind on the smoking ban. If we banned it, we wouldn't have any mechanics tomorrow. My apologies. Gilbert sits down crookedly on a shabby office chair, then begins punching keys on a computer keyboard. He moves the mouse around and apologizes for something Erhard can't see. – You know what, it's probably easier if you saw it yourself. He spins round in his chair and grabs a little red book. – These things are sent to us once a year, but perhaps it'll come in handy now. Let's see.

Erhard spends a few days calling the companies in Gilberto's book. The conversations are brief, and uncomfortable. There's something about their industry – their very nature – that causes them to react hostilely when he rings. At one of the companies, the man who answered the phone doesn't understand how Erhard got the number. At another – a large shipping firm in Spain, TiTi Europe – a woman repeatedly inquires as to whether he's a reporter for a newspaper that Erhard isn't familiar with. Every time he rules out one company, he strikes it from the book. Many don't pick up the phone and he has to call back later.

He's nearly through the entire list when he realizes that the companies are responding strangely because they don't want to get mixed up in anything. During each call he asks whether or not they've had an accident on board one of their ships in the past three months. None have. In fact, they've never had *any* accidents. In the beginning Erhard crossed off all the companies, but the more that refuse to admit to ever having had an accident, the more he knows they're lying. He's not sure which companies are lying, but he knows that some of them are.

And he knows why. They have no reason to tell him the truth. When Erhard calls, it's easier for them to say *No, we've not had any accidents*, than to investigate the matter. TiTi Europe was close to transferring him to their CEO, so he could explain their mistake-free business model. But then the woman changed her mind and lost interest in transferring him. Finally he had to hang up.

He'll have to do something else to get an honest answer. He needs to start over, but ask a different question. He spends most of the afternoon thinking of another way forward, but he can't come up with anything. He's given the vehicle contracts to Ana and expects Marcelis to visit him at any moment, indignant and hurt, the paperwork in his hand.

But he doesn't. The office is dead, the corridors are empty. And that afternoon, for the first time, Erhard misses sitting in a car without knowing who'll be his next fare.

He wants to see Aaz again. And Mónica.

His downstairs neighbour still hasn't listed her name on her door. Every day he hopes to run into her on the way up or down. Just to see her, to ensure that she lives in the house and isn't a prostitute going door to door. It's possible her interest in him was completely sincere.

Tuesday. Driving out of the underground car park to the high street, he passes the drab-looking office where, from early in the morning, a young man sits in a light-blue suit talking on the telephone. Erhard had always thought it was just some anonymous travel bureau, but now he sees seventeen sheets of A4 paper taped to the window, with one letter on each spelling out the company's name: Mercuria Insurance. Insurance isn't a lucrative business on the island. The residents may be pessimists, but they are sceptical pessimists. Whatever happens, happens. And if it doesn't happen that often, well, there's no reason to pay for it not happening. The island's unique conditions, the wind and weather and the alcoholic population, mean that claims, by and large, are never paid out – and claims are mostly something one hears about when an American tourist collides with a breakwater in his sailboat or an Israeli lands a bacterial infection from a swimming pool. But every now and then, an EU directive goes astray and reaches the island, and then everyone with a boat or who works with transport must suddenly be insured.

Erhard can't imagine anything worse than being an insurance salesman. Not even funeral directors sell a product that you hope to never use. Every business sector has its own terms and conditions. Taxi drivers are helpers. They rescue busy people, or people who don't know how to get where they're going, or who want to get away from some place. As a piano tuner, he saves the beloved instrument; he makes it sound better, bringing order to chaos. Insurance salespeople are the irritating messengers. The one who tells you that, sometime in the future, something awful might happen to you, your family, your car, your house. And if the worst possible thing happened – what you didn't want to discuss or imagine – they'll help you out with some money. Money which seems completely meaningless in the big picture, almost like an insult. Buying insurance is like making a huge wager but one with tiny print. It's a grotesque product for a grotesque era.

Erhard thinks about compensation. Bad luck's lottery ticket. Just hearing the word compensation almost makes one want to tell half-lies or half-truths. That's how it is for most people. Maybe even for larger companies in the logistics business?

Erhard swerves into the lot and parks the car, then enters the Mercuria Insurance office. It resembles an office-furniture exhibition in a modern style that Erhard doesn't like, and it's illuminated by a row of light-blue fluorescent tubes four metres off the floor, which makes the man at the desk seem pale and bloodless. He is on the telephone but looks up when Erhard enters; he's clearly not used to customers dropping in. Erhard raises a finger to his mouth, indicating that he'll keep his mouth shut, while grabbing a business card from the table rack. The name on the card is Jorge Algara. The man continues talking into his headset, but he gestures excitedly with his hand that Erhard can take as many cards as he wishes. He takes only one.

53

Shortly after eight o'clock, he returns to the top of his list. Direct Logistica SL. He softens his voice and tries to speak without an accent. It's almost comical.

– Good morning, my name is Jorge Algara. I'm calling from Mercuria Insurance in Las Palmas. I see that you've got a large claim to be paid out to you, but I'm missing some details about the incident.

Silence on the other end of the line.

– What do you need to know? she says.

Everyone wants to talk to him now.

Some are still sceptical. Many cannot answer his questions and transfer him to someone who can. But most research their logbooks, explaining to him precise details about their shipping schedules. At first he writes everything down, but after a few conversations he begins to draw a map with dates and times. He asks whether they've heard of any wreckage in the area, and requests they provide him with bank account information so the money can be transferred. If they ask for an email address at which they can contact him, he gives them the real Jorge Algara's address at Mercuria Insurance. When the morning is over, he takes a break and studies his drawing. None of the companies have transported cars to or past Fuerteventura in the relevant time period. None have seen wreckage or any scrap from the tsunami. Just one company had an incident involving a collision near the islands; it was in January, but none of the ships involved were damaged. He's learned some useful information, but he still has the feeling that people aren't telling him everything. He examines his list. Nineteen companies left to call.

He sits in the rear of his office talking softly so that Ana can't hear him, even though he thinks she's at Marcelis's desk this morning. But surely she can't help but notice all his activity. She brings him coffee, despite the fact that he's told her repeatedly not to, and slips out again in order not to disturb him. He eats lunch with the telephone girls, who've grown accustomed to him and discuss the actor Tito Valverde, who plays Gerardo Castilla in *El Comisario*, Crown Prince Felipe's divorce, and one of the girls' dog; he had been staying with a neighbour and was given cat food to eat, which seems to shock several of the girls. Erhard hears their voices, but doesn't pay close attention to what they say.

He makes more calls. Since the first time he rang TiTi Europe, he's known that they were withholding information. They were hostile and suspicious. He preps himself to call, walking around his office talking softly to himself. The trick is to get in touch with one of the employees he didn't speak with last time. When the receptionist answers, he immediately requests to be put through to the accounts department.

– Alfonso Diaz, accounts payable.

– Good morning, Señor Diaz, my name is Jorge Algara. I'm calling from Mercuria Insurance in Las Palmas. I can see that you've got a large claim that's to be paid out to you, but I'm missing some details about the incident. This is again followed by silence.

– I don't believe so, he says.

He's the first to begin that way.

– Are you telling me that you're not interested in receiving a payment in connection to a collision in January?

– We've had no collisions in the past fifty-four months.

– Impressive. But you're right. According to my papers, it was a near-collision.

– A near-collision?

– That's a word we in the insurance business use.

– Whatever it is, we've not been involved in anything, nothing like that. But I'm here in accounts payable. I can transfer you to our traffic supervisor. He'll have more information for you.

The traffic supervisor is one of those Erhard spoke to last time, and the conversation didn't go well. If he's transferred there, it's over. – It's accounts payable with whom I need to speak. The other party has just acknowledged its role in the matter and is willing to pay 30,000 euros, at face value. If you would check some information, I will then simply ask you to provide a bank number so the money can be transferred.

The hook is cast. Silence.

– One moment, please. The man on the other end fumbles with the receiver. It's as if he holds his hand over the microphone, so Erhard can't hear his conversation. A woman and a man. He hears the word *no* several times. – Hello, Alfonso Diaz says. – Have you called before? I've been told that you called earlier.

Erhard doesn't know what to say. What would someone say who hadn't called before? – No. I'm calling from Mercuria Insurance.

– Are you the one who called about the Volkswagen Passat?

– I'm calling from Mercuria Insurance.

– We can't help you. Then he lowers his voice. – We're not allowed to provide the information you're requesting. Don't you read the newspapers? We don't operate the *Seascape Hestia*. I can't help you.

– So you're not interested in a payment of…

– Goodbye.

The man hangs up.

Erhard is incensed. He stares at the telephone and can't help but throw the receiver across the room, until the cord stretches taut and the plastic device falls to the floor and shatters. Goddamn them and their secrets. Are there rules for what one may say – or do they know something about the little boy? He can't believe it. To abandon a child is too low-class, too cynical, for any company to cover up. No, they're keeping silent because of something as meaningless as money. These companies, which, even in a recession, earn unimaginable sums importing unimaginable quantities of discount products made by children in Asian sweatshops; these companies, which are controlled by nouveau riche Russians and pampered heiresses who eat Argentinean beef and light their stoves with stacks of euros. Whatever rule, whatever consideration, is about money and making more of it, never less. He has the urge to visit them – no, not visit them – to find their office and break in. Find what he's looking for and set the place on fire.

The door opens, and Ana pops her head in. She looks at Erhard, who's sitting against the wall on the far side of the room, then at the floor where the telephone's smashed to pieces.

– I'd like a new telephone, Erhard says.

– What happened?

She seems shocked, even though she must be used to this kind of outburst from Marcelis, who is known for throwing his pens.

He's too embarrassed to respond.

She leaves, then returns with a dustpan and a small broom. – Telephones are pretty cheap nowadays, she says.

He says nothing.

She peers down at the fragments and carries them out.

– Thank you, he calls after her. – I won't do that again.

The door closes.

Seascape Hestia?

It occurs to Erhard that the man from TiTi Europe's accounts-payable department had actually tried to help him. *Seascape Hestia* must be the name of a ship. A ship that was located between Gran Canaria and Fuerteventura at the right point in time. The man from TiTi must have known there was something about that ship. He didn't even have to look it up; he hadn't enough time for that. He already knew. Something must've happened with that ship, perhaps something everyone knows but no one wishes to discuss.

There was also something about what he'd said: Don't you read the newspaper? The man from TiTi Europe hadn't been commenting on Erhard's lack of information. He'd given him a clue: The ship you seek was written up in the newspaper. Or, put another way: Find old news about *Seascape Hestia* and maybe you'll find what you're looking for.

Shipping routes were seldom in the news, unless a ship capsized. But what if there was a collision? Erhard hasn't even considered research-ing newspaper archives. It's a good idea – except that he doesn't know where or how to start. He would need to study an entire month's worth of newspapers that are more than forty days old. And local or mainland newspapers? Could he go to *La Provincia* and request newspapers from

January? Maybe the library in Corralejo has a newspaper archive he could rummage through?

He grabs his notebook and jots down *Seascape Hestia*, so he doesn't forget the name. While he writes, he realizes that the office – which gets no direct sunlight after three o'clock – has grown dark. He rips out the sheet of paper and shoves it into his shirt pocket, then pulls on his sweater. It's time to have another chat with Solilla, the bookseller, and to get hold of her friend again.

54

A flock of labourers emerge from the harbour and walk up the street. They're not all men, some are women in overalls, still wearing their helmets, their work gloves tucked under their armpits. Standing on an empty construction site behind a linen shop, Erhard gazes across the street at the glass building where the newspaper is housed. It's a dull yellow structure. The door opens, but apparently because of the wind. Or maybe because they're electric doors. Diego exits a few minutes later.

He crosses the street and heads seemingly at random towards Erhard.

– Señora Solilla asked me to find everything published in January concerning the *Hestia*. There were five or six articles, but everything's online, I think. He glances down at the file he offers Erhard. – This was all I could find. The printer protested a bit. But this must what you're looking for, I think.

– OK, Erhard says.

– Still the same case? Diego glances down the street to his left, then his right.

– Maybe.

– I don't know what it is you're looking for, but if there's a connection to the dead boy, I hope you can prove it. This might peck some of the rich boys on their toes.

Step on their toes, Erhard thinks to himself. A journalist who doesn't know his metaphors. – Ouch, Erhard says, suddenly bitter that the journalist doesn't care to write about the case.

Diego shrugs. – Well, good luck, he says and returns to his office.

A Judas kiss, Erhard thinks.

Back in the car, he opens the file and reads it. There are six printouts. Four articles about the same subject. The first is one column on the body of the British engineer Chris Jones, who was found in fishermen's nets off the coast of Gran Canaria. The follow-up article links the engineer to the *Seascape Hestia*, which sailed from Gran Canaria and was expected in Lisbon two days later, but was now docked in Port Agadir, Morocco. The end of the article references a possible hijacking. Then there's a long article from *El País* about the *Hestia*, and the author is clearly fascinated by the muddled case. The only crewmembers left on board were a Ghanaian captain, who claimed that he'd been brought to the ship by terrorists, while the eight-man crew had abandoned ship. According to Spanish authorities, the cargo had consisted of construction materials, plastics, tinned goods, and European cars. But the cargo hold was empty, and the Ghanaian captain didn't know when or how that had happened. The last article is very short. It notes that the *Hestia* was to return to Holland, where it had been registered, and the investigation and search were to continue for the presumed Spanish crew. The Ghanaian captain had been released and not charged with a crime.

Erhard tosses the stack of papers onto the floor of the car. Every time he manages to turn over one rock, he finds new rocks under the first rock. Now he knows that the ship is Dutch. Now he knows that the ship carried European cars. But he can't solve a crime by reading old newspaper articles. Who the hell knows what happened on board that ship? The dead engineer, the hullabaloo surrounding the Ghanaian captain, the missing cargo – it all sounds like a desperate cash-grab.

The car smells like the box of books that's resting on the passenger seat. The books once belonged to a cigar smoker. Although there are more than twenty titles, he figures he'll only read a few of them:

Chatwin, maybe Márquez – whom all Spaniards love and hate. He bought the others as a favour to Solilla. Including a novel about a guitar that survives the Spanish Civil War and World War I, only to wind up in Downing Street, in the hands of Churchill's wife Clementine, who played guitar for Roosevelt's wife when the Germans surrendered in 1945. Sure, why not? Everything is apparently possible. He has followed the car's tracks. They didn't lead up the hill and across the island, but out to sea and north to Holland via Agadir. He starts the Merc's engine.

55

He's out at the house to feed the goats. But he doesn't feed the goats. The goats are nowhere to be seen and he doesn't hear their braying or the cracked bell around Laurel's neck, and he doesn't see them darting among the rocks, their white spines like chalk lines against a cliff. The house is more rickety now. Even a house can be lonely when its resident moves out. The windows are wasting away like eyes, and a slamming door is a quivering mouth begging him to stay another day, another week. Maybe the house has always looked like this. Even when he loved it, even when he longed for peace from the voices in the taxis and the crush of people downtown. Even then it was like returning home to a snivelling lover who couldn't live without him. He observes the house, hating everything about it as he, as in a childhood memory, remembers sitting outside in the rocking chair drinking Lumumbas or enjoying a quick sunset meal of potatoes. If not for the two goats, he would never return. Just as he'd feared, his many years out here have made him angry and unforgiving of the house and its dust, its creakiness, and its clothesline that was always too slack.

He throws the goat food on the ground. That usually brings the animals. The rattling of the bucket, too, especially Laurel, the most approachable of the two. Not just for the food, but for the hand that throws the food, a hand to stroke its back. Erhard likes the animals, especially Laurel. He doesn't have a particularly close relationship with them, but he likes having them around, their random movements – without plan or special needs. One time the two creatures had stood a hundred metres apart and, along with Erhard, formed a triangle. A strange symmetry, which, after a few beers, seemed meaningful.

Wind tumbles across the rocks, and from far away comes the sound of a motorboat or an airplane. Erhard walks around the house. Pausing between the clothesline and a cairn he'd built over the years, he suddenly hears Laurel's bell chiming in the distance. Like a low gurgle, a tinkling that is barely audible, and yet there it is. Though he doesn't believe Laurel knows its own name, he calls for the goat. Then he clambers up on a large boulder so he can see across the fields and up the mountain, and loses himself in the greyish-brown landscape. And there, there's a minuscule movement, a white line, Laurel leaping in the groove between mountain and field.

Something terrible has happened. It happens. It has already happened.

Watching Laurel approach, perhaps looking for food, Erhard's not sure whether he's afraid for Hardy, or another, maybe Beatriz. Hardy because he's not around – and he's almost always with Laurel. If they ever got too far away from each other, they compensated by trotting closer and standing side by side. This tightness seemed even more intimidating on the barren paddock. The rocks made them appear insignificant and vulnerable when they stood together, chewing on whatever they found: cardboard, straw. If Hardy's not around, then he's dead. Both goats are over fourteen years old, so it would hardly be extraordinary if one of them lay down and died. He thinks of Bill Haji. Could a group of wild dogs have attacked Hardy?

He rubs Laurel behind his ear and goes back to the house, casting more food on the ground. Laurel eats calmly, his ears waving like a handkerchief. It makes no sense to grill the goat about what happened to its brother. And yet he asks anyway, repeatedly: Have you seen him? Have you seen something terrible?

56

His unease doesn't abate.

He sleeps as if the telephone will ring at any moment, or someone will knock on the door. But the telephone seldom rings. The doctor is the only one who calls. It's a windless morning, one of those rare phenomena that makes everyone in town stop what they're doing to recite Hail Marys as they stare out at the water, which looks like blue concrete.

When he leaves the flat, the downstairs neighbour is there, wearing the same clothes as the first time he saw her, which are exactly as sexy as he recalls but also pitiful. She doesn't have any other clothes, he thinks.

– Let me guess? he says. – You locked yourself out.

– How do you know?

– One knows one's neighbours.

– Can I stay with you until Rainier comes?

Rainier must be her pimp, Erhard guesses. – Can't you meet down at Luz?

– Rainier's the super, she says, as if she'd guessed what he was thinking. – He'll be here soon. Can I wait at your place?

– Unfortunately, I have to go to work.

– You're a director, right?

– What makes you think that?

– It's on your door.

– No, that's the previous owner, Raúl, Erhard begins to explain before glancing at the door. He's never seen the sign before. *Director Erhard Jørgensen.* The worst sign he's seen in a long time. He doesn't care to explain the situation to her.

– Say hello to Rainier for me, and ask him why he put up that sign.

She remains standing at Erhard's door. Her attempts at seduction are amateurish, but Erhard's afraid that one day he'll succumb, and he reminds himself that it'll only make his longing deeper. Just like the other times. His erection almost hurts, and he trots down to the car park.

He picks up Aaz, still uneasy, as if something terrible has happened. Maybe the Boy-Man swallowed his own tongue, or Mónica forced him to move home. But when he drives up the road, Aaz emerges from the gate, one hand in a bandage but apparently in good spirits. He shows Erhard his hand. The pinky. He points at Erhard's hand.

– No, Erhard says. No, no.

It's just like you, Erhard.

– No, Aaz, it's not just like me. You mustn't…

I know, it was dumb.

– What the hell are you thinking then?

If you can handle it, so can I.

Erhard is completely distressed, he has no idea where he's going or even where they are. He pulls over to the side of the road; the place seems familiar. He flips Aaz's hand over. – Did you go to the emergency room? Did the doctor look at it?

Aaz shrugs. It's just a wound, that's all.

Erhard doesn't know what to say. He can't yell at him, nor does he dare make light of it. He looks him directly in the eye, saying nothing. He maintains eye contact until the Boy-Man's quavering eyes settle and begin to fill with tears. Then Erhard looks away. And begins to drive.

Erhard's racing pulse doesn't return to normal until they are at the airport. Aaz studies the traffic and looks at the planes the way he always does. Erhard tells him about his telephone conversations with the import companies. He also tells him about Solilla and the reporter from *La Provincia.*

You've made progress then, Erhard.

– No, Aaz. I've shuffled some pieces around. It's not the same as making progress.

Imagine. Right now there's only one person in this entire world who's interested in finding out what really happened.

– Hard to believe that the police haven't figured it out long ago. He thinks of Bernal. A cowboy with a lapful of teddy bears.

The police are the good guys. Their job is to find the criminals.

– They don't have time. Or they can't. I don't know which.

Mum says that a person can do whatever he or she wishes to do.

– Your mother's a very fine woman, Aaz.

Erhard turns up the radio. Stan Getz: 'Captain Marvel'. From some club recording. Scratchy and shrill, as it should be. He tries to drown out the anger that's directly underneath his fingers. The island's police force has pretty much done nothing. They've buried the boy. They've confiscated the car. Possibly, they made some phone calls. Erhard guesses that they probably haven't called many people. Not as many as Bernal had said.

The section of road on which they're driving is one of the most scenic on the entire island. The road curves and dips, then continues down the hill and up through a rocky pass.

Liana says that I'm weak and dumb. She says I'm a cry-baby and miss my mother.

– It doesn't matter. You're not weak or dumb because you cry.

Did you cry when you lost your finger?

– No. I've never learned to cry. It's something you have to learn. Your father has to teach you, or your mother.

He goes inside to say hello to Mónica, but she's on the telephone and absorbed in the call. She wraps the telephone cord around her finger and stares into the kitchen wall. Erhard writes a note to her: *Back at 5.* Aaz is already sitting in front of the TV and pointing at the turtle.

Ana has bought him another telephone. It's one of those newfangled kinds with a bunch of buttons and a little display where you can see the numbers when you dial, or when someone's calling you. The phone requires a manual, but he doesn't know how to operate it any more than the last one.

She has placed a thick envelope beside the telephone. There's no name on it or sender. He weighs the envelope in his hand, then peers into the reception area, waving it.

– From Luís, Ana says, when she looks up. – He got a fare to *La Provincia.* The man gave him a little package for Director Jornson of Taxinaria. He must mean you.

He tears open the package with his index finger. Inside he finds some printed pages, an article like the others. There's a pink Post-it note stuck to the top. 'Found this in the printer. BE CAREFUL. D.'

He unfolds the article. It's a long one, and not from *La Provincia* but *El Sol News*. It's about an amendment to European law in the insurance sector, which is being rushed through parliament. *Several insurance companies have forecasted such hefty insurance premiums for the shipping industry that gigantic logistics companies no longer believe they will have the wherewithal to sail fully insured fleets. The issue emerged following the recent spate of hijackings in the waters near the Horn of Africa. In Spain, the problem became acutely relevant in January, when a Dutch-registered vessel, the* Hestia *– which sails for a Canary shipping company, Palalo – was hijacked off the coast of Morocco. Its cargo was stolen. In this specific case, plaintiffs are seeking approximately 55 million euros in damages. A large sum, to be sure, but not unusually so – especially since it involves motor vehicles and construction materials. The security chief for Palalo notes that insurance doesn't even cover the actual loss which the hijacking inflicts on the company, in the form of lost customers and negative PR. First and foremost, however, they are seeking damages to compensate their clients' lost goods and associated costs. In the future, Palalo says it will only sail with insured freight. But the security chief believes that, to a greater degree, individual customers will be forced to insure their own goods, or that insurance will become a direct part of transportation costs. A prospect that could lead to a price increase of up to 15 per cent, which would have to be borne by consumers, who are already hamstrung by the financial crisis. For some products, such price spikes could prove fatal. The problem has been discussed for some time by the largest shipping nations. The EU must now determine whether the states will draw up special hijacking insurance to prevent consumers from being saddled with the bill. The security chief concludes: 'For us, it simply means that our customers, in the future, will be producers of cheaper goods. But for many of the traditional and slightly more expensive export firms, the consequence may be that they will have difficulty selling their products to international markets. And for the Canary Islands, it might alter the selection of products found on supermarket shelves.'*

Although Erhard has seen the headlines about Somali pirates at the kiosk, he hasn't considered how it would alter everyday life on the island. But it makes sense. He pictures the empty shelves in HiperDino around the corner.

He returns to the beginning of the article. The *Hestia*, the Dutch ship, was leased by the Canary shipping company Palalo and sailed with goods worth more than 50 million euros. Palalo. He recognizes the name. He believes he remembers it from the book Gilberto gave him. Was that one of the companies that he'd called? He pulls the book from his bag and riffles through the pages, until he finds what he's looking for: Palalo in Las Palmas, Gran Canaria. He doesn't remember talking with anyone there. Now he sees why. There's no telephone number. In fact, he'd drawn a question mark next to this company, because they don't have a telephone number. Only a website.

He calls for Ana and asks her if she can find Palalo's telephone number. He reads the address aloud.

– OK, she says. And a short time later: – They don't list their telephone number anywhere. All they have is an email address.

Palalo. He gets to his feet and goes out to Ana. – Do you mind? he asks, peering over her shoulder while she manoeuvres around the homepage. He doesn't know what he expects to see, but his head is boiling, and he needs to find something to refute his suspicions. – Can you find anywhere where it states who owns the company?

Ana does a few things on the computer. – No, there's nothing about that here. But maybe I can look it up somewhere else? Boxes expand and shrink on the screen. She types in the word Palalo, and soon after, an overview appears featuring a number of companies. She enlarges the site. Then pauses. – Here's something. It says here that it's owned by Palabras ETVE. Was that what you were looking for?

For a moment Erhard stands perfectly still. What is he supposed to make of that? He knows that Palabras, in addition to what he's most known for – olive-oil production in Spain, with a smattering of the same here on the islands – owns many other kinds of businesses. Some hotels, including half of Las Dunas Beach Hotel in the centre of the protected area on the outskirts of Corralejo, a car-rental dealership, the largest tomato farm on the island, a few packing plants on Gran Canaria, several construction companies, a large chunk of Sport Fuerte, and of course TaxiVentura. And now it turns out he also owns the shipping company whose cargo was stolen from a Dutch vessel and, after a detour, wound up, in part, on the beach in Cotillo with a dead boy in the backseat. It could be a coincidence. It *could*.

– Thank you, Ana. Erhard returns to his office.

But it could be something else entirely. He looks around. The windows are like filthy sheets, and the light outside is dimmed by yellow clouds. What does he actually know about this office? Who furnished it? Why does the globe stand right there, next to the telephone? Maybe he's been sticking his nose in things he shouldn't have for much too long, but what is Palabras's role?

He spins the globe, searching for a microphone. But it's just a globe, a ball of shoddy plastic, and he finds nothing. He sets the globe down and investigates the pen holder, letter tray, drawers – all empty. What does he know about surveillance anyway? Other than what he's read in books? These days, you can probably spy on someone through a computer or a telephone. What does he know? He doesn't understand any of the electronic gadgets that surround him.

He eyes the telephone Ana gave him. She swept up the remains of the old phone a little too quickly, before Erhard could help her. That someone has kept an eye on him since he got here, he has no doubt. Ever since he visited the Palace that first time with Bernal and rummaged through the newspaper fragments, one thing after another has taken a turn for the strange.

It explains everything. It explains why Emanuel was so eager to replace Raúl with Erhard, it explains Emanuel's odd friendliness, it explains the flat, the car, and the contrived party. It explains all too well how an ordinary taxi driver could be promoted to director; it explains why he doesn't need to do anything except dine at the occasional restaurant. It also explains why Marcelis's name was on the contract, not Erhard's. They don't plan to let him keep the director's chair very long.

And it explains Raúl. Maybe Emanuel asked Raúl to get lost. To vanish from the scene for a while. He imagines it. Raúl would defend

Erhard, and the only way he feels he can do that is to leave. To retreat from his father's game. Maybe Raúl and Beatriz argued, maybe she didn't want Raúl to go, maybe she believed that Erhard would have to deal with it himself. Maybe Emanuel's thugs drove Raúl to the airport, Beatriz resisted, and...

He gets to his feet. He can't sit still knowing what he knows. He shoves the business overview and a few other books into his briefcase and snaps it shut. He heads out to the corridor, then down the stairs.

He feels stupid. So stupid.

Palabras lured him in with the smell of money. Or no, not money. Something indefinable, a kind of award, the feeling that he'd done something with his life. A bitter combination of company lunches, a new car, the director's chair, a sense of importance, and a flat with a world-class view. Every time he's gotten something, he's thought of Annette and the girls. But mostly Annette. Every time he's thought: *Now I can show her that I made it.* That in spite of her curses, her hatred, her criticism, and the many thousands of euros he's sent home to Denmark, he's picked himself up and become a man. He has grasped the opportunities that have come his way, and tried to make the most out of them. Palabras must have seen his weakness and somehow pulled all the strings to exploit it. The job, the car, the flat. The downstairs neighbour. Mónica. Who knows what Palabras is capable of?

Since there are still two hours until he needs to pick up Aaz, he drives south through the smaller villages, past the villa with its angry piano owner. In the strange, boxy village of Gual he fills his tank and riffles through some books in his briefcase without finding anything of interest. He stares at the note with Palalo's Internet address.

At the bottom of the briefcase, he finds a business card from one of his customers. He remembers having it handed to him along with the usual farewell: *If you're ever in Düsseldorf or Liverpool or Gothenburg...* He remembers him – the man who was in love. He didn't have the money for the taxi and promised to send it, but he never did. Second Officer Geert Kloewen. The ship's mate. Another man of the sea. Underneath the name and titles, the card only lists a telephone number and an email address; apparently that's how it's done nowadays. Geert was no more than thirty years old. Erhard remembers how he'd waved at him on his way towards the boat, genuinely thankful for the free ride. Maybe he just managed to hop on board before they set sail. They'd probably kept a list of all crewmembers on board and would check each one off, just like in school, when everyone was present and accounted for. Could someone like Geert Kloewen help him find lists from other ships? Like the *Seascape Hestia*?

He doesn't like exploiting such things. Geert may owe him a favour, but they don't know each other, and he might be anywhere in the world. If only he knew someone else with knowledge of ships or who has connections to a shipping line. Normally he would ask Raúl or maybe even Emanuel Palabras. But he'll have to find another network.

He thinks of the Aritzas, whose piano he tunes on New Year's Day. André is the gentle engineer-type, who came into too much money and spends it on all-too-expensive purple shirts and fine things for the house, including the Steinway – the piano for people who don't know anything about pianos. His wife, Reina, has tried a few times to explain to Erhard where their money comes from. Something to do with shipping, computers, satellites. They've been unbearably arrogant to Erhard, and yet at the same time kind and loyal customers year after year for nearly a decade, since the first time the piano-playing niece came to visit. It would be hard to ask them for help. But it'd be better to call them than to call Geert, a complete stranger. If he offers to tune the Aritzas' piano for free from now on, perhaps André will drop that sourpuss he's had the past few years and help Erhard.

He starts the engine and drives to Mónica's place.

57

He hopes for a friendly reception, maybe even a warm one – Mónica giving him a clumsy embrace – but he doesn't dare expect anything. She isn't the type. He calls out to her and Aaz, then enters through the front door. They're out in the garden, where he's never seen them. He watches them from behind the netting. Mónica's absorbed in her plants, Aaz is sitting in a chair gazing at the twittering birds. She's heard him, he thinks, but she doesn't say anything.

– I can pick up food at Xenia's place, he says.

– I don't want to make a habit of it, she says, plucking a large white flower with bright yellow petals.

Erhard can't determine whether she's being serious or teasing him. He decides to believe she's teasing him, then walks down to the restaurant with its confusing name, Taberna del Puerto, where Xenia is the manager, cook, and waitress, while her son assists in the kitchen. It's tourist food, but it's tolerable. He buys grilled fish for Aaz, steak for himself, and, for Mónica, a salad with shrimp and one mussel – which he decides must be a mistake.

Spending time together is easy when food is involved; they sit staring at their plates. Erhard can handle the silence, but Mónica sighs loudly and wishes, perhaps, that he would say something. She drinks red wine. After she's done eating, she carries her wine glass outside and shows Erhard her succulents. He listens at first, but he prefers to study her long fingers as she strokes a cactus without pricking herself on the needles. Some of the plants have been used as love potions, she explains, still without looking at him. When they reach the far end of the garden, he interrupts her to go to the loo.

– Oh, by the way, may I use your phone to make a quick call?

– Use the one in the hallway, it's quieter there.

Aaz is watching television.

It seems as though his favourite television show is always on.

Erhard pulls out his notebook and punches in the Aritzas' number. The line clicks.

– Hello, he says, though no one has answered. He hears a hollow, metallic sound, as if thousands of miles separate the two phones.

– Hello, this is Reina.

She sounds tired. It hadn't occurred to Erhard that someone might be sleeping at this time of day. – This is Erhard Jørgensen, the Piano Tuner.

There's a long pause. – Oh yes, she says, before evidently pulling the phone away and muttering something else.

– Is Señor Aritza home?

– One moment.

– This is André.

He sees Mónica through the window. He turns to face one corner of the room, then lowers his voice. – Good afternoon, Señor Aritza. I'd like to make an arrangement with you. He's decided to sound professional. But he doesn't want to be falsely polite any more.

– What kind of arrangement?

– I understand that you have tight connections to several shipping companies.

– We service the largest shipping lines in Spain, so yes.

– And you probably know a lot of people in the industry.

– I meet with politicians and many of the biggest players in the arena. Tell me why you want to know?

– I need to find the crew list from a particular vessel.

– I can hardly hear you, Jornson. Speak up.

– I need to find the crew list from a particular vessel.

Aritza clatters with the phone, perhaps because he sat down once he realized the conversation would take longer than anticipated. He's a large man who has difficulty breathing. – May I ask why?

– That's not your concern.

Silence. – What do you need my help for?

– I believe you may know someone I can call, someone who knows someone who knows someone.

– Señor Jornson, I don't believe we'll need, how may I put it?… help with the piano any longer.

It wasn't what he'd expected Aritza to say. It must be because of the strange thing he'd witnessed the last time Erhard visited them: André Aritza's arm around his niece. – Have you spoken with your wife about the last time I saw you?

Aritza laughs. Deliberating on just what to say, Erhard thinks.

– I have a friend in something called IMO. If anyone knows anything, it's him.

Erhard ratchets up the pressure. – I expect you to do everything you can to help me.

– I don't know whether one is allowed to share such information with a third party.

– Just find a person I can talk to, Erhard says, and prepares to hang up. Mónica has sauntered up the black-gravel path and is now standing in front of the main door. She's able to hear his conversation.

– How about you stop by my office tomorrow? We'll get this all sorted out.

– I'd rather have a telephone number now, Erhard says, trying to be firm. But it's hard. André Aritza is more practised at this kind of thing.

– Meet me Friday morning, then I'll help you.

He gives Erhard the address.

– I'll be there at ten o'clock, Erhard says, before hanging up. He's nearly wiped out.

When he returns to the garden, she tells him about the plants, as if he's ordered a lecture she's determined to deliver. Some of them hardly need water at all, she says. Being a gardener and having plants that are so dismissive is a real challenge. She insists on taking care of them. Following her, he notices her buttocks behind the thick fabric of her dress. She pauses at a table lined with pots of various colours. Every kind of plant: bristly, climbing, round, sharp. There are some with spikes, others with soft stems and long petals, even some with hair. He runs his hand across a plant that resembles a pale-green rock. She tells him its Latin name, which Erhard quickly forgets.

– We shall not be needing you any more, she says, not to the plant but to Erhard.

– If it has anything to do with my…

– It has nothing to do with you. The nuns suggest that I visit him every other Saturday instead. Now that he's so grown, his social life at Santa Marisa is the most important thing for him. It will calm him, they say.

– He needs to see his mother. You two need to spend time together.

– And we will. I'll visit him on Saturday afternoons.

– I can drive you. I don't do anything on Saturdays.

– It's easier for me to take the bus. I'm used to it.

He needs to stop suggesting other ways to assist her now. Needs to give her space. – I can drive you home. The bus doesn't go to Tuineje Saturday after siesta.

She ignores him. Which feels worse than a categorical rejection. – They play bingo every other Saturday, and I can play with them. They say he's lucky, that he wins every time. They don't know how he does it; no matter what board he has, or whether he has one board or three, he wins. She tears the leaves from a dry little tree stump, whose long leaves stick up like antennae. – Liana thinks it's best for him. She thinks he needs all the stability he can get. These past few months, he's begun wetting the bed. Again. He needs to be comforted now, always needing to be around the sisters, not the other children as he used to. He's more and more isolated in his own world. Except when he plays bingo.

– That's not my experience.

– That's how he is here at home. He'll only sit watching that television. It irritates me. He looks at that turtle more than he looks at me.

– I don't see him that way. He seems lively, open.

– He likes you, he likes to drive.

– And he's tired of the sisters. All they talk about is the Will of God. And morning prayers.

– How do you know that?

– He told me.

– I'm not in the mood for jokes.

– They're his words, not mine.

She glares at him. – You're a strange man, you know that? I don't know whether you are the world's dumbest man or the sweetest or the smartest, or whether you're just out of touch with reality. You're a source of light and a light extinguisher. You are this and you are that. You're a taxi driver, and you're a director. But what are you, actually? Who are you, and what do you want with him? You're a disruptive figure in his life, you know. He's not sure what to make of you. But he needs to know what you want, and whether he can count on you, and whether you're sincere or just helping out to make yourself feel better. You are easy to like, but impossible to love.

Erhard is struck dumb. No one has spoken to him like that in nearly twenty years. In all those years, no one has cared for him enough to do so. All at once, he feels both quite misunderstood and quite understood. Her accusations allow him to be full of mistakes, untidy and rough, but also the opposite: with room for greatness, generosity, and freedom.

Something causes him to step forward and press himself against her chest. Though he hardly recalls what he's supposed to do next, he stops worrying about getting it right, and simply lets himself be driven by a completely surprising urge to kiss her. He's certain it's the wrong thing to do. If things will ever be good between them, this is not how it'll happen. Turning to align his lips to her rather expressionless face, he leans close to her bosom and gets a whiff of her scent, not her perfume, but a mix of the warm aroma of her work with the plants and a strong odour of sweat and fear. He's surprised that she doesn't pull away; he expects her to slap him at any moment. He presses even closer, so that she's forced to arch backwards across the table with the pots of cactuses, silently regarding him without resisting. He's crossed the boundary now. No matter how she reacts, he's altered their relationship. If she slaps him or rejects him, he'll be embarrassed. If she gives in or returns his kiss, he'll be embarrassed later. There's no future, no plan, no meaning in anything besides the kiss he's trying to plant on her lips. He can't remember when he last put so much of his own integrity into such a tiny space. Not since he slammed the door that final time back home in Denmark has he known so keenly what he wanted out of life. And just like back then, it's with a feeling of triumph and panicked anxiety, mixed and shifting like the light through the wine glass – which now topples over, splashing red wine onto the pale wooden table. He doesn't care. Even better, neither does she. She acquiesces. He almost can't believe his luck at how far things have gone. For a moment he feels a child's giddiness, Scrooge McDuck swimming in his mountain of gold coins, giddy over his unbelievable good fortune, then swiftly put in his place by his inner auditor, who tells him that it's OK, that it's his turn to collect some of the randomly distributed rewards in life's lottery, followed by perfect silence, astonishment, almost gratefulness. And then he feels her full lips against his, salty and parted, softer and warmer than goat's milk. Beneath him she shoves pots and plants to the floor, accidentally kneeing his crotch, and he's about to give up. But then her hand glides through his hair, forcing his face to balance on the edge of hers and returning him to the breathless space where all he hears is the smacking of her lips and, in the background, the turtle on the television. He's floating now. Suddenly there's so much he wishes to do that he runs out of breath at the mere thought. He keeps reminding himself to kiss her gently, not to chew on her lips. Even though he has an urge to bite into them like tender chicken. Even though he feels the urge to suck them into his mouth and stick his tongue through her worn, crooked teeth. Already she's moaning, as if he has licked her down there for hours, though all he's done so far is to get his hands underneath her snug-fitting, uncooperative dress. They're both probably thinking the same thing – that the Boy-Man will stay put until they turn off the television; they can continue what they're doing so long as they hear the television. Erhard's back aches. It's not accustomed to this position. He props his elbows on the table to lean over her, to get more of her. She tastes of smoke, maybe she smokes on the sly, maybe she stood behind the white hedge and had a fag while he talked on the telephone. Or it's the shrimp from the salad, smoked or grilled with barbecue seasoning. Her cheeks are so paper thin that he thinks they'll split from the corner of her mouth up to her ear, but she just seems to open wider, gobbling him up with a desperate hunger he knows all too well. Passion is like a dazed experience of skin. He stares into the triangular area encompassing her cheeks, ear, and eye, and tries to breathe its scent, but it's gone, and he knows that it won't return. Such is his sense of smell; it tunes in and out, preferring to smell something once and never again. Unexpectedly, her fingers begin working the buttons of his trousers, which he sometimes struggles with himself. She twists and turns to see. The setting sun is no help. She jerks away from the kiss and lowers her head to get a better look, but it apparently doesn't help. Just frustrates her more.

– I can't see anything, she says.

He has the urge to brutally tear off his buttons and zipper, but in truth he wants to buy some time. He's not erect and knows that it can take time – if he becomes erect at all. He's at the apex of his desire, and he can't imagine being more turned on; he fantasizes his tongue's journey through each wrinkle of her neck, along the broad path between her breasts, between the folds of her belly – he's not naive enough to believe she doesn't have a little belly like him – and through the rough mound of bush to the lips of her coal-black labia, loose and swollen, so that his tongue hardly comes into contact with them before she screams in shock. He's so bloody close to ejaculating, even if his cock hasn't gotten the message, that he feels water or something wet dripping from his asshole, and he doesn't know whether he should laugh or cry.

– Help me, she says. She's on her knees, her glasses on, and worrying the obstinate button as if she'd just locked herself out of her house.

– I'll start, he says, hoisting her up on the table again so he can lift the hem of her dress. She resists briefly, then arches her back. To his surprise she lifts the dress herself and pulls it off, dropping it to the ground, where it lies between overturned plants, soil, and a tiny shovel. He doesn't know what he expected to find under the dress. He doesn't know whether he feared or hoped that Mónica has lived a chaste life, that her years as Aaz's mother indicated a totally sexless life. But the sight of the woman he thought he knew – who in the half-light is lying in what appears to be purple panties or lingerie, as the fashion magazines call it, is at once almost heartstoppingly beautiful and so unforgivably sinful that he can't understand why his dick doesn't react. He can't recall ever having such a strong desire to consume someone. He wants to begin on her rough toes, to continue up her thighs – which are fuller and less pale than he'd expected – and channel all his energy towards her vagina, trapped behind the silky fabric like a hedgehog under a swimming cap. There's no hair sticking out from under the lace, no dark path up to her navel like on the prostitute Afrodita, whose grotesque crotch had been a kind of punishment that Erhard had felt was deserved for old men wanting a quickie. Her breasts are held firmly in check by a small bra, and as a result, they bulge over the edge and seem large, and the dark surfaces of her nipples jut out over the minimal lace edge like an advertisement for what's inside the packaging. There's movement in his trousers now, an involuntary tension in his dick, but it's not enough, not something to show off. Leaning into her vagina, he doesn't want to think about his erection. He's got one chance to penetrate her, and he doesn't want to ruin it with his old penis. Upon closer inspection, her panties are pretty, a shimmery blue, and a dark patch spreads from the lower half near the stitching, then along the sides and finally upward. At first he thinks it's her menstruation, but he doesn't care what the hell it is, whether it's marmalade, blood, or sap from the Tree of Knowledge. He's going to lick it and eat it and consume it on his way to her exposed, waiting pussy. But it occurs to him that she probably doesn't menstruate any more, and again he feels something shift at the thought that she's at least as engrossed, horny, and in the clutches of the pent-up coupling instinct as he. He pushes her panties aside so that he can see her vagina. They're less elastic than they appear, and it takes some effort.

There's movement now in his underwear, and he wishes that he had selected them with more care when he'd changed the day before yesterday, knowing that they'd be pulled off him this evening by a woman. Unthinkable yesterday, unthinkable now, but ultimately meaningless now. For the sight of her muff, trimmed or maybe just naturally, absurdly, exquisitely bristly and lacking a single superfluous hair nestled around the two fiery-red lips, isn't something he remembers Annette ever offered him. With Annette, sex was a kind of education in which she kindly guided them both to a good climax, crawling on top of him as the conclusion of a fine evening. He doesn't remember either of them ever losing their minds or fucking the hell out of each other, like he wishes to do with this woman, whose name he can't even remember right now. Right now he can only penetrate her with his tongue. The bristly hair.

The tart tang of her wet sex. And finally her labia – more compliant than a juicy melon and a hundred times more intoxicating than an absent-minded whore's mechanical cock-sucking. He's not sure if she tastes fresh, or even if she's clean for that matter. He's forgotten how it tastes. But he knows she tastes forbidden, enchanting, as if nature has mixed a drink for the persistent fool who can't get enough of just seeing and touching a woman. There's a depth, a reality in her chemical acridity that seems right to him. He's so absorbed in her taste that he only now hears her whimpers – as if they're emerging not from her mouth but her lungs. It's like the purring of a cat, a supersonic rumbling she herself doesn't even notice. When he increases pressure on her labia just a little bit, or slips his tongue into her, the sound increases by a margin. But if he goes around her labia through her pubic hairs that scratch his tongue, dodging her clitoris – which has risen almost a centimetre above her labia – her whimpering subsides by a margin. He doesn't know what it means, but as he fills his mouth with her, he tries to create a balanced distribution between the deep and the loud. And he feels her body responding, kicking into gear. The sounds come at closer intervals, she responds in kind and without delay. He's never been a great lover or viewed himself as one, but this is something else. For once it's as if his age has made him better. His cock has released him from servitude; he's so curious for what he sees, tastes, and hears that he's totally in the moment – awestruck, probing, panting – and every time he does something, it only intensifies the feeling, and he can practically taste her adrenalin.

He feels a sharp cramp in his legs and is forced to change his position, which causes her to grab his hair and pull his head right into her crotch until he can hardly breathe. The cramp flares up, but it passes quickly. She releases him, clutches the edge of the rickety table, and gathers up her legs, enclosing him within a new kind of silence, interrupted only by the swooshing of the blood under his skin. She begins to shift around. A few plants fall to the floor. The soft flesh of her thigh against his ears. He's never experienced anything like this before. During their fifteen years of marriage, he'd never known Annette to be as unrestrained and strong as this woman. With the women he'd been with before Annette, he wasn't interested in anything else but penetrating them, letting his cock fill them. Still, he has no doubt. Everyone knows when a climax is coming, and Erhard recognizes it with fear and excitement; fear for what's to come afterward, and excitement for nature's incredible reward. There's nothing to do. They're on their way. The table jiggles underneath them. She begins to mutter to herself. It sounds like Basque, but may just be a Spanish dialect he doesn't recognize. A flurry of words, curses, or hoarse battle cries. He doesn't know which, but they merge with the choir emanating from her lungs, braiding into one voice. His tongue is sore. He responds by sticking it in deeper. He's good at this. Her thighs chafe against his ears. Is his entire head inside her now? Liquid, skin, hair, and labia surround him. It's as though he hears her organs shifting, making room for something. Her entire body groans, like an animal on its way through a forest not found on this island; the wood in the table begins to give, a cactus pricks his hip, but it no longer matters. His cock is erect now, it wants out. This is new. His tongue is buried in her vagina; he hears her whimpering again, hollow and low. And finally, her thighs fall to the side, the entire scaffold. They're beneath the open, purple sky, riddled with cactus, juice dripping from her sex, the turtle laughing on the television, Mónica screaming. The table collapses, and he licks her all the way down, his cock exploding, heat pouring out of him, unaccustomed and rich in pain, and he falls into a chaos without form or meaning.

58

They laugh, crawling among the pottery shards and the broken wood, and he lays his head tiredly on her rounded belly. She does not protest.
– You've got the devil's tongue, she whispers.
They laugh again. He's spent, unable to think. They fall silent. The television's still blaring inside. How long has it been since he ended his telephone conversation? The sun has dipped below the horizon, and the

little rock fence throws a shadow across the garden the size of a man. The temperature may have dropped a tad.

He doesn't understand it. His luck. His observations. His complete surrender to her. He doesn't understand how a woman can offer him so much when he doesn't deserve it.

Nor does he understand why he feels such destructive guilt towards Beatriz. It's too bizarre and confusing, but he's disgusted by everything he's gone through. He's not sure whether it's because he's been with another woman. Or because he hadn't thought of Beatriz a single time – which is something new for him. Every pore closes, his enthusiasm hardens. It's like window shopping at a going-out-of-business sale: everything is tallied, put aside, closed down. A terrible thing to witness. He doesn't know what to do, or if he needs to do anything. Should he fall in love with the woman he just made love to? Can't he settle on loving the woman hiding in his flat, regardless of her condition?

He gets to his feet and goes inside the house, having not removed so much as his t-shirt. She remains behind in her underwear. His clothes show no sign of what just transpired, except for some kind of wet, irritating stain on his trousers, though he doesn't know exactly what it is. Maybe just some urine.

– I need to go, Erhard says.

When he enters the living room, he sees that something's wrong. The only light in the room is from the glowing television, which is showing the same kids programme. Aaz is sitting, turned, in his chair. And gazing directly, unwaveringly, at the door. It's as if he's staring directly into Erhard's eyes, but of course Erhard doesn't know what he's thinking. He wants to say something, but no sound emerges. Although he's not sure they're staring at each other in the darkness, that's how it feels. Slowly Aaz spins his chair around without facing the television again.

Erhard remembers that he needs to take the Boy-Man with him. For once, he's afraid of the ride. For the first time, the Boy-Man seems as unpredictable as a gorilla. He sees Mónica getting to her feet out in the garden.

*

As he lets himself into the flat with trembling hands, he hears his neighbour rattling her door downstairs. Only a few hours have passed since he was home, but it doesn't feel that way.

He stands in the bedroom doorway watching the tiny, blinking apparatus on the table and the IV rack with the drainage bag, which are connected via a tube to the humped bundle lying shapelessly under the blanket. What was it that she said? He almost can't remember, but of course he remembers it quite clearly. The words have a frailness to them, as if they can't be said or spelled without breaking in two. The less he tries to remember them, the better he hears them. This makes him believe in them, but maybe he hears only what he wants to hear? Maybe he would like her to talk to him?

A sudden impulse causes him to turn on the lights and pull the blanket from Beatriz, and now he can see her lying flat on the mattress in her sequined jogging suit. He crawls beside her and places a finger on her left eyelid, lifting it so that he can see her eye. The pupil shifts like a loose shirt button.

He wants to call out to her. Where are you, Beatriz? Are you in there? But he can hear the desperation himself. All of a sudden he understands what it was all about.

Up until now, he has felt he was doing a kind, unselfish act – saving her from death, taking care of her, waiting for life to return to her. Up until this moment, he's dreamed of waking her up with a kiss, breaking the spell. But what he's doing is not kind, it's not for her sake, and it doesn't have a happy ending. This has all been about Erhard and his hopeless attempt to sacrifice so much for Beatriz that she couldn't reject him later, when he would require something in return. One final opportunity to sweeten his existence with a woman who would normally never fall for him.

And, in all fairness, he's been curious. What do the words mean? And what will she tell him when she wakes up? She's the only one who knows the truth about the night that Raúl disappeared. Though Raúl will never return, Erhard needs to know whether he was the one who hit her, or whether it was all just some unfortunate accident. Whether Raúl has fled from a crime or a stupid, all-too-human mistake. He needs to know. Partly to understand the person he'd believed to be his friend, but whom he didn't know at all, and partly to reclaim trust in his own judgement.

While he's looking into her eye, he feels unbelievably selfish. All the suffering he's put her through. The degrading dehumanization of being in a coma, every day growing more and more distant from the person she once was and will never be again. Family and friends have said their goodbyes. He's the only one she has: a miserable old man who has decided that she is to live – for his sake, for his ego, for his curiosity.

– I'm sorry, he says. He repeats the apology over and over. Until he lies down on the bed and falls asleep, finally close to her, finally not thinking about sex.

Erhard knows where Aritza's office is. It's in Puerto, east of the Selos District. In something called Parque Occidente. A few years ago, no one wanted to live or work in the area, but now it's the exact opposite. Young people with money have arrived. Erhard doesn't understand what they all do for a living, but one of the island's most expensive restaurants has opened on the street, and the area is packed with big cars and high-end rental vehicles. The only reasonable explanation for Parque Occidente's transformation is the view. The Selos District is surrounded by auto workshops, cheaply constructed buildings, and the remains of the old harbour district. Parque Occidente is nearly the same, except for what's called the fourth flank, which opens towards the sea. Erhard is on his way into one of three drab structures linked in a horseshoe pattern. They have been furnished as luxury offices with a communal lobby, an indoor fountain, and a lounge redolent of freshly ground coffee. He enters the lift and presses the button to the fourth floor, and he's carried soundlessly upward. He stares through one glass wall across the harbour to the sea.

The lift opens to a large office with more than thirty tables, sofas, plants, meeting rooms behind red glass, and computer screens. Plenty of computer screens. People – many of them Indians – are clustered around a pair of long tables, and a number of young men wearing hats. Just as he exits the lift he sees a sign listing the businesses located on this floor, including Eawayz, Aritza's company, to the right. As he strolls down the hall, he sees Aritza inside a glass office, his back turned. He's facing the sea and talking on the telephone. Erhard waits at the door until Aritza sees him and waves him in, concluding his conversation with *bye-bye*.

– Good morning, Aritza says, glancing at his mobile. Erhard sits down on a soft, red, ball-shaped chair. Aritza sits down, too, and now looks at Erhard. – Whatever you think you know, you're wrong. It's nothing, it was nothing. You saw nothing.

– I hope not. For your wife's sake. And your niece's.

– My wife doesn't give a shit. She'll laugh at you if you run to her with such a story.

– Then why are we meeting here?

– What is it that you want?

Erhard scrutinizes him. – To be honest, I've come to you because I don't know anyone else with connections to the shipping industry and logistics. I'm guessing there is sensitive information a person needs a clearance to obtain.

– You could've just asked me nicely.

– That's what I'm doing.

Aritza leans back in his chair. – You want to talk with my friend Robbie, Robert Jamieson.

– I want to talk to someone who can help me find crewmembers of a particular ship.

– Right. But you see, I've already spoken to Robert. He says that the ship you're looking for, the *Seascape Hestia*, was hijacked.

– I know that. That's why I'm looking for the crewmembers.

– Robbie tells me the authorities are also searching for these crewmembers.

– OK. That sounds right, Erhard says.

– So why are you looking for them?

– It's nothing criminal, I assure you.

– It's already criminal. A ship was hijacked. A man was killed. The crew and cargo vanished.

– But I'm not asking for your help to do anything criminal.

– You say you're looking for a person?

– Someone from the ship who can tell me what happened.

– There doesn't appear to be anyone who can. All the crewmembers are gone. What are you planning to do?

– I don't know.

– So, if I help you, you will not…

– I hadn't planned on saying anything. As long as you get divorced and marry your niece.

André Aritza stares at Erhard in alarm. – I…

– Relax. Just help me with this. You can do whatever you wish in your private affairs.

– And you'll promise me that you won't harm my friend or get him into trouble? We'll call him together.

– I'd like to talk to him by myself.

Aritza nods. He glances at his mobile, then lifts it to his ear. His face suddenly changes. – Hey, Robbie, it's André. OK. I've talked to him. He's all right. Yes. No, he won't do that. Yes. OK. Here he is.

Aritza hands the telephone to Erhard.

– Good morning, Erhard says.

Static on the other end of the line. A very British voice speaks. – Good morning. André tells me you are searching for a ship's crew.

– Yes. But not for the reason you probably think.

– Right.

– A boy died here on the island. I believe his death is connected to the ship.

– A boy? Do you mean the engineer?

– No. A 3-month-old boy.

– What does that have to do with the hijacking of a ship?

André Aritza looks a little confused.

– I don't know yet.

– OK. I do not know about a 3-month-old boy. André requested that I find some information on the ship you are looking for. The *Seascape Hestia*?

– I just need one of the crewmembers, someone I could call or something.

– Do you know anything about maritime law and administration?

– No, Erhard says. – I don't know anything about that.

– According to maritime law, any person who signs on to a ship must be listed in a register. In England we do that more or less digitally, but the system isn't standardized. In many countries, crew lists are simply a photocopied sheet of paper with names written in illegible handwriting. In Spain you have it both ways. Valencia and Algeciras, two of the larger ports, have a pretty good handle on it. But even though Las Palmas and Santa Cruz are also relatively good, ships from those ports often sail under the flag of Dakar or Abidjan, and one does not quite need to have one's papers in order there. Not always, in any case.

– So what does that mean for the *Seascape Hestia?*

– Up till October 2008, the Dutch shipping company which owns the *Seascape Hestia* was in charge of registering its seamen. But in 2009, the vessel arrived in Spain and was repeatedly leased to Spanish companies that did not have the same strict requirements. There have been relatively few hijackings on this side of the African continent, so there was not a whole lot of focus on registrations.

– So the company which sailed the ship when it was captured has the list?

– They have an old list, written five days before departure. And several of the names on the list, a so-called IMO FAL number 5, were not on board.

– They found the captain?

– Yes, he and three of eight crewmembers were on the list, but the rest were not. The list was outdated when they set sail. But even if it had been complete, you would not be able to find any of them. In addition to the captain, the other three whose names are known are all missing. The remainder know nothing about the *Seascape Hestia.* Except for one, an engineer by the name of Chris Jones.

The name sounded familiar. – What happened to him? Erhard asked.

– He was supposed to be on the ship, but he was replaced at the last moment by someone he does not know. But when the authorities found the body of an engineer carrying his papers, they believed it was him, of course.

– But it wasn't him?

– No. Chris Jones seems to have been reading the newspaper account of the hijacking at a pub when he saw his name.

– So no one knows who was actually on board the ship?

– It is shoddy and irresponsible, but it shows just how messy the rules are.

– Or that someone purposefully forgot to fill out the paperwork, Erhard says, thinking about the stolen vehicles that were last seen in Holland.

– The Canary Islands' police know more than we do at the moment. They have questioned quite a few of the locals in Port of Santa Cruz, including a colleague of mine several weeks ago. She told me most of what I am telling you now. Much of it is off the record. So no list, no names.

– OK, Erhard says.

– Unfortunately.

– OK.

– May I speak with André again? the Englishman says.

– In a moment. Can you get me information on Chris Jones? His telephone number?

– But he was never on board the ship.

– I'd like to speak with him.

The man is quiet for some time. – André tells me that you are pressuring him about something. I do not care to know what, but if I find Chris Jones's information for you, you will forget what you think you know about André Aritza. Do you understand?

– I need the telephone number today.

– I will find the number and give it to André today.

– Thank you. Erhard hands the mobile back to Aritza and rises, with some difficulty, from the chair. – The Englishman is all yours. He's promised to get me a telephone number today. Call me at this number when he gives it to you.

Erhard lays his business card on the table. Aritza picks up his mobile and steps away to talk.

In the afternoon, he has a meeting scheduled with the director of the water amusement park, but he can't stomach the thought of it. Since the door to Osasuna's office is closed, he asks Ana to change the meeting to next week. She makes a few clicks on the computer. He tells her that if a man named André calls, she shouldn't take a message but send the call directly to him. He's not sure if he can trust her.

– Emanuel Palabras called and was looking for you, she says.

– What did you tell him?

– That you weren't here.

– Good enough.

– Should I call him for you, now that you're here?

– No. I'll call him myself. His suspicion returns that she reports his activities to Palabras or even just Osasuna. – I'll call him shortly.

– Remember to plug your phone in, the new one.

– Right, he says, and goes back to his office. Which now feels smaller than his old Mercedes. He drops to his knees and plugs the phone into the creaky outlet. The line beeps. After finding a book, he tries to read while staring at the dark-green telephone.

Around 3.30 p.m. the telephone buzzes. It's Aritza. He gives Erhard an address on Tenerife. – We have nothing more to discuss, he says.

– I asked for a telephone number.

– You're a piece of shit. Robbie spent hours finding that address for you. There is no telephone number. The man is evidently ill.

Erhard falls silent. He doesn't know what to say.

– But I hope you find out what happened to the boy. Children are the salt of life.

It sounds strange coming from Aritza's mouth.

– Not for everyone, Erhard says.

59

Back to Tenerife. The flight doesn't even take an hour.

He sits rigidly in his chair and stares out the window. A large, invisible wave carries them from one island to the next. The motor is silent, and all is quiet; the small plane's personnel whisper, and they don't serve drinks. They don't serve anything at all; they just walk up and down the aisle smiling and reassuring, looking lovely, even the men. Not like the last time he was on a plane. That too was seventeen or eighteen years ago. He was so blotto that he believed they were about to take off when they landed on Fuerteventura. This is only the fourth time in the intervening years that he's left the island and the second time within the last month. But this time it's on the company's dime. A true pleasure. Part of a little white lie that Erhard has a lunch meeting with a shipping firm.

When he sailed to the island, he fell in love with Santa Cruz. From above it resembles the big city that it never became. The palms are grey, and the buildings are plastered with advertisements. From the plane he can see a large ad on the roof of the airport terminal, for a new perfume made with lime and anise: a young couple clutches one another, their arms indistinguishable.

He takes a taxi directly to the address and is dropped off at a little square with some booths and a newspaper kiosk. It's a sluggish Sunday, and he has an urge to eat grilled lamb at a shawarma bar that reeks of cinnamon and burnt grease. Behind the counter, a Moroccan man is rotating the spit and the flat, dark meat. The meat sizzles, attracting a swarm of men with thick black beards wearing what looks like undergarments, along with some taxi drivers.

He enters a filthy, dilapidated entranceway with dove shit on the stairwell. He hears the birds above him in the rafters, but he doesn't look up. Instead he goes calmly up the stairs to the fourth storey. The letter C. There he finds a flimsy white door that seems as though it'll fall apart if he knocks on it.

From the fourth-storey balcony he gazes across the road at a large oval track behind a tall fence. He raps on the door. Twice. Three times.

– Come the fuck in.

Erhard opens the door cautiously. – Chris Jones? My name is Erhard Jørgensen.

– Come on in! No need to shout! Chris Jones shouts. He's pissed. Laughing. – My God, now that I'm dead everyone's trying to find me.

– I guess I'm lucky you're not out to sea, Erhard says, when he sees the man in the bed. The room is dark and there are dog posters on every wall.

– Hell no, I'm on disability. On the state's bill. The good life.

He would shake Erhard's hand, but he's eating carry-out chicken from a bag. He notices Erhard's missing finger, but says nothing.

Erhard looks around for a place to sit, but finally leans against the wall instead.

– I was lucky. Isn't that what people say? Could you ask for a better life than this? A view of the dog track. Grilled chicken. Homemade whisky.

Jones points at a shelf above the toilet door in the centre of the room. A row of five bottles of brown liquid with a label Erhard doesn't recognize.

– You were supposed to have been on the ship that was hijacked? Erhard asks. It's only been a few weeks, but the man already resembles something that has grown out of cracks in the wall. Decay works fast.

– Everything was set. Hell, I had all my things on board. But some asshole hit me on the head when I came out of a, ugh, nightclub. And by the time I woke up, the ship had sailed and my life was ruined. End of story.

– Who hit you?

He laughs again. – The police want to know that too, but fuck if I know. I didn't see who did it. And I didn't ask. It's that simple. I'm guessing it was that motherfucker who was found with my papers on him. But that's just a wild guess.

– Why would anyone want to take your place on board that ship?

– He was probably one of the goddamn pirates, don't you think? Are you a journalist or what? If you are, I'd like five grand to be part of your little story.

– I'm not a journalist, and I don't have that kind of money.

– Then why the fuck did you come here and disturb me?

– I'm looking for a missing person.

– I can't help you. Bloody fucking hell, don't you get it? I got beat up. He throws his empty chicken bag at the rubbish bin, but misses.

– You must hear rumours. From your friends or others you've sailed with. Seven seamen are missing, as well as a multimillion dollar cargo.

– This isn't a gossip mill. My sister's the only person who cares to visit me, and those shitty newspapers don't know fuck all about what happened anyway. They didn't know I wasn't the dead man, but some other guy. Just about killed my old Mum.

– But your friends. They must've heard something? I've driven a taxi for years, and taxi drivers gossip more than housewives, if you know what I mean.

Chris Jones laughs guardedly, as if he's missing a tooth or two. – Hell, I know what you mean. Who are you anyway?

– I'm just an old man who's trying to find someone from that ship, that's all.

– An old man. A curious old man. But I like that. As long as you're not the police. Or from the newspaper.

– I promise you, I'm not from either.

– Hand me one of those, he says, pointing at the whisky bottles. Erhard retrieves one for him, and the man pours whisky into a dirty cup that's standing on a footstool next to the bed, and he gives it to Erhard. He himself raises the bottle to his lips and chugs a quarter of the liquid.

– What happened to your finger? Jones asks.

He doesn't seem embarrassed to ask the question. It's liberating when people ask Erhard.

– My punishment for a crime.

– Fuck me, what'd you do? Look at another man's wife in the wrong country or something?

334

– Not exactly, but something like that.

– United Arab Emirates?

– Denmark.

– What? The Danes don't do that.

– I did.

It takes a little time before Jones realizes what Erhard means. – That's brutal, he says softly.

They drink.

– Last week, Jones says, after he's wiped his mouth with the blanket. – I met one of the lads that I sailed with. Simao. We share a common interest in dogs. Jones whirls his finger around at the posters. – He came up here and sat in that very chair you're in, stiff as a board he was, feeling real bad about what had happened to me. Then all of a sudden he told me about the *Hestia*. He knew exactly what happened and where they were all hiding and shit.

– Hiding?

– He told me the crew was mixed up in something and was hiding from the police and shit.

– Mixed up how?

– No idea. He was probably just showing off. That's what everyone does. Every sailor has sailed around the world a thousand times, scoring some pussy at every port. Braggarts. Many of the sailors are tiny little men, assholes who don't care to leave the ship when it reaches the wharf. As long as they've got fags and alcohol and Coke, they'd rather stay in their small cabins fucking each other. The scum.

– Huh, Erhard says.

– But Simao said something interesting. He said the cargo had been brought back here. The entire fucking thing returned to where it had started. I'd never heard that. Everyone thinks it vanished in the dark heart of Africa. Blame it on the niggers, you know.

– Interesting, Erhard says, though he's unable to determine exactly what it means.

– It's fucking organized, that's what it is. Rich men in their offices, laughing all the way to the golf club. Isn't that what people say?

– Where can I find your acquaintance? The braggart.

– If he's not out to sea, then you'll find him at one of the dog tracks, you know, the ones with the super-skinny dogs chasing each other?

– Which one?

– The big one north of here.

– What else is he called besides Simao?

– Simao. He doesn't have another name. It's just like Pelé. He has only one name.

– If I do you a favour, will you do one for me?

– That sounds naughty, Chris Jones laughs.

– If you find out where your friend Simao is right now, I'll find out who beat you up.

– I know who beat me up. It was the asshole who took my papers.

– But you told me yourself he wasn't alone.

– I'm busy at the moment, he says, waving the bottle.

– It'll be here tomorrow. Or one of its four friends.

– It's hard to say no to an old man like you.

– That's right, Erhard says.

6 0

The container ship is called the *Nicosia*, and he can barely read the name – it's been worn down by bird shit, wind, and the elements. It's approximately fifty metres long. The wooden gangway is rickety; it looks all wrong, frail, next to the black wall of steel that forms the hull of the ship. He'd figured he could just begin by shouting for the crew, who would be busy on board, but there's no one around. So he saunters up the gangway as if it's all he's ever known.

Even when he's on board he doesn't see anyone. The deck is filled with cranes and containers and thick cables with pulleys that fasten the containers to the ship. It reeks of iron or even blood. For a moment Erhard wonders if he's bit his tongue, but it's the deck that smells of metal, it's the peeling containers, it's the chains that form the railing in several sections, creaky, swinging in the wind. He walks along the railing in search of a door. Maybe the entire crew is having a meeting below deck. Maybe they've not reported to work yet. Find the ship's bridge, Chris Jones had told him.

He sees a door under the stairwell leading up to the roof of the top deck. It's a small door that's raised twenty centimetres above the floor, so that it resembles a closet door, and he expects to find shelves filled with torches and ropes and various other equipment. Erhard doesn't know much about the work, and nothing at all about life at sea. Since many of the seamen he's met – including Chris Jones – are alcoholics, drug addicts, violent, or just plain odd, he figures it must be a depressing, demanding life: boredom, the constant pitching of the sea, the creaky hull, awful food served on pitiful metal trays. Not to mention all the horny seamen in too-small beds.

It's not a closet but a long corridor that runs six or seven yards straight ahead and disappears into the floor. But he's not going below deck. He walks straight ahead until he turns a corner and sees a steep stairwell up to the wheelhouse that rests like a bird house at the top of the windowless box that is the ship's hull. It's more or less what he's looking for.

He climbs the stairs and peers through the door window. The room, which looks like what people would call the bridge, is filled with work tables and large, square computers. Sunlight filters through the tinted windows that run the entire length of one wall, allowing Erhard a view of the ship's bow, the other ships in the harbour, and even the ocean as seen through a gauzy coffee-brown haze that makes the morning sun seem tired. Someone is sitting at a narrow table, his back to Erhard, leaning over a newspaper or some papers. Cautiously Erhard opens the door. The person at the table doesn't seem surprised, and doesn't even react. Somewhere a radio is tuned to a pop-music station.

– Good morning, Erhard says.

It turns out to be a short, Arabic-looking woman with silky-smooth hair and a hat. She glances down at Erhard's shoes. They're cheap trainers, he knows. Not the shoes of a director. Even though he's promised

Emanuel several times, he's not bought himself a pair of proper shoes. –
And you are?

– I'm looking for Simao.

She points to the corner, to another door. – He's asleep in there. But
he needs to get up. We sail in forty-five minutes.

She turns and goes back to her reading.

He pushes open the door. The little room is pitch dark. By the light
from the door he sees a bunk bed and a small man with a full black beard.
As Erhard enters, the man wakes up and shifts beneath his blanket, like
a child. – Simao?

– I'm awake, Simao says, though he doesn't sound it.

– I've never said anything like that, he says repeatedly.

Erhard has just tucked 200 euros into the pocket of his tattered shirt.
Anything over 100 euros would get the asshole started, Chris Jones had
said. He's probably got debts he can't pay back that have accumulated
over the decades; his life is in the hands of the only ones in the gambling
world who don't actually gamble, the masterminds who sit in run-of-the-
mill offices and move millions of euros between the islands and never
pay taxes. The dog-racing sheet is poking out from under the mattress.
Erhard had expected posters on the wall. Of a girlfriend or a child or
topless women in mermaid costumes. Or dogs like at Chris Jones's place.
But maybe the bunk isn't Simao's, just a communal galley the sailors use
when on duty. Simao has gone out on deck. To smoke, Erhard discovers,
while he explains to Simao why he's here.

– I've got a few questions for you. If you answer them all, I'll give you
two hundred more. I know what you've said about the *Seascape Hestia*.
Just tell me the same thing, that's all I'm asking.

Simao gazes across the harbour. – Has gettin' beat up made that poof
stupid? I told him that so that he wouldn't feel bad about… About…

Erhard ignores this. – I'm not a policeman, and I'm not a government
official. Nothing like that. I won't tell anyone that I've spoken to you.

They're standing in the shade between a line of containers. Simao
lights a second fag even as he holds the first. He flicks the smoking butt

over the railing and into the water, then pats his shirt pocket for the 100-euro note.

– It's been weeks now. I was fucking stuck in Casablanca. Waiting for my buddy Ramón, who had promised me he'd be there, innit. But he doesn't show up. I'm at some bar, and I run into a ship's mate I know. He's pissed and high, you know. We have a few shots, and we discuss how to find him a woman. But he's not really into it, tells me his wife will skin him alive if he cheats on her, and so we end up at some local guy's. Smoking, innit. All of a sudden he tells me he'd been part of the crew that had sailed out to empty that Canary ship that everyone was talking about. Everyone's looking for that ship's crew who had all sailed on to West Africa, but no one knows this guy was on board that other ship and he's totally whacked wondering if he should tell somebody. But I tell him he shouldn't, cause then he'd be mixed up in some serious shit.

Erhard's not surprised. – Why did you believe him? What if he was just making it up?

Simao looks at Erhard as if he's an idiot. – You just know. When a sailor's pissed enough, he don't lie.

– What if he was just trying to be entertaining?

– Entertaining? Simao tilts his head back as if deeply offended. – Are you implying something?

Erhard doesn't know what the man means. – No, I'm just saying he might have lied to you.

– He wasn't lying, old man.

– What did you say his name was?

– I haven't told you his name. How should I know?

– You were drinking together, and you've sailed with him before, but you don't know his name?

– Shit, what's it matter what his name is?

– Is he Spanish?

– Yeah, for fuck's sake.

– Did he meet others there? Was he alone?

– We had some shots with a few locals, a few blacks, but otherwise no.

– And you say the pirates abandoned them in West Africa?

– The pirates, yeah.

– What?

– Yeah, the pirates abandoned them in Casablanca.

Erhard suddenly understands the man's slightly off-kilter body language. The way his middle finger rubs his right-hand thumb. He's not talking about a drinking buddy, he's talking about himself. He was the one on board the ship. But Erhard decides not to press too hard yet. – There weren't any pirates, were there?

– Yeah, bloody hell. I'm telling you're there were lots of pirates.

Erhard sizes up Simao. He's still a young man. A boy, really. Thirty-something. That could work to Erhard's advantage – that Erhard seems like a strict father figure. He stares directly into the boy's eyes.

Simao covers his face. – Stop that. I don't know fuck all about what happened to Chris. I swear I don't know who beat him up or who pushed the fake Chris overboard.

He seems to be telling the truth, but Erhard is sceptical. – But there were no pirates?

– Fuck me. No, there were no pirates. Never was.

– Only the crew?

– It was supposed to seem like the ship had been seized by pirates. Some of the *Hestia*'s crewmembers punched each other to make it seem like the pirates had done it. We laughed about it at first. Until Señor P decked one crew member so hard that he lost a tooth.

– What about your buddy? Did he punch someone too?

– No, he didn't. There were four on board. They would've been offed if not for the ship.

– What do you mean?

– The ship they were on was a different kind of ship, and none of the crew were familiar with it.

– So what happened to the cargo?

– Most of it ended up here. The crew was dropped off in Casablanca.

– The crew went to port in Casablanca, but the cargo came back to Tenerife?

The man nods, then inhales so that the cherry on his cigarette turns bright red. – Except for Señor P. He went back to wherever he was from.

– Is it even possible to transfer cargo when not in port?

Simao chuckles. – You've sure got plenty of questions, old man.

– I told you as much. Remember my contribution to the dog track.

Simao eyes Erhard distrustfully. – If you're not Chris's good friend then he owes me a fucking apology. He tamps out his fag and lights a new one. This time he takes a normal breath before raising the cigarette to his mouth. – You can move cargo, sure, but it's not easy. It's dangerous, innit.

– How so?

– Out on the open sea the ships sway and might ram into each other, the cranes too, and you might drop your cargo into the water. It's not good.

– Sounds difficult. Does it take a long time?

– Yeah, if there's a lot that needs to be transferred.

– If there weren't any pirates, what happened to the engineer they thought was Chris Jones? The guy the fishermen found? The newspaper wrote that he resisted the pirates.

– They wrote Chris was the one who'd been thrown overboard, and I believed it. But I hadn't even seen Chris on board. I mean, I, uh, my friend said it was total chaos. It was New Year's Eve. Fireworks were going off along the coast, and you could hear the explosions above the wind. The water over there was fucked up. That's why Señor P was called in. He knows the sea better than anyone, innit.

– So Señor P was the one who pushed the engineer overboard? The fake Chris Jones?

– That's what they said. He arrived on the ship right before it happened. He was drunk as a skunk, muttering strange things.

– Strange how?

– *Lad was angry.* He kept saying *lad was angry.* That the money was burning a hole in his pockets. Crazy shit.

– *Lad?* His own son?

Simao laughs. – What does I know? I talked to him only once.

– Why haven't you mentioned any of this to the police? They're looking for the crew, and believe they're holed up in some basement with a
bunch of Moroccan pirates. Families are missing their fathers.

– I'm sorry about Chris and that chap that fell overboard. But I'm not
getting mixed up in any of this.

Erhard decides the time is now to press him. – They paid you, didn't they?

– I haven't done anything illegal.

– Withholding information is illegal.

– In what country? I'm sailing under the Cuban flag.

The lie is much larger than Erhard had thought. – You were on board
the other ship, and you transferred the cargo.

Simao squirms as if he's been asked to chug vinegar.

Erhard presses on. – Say yes. I won't tell anyone, and you'll get another
100 euros for your little dog.

– He's not a little dog, Simao says sharply. – He's an Azawakh.

Erhard hands him a 100-euro note. – How did you move the goods?

Simao looks down the row of containers. – We were supposed to meet
north of Alegranza, but ended up sailing very far south, just to the west
of Lanzarote. *The Hestia* was delayed. It was bad enough to begin with,
but it just got worse.

– How?

– Apparently, the plan had been to find the same-size ship, but our
captain hadn't found one like the *Hestia*. He'd just hired ours, the *La
Brugia*, because there were only four of us on board. But our ship wasn't
a container ship – it was a general cargo ship, like this one. So the two
ships were unequal, and moving the cargo was fucking difficult.

– And then what happened?

– We sailed directly towards Casablanca, while the Ghanaian man
steered the *Hestia* towards Agadir, innit.

– Was anything brought to Fuerteventura?

– No. Well, the *Hestia* sailed that way. It went north around Isla de
Lobos after we separated. But the Ghanaian man didn't go into port. His
ship was empty. I saw it with my own eyes.

– So you transferred everything?

– Yeah. It was hard as hell. There was lots of shouting, and some of the containers were smashed.

– Smashed?

– Yeah, when they were lifted over the ships. They're just like egg shells if you hit them in the right place.

– On the *Hestia* or on your ship?

– I didn't see it. I was below deck. Down in the cargo hold. They were arguing about where we should drop anchor, with the wind and the current, innit. It took a long time. The Ghanaian guy talked to someone over the radio. An hour later, Señor P came on board. Pissed and vicious, he was, but he was familiar with the waters. He was from Fuerteventura. Knew the sea like the back of his hand, he said. Then they began to transfer the cargo. Shortly after that Chris Jones, or whoever the hell he was, fell overboard.

– What did you do when you found out?

– Not a damn thing. What could we do? We were busy. I sure as hell didn't want the same fate. I did my job. But I was real glad it wasn't Chris but some other guy. Though I didn't know that until I'd returned to Tenerife, innit.

– What's the P for in Señor P?

– Easy now, Gramps, I don't know any more than that. If you keep asking me questions like that, I'll have to ask you for a bridge.

– Bridge?

– A 500 note.

Erhard decides it must be some kind of dog-racing term. – I don't have any more, he says. – Just tell me what the P is for?

– Fuck off, Gramps.

Erhard knows that he's just trying to reassert his self-respect, and he can't really blame him for that.

– Thanks for the chat, Erhard says, and starts towards the gangway. Remembering something, he walks back to the containers. Simao is about to light his tenth cigarette. Erhard hands him his business card. – If you feel the urge to help a little boy who's gone missing, call me. But don't leave a message.

– What. A boy? What does that have to do with this?

– There was a 3-month-old boy on board the *Hestia*. And his mother.

Erhard is gambling now. He still doesn't know whether or not they were on board.

– There's was no boy. Or mother. I know that much.

– Call me if you think of anything else. I won't give you any more money. The next thing you tell me is free.

Erhard leaves. He hopes that Simao will run after him and tell him the name of ship's mate, but he crosses the gangway and is back on the dock before he turns to see that no one has followed him.

61

He walks down a broad boulevard towards the city, but grows tired and hops into a taxi that's parked in front of a hotel. He gives the driver one of the few addresses he remembers in Santa Cruz: 49 Calle Centauro. With a little more than three hours before his return flight, there's too much time to wait at the airport, and too little time to take a ferry. He might as well sit at a cafe, doing nothing. He pays the driver, who promptly thrusts the bills into his wallet as if he's afraid Erhard will snatch them from him. Maybe there are more robberies here; it's a bigger island, with more tourists.

Although he doesn't recognize the street, he decides to stroll around the area. He skirts the fence that encloses the container park. There's quite a bit of traffic in there. Huge lorries, fork lifts, and tow trucks that spit brown smoke out of long exhaust pipes. Another forest of containers. In a flash he pictures the containers being raised onto lorries and ships and into cargo hulls and then onto new lorries and new container parks. A flurry of traffic and goods exchanging places, units shifting around in a vast chain of supply and demand, need and desire, habits. A toothpick from China jammed into an olive from Gran Canaria and set in a martini from Italy, and a vodka from Poland in a champagne flute from Thailand in the hand of an Englishwoman from Portsmouth. The invisible underbrush of infrastructure. Like going to the loo, it's not something people discuss. It's simply there. But sometimes, you have to study the poop to determine the diet.

When he reaches the guardhouse, he stops a moment to watch the big lorries exit the park. An African man sits inside the guardhouse.

– Would it be possible for me to meet the supervisor here?

– Supervisor?

– Palalo, Erhard says, quickly showing the man his business card. – I'm here to inspect our containers.

– Where did you say you're from again?

– Palalo.

He stares at a little computer that's affixed to the inside of a cabinet. – There's no supervisor. But you can talk to Binau, our manager. He's out there somewhere, in the park. I can call him.

– Don't worry about it. I'll find him myself. Where are our containers?

The man checks his computer again. Then he points down one of the corridors between the containers and the rows of storage units which resemble enormous shelves. Erhard nods, then goes through the gate into the park, passing the lorries and the cranes. Noise fills the air, men shouting all around him. The soil is hard clay. Every now and then, a forklift pulls up in front of him and hoists a pallet from one of the shelves six metres above the ground, then drives over to a waiting lorry. He heads in the direction the man had pointed, but he doesn't know what he's looking for, or when he'll know he's found it. When he sees a short man wearing ear muffs, he stands beside him until the man notices him.

– Palalo, Erhard calls out to the man, who hasn't removed his ear muffs.

– Over there, the man says, glancing down at his mobile phone.

– Those? Erhard points at four red containers standing side by side.

– From there all the way down, the man says, his eyes still trained on his mobile. His gloved hand indicates a point right behind Erhard, down a corridor the length of two or three football pitches.

He heads that way, as much as anything to get a sense of the containers, to immerse himself in their dizzying quantity, and to try to disappear
in them. He hopes to run into one of the workers, but there's no one
around. He spots a number of new containers with built-in locks, but
most of the containers are the old kind, with a bar fastened by a padlock.
Some of the containers are stacked, while others are lined up in rows.
Some are divided by a clearing between the red and blue containers, a
space ready to be filled.

He reaches the corner where the fence bends, then continues up the
hill and down to the harbour. He sees, on the other side of the fence,
rocks and a stone marker. From the hilltop he catches sight of some
houses and a tennis court, two players dashing back and forth. There's
a small shed on his side of the fence, four posts with a tin roof and a
back wall. Inside is a chair and a wooden box. Some equipment hangs
on the back wall: ear muffs, a torch, a hammer, bolt cutters, a saw, a roll
of cable, a pair of coal-black work gloves no one would ever wish to
stick his fingers into. Well, Erhard wouldn't anyway. He looks around.
Although he can still hear the lorries, there's no one about. He grabs the
bolt cutters and proceeds to the containers, then snips the locks one at
a time. Once he's cut fifteen, he returns to the shed, hangs up the bolt
cutters, and glances around again. Still no one. Then he opens the first
container. And the next. And then another. Each is filled to the brim with
lamps and blankets and boxes, bicycles and bags of clothes and electrical
cords. Some items rest on pallets, others simply lie on the floor; some
are strapped down, others jammed in.

But in the twelfth and thirteenth containers he finds what he's looking
for: a car, a Seat Leon. It's parked on a set of springs and held in place
by thick straps that crisscross the container. He retrieves the bolt cutters
and clips the locks on the next twenty containers.

In all, he finds fourteen vehicles. Seats, Skodas, and Volkswagens.

When he opens a container and finds a black Volkswagen, his breath
catches. Though it's a different model, the make and colour assure him
that he's heading in the right direction. He crawls through the straps
and over to the driver's-side door, and he's just able to squeeze into the

front seat. The car smells strongly of nylon or leather, like it would at a car dealership. It's dark inside and almost feels cosy. The key is in the ignition. He peers down at the odometer, but it's one of the new digital kinds that doesn't work unless the motor is running. He turns the key, but nothing happens. So he slides out again and exits the container as if he has been inside the belly of a whale, tired but proud.

He closes all the containers and collects the locks, then tosses them over the fence, where they disappear among the rocks. He walks along the fence to gaze down at an empty corridor between the containers, so he can get back without being noticed by too many. He reaches the construction site and suddenly recognizes the place, even though it was dark the last time he was here. To his left is a gaping hole in the fence and the entrance to Café Rústica's kitchen. This is where the dishwasher helped him. He crawls through the hole and walks down the alley.

He orders a Mai Tai to see whether or not they've followed his advice, but it still tastes too sweet. The girl who serves it to him is friendly, but she doesn't flirt.

– It was all I could find, she says, dropping two postcards on the table. The postcards are ads for the cafe. DJ Sundays and happy hour, or what they call Rústica hour. Mai Tais for one euro. No fucking wonder.

He jots down a note: He knows where the car came from. He knows which ship it was on. He knows, perhaps, how it got to Fuerteventura. He knows where the newspapers came from. He knows, perhaps, where the girl – it must've been a girl, not a woman – who abandoned her baby was from.

Because he's so lost in thought about her, he stares at the girls in the cafe, as if he expects to find her among them. As if he can see who among them gave birth then starved her baby. He thinks of Mónica. For some reason he thinks about her as a young woman, with Aaz as a boy, a tiny child at his mother's breast, suckling, feeding like a sick kitten. Or maybe he's thinking of Annette with Lene, the youngest, sitting on a faded-blue sofa on the first floor of Bispebjerg Hospital, showing her off to anyone who stopped in, while he stood behind the glass attempting to place a call at a payphone that kept spitting out his coins. A mother is so beautiful he could cry right on the spot. He thinks of the young mother laying her child inside the cardboard box: her trembling nervous hands fumbling as they swaddle the squirming child in newspapers; she's putting her child into the box knowing that it will die. A mother is so beautiful. It all begins with her, her words that raise the child, and her hands that hold the child. A mother is so beautiful and yet so dangerous. She decides whether the child will live and for how long. One day, a month, a decade. He looks at one of the girls, the kind whose belly will one day, maybe soon, expand and she will become a mother; she's balancing rubbish bags and cardboard that have to be taken out back. In truth she's a little too small for this kind of work, frighteningly pale and thin, sickly. With red hair like a German. She pauses. One of the bags is filled with bottles and is too heavy. Erhard gets to his feet to help her. She tells him no thanks but smiles gratefully. He grabs the larger bag and follows her down the bar, through the kitchen, and out back. After he's thrown the bag into a container with other bottles, she thanks him again.

– I'm not very good at this job, she says. I'm too small and I can't remember all the things I'm supposed to.

– You're great at it.

– Don't tell the boss. That I can't manage.

– Do you mean Ellen?

The girl startles. Then nods.

– Not that I know her, Erhard says. – I met her once.

The girl seems relieved to hear that. – She stops in around four o'clock. She can't see me standing here.

– Why don't you quit?

– This is the best job I've ever had. If only I could figure out what I'm supposed to do. I desperately need this job.

Erhard doesn't have it in him to ask her why she needs this job so badly, but the girl tells him anyway. She's three months behind on rent to her girlfriend, who wants to go home and so on.

Erhard glances down at the cardboard box beside the girl's arm. It's an ordinary box, but it resembles the one that the newspaper fragments were in. The same size, the same corner flaps. The same skinlike colour.

– Have you ever heard of any of the waitresses here getting pregnant? he asks the girl.

She hesitates. – No, I…

– Do you ever gossip about a girl who waitressed here and then got pregnant?

– No. Not as far as I know.

– What about the other cafes nearby?

– There really aren't any others. But there was one girl who had an abortion a few months ago.

– Does that happen often?

– I don't think so. There are many Catholics here, after all. Mostly it's the English, you know, who do that kind of thing.

Erhard hadn't thought about that. – So what happened to her?

– She had an abortion and came back to work.

– Here?

– Yes, but she doesn't work here any more. She went home.

The girl glances up at a window above the cafe. Three windows, actually, large and with no signs of life. A ruined sunscreen covers one window; it's one of those kind of aluminium plates that reflect the sunlight. In another is a desiccated flower, which was once a long-stemmed rose.

– Because of the abortion?

– I don't think so. She didn't seem bothered by the abortion. I lived with her. She didn't sleep at home very often, if you know what I mean.

– So why did she leave? And when?

– Probably a few weeks ago, maybe more. The end of January.

Erhard feels the wind being knocked out of him.

– Are you sure? This is important.

The girl studies him. She's not pretty, but she has freckles, a rarity among native islanders. Her mother or father must have come from the UK. – Well, she had the abortion in November. She was living in my old flat then.

– Other than her, you don't know anyone who's been pregnant? No strangely large bellies or sudden illness or anything like that?

– No, the girl says. She's clearly beginning to lose interest and glances towards the door.

– You should get back. Thanks for talking to me.

She runs inside through the kitchen. Erhard returns to his seat. He considers retrieving the cardboard box that resembles the one from the car, but it's not the specific box that's interesting. What's interesting is that, during a certain period of time, there were cardboard boxes and Danish newspapers less than 300 metres from where the car in all likelihood was parked. He's on to something, he's certain. He empties a packet of salt in his Mai Tai and stirs it with his straw. It helps a little.

Shortly after 4 p.m., he watches someone park a large car across the road and the manager, Ellen, enter the cafe wearing sunglasses. She should remember him, he thinks, but she doesn't. Not all cafe owners remember quite as well as taxi drivers. She sets down her bag and immediately begins to boss the girls around. The music is turned down. She upbraids the small, pale girl because she's drinking Coke behind the bar, practically whispering, so that only Erhard notices. The five other guests are eating breakfast and watching television, unperturbed.

Erhard goes up to the bar and tries to catch Ellen's attention, but she's busy wiping the worktop near the sink and throwing away lemon rinds. – Preparing for a visit from the union? he says.

She whirls round and peers at him a moment. – You again, she says.

– Yes. I'm still trying to find a young mother.

– To each his own.

He ignores this comment. – You haven't thought of any employees or job applicants with a large belly one day and a flat belly a few days later, have you?

She seems to pretend to consider. – Crown Princess Kate, perhaps.

– What?

– Nothing. No, I still haven't.

– How long have you been renting out the upstairs flat?

– We let select employees use it.

She doesn't blink once. Pure poker face.

– So VIPs or what?

– Yes.

Erhard laughs. He laughs for such a long time that Ellen finally starts laughing, too. – That's far-fetched. You know that.

– It's only a temporary solution for those girls who can't find a place to live.

– I'm guessing that all they pay is a symbolic rent?

– Let's talk about something else, she suggests.

– Anything new from your friend Hollisen?

She gives him a sharp look. – No. I've told you that.

– Maybe he sent you a postcard or something.

– No one sends postcards any more.

– I see.

– And if you're still hoping to help your friend, then you should search someplace else. Hollisen won't be back.

– You know that even though you say you haven't heard from him?

– Yes, she says. She stares at him. – He's dead.

– How'd he die?

– Don't know. But people I know, and who he was in contact with, haven't heard from him in months. Not a single word. And that man is always in some kind of a fix, financially, sexually, even mentally. So two months' radio silence is as good as... Her light-hearted tone of voice is gone again. – He must be dead.

– But you're not sure. Maybe he was just captured by some muse on a Greek island and has forgotten everything?

– The only muse that could have captured that man was the Big Groove.

The expression is a little old-fashioned, and that's how Erhard knows it. – Was he an addict?

– C'mon. I don't remember your name, but let the man rest in peace.

– But you don't know that he's dead.

– A woman knows. Plus, he hasn't touched his bank account, and he had several hundred euros in that account. Trust me, Søren wouldn't let the account idle like that. That man didn't know restraint. She smiles at the thought. – Even though he didn't have much money, he always spent what he had partying. Bad habits from his days playing with golden boys.

Erhard scrutinizes her.

– OK. I opened one of his bank statements that came a few weeks ago. He took out small sums until 2 January, and then never touched the account again. There's no activity at all. That sets off alarm bells.

– What do you think happened?

– Who knows? Maybe he drank himself to death or had a disagreement with one of his gangster buddies.

– Are you being serious now?

– Yes. He was always a little nervous about that. The last I saw him, he wore sunglasses.

– When was that?

– December.

– The last time I was here you said you hadn't seen him in a year.

– I didn't really *see* him, you know. He just stood out there staring at the cafe.

– I'm not a policeman, I don't care about your little business or whatever it is, I just want to find a friend, who… who's missing. And Hollisen is somehow involved. Was he staring at the cafe or the flat above it?

She doesn't respond, but walks into the kitchen and returns with a croissant in her mouth. – It was the end of December. I remember, because it was right around the anniversary of my taking over the cafe. I was putting decorations in the windows, and suddenly there he was. He was wearing sunglasses, and seemed nervous. Normally he would come over. I was kind of a big sister to him.

– What was he doing? Why didn't he come over?

– How should I know?

– You didn't go over to him?

– I figured he was tripping or something.

– Did he meet with anyone, or talk to anyone?

– No. Just like that he was gone. I thought he'd return after a few days, but he never did.

– Do you have a photograph of him?

She pulls out her mobile phone and presses a few buttons. It's one of those new smart devices that most young people have. She hands him it to him. On the screen is an image of a young man around forty. He's smiling, pointing at the too-tight t-shirt that he's wearing over another t-shirt. Rústica's logo is printed on the shirt in ornate lettering. He looks like a handsome boy who'd become a tired man. Like one of countless people he knows on Fuerteventura, surfers who refuse to remove their wetsuits, party girls who don't care to return to the suburbs, bartenders who don't wish to take a day off. Like Raúl might have looked if his father hadn't been one of the island's wealthiest men and kept him under wraps. He looks like Erhard himself seventeen years ago.

– There are several photographs here. Ellen sweeps the first image aside, bringing a second forward. – Staff party, one of many. He came of course. That was back when...

He's the same happy boy in several of the photos. But with each one he seems sadder. This insistence on happiness which doesn't seem genuine. He stands in front of the camera with all the pretty girls, but also the cooks and the dishwashers and, apparently, even regular patrons. The party was held in the cafe and spilled out onto the street.

– Were you a couple?.

– No. Almost. But you don't date your little brother, do you? Besides, he fell in love every time some hussy bothered to listen to him for more than five minutes.

The photographs speak their own precise language. In several he's kissing girls on their cheek, and in one he's kissing a woman's cleavage.

– What about this one? he says, pointing at an image in which he's holding a ponytailed girl's waist and lifting her off the floor.

– Lily, she says. – No, she wasn't Søren's type. He tried to get her fired. She says she refused to give him a blowjob on his birthday. It wouldn't surprise me.

– The creepy type. The girl, I mean.

– A fucking bitch, if you ask me. A lesbian, probably, and ambitious. There aren't many go-getters like her on the islands.

Erhard can think of a few. – She'll soon be president of Tenerife.

– Too late. She's back on Fuerteventura. She inherited a restaurant or something from her grandfather.

– What's the place called?

Erhard thinks of Bill Haji, but so far as he knows, he wasn't a grandfather and he didn't own a restaurant. He owned nightclubs and one cocktail lounge down at Corralejo's harbour.

– I don't know the name of the place.

Erhard continues studying the photographs. He recognizes the girl who served him that last time he was on the island.

– That's Millie, the American. Søren liked her. He loved the chubby ones.

– Enough to have a child with her?

– Ellen laughs. – Millie? No, she was, she is, the self-righteous kind of American: all talk, no action. She's in the States now, but she'll be back next summer.

– Do you know all the girls who work for you?

– Yes, most of them. I have many seasonal employees. Girls who just come for a single summer. I'm a kind of mother figure to many of them. Young girls who bring so much emotional baggage from their parents. I know that I'm tough and probably not well-liked by many of them, but at least they know where they stand with me, and I try to teach them a little and give them some responsibility.

– Would they tell you if they suddenly became pregnant?

Ellen considers. – Yes, but they would also know that I think getting pregnant is stupid. We shouldn't put ourselves in a worse position than what we're already in.

– Do you mean women?

– I recommend sex before marriage, lots of it. Enjoy it. Sample the goods. But for God's sake use condoms or pills. Once you have a child, there's always someone who controls you. You can't decide your fate.

What about sex after marriage? What about sex with an older woman on a garden table? His Mai Tai is empty. It's a quarter to five. He has to return to the airport. He throws some euros on the table.

– Speaking to you has been, what can I say, riveting, Señorita Ellen. Have a nice day. He heads out onto the street and towards the water. When he reaches a broad boulevard, he flags down a taxi and climbs into the backseat. He notices everything the driver does, but he doesn't say a word. There's nothing worse than having a know-it-all taxi driver as a passenger.

62

As he's heading down the FV-1, a giant raindrop pelts the windscreen. Erhard studies it calmly, curiously, then notices the dense, grey clouds. Normally he loves the clouds, but for some reason they seem foreboding today. He snaps on the radio and, a few minutes later, hears the DJ on Radio Mucha discuss the weather. When he lived in the old house, he used to hurry home and lash everything down, making sure the tarpaulin covered the roof if he heard rain. If the goats were nearby, he would let them into the shed. The rain made them nervous. Hardy was known to run great distances to find shelter. His instincts might drive him more than three miles south. But the roof is repaired now, and Hardy – who knows where that wretched animal went? Besides, he doesn't live there any more. He's a director now. Although he anticipates more rain to fall, none does, and he manoeuvres the vehicle soundlessly into the basement beneath his building. The windscreen is once again dry.

He's exhausted and impatient in the lift. Even though Beatriz has been alone for only a few hours more than usual, he feels bad. He's witnessed firsthand how she can fill her drainage bag with so much urine that the pressure alone makes it difficult for her to pee. All in all, it's not easy keeping someone alive. It almost seems as if she doesn't wish to live. As if she's trying to make things as hard as possible for him. It's tough to ignore the doctor's admonishment. It's inhuman, what he's doing. It's undignified. He almost agrees with the doctor, but he knows the turning point could come at any moment. The doctor says there's a chance she will survive. A chance. If that's true, what else can he do but assist her, regardless how small that chance might be?

He pulls out his key and lets himself in. He notices that the door mat, a thin, black rubber mat, has been knocked out of place. He checks the extra key, but it's still taped under the stairwell. Maybe the doctor stopped by without telling Erhard?

He locks the door behind him, then hurries to the dark bedroom. He hears a strange beeping sound. He runs his hand along the wall and finds the switch that turns on the two reading lamps. The respirator's warning lamp is blinking and the IV rack has been knocked over. Erhard's side of the bed is made, but Beatriz's is empty.

Then he sees her right hand. Still attached to the IV, it's raised clumsily in the air, so that it appears she's waving at him. She's lying on the floor.

He hops onto the bed and grabs her as if she'll disappear if he doesn't. She's curled in an impossible position between tubes and cords, but her eyes sparkle. Both of them. Her mouth quivers, and her hand almost feels warm.

– Bea! My Bea.

She doesn't respond. Erhard shifts closer, so that he can see her face, her eyes. At first he thinks her pretty face is still pretty, that it still surprises him with its straightforward simplicity, no make-up, no earrings. But then he sees that it's all ruined. That there's nothing left to save. He doesn't know what has changed, but her face is like a mask. As if her eyes and the person behind her face belong to someone else entirely. She blinks. Her eyes have a glossy sheen to them, and her pupils are slightly dilated as though in darkness. They are the eyes of a living being, just not the person he knows. He wants to say her name, to embrace her, if for no other reason than to do so one final time, but it doesn't seem important. There's nothing left to embrace, just cells. Assisted by machines, the body breathes, but it's not Beatriz. Still, as a polite gesture, he strokes her coarse, greasy hair.

– E.

Erhard's nearly certain that it was the machines that beeped. Her lips don't move, but a sound emerges from between them. – *E.*

– Bea, is that you, Bea? Are you there, Bea?

He stares at her lips. They're parted slightly, and dry. As if she can't lick them.

– *Em…*

– Can you hear me, Beatriz? Nod or say yes if you can hear me.

– *E.*

– Beatriz, who did this? Who hurt you?

– *Ema.* The sound emerges as if it's been forced over her tongue with great effort. Her eyes have begun to flicker. He can't bear it. All the pain in them. Tears well in Erhard's eyes.

– It's important that you answer me, Beatriz. Try. Who did this to you?

– *E.*

Then the sound stops abruptly.

A few seconds pass. Erhard doesn't dare move. Her eyes remain open, immobile. Erhard sees the red lamp glowing above the bed.

With some difficulty he crawls over and picks up the telephone. He has memorized the doctor's number, but his fingers struggle to press the big square buttons. It rings far too many times before the doctor answers. Erhard is so relieved he begins to shake.

– Michel, it's me. She's talking.

Silence on the other end of the line. – No, he says simply.

– But now she's… she's gone again, and the machine is making noise, beeping.

– Is everything in working order?

– No, she fell out of the bed and is wrapped up in tubes and cords.

– Get her back in bed, stabilize her, and let her rest. She might wake again. It may have been her body sending a signal.

– A signal? What do you mean?

– Some patients wake up for a short period during a coma, just before they get a blood clot in the heart or the brain.

Sometimes he despises the doctor's cool assessments.

He slams the receiver down and pushes himself out of bed, then crosses to the other side of the bed, so he can lift her up. He checks the catheter and the cords, as he's been taught, places the mouthpiece over her lips, and hears the respirator kick on. Her pulse is low and irregular. The beeping ceases, but the red warning light that illuminates the top of the monitor continues to blink. Her pyjamas have been torn, and he can see her beige-coloured chest, her flabby breasts. Erhard feels terrible; he's sickened by the sight of his friend, and by the fantasies he entertained about her body. As if her body was what he'd wanted, not her. But now he can see that it was the other way around: since only her body remains, he understands just what it was he'd lusted after. Even her skin is grey like cheap flour.

The drainage bag is nearly full; he finds a new one in the loo and unfastens the old one.

Ema. Her speech had been unintelligible and stuttering, but impossible to mistake. Ema. He wishes she was in a private hospital, far away from here, from Ema, from him. It's too late for regrets, but maybe he could take a different tack. Maybe he could…

There's a knock at the door. A cautious, rhythmic knock.

He has no idea who it might be. But it has only been, at most, five minutes since he returned. He sets down the drainage bag and sits quietly, expecting footsteps to trundle down the stairwell, or the lift door to open and close. But he hears nothing. Cautiously, he emerges from the bedroom and crosses to the front door. Another knock.

Erhard retreats a few steps and turns away from the door. – Who is it? he shouts from the living room, so that it sounds farther away.

– Señor Director, are you home?

A dumb question. It's the downstairs neighbour. She knocks again.

– One moment, he says. He closes the bedroom door. He doesn't know what to think about this neighbour. If she's a hardboiled prostitute she seems almost comically naive. But she's suspiciously persistent. She could be doing some house calls. Or maybe she's just lonely.

He opens the door, but only enough to peer out.

– Am I disturbing you? Are you alone?

She laughs. She's wearing the same clothes she wore the other times he's seen her. She appears to be under the influence of something; her nose is crimson.

– It's OK.

– Are you alone? she repeats.

– Yes, I…

A man suddenly appears. He'd been hiding along the wall and now forces his way into Erhard's flat. He grabs Erhard's shirt and shoves him against the wall. But Erhard slides free and stumbles down his corridor, the man at his heels. Erhard's surprised, but not shocked. His neighbour's strange questions seemed like a warning of some kind. He has seen this man's face before: a narrow, bearded face concealed by dark sunglasses – like someone from an old Italian comedy. All he's missing is a straw hat and a cigar. He's lean and muscular, and there's an angry, controlled force in his hands that have just torn Erhard's shirt to tatters and now reach for Erhard's throat and shoulders.

Erhard backs up against the bedroom door; here, the long corridor is dark. He sees the girl behind the man's shoulder, unperturbed, watchful, as if she's waiting for this to be over with. He doesn't even bother calling for help. She's the only one who can hear him, and she won't help him at all.

He wants to ask why. Why are you doing this? But he already knows the answer. The man is there to get rid of him. It has something to do with the boy. It has something to do with the ship and the sailors and Emanuel Palabras. Maybe this man is the boy's father? Or the boy's mother's boyfriend? Maybe he's one of the men from the ship? Maybe he's been sent by Palabras himself, just as his neighbour was probably bought and paid for by Palabras from the very day Erhard moved in. The most confusing thing is that he's seen this man before. What if he's been following Erhard for a while? What if he saw him on a plane or in Santa Cruz or in the rearview mirror on his way to the office or down the street? Or what if he was some interesting-looking customer he noticed at Silón's shop? Shit, for all he knows the downstairs neighbour is the boy's mother.

It has been at least eight years since Erhard was in a fight. Even then, it didn't turn out too well for him. Even then he was too old to do much damage. He'd split his eyebrow and hurt his knuckles. Today might be much worse. Today it'll hardly be a fight – more like a wrestling match. What's important is sheer strength and durability. Erhard can't compete with this compact, muscular man. Through the man's light-blue shirt he can feel his arms like steel pipes, and he can smell him, too: roasted chestnuts, or smoke, and sweat on the far end of the sour spectrum. The sweat of adrenalin. He tries to recall the man's face beneath the sunglasses, but – despite Erhard's ability to remember faces – he can't place this man.

Erhard wriggles from side to side, trying to knock the sunglasses off so that he can see his eyes – he pictures blue eyes – but the man resists him. It's not really a wrestling match, because the man's not interested in fighting. He's holding a strip of hard plastic, and he tries to loop it around Erhard's throat. Twice he misses, and the strip sweeps through Erhard's hair. The third time he finally slips it over Erhard's head and down to his neck.

– Fucking dog! Erhard shouts, throwing punches with all his might at the man's face and managing to pry the strip away from his neck.

But the man quickly shields himself with his elbows and forearms. Suddenly, the bedroom door swings open and both men stumble into the dark room. Erhard has a small advantage because he's familiar with the space; he steps to the side and hears the man thump against the low bed rail. He leaps at Erhard and once again wraps the strip around Erhard's throat, harder this time, and friction alone causes his skin to burn. Erhard cries out, drained. The man crosses his arms and yanks on the strip of plastic, tightening it. Erhard feels a burst of pain, and now he's frightened, surprised at the man's brutality. He almost wants to give up. Giving up seems the easier path. In a way it already is over; he can't win. He glides down the wall and the man constricts the strip even further. Erhard lets go of the man's hands. As long as he doesn't gasp for breath, he keeps his panic at a distance.

The girl switches on the bedroom light and shrieks. – What the hell? She must have seen Beatriz.

– What the hell is *that?* she screeches like a banshee.

The man turns his head slightly and looks down at the bed. For a moment the strip around Erhard's throat goes slack, allowing Erhard to gasp for breath. His fingers and brain tingle with oxygen until the man turns his attention back to Erhard and now, in earnest, twists the strip. Erhard imagines it slicing through the loose, old flesh of his throat like a cheese slicer.

When Erhard drops his hand to the nightstand, he touches something warm and soft that at first he thinks is Beatriz. But then he realizes what it is and, sparked by the energy from his last burst of oxygen, he lifts the drainage bag and smashes it against the man's face. His sunglasses fall to the floor, and the warm liquid splashes on his head, runs into his eyes and down his neck. At first it doesn't seem to affect him, just irritates him, then all of a sudden his face begins to twitch. Under the light of the lamp Erhard sees his blue eyes, and he remembers those eyes. He *has* seen them before.

The man's eyes darken and he squeezes them shut, screaming shrilly. The stench is stronger than urine. It's a sickening, hideous, rotten odour, and anyone would flee from it.

After a few moments, the girls screams again. – What the hell is that? But she doesn't stand in the doorway long enough to find out. Erhard hears her footfalls, her curses and screams. – You said it would be easy, you said…

Erhard doesn't listen any more. He gets to his feet without knowing where this energy reserve was stored, and shoves the man back, back, back. The strip of plastic drops to the floor and the man, absorbed by the stinking wetness that clings to him, stumbles backward to gain his footing. With all his might, Erhard shoves the man against the edge of the doorframe. He hears the man's ribs crack, and the air exiting his body with a dry pop. The man gasps for breath and stands vulnerably as Erhard – not knowing what else to do – picks up the IV rack that's leaning against the wall and smashes it into the man's head, the five metal wheels landing with a solid plunk. Erhard regrets it immediately. Watching the rack travel towards the man's confused face, he thinks, *Shit, I'm going to kill him, I'm going to kill him now.*

The rack slams against the man's head like five baseball bats simultaneously striking him, and blood gushes from his face. Erhard expects to see him fall to the floor, but he drops to his knee and turns, half-stumbling, half-running out of the bedroom and into the corridor. Erhard considers all the knives in the kitchen and somehow finds enough strength to chase the man, shouting and screaming angrily, desperately, even using a few choice Danish words – words he hasn't uttered in years.

Just as the girl's about to open the front door, she screams at the man stumbling towards her and following her out. *Bloody fuckin' 'ell,* Erhard hears the man say in a low, furious voice while the pair run down the stairwell. He considers chasing them, but doesn't know what the point of that would be. Beatriz has, in a way, saved him. He closes the door and locks it, then hustles back to the bedroom to rearrange all of her equipment. The foot of the IV rack is broken beyond repair; two of the wheels are bent, but if he clamps the rack under the bed, it will still stand. He slips into the bed beside her and begins to feel his pulse racing, then falling. The memory of the strip of plastic around his throat slowly fades, as if the blood cells in his skin are only now returning to normal. The stench of urine fills the entire room, but he doesn't care.

It occurs to him what it means.

It means he can no longer stay in the flat. Surely the man will try again. And maybe he'll get others to assist him next time. He will return. He will be better prepared. Humiliated now, he will be angrier than Erhard could handle.

Erhard can't go back to the house. It would be too easy to find him there. He would be alone and exposed. He needs to keep busy, and close to others. That would be best. The only way. Better yet would be if he disappears, if he boards a plane or a boat as quickly as possible.

But what about Beatriz?

He needs to move Beatriz before something happens to him. The doctor won't take her, he knows. He has to find a place for her where she can be taken care of if he's not around. He thinks of a few options, but none are any good. He wishes Emanuel Palabras was an option. It's his daughter-in-law, and he has the means to take care of her better than Erhard ever could. But Palabras. The heavy-set man in his bathrobe-like Bordeaux silk jackets is a manipulating, shameless devil. Erhard doesn't know why he's done it or how, but it's surely no coincidence that his name crops up everywhere. He's the man pulling all the strings.

Erhard wants to stand up and do something, but he can't. He continues to lie there, stiff and immobile, feeling weeks of exhaustion weighing him down on the bed, extinguishing everything.

THE LIAR

18 February–22 February

63

Daylight. It's not morning, more like early afternoon.

He crawls out of bed.

He's got to get going. Down to his car, then on the road. Although he reeks of urine, he doesn't care to waste time with a shower; he washes his face with scalding water and runs his hands through his hair. There are sausages and olives in the fridge. He tosses them in a duffel and takes the lift directly to the basement. He trots to his car, jumps in, and speeds out onto the highway, through the Dunes, away from the city.

He drives all day, trying to come up with a plan.

He'd prefer to go to the police. He feels this childish need to cry it all out. Let them catch the criminals. It's grown too big and dangerous for him. When it was just Raúl, Beatriz, and Alina – and the doctor, the forensic technician, the sailors on Tenerife, the images of the boy in the cardboard box – he could handle it then. But not now. Not with Emanuel Palabras, guerrillas, violence. Christ, even the *thought* of the man in sunglasses makes him want to vomit. But he can't go to the police, of course, because he can't tell Bernal anything without telling him about Alina and Beatriz. Then he would be in another heap of trouble.

But he's too afraid and too disorganized to think of anything coherent. Usually he drives around Esquinzo and back through La Pared and up along FV-605. Not today. He's never been on these roads, and to kill time he drives slowly. Late in the day, he circles Tuineje a few times, then finally tanks up the Merc at a petrol station in town. He asks the attendant if he can use the loo, but they don't have one. Go around back, he's told. But Erhard doesn't want to go around back, where some cats are busy devouring the carcass of a large bird. The attendant prattles on about the rain. – The gods have it in for us today, he says, taking Erhard's money without giving him change.

– Don't they always? Erhard says.

Mónica lives right here.

Idling in his car, he stares down the potholey road leading to her house. He needs to speak to someone. Especially someone like Mónica, who's a great listener. He doesn't know what he'll tell her, or what will happen when he opens his mouth, but he's afraid of what will happen if he *doesn't* tell her. He has the feeling that he if he doesn't tell someone, he'll fall apart.

At the same time, he's afraid. Of involving her. Of leading the man right to her door. Of her being harmed because of him. After parking the car around the corner where it can't be seen from the main road, he walks to her house.

When she opens the door, she's confused. She hadn't expected him.

– Did we have an appointment?

– I was in the area.

– OK, she says, stepping aside so he can enter.

It's dark and untidy inside the house. Quite different from when he drops off Aaz on Wednesdays. The curtains are closed, and there are clothes scattered on the sofa, which she gathers up and tosses in the bedroom. It occurs to him that she might spend a lot of time picking up the house before Aaz's weekly visits. He'd thought the house was always spotless. With fresh flowers and a smooth, wrung-out dishcloth by the kitchen sink, but maybe she only does that once a week. For her son. Or maybe even for Erhard.

She scrutinizes him. – Well, here we are.

– I was in the area.

– Right, but it's not Wednesday.

– May I sit down? He plops into a dining chair. On the table is a deck of cards and a half-empty glass of red wine. – Are you playing Solitaire?

– Not really.

Only now does he realize how well dressed she is. She's wearing a dark-blue dress and tights, and her blouse is so revealing that he can see her cleavage and a necklace with a small anchor attached. She must be on her way out, downtown, probably to dinner. He wants to have her again, like before but more desperate this time, one final time, inside the house, in every room, loud.

– What do you want? she says sternly.

– I just thought I'd stop by to chat.

She laughs. Not a good sign. – You want to chat. It's bad timing.

– I realize you're about to go out.

– I'm just so tired of waiting.

– Excuse me?

– I've waited, but I won't any more.

Erhard recalls a memory: his parents talking about him though he sat right beside them. – I don't follow, he says.

– Isn't that the problem? I've waited for something to happen between us. Then something happens and nothing changes. Five days of silence. At my age it's too much. I don't want any part of it. I'm moving on with my life.

– I didn't know you were waiting.

She laughs again. Not a pleasant laugh. The she drains her glass of red wine. – Oh, Erhard. Let's not fight.

– Why would we?

– What did you want to talk about?

– It's not important. Some other time.

– Tell me, Erhard.

– Not now.

– Tell me or I will… I will…

He doesn't wish to mention Beatriz now. Doesn't wish to get Mónica involved. – I can't drive Aaz any more. It's like you said. I need to get away, take care of some things, and I can't drive him any more. Just can't.

– Fine, she says, setting her wineglass on the table. – It's better that way.

– Do you mean that?

– You're a no-good louse, that's what I mean. My boy trusts you more than anyone… Even me. And now you're just abandoning him.

Erhard stiffens. – I'm not abandoning him.

– Oh, no need to explain. I knew this would happen. First Lui, and now you.

Erhard doesn't know who Lui is, but he guesses that it's Aaz's father or some other significant person in his life. – I never made any promises. I'm a… a taxi driver.

– No you're not, you bastard. You're a, you're a…

He knows what she means. – I'm not his father.

They fall silent.

He watches her lock the door behind her.

– Let me drive you, he says, and kind of hopes she'll say no.

– No thanks.

– Mónica, I didn't know you felt this way about us.

– You're blind to what's right in front of you.

– I've been busy the past few days, I've been…

– You've been out playing detective. Trust me, I've called your office. Your secretary doesn't know where you've been. She tried to cover for you.

She's right. He has been playing detective. When it comes right down to it, he's just a tired old man.

– You want to ride with me? he says. – My car's right around the corner.

– And you can stop pretending to be a gentleman, too. She starts walking towards the road, probably heading to where the Puerto bus stops. The bus Aaz isn't allowed to take. – You're not as friendly as you look.

– We had a good, um, time recently. What happened?

His legs are longer than hers, but she moves swiftly and he's forced to trot beside her like a desperate street peddler.

She says nothing. When they reach the road she stops abruptly, and a lorry rumbles speedily past them.

– Nothing happened, Erhard.

– What about all that talk of yours that you liked quiet men?

– That's just something women say to get quiet men to relax, to talk. No one likes quiet men. Not even quiet women.

– I can drive you wherever you want to go. The bus might not be here for another hour or two.

She glances at her slender wristwatch. The road is deserted. The attendant at the petrol station watches them. Tuineje is one of those towns tourists don't dare visit. The people who live here prefer to be left in peace, but they're too afraid to leave civilization behind. Erhard would hate to live here. He'd rather have the genuine article: the life, stench, and colour of the city or the silent, empty expanse of desolate country.

– OK, but I still think you're an asshole.

They walk to his car. He wants to open the door for her, but he doesn't. They climb in, and he drives towards Puerto. When he asks her where she wants to go, she says downtown, close to Juan Tadeo Cabrera.

Erhard feels an urge to explain why he should no longer drive Aaz, but he's afraid to make her even more uncomfortable. Besides, she's too upset, and she takes things personally. Still, he can't help himself. The words stumble from his mouth. – It's for Aaz's sake, he says. – And yours.

– What kind of ridiculous excuse is that?

– If something happened to him, it would be… it would be unforgivable.

– You're scaring me, Erhard. What do you mean?

– If someone were to mistakenly… or if someone wanted to hurt me… if he were to… or if my car… or… I don't know.

– What are you talking about?

Her voice trembles with anger bordering on hysteria. She starts to hyperventilate.

– Stop, he says. – Nothing's going to happen to him. That's why I'm telling you all this. He's not going to get mixed up in anything. Nor will you.

Her eyes are wet and smeared. He finds some Kleenex in the glove box.

– It's just a precaution, he adds. For now. Once this is all over, maybe I can drive him again.

– No, she says. – No more. The boy... He's been through so much. He doesn't need any more part-time fathers or people who let him down.

Welcome to reality, Aaz, Erhard thinks.

– What if we tell him that I'm on a trip? That I won't drive him for a few weeks?

Erhard hates it when he tries to solve problems and comes up with a solution he himself doesn't even like.

– All or nothing. And since you've just told me that you'd be putting him in danger, the answer is self-evident.

– I didn't say he'd be in danger.

– But that's what you mean, isn't it?

– I don't know, Erhard says.

But deep down, he knows that's exactly what he means. If Ema is Emanuel Palabras, and if Emanuel is somehow behind the hijacking of the *Seascape Hestia*, and if he's given his gorilla orders to kill Erhard, and if he's exiled his own son or whatever the hell happened, and if he's tricked Erhard into his position as director for God knows what reason – perhaps to keep an eye on him, which means that Palabras knows as well as Erhard that right now Emanuel Palabras's name is all over this case – then Erhard is in danger now, and so too are Aaz and Mónica. Or maybe he's blowing things out of proportion, and maybe it's just a coincidence that it was Emanuel Palabras's cargo that disappeared. It's possible that Beatriz mouthed Emanuel's name because she wanted to speak to him. It's possible that Palabras offered the directorship to Erhard because he'd earned it.

– I just mean... I need to get some things under control. It would be better if I focused on them for the next few months. As soon as I've managed that, I can drive Aaz again. I promise.

– So you're telling me he's not in danger, but you'd prefer to have it your way. Other children might understand that, but not Aaz. He needs you. He... He thinks the world of you. One can't just pick and choose one's friends.

– Are you saying that, or Aaz?

– Listen. When you act like this, we're just not interested in your company. We're through. You're not to drive Aaz any more, you're not to stop by just because you happen to be in the neighbourhood, and you're not to invite us to dinner. I'm letting you go.

They arrive in Puerto. Mónica's remark would've been better timed had she been getting out of the car at the same time, but they're racing along at fifty miles per hour.

– And if you haven't already figured it out, she says, if you're worse at catching signals than some broken antennae on some shitty TV, then I have a date now, right now. With a man who is handsome and success-ful and… nice.

– Close to Juan Tadeo Cabrera, you said? Which end of the street?

– Are you a taxi driver again?

– I promised to bring you, and that's what I'm doing.

She rummages feverishly in her purse and throws some bills and euros on the floor. – Then here's your money, you asshole. Keep the change. We want nothing from you.

– Didn't you tell me that there wasn't room for a man in your life? What did I misunderstand?

– Oh for God's sake.

They are stopped at a red light; she opens the door and leaps out, dashing across the street as a car honks its horn behind Erhard. He watches her go, but when she turns the corner, he doesn't dare follow her.

For a moment after the light turns green, he makes no effort to drive and lets the car behind him honk. He stares down the street expecting the sea to swallow vehicles, shops, and the chain-smoking washer woman on the corner with her laundry basket and two dogs. Maybe the entire island will flood and the earth and everything on it will be rinsed clean. Beginning with him.

64

He arrives at the office and heads down the corridor as if he expects a group of men in sunglasses to jump him at every door. He doesn't know where else to go – and he figures Palabras won't try anything here. Surely it's no coincidence that they attacked him at home.

Just as he's taken his seat and regained his composure, Ana enters. She's working late on a Saturday. If Marcelis was here, they would probably be shagging.

We've got problems, she says, then proceeds to explain how three drivers are criticizing the deal they'd struck with the harbour. They are arguing in the courtyard. Where's Marcelis? he wants to know. At home, she says, and the look on her face suggests that she's called him several times. For a moment he wonders whether it's some kind of ambush. Perhaps Palabras and his sunglass-wearing friend are waiting for him down there. But the secretary seems genuinely shaken.

He follows her to the workshop. She sizes him up strangely, as if there's something she wants to tell him. But she says nothing, and once they reach the courtyard he loses interest.

He's spoken with these three men a few times. They're standing off to the left side of the workshop, puffing out their chests and gesturing wildly as four or five others look on. Gustavo, a dark-skinned man with a beard, was to pick up a customer down at the harbour. By request. But Luís – loudmouthed, slightly cross-eyed Luís – apparently believes that Gustavo should have to park in the queue like everybody else. Manni somehow agrees with both Luís and Gustavo, or maybe he's got an entirely different opinion altogether, because he's standing between the two men and yipping at them as if they've misunderstood something. He might be trying to mediate between them by working them into a lather. It's a heated confrontation that appears mere seconds away from breaking into a full-blown fight.

– I remember you, Luís Hernaldo, Erhard says. They hadn't noticed him arrive, and they turn to him, surprised. – I remember how you were the one always saying that good drivers earned the regular customers. We need to be where the customers are, you said. Isn't that so, Luís?

Luís eyes Erhard. – What's your point, Hermit?

– Now Gustavo is you, and you are me. Ambition comes with youth, justice with age. Isn't that what people say? Erhard has sidled between the three men. – Thanks, Manni, Erhard says, shaking Manni's hand, deliberately formal. As if to say, Management is now officially involved. Manni shrugs, then lumbers to his car.

– I'll give each of you one minute to tell me what happened. This isn't a trial. You won't get to defend yourselves, just explain your position. You first, Luís. You've got seniority.

Erhard doesn't care about seniority, but he knows that many drivers do, feeling that they merit respect, especially after years of working in a low-status occupation. And he knows that Luís – who loves everything about General Franco, big-bosomed babes in cheap magazines, and watching boxing matches on the widescreen TV down at the Yellow Rooster – needs to hear this sort of thing. It helps him to relax.

He listens to their accounts. What becomes clear is that Gustavo simply provided good customer service. The customer had been in Gustavo's taxi before, and liked him; he'd gotten his mobile number, and he'd specifically called to request a pick-up at the harbour when the ferry from Lanzarote arrived. Luís says it's disloyal of Gustavo, that it's against the rules the drivers have established; they're supposed to share customers. This is an old argument, but Erhard can tell that, for Luís, much more is at stake. He doesn't feel cheated, he feels dumb.

– You raise a good point, Luís, Erhard says. – If anyone has sacrificed for the system, it's you. Surely you've rejected many of these kinds of rides yourself in order to be loyal to the rest of us.

Erhard knows, of course, that he's manipulating Luís. Luís never turns down a customer. He has very few regulars, and those he has are mostly whores or sick people, who pay him extra to be picked up whenever they're in dire need of a lift. While Erhard talks, he keeps his eye on Gustavo. It's difficult to read his face.

– At the same time, Luís, you also provide the best customer service that you can.

– We don't want to lose revenue because of a few cheaters, Luís says. Again. Some of the others grunt in agreement.

– No. Instead, you hope for even more, Erhard says, watching Gustavo blink, confused.

– Exactly, some of the drivers say.

Luís looks around as if victory is his.

– It's only fair that everyone gets more when a good driver does the work.

– That's right, the drivers say, even though a few have begun to sense that the argument is headed in a different direction. But not Luís. Like a union boss who's just won a settlement with the company, he shouts, YES!

– I would like, this company would like, to put three euros in the communal pool for every driver who calls in a customer. Which is to say that drivers like Gustavo, who have a big network, can now earn money for those of you waiting in the queue.

Silence. Gustavo stares at Erhard, puzzled, a hint of a smile in his eyes.

– Good idea, one of the other drivers says.

– Where will the money come from? another says.

– We'll just have to find the money somewhere, Bilal says. He's a mechanic, but he's got more business savvy than most of the others.

– That'll be my problem to deal with, Erhard says. – It won't affect you. Trust me, I've been in your position. I want to make sure this is a good place to work, and it's only the beginning. I'd like to change other things as well. But is this a compromise you can accept, Luís?

Luís has no other choice but to say yes. Though he doesn't seem to understand the math, or what it means for his wallet. But since the others are excited, he nods at Erhard, then steps out of the circle.

Erhard walks over and shakes Gustavo's hand. – I hope you know you've made the right choice. Drivers should never be punished for good customer service.

– But you're not giving out bonuses for it, either. You're just giving the others a cut to wait on customers?

– Yes, because they don't know any better. When you start bringing in fifteen to twenty euros more a month for them, things will change. You'll be their hero. Everyone wants to be the benevolent provider. What's important is that you don't stop doing what's right.

– What if a driver picks up someone who'd hailed him but calls it in saying it was on request? Will you pay three euros without checking?

– I haven't thought it completely through, but I'm sure we'll figure it out. Maybe you can help me find a solution?

Gustavo laughs, then turns serious. – I've only been a cabbie for three months and you're asking *me*? The only reason I'm driving is to earn a little extra cash on the side.

– On the side of what?

– I'm a musician.

– Drummer?

– How do you know?

– The way you move your arms. They seem a little more dexterous. Gustavo laughs again. – If you want my help, I'm happy to do so.

– I'll come get you next week, and then we'll discuss all this.

Erhard heads back to his office. It's not until he reaches the stairwell that he realizes Ana is still behind him.

– You took care of that rather well, she says softly.

– Does that surprise you?

– A little. Marcelis hates Luís.

– Everyone hates Luís, but he's been a taxi driver for more than twenty years.

– Marcelis would have fired him.

– And that would have been a mistake.

– Where will you find the three euros?

– No idea. I thought I'd peruse our agreements with local businesses. Maybe we can squeeze more money from them?

– We're already more expensive than TaxiVentura.

– And so far as I know, they sell too low.

– Marcelis isn't going to like it if you don't know where the money's coming from. Just letting you know.

Erhard is suddenly invigorated. He takes two steps at a time, forcing the younger Ana to jog after him.

– You have a meeting with Alphonso Suárez this afternoon, she says once she catches up to him. – At 5.30.

– Isn't it too early for that? The casino hasn't even been built yet.

– I don't know. Marcelis was the one who asked me to schedule the meeting. And it had to be on a Saturday, because Suárez likes to go out on Saturdays. Marcelis said it was important to strike a good deal.

It'll be another two years before they've completed construction. Such long-term planning is beyond Erhard's comprehension. – OK, he says, closing his office door. For the first time, he feels an urge to study the accounts folder, which is lying on the table. For the first time, he feels an urge to be the director.

But when he sits down at his desk, his unease returns.

During the ten minutes his involvement in the drivers' argument lasted, he hadn't thought about the incident in his flat. But when night falls and he has to leave the office, he doesn't know what he'll do. Unfortunately, there aren't too many possibilities available to him. One by one he has shrugged off fragments of his old life, and there's not much left. It's his own fault.

He needs to find a new place.

He can't stay in the flat. His downstairs neighbour is surely keeping tabs on him, and who knows how many men they'll send next time? He can't stay at his own house, either. All that he once appreciated about that place – the isolation, the distance to his neighbours, the whistling of the wind – is very much a disadvantage when one is being hunted by thugs and murderers.

Miza, Solilla. The only two people remaining in his life, the only ones who trust him, who would let him sleep on their sofa if he asked. But he doesn't want to involve them. Not the way it's going now. Who knows what will happen when Palabras and the man with sunglasses grow even more desperate? It's kind of embarrassing to tally up his friendships and only get to two, and it's not like he's close to either of them. Until recently, he'd felt that he had more friendships than he could spare, but now they've all ground to a permanent halt. He's a superficial person, he thinks, who never ventures to that level where things become meaningful. Usually, this recognition triggers one of his more unbridled benders; he'll find his keys in one place, his wallet in another, and himself in yet a third. But today, such a thought holds no appeal to him. Today he'd rather be wide awake and miserable than numbed by Lumumbas.

For a brief, brief moment, he considers returning to Denmark. He could leave without telling anyone. He could live in a little house in North Jutland – far from Annette and the girls – raising chickens, ploughing snow, driving a taxi, and tuning pianos. Annette would wonder why the money's coming from some place new, but she probably wouldn't even care. Just as long as he keeps sending her money, stays far away, and doesn't contact the girls. But he can never go back to Denmark. He knows that. He studies his hand. Twenty years ago he exchanged his finger for a new life far away. There are no tradebacks. Besides, he's quit Denmark in the same way one quits smoking or gawking at girls in bikinis. He's grown too old. Not completely, but more and more.

He considers other possibilities, places to sleep, live, spend the night, park the car. None are any good.

And what about Beatriz? She can't stay in the flat. In all likelihood, Sunglasses has told Palabras about the woman in the bed, and even though Palabras couldn't possibly know who it was, or how she got there, he would doubtlessly suspect that Erhard was hiding something.

Ema.

He checks off possible and impossible places to go and eventually narrows his list to one: Hotel Olympus, the abandoned hotel south of Las Dunas. Partly because he can drive all the way around the building and sneak into the unfinished car park. Should anything happen, there's a second exit with access to a narrow footpath that he's crossed before and which leads to the beach. The Greek company responsible for building the hotel abandoned its shell in such great haste that it left tools, cement-mixers, and materials worth thousands of euros behind. Anything of value has long since been nicked and sold on the black market, but to the delight of the homeless who live there, the water and electricity have not been shut off. One of the homeless, Guillermo Trajo – best known as the man who looks like a woman – once told Erhard that he watches TV and blows his hair with a hairdryer. He can put Beatriz on the backseat and park the Mercedes close to the distribution board, and in that way the respirator and the catheter will both have access to electricity. It's not a perfect solution, but it's the best he's got.

But he needs to pick up Beatriz now, before Sunglasses and the downstairs neighbour and Palabras break into the flat to find her. Or before they lose their patience and come looking for Erhard.

He grabs his briefcase and leaves the office as if he's going home.

– Did you get my message? Ana says.

Erhard looks at her.

– Someone called and left a message yesterday. It's on your desk.

He returns to his desk and finds a yellow Post-it note. He doesn't know how he could've overlooked it.

Juan Pascual = P.

He goes back to Ana. – What is this?

– I don't know, but he asked me to write it down for you. It took him a long time to spell it. I think he was dyslexic.

– Who was it that called?

– Simón or Simone, something like that. I was so busy trying to write that other name that I didn't really get his.

So he'd called after all. Juan Pascual was Señor P, the ship's mate who'd boarded the *Seascape Hestia*. The man from Fuerteventura, as Simao had said. Mean and pissed.

– He lives here on the island, this Juan Pascual. Can you look him up for me?

Ana taps a few keys. – Maybe. Not everyone is listed. Assuming he spelled the name correctly, there's only one Juan Pascual, and he lives here in Corralejo.

She snatches the Post-it note from Erhard and writes the address under Pascual's name.

– 15 Lago de Bristol. Weren't those buildings torn down?

– Possibly. Some of the addresses here are old.

He nods, then leaves the reception area. Ana watches him go. – I don't mean to interfere, but…

He pauses. – What?

– It's OK to dress like that for the drivers, they don't even notice, but don't you think you should change your clothes before you go to your meeting?

Erhard glances down at himself. His shirt is wrinkled, and there's a huge brown stain – which looks like sauce or shit – in the centre of his chest. He hadn't noticed that, or even considered his clothes since the scuffle in the flat. He'd rather come across to Ana as unaffected, deliberate, but instead his irritation gets the best of him. That feeling of his returns: he's a piece in a giant puzzle. – I'm not going to that meeting, Ana. I've got other things to worry about besides that shitty meeting.

Alarm creases her face. – Should I postpone it? she asks softly.

– Of course you should. Postpone the rest of the week while you're at it.

– What's happened? she calls out after him.

On his way to the car he hatches a plan to get Beatriz out of the flat and into his car. It's a horrible plan, but it's the only one he can think of in a rush. The car park in the basement is out of the question, so he needs to walk right in the front door and use the stairwell. That's the only way, maybe, that he'll be able sneak past the downstairs neighbour. But he needs some assistance. From one of the city's most ridiculous charlatans. Silón, the man who sells briefcases.

65

Silón's shop is directly opposite the entrance to his building; it's so close that when one exits, one can see through the shop and the muddle of paraphernalia that Silón sells – discount bags and cases in garish colours, inflatable animals, woven beach mats – and directly out to the car park behind the shop. Erhard knows that, if he parks in that lot, he'll have to walk about thirty metres from the lift to his car. Through the store. Silón sells large, very large, square suitcases, some with wheels.

He enters through the backdoor and glances around the miserable shop. As usual following siesta, Silón is out front smoking small, hand-rolled fags that smell like something other than just tobacco. Erhard hopes the man has smoked so much that he's easier to persuade. He's sitting with his back to Erhard, shouting at someone farther down the street. He knows everyone in the city, or wishes he did. Erhard rings the bell, and Silón hops off his stool just as Erhard had hoped he would and comes running into the shop. At first he seems agitated, the dark circles beneath his eyes darker than normal, but as soon as he sees Erhard, he relaxes and grins almost apologetically.

– Raúl's friend, he says, gesturing for Erhard to have a look around.

– I need a very large suitcase, the biggest you have.

Silón points at a red one hanging from a wire attached to the ceiling.

– No, I'd like one that's more like a chest.

They turn to the wicker trunk in the centre of the room, which is stuffed with small bags of swimmys, beach balls, and stuffed dolphins. – It's my display trunk, Silón says. – I can't. What would I do with all those things?

– I'll give you 100 euros for it.

– Two hundred.

– One hundred and fifty.

Silón has already begun to empty it. He pours everything, dust and grime included, into a cardboard box.

– And I'm going to need your help carrying it.

Silón shows him how easy it is to carry. But it has no wheels. Silón appears to be stoned or perhaps just tired, and that's fine with Erhard. It would be best if he doesn't remember this tomorrow.

– No, wait here. When I come back down in the lift, I'll need you to help me take it to my car.

– Are you moving out?

– Just some books.

– You have a lot of books, Silón says, edging behind the counter.

– I'll pay you when I come down, and once you've helped me to the car.

– OK, Raúl's friend, he says, without realizing what he's getting himself into.

Erhard lifts the trunk. Silón is stronger than he looks; it isn't nearly as light as Erhard had hoped, and the trip upstairs is difficult. Once again he considers taking the lift, but he's certain that the noise will alert his neighbour. It would be better to wait until he's ready and Beatriz is in the trunk. The neighbour will think he's going up to the flat then, not down. That's what he's counting on, anyway.

– Keep an eye out for me. Over there, Erhard says, pointing at the stairwell. – I'll be down in three to five minutes.

He readies his keys and grabs the suitcase. Then he walks out of the shop and swiftly crosses to the stairwell.

As he's peering down the street in the direction of the harbour, he spots Charles, Emanuel Palabras's broken-legged henchman, standing not ten metres from the stairwell. His back to Erhard, he's scrutinizing the neighbouring cafe's selection of ice cream, visible in the refrigerated display counter decorated with a purple flamingo. But just as Erhard's wondering how fast a man in a leg cast can run, Charles turns and stares directly at him. He doesn't seem gruff or particularly agitated. In fact, he waves at Erhard. Which scares Erhard even more. So much so that he fumbles with his keys and practically stumbles over the trunk, which suddenly seems huge and square.

Charles is heading his way.

Erhard makes a snap decision to drop the trunk and run, but instead of heading directly through Silón's shop, he bolts down the street and right into someone wearing sunglasses. Although it's the middle of the day and the sun is shining, and the street is teeming with people, Erhard steels himself to fight and scream like a feral cat. Then the man lifts his sunglasses and rests them on his head, studying Erhard intently. They're not the same kind of sunglasses, and it's not the same man; it's Hassib, the young policeman. Another, older officer is with him. Erhard has seen him before, but he doesn't know his name.

– I told you I wasn't through with you, Hassib says, as if they've just had a long conversation. Erhard doesn't know whether he's afraid or relieved to see him.

– Can we talk another day? Erhard says, glancing towards Silón's shop. To see whether Silón's still there and to see in the reflection of the shop window what has become of Charles.

– I've come to take you in, Erhard Jensen.

– Jørgensen, my name is Jørgensen. You don't want to bring in the wrong person, do you?

– Potatoe, potato, Hassib says. – You're the one I'm looking for. You were the one in the flat when we found Beatrizia Colini.

– But why me? Erhard says, trying to draw the conversation out, so he can determine what's become of Charles.

– Where were you going with that trunk?

– Nowhere. Up to the flat.

– You look like someone in a hurry to get away.

– I'm hungry. I thought I'd go shopping.

Erhard hears how ridiculous he sounds given that he dropped the trunk and ran.

– You need to come with us.

– Only if I'm arrested.

– Just come along with us, Jensen, the other officer says.

– You're wasting your time. I've told you. Beatrizia was my friend. I haven't done anything to her.

– Others tell a different story. That's what we wish to discuss with you. We want to hear it straight from the horse's mouth.

– Just a moment, Erhard says, turning towards Silón's shop and gazing down the street. Charles is gone. He must have been able to run after all, despite his broken leg. – You'll have to drive me back again.

– We'll see.

66

It feels wrong to be used to the Palace. Maybe he's not used to it, exactly. But the reverence is gone. Neither the arched ceilings nor the predominant Renaissance style impress him any longer. Now he notices everything else: telephone cords in unmanageable knots under the desks, overfilled bookshelves made of cheap metal, chipped plaster, office furniture of various origins, tottering rubbish bins. Above all else, he notices the lack of daylight. No windows, no doors. The air is stiflingly warm like in a pizzeria.

They pass the table where he once sat opposite Hassib, then enter a boxlike room in the centre of the building. He hasn't even taken a seat before they start in on him. Hassib does all the talking, while the older man leans against the wall checking his mobile phone.

– Tell me about the last time you saw Raúl Palabras.

Erhard tries to recall. – It was the night, the morning, before he disappeared.

– The night of Saturday, 21 January?

– That sounds about right. It's hard for me to remember such details.

– And you haven't seen him since?

– No.

– Raúl Palabras hasn't visited you since that day?

– Is that a question?

– Has he or has he not?

– No. He hasn't.

– You just said that you don't recall.

– I can't remember the date, or the details of what I was doing, but I know that I've not seen Raúl since the day I found Beatrizia Colini in his flat.

– You're certain of that?

– Yes.

– He hasn't visited you in Majanicho?

– He's visited me out there, sure, but not after all this with Beatriz. C'mon.

– Did you collaborate with Raúl Palabras by hiding him in your house while you lived in his flat?

That was a new one.

– No, Erhard says, startled at the notion. – You can drive out there and see for yourself.

– We have.

– Did you find him?

– Raúl asked you to move into the flat. In fact, he also asked you to get rid of Señorita Colini.

– No. None of that is true.

– How would you explain moving from your house, a shed, let's be honest here, and into one of the city's most luxurious flats?

– Emanuel Palabras asked me to move in until Raúl returned. The man was grieving, so I thought, Why not?

– So you helped a poor father in need? Hassib laughs.

The older officer, still absorbed by his mobile, doesn't join in the laughter.

– Well, I guess you could say that.

– That's not how Emanuel Palabras remembers it, the older officer suddenly interjects. Hassib gives Erhard a chilly stare.

– What?

– Señor Palabras would also like to know why his son let you move into his flat.

– Then he's lying. Palabras was the one who...

– But we're more interested in Raúl, where he is now, and we believe you know, Hassib says.

– I don't know where Raúl is. I swear...

– That won't help you, Hassib says. – I hate it when people swear. Usually means they're lying.

– I'm not lying. Raúl Palabras was my friend.

– Stop, Señor Gorsensen. Now listen to me. No more excuses. We have a witness who saw Raúl Palabras at your place in Majanicho on 20 January.

– I don't know anything about that.

– The same day you found his girlfriend, supposedly after having fallen down a stairwell.

– I don't know what he was doing out there. I haven't seen him.

– The witness reports the two of you were having an argument.

– Who's the witness? A goat? Who the hell walks around out there and randomly finds two men arguing?

– So you were arguing?

– No. Your witness, whoever it is, must be mistaken.

– But you met with Raúl Palabras?

– No, for God's sake.

– Relax, the older officer says, stepping forward.

– It's possible that Raúl was at my place without my knowledge. It's possible someone saw him. I can't refute that, but I know I haven't...

– Sure, sure, Hassib says.

– He's my friend. I'd also like to know where he is. He left the country.

– How do you know he left the country?

All of a sudden Erhard is no longer sure. Had Papa Palabras told him? – I think your colleague Bernal was the one who told me that. He'd been spotted in the airport.

– That's news to me. Have you heard that? Hassib asks, turning to the other officer, who just grunts.

– We've also heard that you and Raúl Palabras were involved in a scuffle on 17 January, the Tuesday a few days before he disappeared. What was that about?

Erhard is caught off guard. – I don't know what you're talking about.

– You don't know. Hassib glances at a sheet of paper. – A young musician was beaten up, his clothes were burnt, and his money and mobile were stolen. By an older gentleman with four fingers on his left hand.

Erhard stares at the tabletop, his misgivings making his heart pound too fast. The musician apparently went to the police and gave his own peculiar version of the events. He hadn't expected that. That case could link him to Alina.

– What happened to him sounds terrible, but I don't know anything about it.

Hassib laughs. – Must be another older gentleman with four fingers.

– I'm sorry, young Hassib, but it wasn't me.

– What were you doing here at the station on 29 January?

Erhard can't remember the date.

– Let me help you remember. We ran into each other at the front door.

The day he stole the cardboard box filled with newspaper fragments.

– I was delivering a package, he says.

– That someone had asked you to drive where?

– I can't remember.

– You said Morro Jable. Does that sound right?

– Yes, if you say so.

– Who asked you to deliver it?

– I don't know, someone named García.

– That's interesting, Gorsensen. Hassib glances at his colleague. – But funnily enough, no one here at the station or in Morro Jable requested a package or received a package that day.

– Quite a mess, Erhard says. He doesn't know how he might begin to explain. – I was just doing what I was told. García in Morro Jable accepted the package right outside the station.

Hassib blinks. – So you're saying that one of our officers is lying to me? Telling me they haven't received a package that you delivered?

– What do I know? They're your colleagues. I don't know why they're lying.

Hassib sucks air through his teeth. – You're the one who's lying, you fucking old idiot. The more you lie, the deeper you bury yourself in shit.

Erhard buries his head in his hands. It's as though his face is connected to the policeman's hands by hooks and wires, and every time Hassib jabs his arms or slams his desk, Erhard is pulled in all directions at once.

– Were you in love with Beatrizia Colini?

A new tack, Erhard thinks.

– She was like a daughter to me.

– Were you in love with her?

– No. But I was very fond of her. *Am very fond of her*, he thinks to himself.

– It must've been difficult for you with a woman like that, eh? To look but not touch?

– What do you mean?

– Come on, Gorsensen. A *pibón* like that with knockers out to here. My colleagues tell me there were racy rumours about her down at the Yellow Rooster.

Hassib's just saying that to provoke him, but Erhard can't help but picture Beatriz; she could be very provocative, bordering on vulgar, with her long nails and her bright red lipstick, or the way the edge of her bra was visible. But always in an innocent way.

– I don't know anything about that. For me she was a friend, nothing more. I was twice her age.

He has to strain to remember to keep it all in the past tense.

– You've been strangely busy recently, haven't you?

– I'm a director now, Erhard says, though he's pretty sure that's not what Hassib is referring to.

– Travelling around, meeting with journalists in odd places.

The police aren't as misinformed as Erhard had presumed, and it unnerves him. – It has nothing to do with that.

– To do with what?

– With Raúl. I went to Tenerife to talk to some people.

– What kind of people?

Erhard holds Hassib's gaze. He has a powerful urge to tell him everything. About the boy on the beach, Alina, Emanuel Palabras, Beatriz, the hijacking. Everything. But he's afraid that it'll sound too incoherent, too crazy. So he keeps his mouth shut, and waits for Hassib to turn away.

– When were you last on Tenerife?

– Um, a few days ago.

– When were you on Tenerife before that?

– I don't know. A fortnight ago.

– It was 31 January. Precisely eleven days after Raúl Palabras was seen at your place.

– He wasn't at my house.

– So you say. What were you doing on Tenerife?

– Talking to some people.

– You think we don't know what you were doing?

Once again Erhard feels the hooks and wires in his face. It's as though his eyes are completely bloodshot from the strain.

– How many times in the seventeen years that you've lived on this island have you made the short trip to Tenerife to talk to some people? You don't need to answer that. Zero. Zero fucking times. And you want me to believe that you're not up to something? That you're not hiding something?

– You've talked to Bernal. You know what I'm doing. I'm doing *your* job. I'm doing what you should have done from the very start.

– That's what you say, and that's what everyone thinks you're doing. But how's that going for you? Have you found the mother? Have you solved the mystery of the boy's death?

– No. But I've found out more than you were able to.

Hassib grins. – You'd like to think so. Please also figure out why some 17-year-old idiot killed himself by driving into a light pole the other night in Villaverde, or why a young girl choked on her own vomit a few weeks ago.

– That's not my problem.

– So you say. The fact is, you're involved in a number of very suspicious activities. Suddenly. Right after Beatrizia Colini dies and Raúl Palabras disappears. Something's going on. You're acting peculiar, and there is a connection. Cause and effect.

– I've tried to find out what happened to the boy.

Hassib gives the older officer a long look. – Every housewife on the island is talking about the *extranjero* who's searching for the boy's mother. One might think you were using the story as a pretext. Listen. We have proof, P-R-O-O-F, that Raúl was at your house in Majanicho. And we have witnesses who tell us that you, the next day, went to the auto workshop and spent an hour and a half cleaning your car. Thoroughly. Very thoroughly.

It must be a bluff. Erhard can practically read it on his face. Hassib likes to take such risks. Because there's no proof. Of course there's no proof. Unless someone planted it. Unless someone's out to frame Erhard for Raúl Palabras's murder.

— Witnesses and proof, Erhard says. — Seems as though you're building a case against me. But you're missing the last piece. You know, a confession.

— That would be nice, Hassib says, grinning the grin of a poker player.

Erhard leans forward. Last try. He has nothing more in the tank.

— It wasn't me, Hassib. I know you don't believe me, but look at me. I'm almost seventy, I'm a shrimp, and I'm not even very intelligent. And if that's not enough, I'm also friends with the man you think I killed, not to mention his father. How? Why? Isn't that the kind of thing one asks when trying to solve a crime? Here's your confession: It wasn't me. Regardless what anyone says, and regardless what you find in my house or in my car, I didn't do it.

67

They lock the door. Erhard expects them to open it again. But they don't. The walls are ashen. He's in a section of the Palace that's been remodelled with blocky grey cells, high ceilings, and huge armoured doors.

He remains standing for some time – as though sitting equates to an admission of guilt. But after an hour or so, when his legs are so tired they've begun to tremble, he's forced to lean against the wall and glide into a squat. He doesn't know what will happen to him. When they told him they were arresting him, he stopped listening and simply went with them, down the dreary staircase and through long corridors. He no longer has any sense of where he is in the building. But he guesses they're going to let him sweat, figuring he'll blurt out his confession once they stretch the time. Maybe they're right. Not because of the room or the facilities, the bare, humiliating walls – he's pretty much OK with all that – but because he feels trapped. He can't just walk out the door.

He closes his eyes. Squeezes them so hard that he sees explosions of colour on the inside of his eyelids, and he pictures a hot day. Rocks, shimmering heat, his house in Majanicho. The goats trot off ahead of him, as if he's moving forward, as if he's a thirsty wayfarer stumbling towards the house. He sees Raúl standing at the front door, Raúl seated in the chair out back, Raúl between the clotheslines, Raúl floating in the air. It's like a test run, his thoughts striving to eliminate the possibility that Raúl was at his place. But there doesn't seem to be enough colour to describe the scene. As if the unreality of the image is telling him that Raúl couldn't have been there. He imagines following Raúl into the house. And he finds Beatriz lying in his bed – in Erhard's bed – underneath the blankets and sheets. Raúl leafs through the blankets to find her, but she's no longer there.

He wakes up, or perhaps he just opens his eyes without having slept. Something is scuffing along the walls, but there's nothing in the cell. Except for his own breathing and the flickering white lamp.

Hassib opens the narrow window in the door to ask how Erhard's doing.

– Terrible.

– Good, the policeman says, and leaves.

He's served mashed potatoes or maybe they're just regular potatoes. As he eats, the guards laugh so loudly that he suspects they've urinated on his food. This whole experience has been a fucking violation of his human rights, and Spanish law, but he hasn't the strength to protest. He hasn't the strength to do anything but sit quietly on the floor holding his water. He doesn't want to relieve himself down here. If he lies wedged in the corner, he can keep the pain at bay. Hours have passed since the last time he'd had a slash. It was on Tenerife. And his body recalls – the tip of his dick recalls – how it was to empty his bladder: searing pain. Before long it will surrender, before long he won't be able to hold it any more. His last slash was at the cafe, after the Mai Tai. He'd stood at the black-painted toilet, which reeked of cooking oil, and glared at the small painting of the cafe, while the warm urine ran through his urethra like apple juice through a transparent straw and round and round and finally through the few inches of his dick before squirting into the urinal, splashing first against the wall and then the dark concrete and grate. For minutes he plays out this recollection, and in doing so forgets that he has to go, but then it returns: the feeling that his urine is burning in him or sickening him from within. He doesn't want to do it here.

It's their way of getting to him, he knows, their way of breaking him. He's watched the crime shows, and he's seen *The French Connection*, the one in which they work over an innocent street urchin until he bursts into tears. That's what they're going to do to him, he knows – he can sense it. They've probably put some diuretic in the mashed potatoes, and they're laughing at him behind the door.

Hassib returns to ask how it's going.

– Terrific, Erhard says.

But the policeman can tell this isn't the case. The policeman sees Erhard opening and closing his eyes, his dogged struggle to blink himself to forgetfulness.

– Are you in pain, Erhard?

– What the hell does it look like to you?

– Good, Hassib says, slamming the window shut.

More food arrives, soup this time, and Erhard is certain they've urinated in it. It smells, it's lukewarm, and it's sour. But though he's hungry and would hardly even care if they'd shat in the soup, he doesn't want any more liquid in his body. All he wants is to get out of this cell and back to the interrogation room, so he can have a slash there, have it in his trousers, have it all over the damn floor, emptying his bladder. It's like holding his breath, only worse because it burns and stings. He can keep it up. Has to. He's survived on cheap tinned food for weeks before; he's lived on garbage and mouldy bread and tiny fish. He doesn't need anything. He doesn't need food. He won't eat.

After he ignores the third meal they bring him, they finally escort him back to the interrogation room. He can tell by the older coppers, their faces, that they're not too happy about the situation. They give Hassib uneasy looks. Hassib, who's in charge. Hassib, who glances at his telephone as though he's just received an interesting message. They prop Erhard in the chair across from Hassib, and instantly he relaxes his muscles and releases his bladder's firm grip, and with shooting pain – as if his urethra has been dried out and sealed up for many years – he watches a dark stain spread from his crotch all the way down to his ankles. The others snigger. Wonderful, one says. But Erhard feels no sense of relief, no exhilarating release. The pain is too great. And it continues to sting long after he's stopped.

Then comes the exhaustion. The urge to make water had kept him awake. Now he's so tired he can can barely sit up. Hassib notices and shoves him back in the chair. He talks to him, calls his name. Erhard knows he's being interrogated, he knows they're trying to drag a confession out of him, but he's so exhausted that he's willing to say whatever they want just so they'll let him sleep. This surprises him. He's always thought it would require more to break him, that he was a tough nut to crack, but he's broken. Snapped right in half. His will to do anything but sleep has drained completely out of him. Finally, after several hours, or what seems like several hours, Hassib comes to the point.

– So you admit meeting Raúl Agosto Palabras at your property, Via Majanicho, on the afternoon of 20 January?

– No, y…

– You admit having an argument with Raúl Agosto Palabras at your property, Via Majanicho, on the afternoon of 20 January?

– No, ye…

– You killed him and transported his body in the boot of Señor Palabras's Mercedes on the evening of 31 January.

– Nyo.

– We have a witness who reports that you carried a large object in the basement below the flat in Calle el Muelle. Is this true?

– Nyo.

And so it continues. He doesn't know which questions he's answering, why he's answering them, or how he should answer. Irrespective of what they say, and irrespective of what he says in his current condition, he's certain that he'll be able explain everything later. All he needs is a little sleep, just close his eyes. Just a little.

The chair slides out from underneath him. On the way down, he falls asleep.

68

He has a bulge above his left eye, which is so swollen that he can hardly see. His head is heavy, but he manages to eat a dish consisting of clumps of rice and beef. The urinaters leave him alone. One even enters his cell to help him sit and to put a bowl of food down beside him. He told Erhard he would soon be taken to the basement, where he'd have a bed, a table, and a chair. Maybe even a sliver of a harbour view. All they need is the paperwork. Then you're allowed guests, the guard had said, a man who resembled a huge mouse standing over Erhard and blocking the light. A bed sounded nice. I'd like you to know, the mouse had said as he headed out the door, that we understand you. Rich people do whatever they please, and sometimes it's the little guy that has to put an end to it. Although Erhard didn't exactly know what he meant, he could feel the bulge on his forehead, and he decided it was his punishment for having lived the high life. In Raúl's flat. In the director's chair. For peeking underneath a dying woman's robe.

The food makes him feel better. After some time, impossible to say how long, it dawns on him where he is. The cell is made entirely of some kind of hard wood, unpolished and untreated, so that it hurts a little to lean against the walls. You could easily imagine being inside a container making its way across the Atlantic, a tranquilized, toothless hyena en route to some debt-ridden zoo. At the top of the tallest wall is a round ventilation grate. In the left corner of the cell, a sleek miniature sphere hangs from the ceiling: a surveillance camera. The door is some kind of lightweight metal, with a square window in the centre which can be opened from the outside. He glances around the cell, as if he'll suddenly discover a hidden passageway or crowbar that no one has ever noticed. But there's nothing, of course.

After some time braced against the wall, his back and neck ache.

He scuttles to the middle of the cell and lies down flat, stretching his arms and legs like the Vitruvian Man. He considers removing his clothes to complete the image, but he's not sure it would surprise anyone these days. Already he's been classified as a sad sack, a mad man. Lying on the cool cement it's as if he's clinging to the world, or merging with the Palace, the old stone flooring, the shoddy office furniture, the stacks of reports, and the teeming rubbish bins stuffed with half-eaten pastries. He senses life buzzing around him: footsteps and telephone conversations, a toilet flushing one storey above, coins clinking on a counter at some harbour bar, a car somewhere in the city swerving too close to the pavement. Above all else, he feels Mónica's pale, wrinkled flesh as she awakes, and the rock-hard bed underneath her soft tush, and the beats of her heart, irregular, staccato. Her home is peaceful; outside her window, a flower sprouts. A bottle washes up on shore again and again. The sleepy eyes of his goats blink against the sun before they sleep. Laurel's bell tolls among the rocks, a place the goats never go, because it's shady down there much of the day and far too cold at night. The heat from his cabin, which is ablaze, the five-metre-tall flames that have transformed everything to ash. No smoke, just flames. And when the flames settle, when they finally flare out with a whoosh, he's back in his cell and all that he feels is the hard, indifferent floor beneath him.

Following his next meal, a gummy dinner of white fish flaking in chunks, papers are thrust through the window of his cell. The charges, the copper tells him. And your confession. Once you've signed your name, you'll be taken to a larger cell. With a TV.

It's a hazardous document. At once so formal and so meaningless that he almost considers signing it unread. But Erhard's admissions are so detailed that his signature would make any other interpretation of the case difficult to believe, if not impossible to explain. He makes no sudden movements, but he becomes alert when he sees what he confessed to during the interrogation. His statement is accompanied by witness claims and actual physical proof that Erhard doesn't know anything about. He needs to think this through. He needs a solicitor, an outsider's help. Someone. Anyone but Emanuel Palabras. Erhard is convinced that Palabras is the mastermind.

The guard raps on the door. Only a few minutes have passed since the papers were thrust at him.

—Just a moment, Erhard says. He glances at the box where he's supposed to sign, then the pen he'd been given, and he scribbles the name Emanuel Palabras. He hopes that will delay the process enough that he can have another meal, get his head right, and find someone who can help him.

— I'd like to make a phone call, Erhard says to the guard when he hands the papers over. The guard doesn't even glance at the signature, just takes the sheets and looks at him. Exactly what Erhard had hoped he would do.

— Sure, the guard says, as though his life just got a whole lot easier. He tromps off, and the corridor is silent.

Once again Erhard tries to think of people he knows, people who could help him, but there's no one, not a single person.

He needs to call the doctor. They've confiscated his notebook, but he remembers the number. The doctor has got to check on Beatriz, and he'll have to take care of her now; he'll have to admit her to a hospital. Emanuel Palabras won't be thrilled to discover that his daughter-in-law is still alive. That's what she'd said: *Help me.* She was afraid of Ema, and for good reason. The man's power stretches all the way into the prison.

Commotion outside the cell. They're coming to get his real signature, they're coming for the last time.

— Out, someone says.

Erhard recognizes the voice. It's Bernal's.

— I wish to speak to a solicitor, Bernal.

– You'll be speaking to yourself, you will. You're going to the basement.

– But I haven't signed anything yet. That wasn't my signature.

– Doesn't matter, Bernal says, as if he hadn't even heard Erhard. He opens the cell door. – Turn around.

Erhard turns. He tries to think of something to delay his transfer. But he can't think of anything. Bernal handcuffs him, then shoves him down the short corridor and into the office area, where it's suddenly quiet. Erhard doesn't dare look up, just walks between the desks, ahead of Bernal.

– Now you'll fucking learn what we do to people like you, Bernal hisses.

A murmur runs through the office, but Erhard ignores it.

– In, in, in, Bernal says, driving him into the lift so roughly that his shoulder strikes the wall.

Erhard tries again. – Bernal, I haven't done any of this. I want a solicitor. I am entitled to a…

– Just shut the fuck up, Bernal says, strangely loud. The doors of the lift slide closed.

– I have the right to a…

Erhard feels Bernal's hand firmly gripping the handcuffs as soon as the lift begins to move.

– Wake up, Hermit. Emanuel Palabras sent me. He wants to help you. In a moment we're going to reach the ground floor, and I want you to punch me and run. One of your colleagues is waiting in the car park. Jump into his car and lie down flat on the backseat. Ask him to drive you to Raúl's flat. You have ten minutes to pack your things and vanish.

– What the hell? Erhard says as the handcuffs loosen on his wrists. He turns to Bernal.

– Do you want to prove your innocence? Or stay here and prove your guilt? Now, punch me as hard as you can.

Bernal points at his nose. His fine, hooked nose.

Erhard's not sure he has enough strength.

– Now! Bernal says, just as the lift prepares to stop.

Erhard doesn't even think, just slams his knuckles into Bernal's nose. Bernal stumbles backward and thumps his head against a rail affixed to one of the walls. Erhard's not sure if Bernal is acting or genuinely injured, but he lies still, crumpled on the floor of the lift. The doors make a plinging sound, then glide open.

LUCIFIA

23 February

69

It's Gustavo, the taxi driver. Erhard doesn't know what he's been told, but as soon as Erhard crawls into the backseat and gives him the address, he snaps on his turn signal and tears off. He asks no questions, and doesn't look at Erhard. He just drives. Erhard can't bring himself to speak or explain; he wouldn't know what to say.

There are no sirens. And after five minutes, when they're on FV-10 heading towards Corralejo via Oliva, Erhard peers cautiously through the rear window. No one is trailing them. All that he sees is a dry, barren stretch of highway.

– There's a duffel bag with a few trousers and shirts, a jacket, and a pair of sunglasses, Gustavo says.

He wonders why he should change his clothes. Possibly so that he won't be easily recognized if his description goes over the police radio. His shirt is stained, and his trousers smell of urine. Those are good reasons. Removing his trousers and tugging on a new pair, however, is nearly impossible. They fit him well enough, they're a just little too large for him. The sunglasses are the cheap kind that can be purchased on the street for five euros, and the jacket is a sports jacket, maybe Gustavo's own. This escape was better planned than he'd first thought.

– There are too many people out today, Gustavo says, so I'll have to drop you off near Escámez.

397

– What? Why? Erhard doesn't want to walk very far if the police are after him.

– Virgin del Carmen. It's already begun.

Erhard realizes that he's been at the Palace for three days. He'd counted his meals and thought it'd been two days, but apparently he'd been given only one meal per day. The festival is the biggest in Corralejo. It begins early in the morning and ends around midnight with fireworks on the beach. Last year, he watched the fireworks from Raúl's rooftop terrace with Raúl and Beatriz. It'd been a peaceful evening with one-too-many vodka-tonics. They had watched the sunset, gobbled grilled shrimp, and gotten pissed. *For Carmen! Every man's favourite whore*, Raúl had shouted from the roof.

He pats Gustavo on the shoulder and climbs out of the taxi, his filthy clothes bundled in his arms. Then he merges with the throng of people. All around him, children walk hand-in-hand with their parents, and Erhard has to continually dodge them and stay oriented so that he doesn't wind up near the stage, where there is some sort of song competition going on. Children perform, their parents applaud. Farther down the street, people stand even more densely packed, clustered around a troupe of dancers, jugglers, and dice-throwing Moroccans who pound sticks against buckets made of sheet metal. There are also small booths selling cheap mobile phones in transparent cases or figures of Carmen in every shape and size: mermaid Carmen, buxom beach-blonde Carmen, mother Carmen with her little boy on her lap, Carmen with dolphins. He feels an urge to buy a figurine for Aaz. Erhard may not believe in the guardian of sailors or her saintly peers, but Aaz does. Automatically, he reaches into his pocket to see if he's got enough cash to buy the Carmen as mother. And it's then he realizes that his keys to the flat and his wallet are back at police headquarters. They'd emptied his pockets and confiscated his things before he'd been led into the first cell. He's locked out of his building.

All at once he needs air. He tries heading down one of the smaller streets, thinking there'll be fewer people, but it's even worse and he pauses in a doorway to catch his breath. Since hopping into the taxi at the Palace, he'd almost forgotten how tiring the past few days have been, but now he's overcome with exhaustion. He's about to sink to the floor of the stairwell, giving up right here and now, letting the police capture him, when his fingers touch something in his jacket pocket. He unzips the liner pocket and shoves his hand in. Someone has stuffed a stack of fifty euro bills in there. He glances around while counting the money. The noisy street is teeming with people and dogs, but no one notices him. He's not sure what's going on. He's got 3,000 euros. When he returns the notes to his pocket he discovers a yellow slip of paper sticking to the reverse side of the stack. There's a note in handwriting that he recognizes:

Leave the island. Find the Lucifia. *EP.*

Emanuel Palabras is a criminal and a liar. Why would he suddenly help Erhard? He wants to accept Emanuel's assistance. Unless he intends to sit in prison for something he hasn't done, he *needs* to accept Emanuel's help. Growing hot, Erhard feels the confusion and anger swirling in him. He forces his way through the throng and up the street towards the flat, the current strongest near the harbour because everyone is eager to score good seats to watch as Carmen is sent out to sea, and the fireworks that follow. Swiftly, without a glance inside, he walks past Silón's shop. Since he doesn't have the key to the building, he hurries to the basement and takes the lift to the fifth floor.

Underneath the stairwell he finds his extra key.

Cautiously he unlocks the door, listening for the slightest sound. The flat is stranger, more dangerous for Erhard than it has ever been. The rooms seem forsaken, and there's a smell of autumn soil and chestnuts – insistent odours on this island. He inspects the living room, the office, the kitchen, and the dining room he's never used, then the bathroom – the most luxurious of all the rooms – and finally the bedroom where Beatriz is lying exactly as he left her. He repositions her, scrubs her catheter, and inserts a clean bag containing a nourishing grey substance on the IV stand.

He changes his shirt, taking for the first time one of Raúl's from the large wardrobe, then tugs on a new pair of trousers. He packs a bag, as

Bernal suggested, a little backpack that seems to have been Bea's. He doesn't want to bring much: a short-sleeved shirt, an undershirt, underwear, comb, toothbrush, and some practical kitchen items like tinned food, a tin opener, a sharp knife. He can't think of anything else. They're ridiculous items, especially since he doesn't know where he's going. He's taking a boat, but to where? He's reminded of that day almost eighteen years ago when he packed a bag and left the house on Fuglebjergvej. Now he's running again. Patterns first become patterns when they're repeated. Why is he doing this? Why do all roads end like this for him? With a cheap backpack filled with random objects and no idea where he'll be a month from now, or a year? He's been content here on this island, he knows now, as he stares through the window at the harbour. In the bay are hundreds of boats of every shape and size, including children in rubber dinghies and families in row boats. On the deck of a huge speedboat, two young women sunbathe, while their boyfriends dance in the cockpit behind them. Probably pissed, high as kites. He sees Isla de Lobos beyond the speedboat. On the window sill in front of him, the desiccated husk of a basil plant, charred nearly black.

Far and near.

It doesn't feel right, it feels wrong.

He'll never return to the island. Life as he knows it is over; he'll live in Morocco, or wherever they're sending him, like some common beggar. The two or three thousand euros in his pocket won't help him any. He won't be able to send money to Annette and the girls. He'll have to break off all contact with them.

A clear vision of his life on a chute towards hell emerges. Life is tapering into something very narrow, the pattern writhing, distorted. His exile to Fuerteventura made him lonely, a pariah of sorts, and yet he retained a certain dignity and strength. Now he'll travel to Africa with neither dignity nor strength. He'll be a finished man. Something more ridiculous and miserable than a poor black man – namely a poor white man. A man given every opportunity to succeed, but who wasted them one after another. He can't step on board that cutter, but that's what he must do.

He has no other choice.

If he stays in Fuerteventura, the police will nab him. Although the judicial system is supposed to be a relatively fair arbiter, it wouldn't be able to overlook his confession, his escape attempt, and a whole shitload of bizarre circumstances. Even if he were capable of explaining the boy in the cardboard box and Beatriz and Alina so that the connection between them was clear.

But why would Palabras let him go? Because he knows that Erhard has gotten too close to the truth. If Erhard could continue his investigation, he would discover that Palabras had stolen his own cargo – God knows why – and people had been killed. The fake Chris Jones was thrown overboard when he tried to stop the hijacking, and maybe Raúl was disposed of when he began to suspect his father was involved. They probably took Raúl somewhere and killed him, leaving Beatriz for dead in the flat.

Palabras had first tried to pin Raúl's murder on Erhard, but perhaps he'd worried that Erhard might tell the police about the boy and the hijacking, and so he chose to help him escape prison and the country instead? The more he considers the situation, the more he thinks one of Palabras's thugs is probably on the *Lucifia*. A pair of strong hands to force Erhard's head under the water. His corpse would float on the current around the Cape of Good Hope, and it would never be found. Case closed.

Since his choice is between going to prison and drowning, he decides it's better to risk the latter and get dropped off in Agadir or, more likely, Tarfaya, which is four or five hours away by boat. But if he is to survive the journey, Erhard will need some insurance. Something that can stay Palabras and his goons' hand from burying him at the bottom of the Atlantic Ocean. He doesn't have the strength to write the entire story; with his poor, cumbersome handwriting, it would take too long. He considers contacting Solilla again, not her young journalist friend. She would ask the sharp, irritating questions that dredge the details from Erhard's thick head, and she could stitch together an article. That would take time too, more than Erhard has. What he needs is a video camera to record everything. One of those new kinds customers sometimes use when they sit in the taxi filming the beach and the surfers. Surely Raúl has one of those things lying around – he was always obsessed with the latest in modern gadgetry – but Erhard probably wouldn't even know how to turn it on. Too many buttons. He drops the thought.

Unless.

He hustles to gather his things, so that he can get down to the street. He's already spent too much time in the flat.

He needs to call the doctor and convince him to assume responsibility for Bea, but to also keep her concealed. Maybe Michel with his network and his resources can get her away from this island and to a hospital elsewhere. Under the name Angelina Mariposa, Alina's real name. An available identity.

He zips up the backpack and counts the bills in his pocket once more. He lays one thousand euros on the table beside the bed. Then he snatches up the telephone and calls the doctor.

Let me go.

He hears Beatriz's voice for the first time in a long while.

It's so faint that it sounds more like a vibration.

He scrutinizes the grotesque body that's drawing uncanny nutrition from a beeping machine. The creature he's produced by hiding her and keeping her alive, even though hers can hardly be called a life. He loves her, and yet he forgets about her from time to time and lives apart from her. Her body manifests nothing to him, only a recollection, like a souvenir of flesh and blood. She's not alive, she's not dead. She's his now; she no longer belongs to herself.

There's only one thing left to do.

– *Hola*, the doctor says.

Erhard can't speak. He holds the receiver to his ear while he switches off the machines. As if he needs a witness, someone to support him in doing the right thing. He can hear the doctor's breathing and the sound of children behind him. The respirator whines until he clicks off the switch. Then that sound, too, falls silent.

– I love her too much to let her live. I'm turning off the machine. I'm turning it off now.

– Jørgensen, the doctor says. – You can't do that, goddamn it.

There's still moisture in the mouthpiece she's wearing. But it's decreasing by the minute. Erhard removes the mouthpiece and adjusts her position, until she's lying straight and long, a collection of limbs, a space alien before the final dissection.

– *Buen viaje*, he says, and hangs up.

70

He rejoins the throng and heads towards the harbour. He'll ask someone washing boats whether or not they know of the *Lucifia*. Dockworkers know everything that happens in the harbour, just like taxi drivers know what's going on downtown.

The streets are packed. Everyone wants to be part of the festival.

It's the major event of the year, attracting visitors from all over the island, and even from Lanzarote. After sunset, people gather in houses to celebrate. But the big attraction is the procession – entertainment for the entire family – when the effigy of the Virgin del Carmen is borne around the city. Her name means Fortune, and all shop owners are eager to have her blessing; they greet the procession with songs and miniature tableaus, and place large bouquets, jewellery, and gifts at the feet of the effigy.

On his way through the crowd, Erhard runs into several people he knows. He tries to keep his head down to avoid being seen, but it's useless. The drivers with their families recognize him, as do long-time customers and some former piano clients. Luckily, it's impossible to carry on a conversation within the chaotic mass of people, so he just raises his hand in greeting and pushes on.

But down at the piers, the crowd thins some, and there's hardly any queue at the ticket booths for the ferries to Lanzarote and Isla de Lobos. He asks three dockworkers before one recognizes the name *Lucifia.*

– Yeah. She's been docked here for a few days, the man says, and gives Erhard the berth number. – You can see her from here, he adds, pointing at a shrimp boat that appears to have once been red but is now a lustrous ochre.

Erhard thanks him and proceeds to Berth 5, then marches onto the pier and tries to determine if anyone's on board. The sun is at its zenith; it shines directly on Erhard's bald spot. The shadows are gone; all that's left is the white, shimmering light – the sea's thousand crystals of light – and the shrimp boat. He doesn't go down to Berth 5, but observes it at a distance. The boat is larger than he'd expected, and it has been many years, clearly, since it was actually used to haul shrimp. Now it's a tourist boat carting the English out to sea to catch grey mullet and stingray with a beer can in their hand. No one's on deck.

That means he's got time. A half-hour or an hour, anyway.

Erhard hops off the pier and returns to the swarming mass of people, dodging elbows and purses and backpacks, searching for gaps through which to walk. Always moving forward. He passes the Yellow Rooster and the fishmonger's shop. He turns and seems to hear someone calling his name, but no. He bangs his arm against a mother's picnic basket, causing a long red scratch up to his elbow. *Oops*, she says, but he's already moved on. Soon he's out of breath and has to find a place to rest. He dashes into a little tourist trap where they sell small jugs, Mickey Mouse towels, porcelain donkeys, and glittering dolphins. At the far end of the shop he squats down as if to tie his shoelaces. The owner's in the neighbouring shop drinking red wine. Erhard's hands are trembling, and he attempts to calm his breathing. Two teenagers trying on sunglasses cast pitying glances in his direction. He probably looks like a confused old man. He feels like a confused old man.

After a few minutes, he gets to his feet and snatches a Barça cap off one of the racks. There's a large royal crown on the front of the cap, and Aaz would love it. Erhard would pay for it, but the owner's still next door, and he doesn't want to arouse any more attention than necessary. He tugs the cap onto his head and exits the shop, heading down along the harbour. He passes the narrowest section of the promenade, where the throng is especially dense; people stand quite still, mashed in a bunch outside of Bill Haji's old nightclub, Azura. The place has been remodelled and is now a cafe and bar, a trendy-looking spot where only the wealthiest tourists care to go. Of course, there are many of those today. It's decked out for the day's events, and the staff are dressed in robes like the Virgin del Carmen – complete with fishnet and crown. Lined up in a row, the waiters and waitresses sing and crack oyster shells, like chestnuts, as they wait for the procession. He recognizes the tall girl; she walked beside Haji's sister at his funeral. He's heard that the place is now run better than when Haji owned it. It reminds him of something.

He turns up Avenida Maritima and jogs on the narrow pavement as far as his body will allow, underneath hanging flowers and umbrellas poking out from balconies. Some shops are closing up for the day, their grates slamming down, but many shop owners are ignoring the siesta in the hope of earning some extra money. He makes two turns and reaches Nuestra Señora del Carmen, which is just as busy. The city is in free fall as evening approaches, with families parking illegally and emerging from their vehicles dressed in white, and youths with oversized beer bottles shouting from balconies. He comes to Cormac's electronics shop and edges past a group of children gawking at some colourful boxes, then enters the store.

It's crowded. Ruddy-faced Cormac is busy helping a man purchase a mobile phone. They're in the middle of the transaction. A young man with thick blonde hair stands behind the counter ringing up a woman's order. Erhard heads to the video cameras that are affixed atop tripods. He tries to get Cormac's attention, but he's busy showing his customer something. Cormac doesn't see Erhard until he has put the mobile phone inside a box and run the man's credit card through the machine. He gives Erhard a curious look, and Erhard saunters towards the back of the shop.

– The strong arms of the law slipped you loose, did they? Cormac says, peering across the shelf of video cameras.

– How much do you know? Erhard says, low, glancing in the direction of the shop's entrance.

– The crazy suitcase man saw you in handcuffs.

– I wasn't in handcuffs, but yes, I'm no longer in police custody.

– You look a little worse for wear, Cormac says.

– You have to help me.

– Come this way, Cormac says, nudging Erhard through the beaded curtain and into the backroom. – What's going on?

– I need to borrow one of your video cameras for five or ten minutes.

Cormac doesn't seem thrilled. – It's the Virgin del Carmen Festival. I'm busy.

Erhard looks at him. – You're my only hope.

– For what?

– To confess my sins. I need to record them.

Cormac's face grows solemn, then he begins to laugh. – What have ya done? Has it something to do with the dead boy's mother?

– You could say that.

– Where do you wish to record this video? Here in my shop?

– If I can. As long as I'm not disturbed. As long as no one can hear me.

– You can use the storage room. No one's out there, but the light is shite.

Erhard exhales in relief, then collapses against the wall.

– And then what? What are you going to do with your little confession?

– I'll take the tape with me and hide it somewhere.

– Tape? There's no tape, my friend. That was years ago.

Erhard doesn't know what to say. – So I can't record it?

– Of course you can. But it's all digital now. You'll have to put it on a computer or something. I can save it to a USB drive and you can take it with you.

– As long as I can have it right away.

– You can, but it'll take some time to transfer the file.

– How much time?

– When you're done with the recording… maybe fifteen minutes.

Erhard does the math. – That's too long. I'll miss the boat.

– Boat?

– Can you send it via post or deliver it for me?

– I can, Cormac says, but he still seems sceptical. Unconvinced.

Erhard takes a chance, lowering his voice so that it can't be heard on the storeroom floor. – If you record me with your camera and hear me out, you can decide whether you wish to help me. If you don't wish to help me, I'll take the recording with me. If you do wish to help, then you can send the recording to one of my friends.

Cormac glances into the shop. – Then we'll need to do it now. Right now.

– I'm ready, Erhard says.

Cormac retrieves one of the larger cameras from the shop. He presses a few buttons and runs a cord under the door of the storage room, where he sets up the tripod. He positions Erhard against a shelf of boxes and switches on a waxy yellow ceiling lamp.

– Let's go, Cormac says. – I'm recording.

Erhard has no more time to consider.

He starts from the beginning. He's afraid he won't have enough time to squeeze everything in. Speaking quickly, sometimes incoherently, he discusses the Chris Jones who was beaten up, the hijacking, the removal of the cargo from one ship to another – and the container that broke apart – and the fake Chris Jones, who drowned. A ship's mate by the name of Juan Pascual, who lives here in Corralejo. He goes on to mention the car on the beach, and the boy in the cardboard box.

– What? Cormac says.

– The car floated for four miles and then washed ashore in Cotillo.

Staring straight ahead, Cormac lights a cigarette with an old-fashioned petrol lighter.

Erhard continues: The cafe in Tenerife and Hollisen. Hollisen is missing. Emanuel Palabras stole his own cargo, sold it, and will probably win an insurance claim. The crew is nowhere to be found, but Erhard spoke with a sailor who was on the second ship. He reports that the cargo was returned to Tenerife and the crew was dropped off in Morocco. To cover it up, Emanuel Palabras murdered his daughter-in-law and probably his son too, then tried to pin their deaths on Erhard. He doesn't mention Alina. He doesn't say anything about Beatriz lying in Raúl's flat. He closes with the man in the sunglasses who tried to choke him, and the police's interrogation, which ended with his false confession. And finally, his flight from the police and the ship waiting for him down at the harbour.

– Holy fucking Christ and the mighty Mother Mary, Cormac says after a moment of silence.

– How long did that take?

Cormac checks the camera. – Seventeen minutes.

– I have to get going.

– How do you know it's all connected?

– I just do.

– I'm no fan of the police, but I think you'll need to find a few missing pieces of this puzzle before they'll trust you. Like the part about the car.

– The Volkswagen. What am I supposed to say?

Cormac grins and sucks on his cigarette.

– What else can I do? Erhard says. – For fuck's sake, I can't go any further. I've come as far as I can, but it's over now. This recording is my only assurance that I won't be thrown overboard in the middle of the ocean. Others will have to pick up the thread. Would you care to?

Cormac stiffens. – I have my shop. And my new girlfriend.

– Everyone thinks about their own fucking selves. I've told you everything, so now I'll give it to my friend. She's a journalist who lives in Puerto, a good person. She'll pick up the slack. I doubt she'll want to, but if anything happens to me, she'll do it anyway. Will you send it to her for me?

Cormac looks at Erhard. – Sorry, my friend. I've helped you, but I can't get involved. I've lived on this island half of my life. I have my ex-wife, my sons, my new girlfriend, and my shop to consider. I just can't do it. I'll download your video to a drive, but give me a moment. Cormac takes the camera with him when he goes, leaving Erhard alone in the storage room.

71

He heads back to the boat. What he wants most of all is to be done with all this. He's tired and confused. His body is guiding him forward like a machine, but it's broken down and sore all over. If they try to drown him, he'll be unable to resist. He doesn't even care.

The little USB drive Cormac gave him is lying in his pocket; it feels like a knife against his thigh. Somehow, he needs to pass it on to someone to give to Solilla, or send it to her himself. He studies the promenade, looking for a kiosk where he can buy an envelope and a stamp, and finds a combination ice cream booth and souvenir kiosk. He gets in line underneath the sunshade as the place fills with people, happy children eager to gobble ice cream and watch the Virgin del Carmen pass by. A few of them sing of the protector of fishermen, the lovely Carmen who wanders the sea. Even the dead sailor, drawn to his death in his own nets, walks on the beach among his loved ones with Our Patroness Carmen at his side. The song is 'Our Carmen', and it's taught to schoolchildren and sung at the festival every year. This choir sounds slightly amateurish to Erhard's ears; they sing completely off-key and without rhythm, and yet with enthusiasm and sympathy, as if they really wish to bring the patroness to life. A pair of adults shush a screeching boy who demands ice cream.

Erhard is next in line. From the kiosk, he can see over at the Café Azura, and the tall young woman. This face. This face on a slightly troubling and pale woman in her early twenties. She's nicely dressed, her hair pinned back in a whiplike ponytail. Her lips are painted so thickly red that they appear to be black. She doesn't seem comfortable in her clothes, as if she would rather wear a tracksuit and trainers. Now he suddenly remembers where he's seen her; it wasn't at Bill Haji's funeral: it was at Café Rústica. The cafe owner had called her a bitch. According to the owner, she was probably a lesbian too. The Bitch had returned to Fuerteventura because she had inherited something. And now she winds up at Bill Haji's cafe wearing an ironed dress. The islands live up to the worst stereotypes. A bitter mix of the same people.

She knew Hollisen. She knows what became of him.

Erhard scoots out of the queue and crosses the street to the cafe.

– Just one today? The Bitch asks. She guides him to a small table half-shaded by the cafe's awning. People are everywhere, between tables and up at the bar and along the wall. She pulls out a chair for him.

– Do you have a table a little farther from the street? In the shade?

– Do you mind sitting near the loo?

– I'm used to it.

– That doesn't sound too nice, she says, and Erhard nearly bursts into laughter. She's funnier than she looks. She tries to stand the menu on the table.

– Do you have any specials from Tenerife? Erhard asks. He sits down and shoves his backpack under the table.

– Mostly from Madrid, London, and New York.

– I went to Café Rústica once. Do you know the place?

The Bitch takes a step back and regards him. – Just a moment. María, can you pick up table seven's check? Then she turns her attention back to Erhard. – You've been to Rústica?

– A couple times.

– On holiday?

– Something like that.

– You live here?

– Yes, but not for long.

– You need a cold beer?

– A San Miguel.

– I'll give you an American beer. Better for you.

She walks off and returns with a bottled beer, an American brand he doesn't recognize. Also a bowl of fresh shrimp with some kind of dressing that he can dip them in. – In honour of Our Carmen, she says.

Erhard watches her come and go. He wants to ask her if she's seen Hollisen since leaving Tenerife. Or if she's heard from him. Since she didn't like Hollisen, chances are good that she'll gossip if she has any information on him. For a while, she responds to his stares with a professional smile; but when he keeps at it, she stops peering in his direction and begins wiping tables, mixing blue drinks, and conversing with one of the cooks, who stands with his head poking through a little window.

The shrimp are surprisingly good.

He's invisible from the promenade. There is minimal risk of the police entering every single cafe on a day like this. Broken-legged Charles and Palabras's other men are no doubt searching elsewhere. They're probably already livid that he hasn't arrived on the *Lucifia* yet.

Before he even finishes his beer, he has to use the loo. From the toilet he can see a large aquarium holding a lobster and a couple of big red fish peeking around long blades of green algae. A thick layer of black slate rests on top of the aquarium, but one corner has been left uncovered. He finishes his business, washes his hands, and taps on the aquarium with his index finger. When he returns to his table, he glances around for the Bitch. She emerges from the kitchen, her lips fresh with lipstick, and trailed by a powerful odour of cigarettes and cooking oil. He raises his hand for the bill; she prints it at the register and hands it to another waiter, who delivers it on a small plate without a word. She remains behind the bar discussing, with a colleague, which tables need to be wiped down, her ponytail swinging. Now, suddenly, he sees the resemblance. She's got Bill Haji's smile, and the same arrogant tilt of the head he'd make after he'd told a joke or lifted one of the dancing girls onto his lap. That was something he did to help his business, putting them on his lap. Bill was as queer as they come. The entire island followed his love life with keen interest, the women especially; they sighed for Bill every time some man left him or cheated on him. The men snorted, and the more homophobic among them swore at the old queer, wanting him gone. Erhard had heard it many times. From the backseat of his taxi, in the break-room at work, on the street, at the hairdresser's. Because Bill was so damn interesting and lively and extreme, people talked about him – and now here's a girl who is his spitting image. The grandchild. To Erhard, she looks more like his daughter than granddaughter. But she's avoiding him, staying behind the bar polishing everything there is to polish. He needs to find another place where he can talk to her.

He pays at the bar. When the waiter brings his change, Erhard leaves the money on the plate and requests a small plastic bag and a rubber band. The waiter goes back to the kitchen and returns, then watches curiously as Erhard ambles to the loo. Once Erhard makes sure he's alone, he pulls out the little drive Cormac had given him and throws it into the bag. Then he squeezes all the air from the bag, knots it, and wraps the rubber band around it as tightly as possible, until it's a small, hard cocoon. Keeping the door of the loo closed with one foot, he carefully sticks his hand in the cold water and sweeps it into the back corner of the aquarium before dropping the bag and watching it sink to the bottom, where it nestles between the green plants. It's not as well hidden as he'd like, but unless someone squats low and stares in the back corner of the tank, no one will ever notice. A child might. But no one taller than three feet. For a moment, he wonders if the lobster will try to poke the bag. Then he realizes that half of its claws are missing.

He taps once on the glass, then leaves the cafe.

He hurries down the street, his head down, and darts into a narrow alley filled with mangy cats and crushed bottles. Two men with crusted blood under their noses are sleeping on a stack of cardboard boxes. The alley emerges onto another that skirts behind all the bars and cafes, one used by rubbish trucks, schoolchildren, dogs, pushers, and locals taking a shortcut. He makes his way to Azura's rear entrance. There he finds a vandalized bar stool on a carpet of cigarette butts.

He perches on the stool and inspects the alley, which is quiet except for some snoring drunkard sleeping on a collapsible chair. After half an hour, he hears footsteps.

The back door flies open. The Bitch bursts outside, leans against the wall, and vomits a soupy red liquid that drips down the wall onto a patch of withered grass. With her head still down, she turns towards Erhard. – You're not a stalker, are you? I don't have the energy to deal with that.

– Are you OK? What's wrong?

– Too much partying, too little sleep, she says, wiping her mouth with the back of her hand. – And who are you?

– One of Bill's friends. Erhard. He offers his hand. But she sees his missing finger and clutches his hand awkwardly.

– So many people are friends with him all of a sudden, and they're coming from everywhere. Talk with Ernesto. He's the one who handles that kind of thing.

– I was the one who found him. After the accident.

She doesn't respond to this, just rummages in her waist apron for her pack of fags.

– And you're his granddaughter?

– My grandfather, a first-generation homo. From a family of homos, if you ask me, who have children without knowing why.

– I didn't realize he had kids, or grandkids.

– He probably didn't either.

– But you inherited this place?

– It went to my father. And he gave it to me. That's the short version. The sanitized version.

– Does your father work here too?

She laughs once more. This seems to cause her pain, and she clutches her belly. – You're no journalist, that's for sure.

Erhard takes that as a no.

– So you stopped working at Rústica and came home to Tenerife when Bill died? Have you seen anyone from there since?

She shakes her head.

– Do you know Søren Hollisen?

Something changes on her face when he says Hollisen's name. It's not a positive change, it's not even surprised.

– You've asked me that before, and I told you that everyone who works at Rústica knows that fucker.

– What did he do to you?

– You mean, what didn't he do? He's fucked with everything and everyone, that's what he's fucking done.

– Do you know what became of him?

413

– I'm sure he went home to Denmark. That's where you'll find him, *Extranjero*… Good luck.

– Is he violent?

– That psychopath is capable of anything. That's all I can say.

– Your old boss told me he was very popular.

– Of course he was popular. Like all psychopaths. She lights a fag. – I need to sit down. She points at the stool, and Erhard stands up. She seems suddenly exhausted. – He must've done something stupid since you're here.

– He must've done something to you since you're answering me like that.

– Touché, the Bitch says. Smoke slowly escapes her lips; it spirals past her nose and into her eyes, forcing her to squint. Again he recognizes Bill Haji in her rather elongated face. Everything about it seems too large, too long, too hot-tempered to be attractive. It's like a face seen through a magnifying glass.

– Do you know if he got a girl pregnant?

She shakes her head. – The poor girl.

– What do you mean?

– Growing up here is a form of child abuse. All of the crazy idiots a girl has to survive. On some of the islands they eat children, did you know that?

– I didn't know that, Erhard says.

– Any child of Søren's can only be fucked up.

– So he had a kid?

– I didn't say that.

Erhard's alarmed by the way she's seated on the stool. As if she's sagging because she's ill.

– Are you sick because of him? Did he infect you with something?

She laughs, and smoke sprays from her mouth and nose. – You don't think I'd fuck that psychopath, do you?

– Why not?

Erhard wonders if maybe she's a homosexual like her grandfather.

– You're funny, she says mirthlessly.

– You look sick. I don't mean to be cruel. You look like you're in pain.

– That's my problem, not yours.

– If you die while I'm here, then it is my problem. People tend to die in my presence.

– Relax, old man. I'm just not feeling well.

– How old are you? What's your name, actually?

– Twenty-seven. No more questions. I don't want to answer any more. I'm working until four in the morning. Our Carmen, you know.

She stands.

– Why do you think he's in Denmark?

– He didn't like to stay away from Fuerteventura for too long at a time. So he's got to be long gone. That's what I think.

– Have you searched for him?

– He owes me money. I could use it now that I run this place.

– Your old boss said that Hollisen had money troubles.

– Doesn't everyone? But let me tell you something, if you find him I'll give you a reward.

When she opens the door, kitchen sounds pour out. She steals a quick glance at him, a confused flash of a smile on her lips.

Only then does he notice her silhouette, her belly, swollen underneath her black dress. On such a slender frame as hers, it looks as though there's a turtle on her stomach.

– You're the one, Erhard says.

– What now?

– You're the mother.

72

The boy.

He has never really thought about the boy. Never really imagined him. In a little hollow, in a little coffin, in a little cardboard box, in a little playpen, in a little bed. He hasn't thought of him as a boy, only as a cheap doll, like those Lene played with, one of those with a body made of soft fabric and hands and feet made of pink plastic.

Now, all of a sudden, he sees him. Lying in the darkness of the box, pale, luminescent. Lying between the shreds of newspaper like a chick on a nest of thorns. His hair merges with the darkness. His brown eyes are hard and exhausted from crying. He's not screaming, he's quiet, touching his chubby fingers against the sharp edge of the cardboard. Scraped from his mother's life, not after twelve weeks in the womb, but after twelve weeks in the world. A failed abortion with hair and thumbs. The worst part isn't that he's dead, that his parents killed him, but that they let him live, that they kept him alive for three months before they killed him. They gave him three months without love, three months without eye contact and proper care, without a pacifier or teddy bear and whispered kisses and loving glances from the edge of his crib, without a hand caressing him in the darkness. Three months of indifference before they abandoned him, stuffed him into a box, and sent him away like a package with an unknown addressee.

The Bitch stands in the doorway. Though she clearly prefers to go inside and close the door, she stays put, eyeing Erhard.

– Did Hollisen kidnap your son?

– He wanted it.

– What do you mean?

– I didn't want the kid. That's what I said. But it wasn't free. Nothing is.

– So why were they on the ship?

– Ship? I don't know what you're talking about. All I know is that he ducked out on our agreement. I thought he'd flown home to Denmark.

– What was the agreement?

– I'm not proud of it, but it was business, that's all.

– What kind of agreement was it?

– He wanted to keep the baby so fucking badly. But not me. I'm from a family of abortions. But that's why I wouldn't give it to him for free.

– What do you mean? Was he supposed to give you money?

– He promised twenty thousand, but then he bailed on me. Just took the kid and left. Ticked me off.

– What did you do?

– Not much. I didn't want anyone to know about it. I didn't want to keep it.

– So you did nothing when he took your son?

– Not a damn thing.

– Did you talk to anyone?

– I did everything I could to make sure no one would find out. If I'd said anything or shown myself in public with a baby, I would've been fired on the spot and kicked out of the flat. That's the truth. And my family may be full of homos, but we're very religious, especially my aunt. I ate practically nothing. You couldn't tell that I was pregnant. Fuck, I didn't even know it myself until I had a bleeding episode. But by then it was too late.

– What do you mean too late?

– It was too late to have an abortion. So I drank and I smoked. But that little monster held on. And then Søren said that he'd take it, that he would pay for it. So I said fuck it, and went to term.

– What did Hollisen do when the baby was born?

– He was involved in everything. He wanted me to breastfeed, but I didn't want to do that. Søren fed it. He talked to it as if it understood what he said. After seven or ten days, he bolted. I went out to have a fag, and when I came back in he was gone. As if he'd planned it that way. Really ticked me off.

– Ten days? When was it born?

– I think it was 21 October.

– Hollisen ran off with your son at the beginning of November?

– Something like that. I can't remember exactly.

– What happened then?

– He kept calling me, telling me I could get another chance. But I didn't want another fucking chance, I just wanted my money. But he didn't have any money, he didn't have shit. He kept saying he would leave, that he would fly away, but he had no money. Not even for food.

– You didn't consider reporting him to the police?

She laughs, and smoke billows out of her mouth and nose. – I didn't want to involve anyone, don't you get it? I never should've told my grandfather. He went ballistic. He was really looking forward to seeing the kid. He knew people, he said, who could find it. But then he was killed, and I didn't pursue it any further.

– When was this? Erhard says. He has a strange hunch. He glances down the street as the drunkard falls to the ground.

– Grandpa called on New Year's Eve to say Happy New Year, you know, and I was pissed and tired and I told him what happened. It made him crazy, so unbelievably crazy.

A police car has turned down the alley and is now heading in Erhard's direction. It's driving slowly. The officers inside seem mostly interested in the drunkard, who's standing on a low wall and having a slash in a bucket. One of the officers stretches his arm out the window, trying to force the man down. Erhard pulls his Barça cap lower over his forehead.

– So you don't know what became of Hollisen or your son?

She shakes her head, sucks the fag right down to the filter, and lays her hand on her belly.

– Do you know a guy called Rick? Erhard asks.

She stares at him with her dark eyes. Shakes her head again.

Erhard considers letting her know, right now, about the boy in the cardboard box, his dried-out eyes and broken fingers. But she doesn't care. She's so fixated on her own anger, whose source is elsewhere, that she feels nothing for the boy. If only she had been on drugs or retarded, she'd have an excuse. This is just deplorable.

– If you find him, tell him he owes me money. I don't know why you're looking for him. Did he cheat you, too?

Erhard can't help himself. – The man sounds like a saint right now, he says.

She begins to speak, but Erhard turns away. The police car is approaching, and one of the officers is gazing intently through the open window. With his face concealed by his cap, Erhard walks calmly around the corner. He hears the word *Stop!* But as soon as he's out of sight, he runs down the same narrow passage he'd taken earlier. He disappears in the crowd heading towards the beach to watch the Virgin del Carmen being pushed out to sea. Ducking his head, making himself shorter, he lumbers alongside a family with young kids who snap photographs with their cameras above their heads. *Pardon me, Pardon me*, he says softly to everyone who bumps into him. There's a pushchair with two blonde girls in his way, and he almost has to step over it to keep moving forward.

– Hermit? he hears someone say behind him. – It's the Hermit!

– Where? Where?

Erhard glances over his shoulder and thinks he spots Charles and his crutches.

He pushes his way through bodies, people, faces. They come like waves crashing over him: arms, legs, flowers pounding against him, knocking him around and around so that he doesn't know which way is what. The sea, life, and the relentlessness of humanity, the eternal flow of energy. How does one ever get a chance to become whole?

He finds himself standing on a side street leading downtown, confused, catching his breath. The easiest thing would be to give in, to let himself be pushed along by the current, down to the boat and out to sea. To let himself be overwhelmed and washed away. That's what he usually does. Life washed him all the way out here, and he crawled onto land, started over. Now it's happening again, and there's nothing to suggest that he'll make a difference, that he'll be the one to keep the wave at bay. But he has succeeded so far. For two months he has held his breath and survived everything that came at him. Every time an obstacle was put in his path, he managed to find a way around it.

The *Lucifia* will have to sail without him. He won't give in. Not until he's got such a firm grip on that child-murderer and criminal Palabras that he drags him into the depths with him. And he knows just the right person to knit all the threads of the story together, so that the police will listen and Palabras won't dare touch Erhard. *One* person who knows what became of Hollisen, and precisely what role Palabras played. Juan Pascual. He angles away from the harbour, heading downtown. But first he has to do something about his appearance.

73

When he gets to the hair salon, Petra is sweeping the floor.

– Unfortunately, my dear, we're closed for the day. Virgin del Carmen calls.

– Let her wait five minutes, Petra.

She puts her broom aside and regards Erhard. – What's with you? You smell like a homeless man, your clothes don't fit you, and… that hat.

– I know, I know. Please, Petra, you have to help me. Five minutes, that's all I need.

– Who says I want to, or even can?

– I know you can. Just do what you always do.

Petra shakes a styling cape and retrieves her sheers from the counter.

– What happened to you?

Erhard pulls off his hat. – Get your electric razor. I need a buzz.

– I don't do that to men over sixty. It makes them look like idiots.

– Then make me the nicest-looking idiot you've ever met, Erhard says, climbing into the chair.

Petra scrutinizes him in the mirror. – Just this once. Next time you'll have to go to Hussein. He'll do it for five euros.

Erhard just stares at her. Then she shaves his head.

She begins at the nape of his neck, where it tickles the most, and runs the razor over Erhard's scalp. Thick clumps of grey hair fall to the floor. She repeats the same motion, then trims left to right. She's very thorough around his ears, but she's not happy about it. She switches on the hairdryer and blows hair off his shoulders. Erhard removes his sunglasses from his pocket, then pops out the lenses to make them look like ordinary glasses.

Petra steps back, startled. – You look like that agent from *Three Days of the Condor*.

– Robert Redford?

– No, the bad guy. Max von Sydow.

– As long as I don't look like myself.

– There's nothing wrong with that. What kind of trouble are you in? Does it have anything to do with that boy who was found on the beach?

– No.

– I knew you shouldn't get involved in that. You're not a policeman.

– Thanks for your help, Petra. I owe you. He's already on his way out the door again. The nape of his neck itches.

– I don't want anything for such a silly haircut. If anyone asks you, I had nothing to do with it. Where are you off to?

– The laundry, he says.

The machines are quiet. It's been hours since anyone washed a load. He opens the six large dryers one at a time. Clothes tumble out the fourth machine, underwear mostly. The sixth machine has more of what he needs: t-shirts, undershirts, socks. He quickly picks through the clothes and selects a green shirt that reads *Viva La Evolúcion*. He tosses the rest back into the dryer and changes his clothes. Then he hustles through the streets like a new man, pausing to examine himself in a window reflection. All he can see are his hat, glasses, and his gaudy t-shirt, but no one would notice that he's almost seventy. He looks like a tourist, just as he'd hoped. Maybe even an American tourist. Neither Charles nor Emanuel Palabras would recognize him, even if he sauntered right past them. It's liberating, and he feels strangely elated.

Number 15 on Lago de Bristol is a low, long, two-storey building. Each flat has a small terrace or balcony overlooking the bay and its windmills. The warm air is moist from the water that pounds against the shore. Seagulls squawk, but otherwise it's quiet. Everyone is downtown.

He has plenty of time, he tells himself. Juan Pascual has to return home at some point, exhausted from the festival, with a girl or two on his arm. But then he remembers that Pascual's a ship's mate and might be out to sea. If that's the case, he might not be home for several weeks. Erhard approaches the broad gate and finds a series of names fastened to a large sign underneath the number 15. Pascual's name is on the bottom. Does that mean he lives in the last flat? Top or bottom?

Peering over the nearly two-metre-high brick wall that encloses the courtyard, he studies the bottom flat. The balcony door is closed, and there's a table on the red flagstones along with three wrought-iron chairs. He notices a long, meaty bone next to the building, the kind that medium-sized dogs like to gnaw on. If Juan Pascual lives alone, then he doesn't have a dog. And if he lives with someone, surely there would be two names on the sign. Erhard glances up at the second-storey balcony; the door is ajar, and a curtain flutters like a flag. He creeps among the trees and steps onto a small wooden box that's beside the wall. In many of the flats, towels hangs on racks, and there are potted plants or small patio tables with umbrellas. But not this one. This one is unused. A man who does not wish to gaze at the sea lives here. A man who does not wish to sit in the sunlight.

A sailor.

If he stands on the wall, Erhard believes it's possible to reach the second-storey balcony, to grab hold of the balustrade. But the only way he can scale the wall is from this very spot, which means that he will have to walk seven or eight metres along the top of the narrow wall – the entire time visible from the other flats and the street. He might fall, too. It wouldn't be a long drop, but his knees would feel it; they would immediately buckle, and it would be difficult to get to his feet again.

He clutches a branch, lifts his leg, and clambers up on the wall. Once on, he balances a moment to regain his equilibrium. Standing atop the wall doesn't seem that difficult. It's a simple brick wall, about twenty-five centimetres wide, polished and painted. But it's rounded and slick, and he feels strangely vulnerable. Like one of the bears in the Bear Hunt game at Tivoli in the old days, the ones he would shoot in the belly with a red light, causing them to roar and spin. The wind suddenly picks up. Putting one foot in front of the other, he edges towards the middle. A gull swoops past. Cheers and applause from the festival echo between the houses. Though he doesn't dare look up, there must be only four or five metres to the building, where he'll be able to brace himself. Still, it takes time to get there, and he begins to sweat. It's hard to stay balanced.

He has to continually shift his weight, forget where he is, and feel his way forward with his feet. Like a crow. Ahead of him, and above, is the balcony. He hasn't considered how he's going to manage it, but now that he's almost there, he knows there's only *one* way. And he's not sure he can do it. Somehow he has to get his legs onto the balcony, and that will require him to lift himself with his arms. He leaps up and clutches the balustrade in both hands.

Loud music blares in the distance. Samba rhythms with flutes and drums. Two flats down, the balcony door swings open, and an 8- or 10-year-old boy appears. He's munching on a biscuit. Women's voices debate excitedly in the flat behind him, but no one speaks to the boy or tells him to get back inside. Not wanting to attract attention, Erhard stands motionless, but before long the boy shifts his focus and stares directly at him. Knowing that he'll have to lean forward and hope that his arms are strong enough to pull him up, Erhard jumps up, grabs the balustrade, and dangles in mid-air.

– Mama, the boy says.

Erhard can no longer see him. He's too focused on holding on for dear life.

– Mama?

Desperately, Erhard swings his legs to the side and kicks one foot so that it strikes the edge of the balcony. But it slips free and dangles again, forcing his hip to slam hard against the building.

The mother responds to the boy, but Erhard can't quite make out what she says, and the boy ends up calling for her again. – Come see.

Erhard tries a second time, jerking his left leg up and jamming his foot under the metal balustrade. Then he hoists himself up, kicks his other foot up onto the railing, and climbs over. His body aches. It's not used to using its muscles like this.

The boy calls for his mother a third time, then runs inside to find her.

Erhard crawls over the railing, pushes open the door, and enters the flat.

74

He's still not sure he's in the right flat. He's not sure what he expected to find. Old nautical charts on the walls? Ships in bottles on shelves? Ashtrays filled with foreign coins? Timetables on the refrigerator door? Or just a tired sailor snoring on the sofa?

Instead the flat looks like temporary living quarters, as sterile as a waiting room. Clothes are piled on the floor along with colourful computer games, a Real Madrid team-photo towel from 2009, and sweet wrappers. Erhard's nearly certain that the black-and-white photographs on the wall were there before Juan Pascual moved in. The living room and kitchen are one room. From the kitchen table there's a view of the bay. The cupboards are bare. Well, except for paper plates, paper cups, plastic cutlery, microwaveable meals, boxed wine, salt, and so on. How long has Pascual lived here? Apparently long enough to be listed in the telephone book. Four or five years? Still, it's as if the man is waiting for something that will change his life. Maybe he's a junkie? Erhard has seen how junkies live: sad, filthy, disgusting. But here the sadness seems desperate. A person who has a very poor quality of life. A rootless person.

He opens a few drawers and the flat's only cabinet, but finds nothing. No papers. No letters or telephone bills. Nothing to confirm that Pascual lives here. Nothing to help Erhard at all. He grabs a beer from the fridge. He might as well. He sits down in the chair nearest the front door and waits for the man to return.

Even though the beer is a watery, tasteless San Miguel, it knocks him out cold. The events of the last two days whirl him into a hole. He keeps his eye on the door, blinks, watches, blinks, and then his eyes close for good. He runs his finger along the rim of the bottle and jams it into a magnetic darkness. In the dream everything is nice, simpler. There's a table with a white tablecloth and candelabra. The waiter is setting the table for two. He pours white wine from a lamp. At the same time, he feels the grotesque, in-the-dream recognition that the dream is better than reality. He lifts the glass to his mouth and white wine runs under his tongue, down into his small intestine, and across his belly membrane. Everything quivers and grows, his body smells of sweets, bubbles.

He stands up dizzily.

His bladder has lost patience with him; it complains as soon as there's liquid in his system. He hurries to the loo and notices how the daylight has changed. He's slept for more than ten minutes. Maybe an hour. Or longer. He quickly unzips his trousers before his urine gushes out. It emerges hot and greenish. Maybe it's the light playing tricks. There's a musty odour around the toilet, which reminds him of the smell of goat excrement back home in Majanicho.

He opens the cabinet above the sink. Apparently, Pascual has a bad stomach. There are four or five packages of Fortasec and some bottles of Pepto-Bismol, along with a couple of empty plastic pill bottles. He sees different names on the labels, none of which are Pascual's. One's called Clomipramine. Erhard's unfamiliar with it, and the label doesn't say what it's for. He finds a mobile phone on the lowest shelf. A small cobalt-blue device with black buttons, one of the popular brands. Nokia. The kind Beatriz had. It's powered off. And there's a small box with of some sort of transparent rubber plugs that look like toadstools.

He finishes up and flushes the toilet. As he's washing his hands, he spots a rubbish bin underneath the sink. It's actually just a cardboard box with a plastic bag inside. Toilet paper is heaped on top, and gauze-coloured tape. He picks up the box and removes the paper. It takes him a few seconds to realize what it is he's looking at, some thin strips of hard plastic. The kind one binds around a package or a pallet that needs to be transported. Almost instinctively, Erhard reaches for his throat. Beneath more paper he finds a pair of sunglasses, slathered in what looks like brown paint. This is the source of the smell.

He hears a key in the lock. He just manages to turn off the light, then stands in near-total darkness apart from a thin stripe of light entering through the door, which is ajar.

75

Juan Pascual has shaved off his beard and looks normal, friendly even. But Erhard has no doubt that this is the same man who assaulted him. Although a lot has happened since, and he hasn't had time to think it through, he also wonders if he'd seen him before that. Down at the harbour? In the rearview mirror? At Greenbay Jazz bar the night that Alina went off with the band?

Pascual's in a hurry. He dashes into the living room, talking to someone. At first Erhard thinks somebody is waiting for him in the corridor, but then he hears him answer unheard questions, explain, argue. He's talking unusually loud.

– I've been everywhere, he's saying. – Shouldn't I just stay on task? I've promised to… No. She's in Arrecife. Yesterday. No. I'll do it now. We don't need to… It's tough when the city… No. Not at all. He can't. No. I'm not complaining. I'm not complaining. All I'm saying… all I'm saying is… why out there? I'd rather meet downtown. What about tomorrow? I'll do this first and then…

Silence.

Glass shatters. Must be the bottle Erhard had left on the chair's armrest.

It won't be long before Pascual comes to the loo to have a slash or fetch his pills. Erhard squeezes himself against the wall and lifts one leg, so that he can shove the door into the man's head as soon as he enters. The refrigerator door bangs shut, and Erhard hears a beer can cracking open. Then footsteps approach. A shadow passes beneath the door, and Erhard raises his foot above the knob, preparing to kick the door like a donkey. He wants to crush the man's head.

Instead the shadow retreats, and Erhard hears the front door thump against the wall, then slam shut. The lock clicks and Erhard stands stockstill, wondering what to do. He'd imagined that he'd get the chance to talk to Juan Pascual, to ask him probing questions about that night he went aboard the *Seascape Hestia*, and about the hijacking and the fake Chris

Jones. But now he's leaving, Juan Pascual or whatever his real name is, and this time maybe for longer than a few hours, and Erhard can't think of a single thing to do.

Suddenly he sees the man's face at the cafe.

At the cafe that morning Bernal asked Erhard to go with him to the Palace and read newspaper fragments. He'd sat in the back of the room, apparently either hung-over or tired as hell, but Erhard is sure it's the same man. A man called Pesce. Raúl had mentioned him, liked him, drank beers with him. Pesce, who knew the best fishing spots near the coast. Pesce, who could sail to Lanzarote and back with his eyes closed. Of course. What had Simao said about Señor P? The man knew the waters better than anyone.

He hurries from the loo, crosses the living room, and dashes onto the balcony. He grabs the railing and lifts his legs over it, then carefully lowers himself until he's hanging in mid-air. Erhard's knees buckle and crack like soft twigs when he lands on the ground. But he doesn't have the time to deal with it; he shoves the wrought-iron chair against the wall and climbs over. Beyond the tree, whose low branches practically conceal the wall and two parking spaces under its light-green foliage, he sees Juan Pascual racing past in a dark-blue delivery van. A rental.

Out there, he'd said. *Out there.*

Usually, *out there* means Las Dunas. People don't say *out there* about Puerto or other cities. They say *out there* about a barren, abandoned landscape. Unless he decides to drive down Alejandro's Trail, *out there* means that Juan Pascual will take the FV-1 or FV-101. Both roads begin at the roundabout near the stadium, and Pascual would almost certainly take Avenida Juan Carlos to avoid city traffic. If Erhard can hail a taxi within the next two minutes, he can drive up Carmen and, with even greater luck, reach the roundabout at the same time as Pascual, then follow him until he gets the chance to stop him. If Erhard is really lucky, he'll see Pascual meeting the person he spoke to, probably Charles or maybe even Palabras himself.

He picks up the pace down Calle Galicia and crosses the street to Calle Pizarro, but his body is sore all over. Evening has fallen, and the music is louder. There are no taxis, only mopeds with too many riders. He has to go all the way down to General García to find a taxi stand. If only he'd swallowed some of the pills in Juan Pascual's cabinet. The road curves. A couple of noisy vehicles with young men and women zip past waving flags out of windows. He pulls his cap down tighter and walks faster, reminding himself not to seem nervous.

At the corner of General García, he glances towards the taxi stand and the lone taxi in the queue. It's Ponduel, lazy Ponduel in his beloved Lexus. Shit. What choice does he have? He rushes to the car and gets Ponduel's attention before hurling himself into the passenger seat. Ponduel's watching sports news on his mobile. He lays the device between the seats and regards Erhard coolly.

– The stadium. Now.

– I don't drive traitors.

– Shut up and drive, Ponduel. Erhard can hardly speak, but he fumbles with his notes and waves a hundred euros.

– Why should I? Ponduel asks, putting the car in gear and snapping on his turning lights, before merging onto General García.

– I'll give you two hundred if you put the pedal to the metal.

As they turn the corner onto Isaac Peral and swerve to avoid a queue that's formed outside the restaurant Le Provençal, Ponduel glances at Erhard. – What are you up to, Hermit? I heard you got busted.

– They let me go.

– Why should I hurry? Why should I get a ticket?

– Just drive, Ponduel. Act like a taxi driver.

Ponduel drives faster through the smaller streets than Erhard ever would have dared. He may not be very bright, but as far as Erhard has heard, he's a good driver. And the Lexus is much faster than a delivery van.

– How's the traffic on Juan Carlos?

– It's fine.

– Can you get someone to park by the Rusty Arrow?

That's the name of the sculpture in the middle of the first roundabout that Pascual will have to drive through.

– What?

– Get someone to park in the middle of the roundabout or something.

– Why?

Erhard presses the button of the radio and says loudly: – This is twenty-eight. To all the vehicles in Cɪɪ, can one of you park in the roundabout? We have a C & C on the way south on Juan Carlos.

A C & C is an unpaid account. Either someone who's failed to pay a fare or an ordinary motorist who's run from an accident. Taxi drivers hate them more than anything.

Ponduel shoves Erhard in the face, knocking his hand off the button. – Fucking hell, what do you think you're doing? You're with the enemy now. You're not going to...

– I'm sorry, Ponduel. I need this. I need to stop him.

– Is it a C & C? Where is your car? Did he total it?

– No, it's not a C & C. That was the only thing I could think of. I'll explain later. Erhard pulls out 250 euros. – Here. Just drive. Drop me off near the stadium. But don't tell anyone you drove me.

Erhard knows that will prove difficult for Ponduel, perhaps impossible, but he has to give it a shot.

Ponduel accepts the money. – You're not well, he says.

The taxi climbs to 100 mph, and passersby glance up, fearful, as the car roars past. If anyone were to step onto the road, there would be no time to swerve or honk the horn.

They turn off Carabela and onto Fuente, passing the water park.

– Car seventeen here. I've got some engine trouble that'll take a few minutes to fix. I'm at the Rusty Arrow.

It's Sebastiano.

– That was fast, Ponduel says, and can't help but smile. The truth is he loves this kind of stuff. Drama, disobedience, having a slash on the powers that be.

It was fast, yes, but Erhard's not sure it was fast enough. If the traffic on Juan Carlos is like it normally is at this time of day, then Juan Pascual is already on FV-ɪ or FV-ɪoɪ.

They drive in silence, and the car swerves through the little roundabout near Oasis Dunas. This is a gamble. For all he knows, Pascual took another route. But Erhard has convinced himself that Pascual's taking the highway out to the big roundabout. There's still a slight chance he'll be able to stop him. He just doesn't know how yet.

– Seventeen here. A few cars are veering around the blockade. Twenty-eight, what does your C & C look like?

Ponduel looks at Erhard, then presses the call button to let Erhard speak. – It's a blue SEAT delivery van, a rental.

The radio crackles. – Seventeen here. That vehicle just slipped past.

– Fuck, Erhard shouts, the button still pressed down.

– Jørgensen, is that you? Sebastiano says.

– Yes, it's me.

Erhard sets his eyes on Ponduel, who raises an eyebrow in irritation.

They come to the roundabout, and just as they speed into the circle, Erhard sees the delivery van a few hundred metres up the FV-1. Unable to speak, he simply points.

– Is that him? Ponduel asks. The taxi's left wheels are up on the kerb. Ponduel jerks the wheel and continues straight, cutting off a car that's approaching from the right, then races onto the FV-101. The delivery van is now three car-lengths ahead of them. – What do you want to do now?

– Just drive. But don't be aggressive. It's best he doesn't notice us.

The delivery van and the other cars ahead of them settle in at approximately 60 mph, barely slowing as they pass Geafond. Sighing as if all this is aggravating, Ponduel snaps off the radio. – How far are we going? I have to get back by 9.30 p.m.

– Not much farther, Erhard says, though he doesn't really know for sure. *Out there*, Pascual had said. Not down there, not over there. But *out* there. Out in the middle of nowhere. Pascual hadn't uttered the address out loud, and he hadn't asked for time to jot it down. Which meant it was some place he'd been to before. *Out there*.

Erhard removes his hat and wipes the sweat from his head. Ponduel gives him a funny look when he notices his new 'do, but he says nothing.

The landscape just south of Corralejo, east of Majanicho, is the flattest and most rugged on the island. Some farmers' meaningless stone dikes divide the area into small, skewed squares. One can almost see the wind whip across the pale, grey rocks and dried clumps of soil before gathering speed for the trip up Montaña Colorada a few miles to the west, a mountain where the edge of the island seems drawn up to a point, like a blanket lifted from underneath by a knee. The delivery van takes the next right, on La Cappelania, but the other cars keep straight. Erhard's just about to ask Ponduel to follow the van at a distance, but Ponduel's one step ahead of him, lifting his foot from the pedal and letting the Lexus coast, until the two vehicles are once again separated by a few hundred metres. La Cappelania is an asphalt-covered cluster of houses with palm trees, water sprinklers, and a community pool. Erhard expects to see the delivery van stop in front of one of the houses, but instead it turns down a gravel road and heads away from La Cappelania. Ponduel brings the taxi to a halt, and the two men watch the blue van drive towards Montaña Colorada.

– Do you think he saw us? Do you think he's trying to get away from us?

Ponduel looks to Erhard for guidance, and Erhard can think of nothing else to do but to continue following the van.

– Wait here a little. Let's see what he does.

The gravel road curves across the barren landscape and continues up the mountain. The van almost vanishes from sight, but Erhard can still see its blue roof like a magic carpet flying up, up, up.

– He's going over the mountain. We've got to follow him, Erhard says.

Ponduel glances at his watch and turns onto the gravel road.

76

They follow a cloud of dust. Can't see the delivery van anywhere. Carmino Calderas is a narrow, difficult road made for lazy tourists. It winds around the largest volcanic crater, Montaña Colorada, and continues towards Calderon Hondo and over to Lajares. Ponduel mumbles something about the rocks spitting against his nice Lexus, then turns on the windscreen wiper and sprinkler to wash off the film of dust. One good thing about the dust cloud is that Pascual won't know they're trailing him.

They drive slowly and cautiously. As the delivery van continues past the houses at the base of the mountain, Erhard becomes more and more convinced that Pascual detected them and took this route to shake them off. Why else would he choose such a difficult road to Lajares? He might also be on his way to Cotillo. Driving up the hill with the narrow road balanced between the crater on the right side and another, steeper drop into a small valley on the other.

The cloud of dust suddenly clears.

Ponduel slams on the brakes.

The last of the dust settles. The road is deserted; they can see all the way to the motley collection of houses that makes up Lajares.

– Fucking hell, Ponduel says.

– There, Erhard says, pointing. The delivery van is parked a hundred metres ahead, within a cranny in the rocks. And they see, a short distance beyond the van, almost invisible against the light-brown soil, Pascual making his way up Calderon Hondo.

– What's he doing? Erhard asks.

– Maybe he likes volcanoes.

Native-born islanders love their volcanoes. As children, in school, Sunday school, and whenever their families visit from the mainland or the other islands, they're dragged to them, around them, and into them. Calderon Hondo is the most beautiful of them all; it's almost perfectly formed, and its rim is so sharp and pure that it appears as though it could slice skin. At the same time, it is smaller and not as overrun with tourists as Montaña Colorada, which is as shabby as a soft old hat. Maybe Ponduel's right and Pascual does like volcanoes.

Of course, Erhard wants to point out to Ponduel that Calderon Hondo isn't a volcano but a meteor crater. This is a sensitive topic that's regularly debated here. Some years ago, the discussion grew so heated that it split a local tourist bureau into two camps: the volcanists and the meteorists. Erhard sides with the meteor-theory, especially as it's described in Belgian scholar Norman Zectay-Bidôt's two-volume *Circle of Life* from 1972, which he's read twice. He imagines the fifteen-stone meteor, not much larger than a beach ball, slamming into the island thousands of years ago. Had someone been standing on Africa's coast at that moment, he or she would have seen a great mushroom cloud of dust rising from the surface of the water.

– Stay here, Erhard says, getting out of the car.

– I have to head back. My wife and I are celebrating Carmen, Ponduel says, though without conviction.

Erhard leans through the open window. – Wait ten minutes. If I don't return, go ahead. And forget that you ever saw me.

As harsh as Erhard's words are, Ponduel appears to be falling asleep. Erhard remembers something. He'd wanted to borrow Ponduel's mobile to call Solilla and tell her about that computer gizmo he'd lowered into the aquarium. Too late now.

– Do me a favour, Ponduel. Tell Solilla at 46 Calle Reyes Católicos that I've put something in the fish tank at Café Azura in Corralejo. In the loo. It's important, Ponduel.

– In a fish tank? What the hell are you talking about?

Erhard pulls out his roll of euros again. – If I don't return, this is yours. He tosses the notes on the empty seat. – But you must, *must* give Solilla the message.

Ponduel takes the money without a word.

After repeating Solilla's address and the name of the cafe, Erhard starts up the mountain in the same direction as Juan Pascual.

Erhard expects to hear Ponduel starting the engine and backing onto the road, but he doesn't. And when Erhard's almost halfway up to the rim of the crater, he sees the Lexus still waiting – the white vehicle now the size of a fingernail. Erhard approaches the crater, then falls to his knees. He crumples himself into a ball as much as he can without injuring himself. He was never a soldier; in his youth he'd been a conscientious objector. But right now he wishes he knew more about soldiering, so he could sneak up to the crater without being seen or heard. He shifts a little to his left, so that he doesn't emerge on the tourist path that's visible in the trampled earth.

Juan Pascual is gone.

Erhard reaches the rim, squats down, and glances into the huge bowl, rough and raw, beige-coloured with black blotches, pounded smooth by thousands of tourists but still as innocent and otherworldly as the day the meteor struck. Zectay-Bidôt wrote that the rock formations in Calderon Hondo, compared to its neighbour volcanoes, had been crushed to a far greater extent. Like in a mortar. This is clearly evident. There are no large rocks on Hondo, but the long, thin stems of plants poke up here and there, and a goat grazes on the other side of the crater, munching restlessly on the grass.

How did Juan Pascual manage to disappear behind the rim of the crater? But he has. Like sleight-of-hand. Erhard sits quietly, his eyes darting around the crater, examining every shadow or rock formation. But there's nothing large enough to conceal a man. Maybe he leapt into a recess and covered himself in loose stones. Erhard focuses on the area directly below him, and to the sides, and scrutinizes every square metre. His eyes hurt from the strain. But there's nothing to see.

The goat is heading towards him. It's not trotting in a straight line, but a zigzag, now running, then pausing, now springing. His own goats had needed years to feel comfortable enough to approach him. In truth, it was only when he rattled the pellets in the bucket that they came to him.

He walks a short distance to his left, slowly, his eyes focused on the crater. What is Pascual doing here anyway? It sounded as though he was going to meet someone. But clearly there is no one here but Erhard and the goat. Could there be a hidden cave or something that Juan Pascual leaped into? Where Emanuel Palabras or whoever it was on the phone had been waiting for him? The goat continues towards Erhard, running. Odd behaviour. Maybe the animal is so hungry, or social, that it will do whatever. It's almost as though someone is driving the animal towards Erhard, or a strong wind. But Erhard sees nothing, and there's little wind in the crater.

He might as well head back to the car.

He hears a couple of loud honks, probably Ponduel reminding him how much time has passed and that it's time to go home. Our Patroness Carmen is expecting him and his family downtown for crabs. But why does he keep honking?

Erhard returns to the rim and glances briefly at the goat, now running almost directly towards him, hobbling on one leg, and yet tumbling forward. Then he notices the dark figure of a man, a silhouette against the light-yellow sky, charging at him from the left side of the crater. Ponduel has now, apparently, pressed his hand down on the horn, and keeps honking until the man ploughs into Erhard, knocking him backward. The two men roll down the side of the crater. Erhard focuses on protecting his head, and bracing himself with his arms, while the other man – who must be Juan Pascual – manages to punch his jaw and ribs even as they're rolling downhill. At last Erhard's lying still, confused and mashed against the warm gravel.

Juan Pascual hovers above Erhard adjusting something on his head, a little contraption affixed to his ear. A hearing device the size of an insect. It must have fallen off when they were rolling around. He seems irritated.

When he's done adjusting the device, Pascual punches Erhard with clenched fists, his hands like knots of old rope. The first blows hurt, slicing his face and bruising his ribs. He can't feel any of the blows that follow, just hears them.

– Macho, why do you keep getting in the way? Juan Pascual says, punching Erhard's ribs.

– I... have told everything. To a journalist.

Juan Pascual lowers his head to Erhard's mouth. – No, you haven't. You were in the lockup. He slaps Erhard to get his attention. – How did you find me?

– I know everything. About the hijacking. About you. About the dead ship's mate. And the baby.

– Baby? You mean the boy? I don't know shit about that boy.

– Tell Palabras that... I'm exposing... everything.

– Palabras is gone, and you're not exposing shit.

There's something about the man's eyes. It's as if he's stood too close to a fire.

– You're sick, Erhard guesses. – You… are sick.

Erhard remembers Pascual at the cafe that morning many weeks ago, how he sat hunched over. And he remembers something Raúl once said about his friend Pesce. That he'd been to hell and back again. When Raúl told him, Erhard had thought it meant that he'd been to war. Maybe the Balkans in the nineties. Many young Spaniards had been deployed back then. But now he's not sure. There's something wrong with Pascual.

The look on Pascual's face changes, just a fraction, and he fumbles in the pocket of his thin windbreaker. He quickly throws a plastic strip around Erhard's throat and cinches it, then tightens it until Erhard feels it cutting into his flesh. Every time he tightens it further, the little lock clicks. Erhard manages to take a deep breath, but now he can't exhale. Only a tiny portion of air escapes.

Without a word, Pascual stands up.

Erhard sees Pascual's silhouette against the rays of sunlight. Like the outline of a new coin, stamped in dust and clouds. Pascual kicks him with what feel like steel-toed boots. A second time. A third. He would probably survive the kicks if not for the fact that each one also knocked more air from his lungs and pushed it up his throat where it can't escape. He feels like a bubble in a section of bubble wrap, stretched to the breaking point, ready to explode from within.

Suddenly Pascual grabs his waist.

– Let's give La Policia something to work with. You think a little accident in your taxi will keep them busy?

Since Erhard can no longer feel his limbs, he wonders if he's losing consciousness – or if he already has. Pascual drags him down the hill. Erhard's feet scrape the ground; he can hear them, but he can't feel them. He's not sure what's going to happen to him, but he knows something's not right. Doesn't Pascual know that Ponduel's in the taxi? Didn't he hear him honk? Will Ponduel see Pascual dragging him and wonder what's going on? Will Pascual kill them both?

They reach the path, and Pascual walks faster, Erhard like a mannequin in his arms. – You're a sad sap, he whispers almost tenderly in Erhard's ear. When they reach the car, Pascual drops him to the ground.

– Do you have the keys or what... Pascual pats Erhard's pockets, but there's nothing there. Then Pascual goes to the Lexus and opens the door. He climbs in, and Erhard is confused. His thoughts swirl. His body is in a state of emergency. Where's Ponduel?

He gasps for breath, but it never seems to be enough. Did Pascual take care of Ponduel before attacking Erhard? Pascual starts the engine and drives onto the road. Then he hauls Erhard into the driver's seat, propping his feet on the pedals.

– There you are. Now you can drive.

Pascual jerks the gear stick, and the car begins to roll. Erhard wants to glance up. Wants to put his hands on the wheel, his foot on the brake. But nothing. He can. Do nothing.

– *Buen viaje*, Pascual says.

Erhard expects to hear the door slamming shut. Instead he hears a strange sound: Pascual moaning.

– Fucking hell.

Thump. Thump. Something strikes the car twice, but it continues to roll, downward, over gravel.

Erhard manages to get his hands on the wheel, but they just slide off the warm leather onto his lap. He forces himself to look up, struggling for air. But when he raises his head, the plastic strip bites into his neck. The car continues to roll. Faster. He can just make out some light, the path's yellow gravel, and something purple, the evening sky, as if the path is vanishing heavenward. If he could scream, he would. He presses his weight down, first on the gas pedal – which causes the car to pick up speed – and then the brake. The Lexus slows down, but only just. He hears footfalls to his left, someone running alongside the car. Pascual.

He raises his head and sees how the path curves up ahead, but he's unable to keep the car on it and continues straight through the curve.

He holds his breath and hopes he'll faint, so that he won't feel anything. Only fifty or one hundred metres to go before the Lexus reaches the cliff. The car is picking up speed, and he can no longer see the path, only the sky.

The windscreen is like the flap of a box closing in on him. His vision flickers. He wants to leap out of the box, but he's held down by some kind of invisible lid.

At that instant someone reaches in, grabs his shirt, and yanks him out. His head bangs against the door frame, and when his shoulder slams against the ground, followed by his head, legs, and the rest of his body, pain flares in him. All the wind is knocked out of him, his energy spent. The car's gone, tumbling down the path. He hears it flipping thunderously end over end. He goes out like a light.

77

– I won't be home by 9.30, Ponduel says.

These are the first words Erhard hears. Before he realizes that it was Ponduel who'd just resuscitated him. Ponduel's standing with the plastic strip in one hand and a pocketknife in the other. – That *maricón* was seriously unhinged. What the fuck was going on? He wanted to kill you.

Erhard sucks up great impatient gulps of air and feels something wet rolling down his forehead. He fingers his throat where the plastic strip was wound.

– Your car, Erhard stammers.

– You owe me, you sick old man. And we'll never find those 875 euros you gave me in the wreckage.

– Where were you?

Ponduel explains. He'd been sick of waiting and was about to drive off, but then he saw Juan Pascual running along the rim towards Erhard. Ponduel had honked to warn Erhard. He couldn't tell what was happening, and grew uneasy. He decided to go up to the crater to see what was going on, but he got lost on the way and came out in the wrong place, just in time to see that crazy asshole – Ponduel's words – dragging Erhard down the hill. At first Ponduel thought Pascual was going to drive off with Erhard, and so he ran down the hill to block the van, but instead he watched him back the Lexus onto the road. That irked Ponduel, so he found a big rock and ran around the car to hammer it on the asshole's head. But before he got there, Pascual had put the car in neutral and shoved it down the path. Ponduel slammed the rock in the man's in the face, but the guy punched him like an angry bull and knocked him down twice. In the end, Ponduel managed to shove him off an outcropping. He struck his head and went out like a light, and then Ponduel ran after the car to save it. Save Erhard, of course.

– And not a moment too soon, Ponduel concluded. – You've got a little blood on your neck, because I had to put my Swiss Army knife under the plastic to cut if free. And I had to pound your chest once to get you breathing again. *Lo siento.*

– Where is he?

– Up there. He had another one of those plastic strips on him, so I used it to tie him up. He can't get away. I would call the police, but my mobile's in the car. You don't have one, either.

– I saw him talking on his mobile. Erhard's inhalation is returning to normal, and it no longer hurts to breathe.

– Maybe it's in the van. I haven't checked. But I have the keys right here.

Erhard sits quietly for a moment, then pushes himself onto his elbow and looks at Ponduel, shaking his head. – No police. Not yet.

Ponduel throws up his hands, but says nothing.

Erhard tries to stand. His body feels like fragments, wired and taped together but otherwise broken. He takes a few cautious steps, but can't continue.

– I'll get the van, Ponduel says, and starts briskly towards the road. Erhard has never seen him move that fast. A few minutes later the blue van noses down the path towards him. Ponduel parks and leaps out to help Erhard into the passenger seat, waving a black mobile phone that he's found in the van. Then he turns the van around and drives ahead twenty or thirty metres. Erhard spots Pascual lying in a ditch at the foot of a small outcropping. He doesn't seem to be awake, despite the awkward position he's in: hogtied.

– What do we do with him? Ponduel asks.

– We have to take him to Corralejo.

Once again Ponduel has to climb out of the van. He drags Pascual from the ditch and up the hill, then dumps him in the back. Erhard can't see the two men, but he hears Pascual groaning in protest.

Then they head back down Calderon Hondo. Erhard reclines in his seat, his body sore all over. Ahead of them, the sun is sinking below the horizon. The smashed Lexus irritates Ponduel more and more the closer they get to the city. He doesn't know what he's going to tell his wife, doesn't know how he's going to earn a paycheque the next few days. Erhard tells him to report the incident to the police as soon as he gets home. Tell them how that crazy Hermit took him hostage and stole his car. The police would believe him.

Ponduel's not so sure. The wife's got a sixth sense for lies like that. That's how it is with *majoreros*. They know a lie when they hear one; it's a skill they pass down from generation to generation. That's women for you, Erhard suggests, but Ponduel just snaps at him, telling him that he looks like a homeless man with his buzz cut, like a fucking beggar.

They drive to Hotel Olympus and the unfinished car park. Ponduel slams the door and wanders off. Vanishing in the darkness, probably down one of the paths that run behind the luxurious villas to the block of flats where he lives with his young wife. Erhard isn't sure what to do with the van or with Juan Pascual, who has begun to stir.

He flails about, cursing and shouting. – Hey, who's there?

Pascual doesn't know who knocked him out, Erhard realizes, or threw him in the van. The roles are reversed.

Erhard revs the motor by stepping on the gas. He pulls his t-shirt up to his mouth and barks above the din, impersonating Palabras. – Scream all you want, my friend. No one can hear you.

– I've done everything you asked me to do. Everything. I took care of the old man. Now I just need the woman. Let me finish the job. Give me a chance. I need my medicine, otherwise I'm going to be sick.

Erhard considers. – I'm not giving you anything until I know for certain that you won't go to the police.

– I swear by Mother Mary. You can trust me.

– What if… what if the old man spoke to someone? Erhard ventures, pressing down on the gas until it's nearly impossible to tell what he's saying.

– What? Pascual says.

– What if the old man talked? he yells even louder. Must be the hearing aid, Erhard thinks, or maybe he lost it in the tumult.

– I've kept my eye on him.

– People have seen you, you stupid sailor.

– Who? When did they see me?

– When do you think?

– What?

– In the flat. When Beatrizia Colini was beaten up. A neighbour in the building across the street saw you.

Silence.

– I told you it wasn't me. Raúl was upstairs making a phone call. After the incident with the whore. I waited outside after we returned, and he started to argue with Colini. I tried to stop him, but he didn't let me in until it was too late. I told him I'd take care of the old man, who was lying upstairs. But Raúl said no.

Erhard's head is swimming. – What did you do to the whore?

– What?

– What did you do with the whore?

– I've already told you that. You know what I did.

– Remind me.

Silence. Then a thump on the floor. – Fuck you. Who are you? Is it you, Palabras?

– You killed her.

– What the fuck? You know what…

441

Erhard revs the engine and quickly hops out of the van. He feels terribly nauseated, and expects to vomit his afternoon shrimp. But gasping for breath, he tastes the sea salt and inhales the smell of cool cement, and that helps. The nausea passes.

More pieces of the puzzle have fallen into place.

Of course Alina didn't jump off the roof herself, of course she was pushed. Why hasn't he considered that possibility before? He'd thought that no one knew she was out there, but Raúl knew. Erhard told him as much. A mixture of relief and anger tumbles around inside him. Erhard didn't caused her to jump; it was Raúl or his friend Pesce. They let her hang herself like a hunter's deer. With premeditation. They killed the confused, dumb girl, and they hoped Erhard would take the fall.

He walks away from the delivery van, then through the unfinished hotel. In many ways, the hotel is representative of the island's grand ambition, its widespread corruption, terrible public administration, and planning. But it's also a rather poetic feature: a pile of rubble revealing some poor architect's late-night elbow grease and drawing-board ideas removed of varnish. By the glow of headlights, he catches a glimpse of what would have been a restaurant or a cafeteria with a stairwell, a landing, and a wall of windows facing the sea. German housewives and smug Russians could have circulated around the buffet table, while twenty or thirty West Africans and young Spaniards ran about filling the empty trays with fresh figs, steaming tortillas, and locally harvested shellfish. The guests could have sat in plush chairs drinking champagne as they enjoyed the view of the bay and the city. Because of the shrubbery and the giant rocks, it's impossible to see the ocean from here, but surely those would've been blasted away with dynamite when the hotel was completed. In a changing world, it feels good to stand in the centre of something unchanging. A construction site: a work in progress that, in all likelihood, will never amount to anything. One day it'll be razed to the ground.

He kicks at a crumpled-up plastic bag from HiperDino, the silly green dinosaur logo with its fiery-red tongue. What he really wants to do is to haul that bumbling fool Pascual out of the van and beat him senseless. Find an old pipe and flatten his head with it. But what good would it do? The sailor didn't do anything but carry out orders, and those orders came from Emanuel Palabras. Must have.

I only need the woman, Pascual had said. The woman. He must mean Mónica. They must think Mónica knows something.

Erhard scoops up the bag and puts it over his head, testing how it feels. It smells musty. Then he jogs to the van, opens the door, and scrabbles in the back. Pascual's a dark lump in one corner, and he hardly moves when Erhard climbs in. He swears once before Erhard grabs hold of his throat and pulls the bag over his head. – Why did you push the ship's mate overboard?

– Who the fu—?

Erhard kicks him as hard as he can in the kidneys. The plastic bag rustles; it's begun to expand and retract with Pascual's breath.

– Why did you kill him? Tell me and I'll remove the bag. Erhard can no longer see his face.

Pascual gasps for breath. – He couldn't sail, a... fucking liar, a junkie. Take it off, take it off. The bag tightens across his mouth.

– He tried to keep you from moving the containers.

– He was useless, and he kept shouting incoherently about the boy. It was all so chaotic, and we had work to do.

Erhard kicks him again. – The woman, what will you do with her?

– What do you mean?

Erhard unleashes his fury on the lump, shouting, – What will you do with the woman?

Finally the lump goes quiet. One of the plastic strips he'd tied around Erhard's throat lies on the floor of the van. Erhard picks it up and considers returning the favour. But instead he sticks the strip in his back pocket, rips the bag off Pascual's head, and hops out of the van.

Only one person can stop things going any further.

Pascual's mobile is beneath the handbrake. Erhard opens it with a click and stares at all the buttons. He inputs Emanuel Palabras's number, but nothing happens. Then he presses the large green button, the one with the telephone symbol, and hears the line beep.

It beeps six, seven, eight times. Then someone answers.

– Yes.

The voice is simple and clear. It's Palabras. Measured, waiting.

– You fucking bastard, Erhard says. He can't think of a better way to start the conversation.

– Why couldn't you just leave well enough alone? Why did you have to play the hero?

– I wanted to expose you. You and your fucking sick game.

– Well, I'm glad you called. I was wondering when I would hear from you.

– Shut up, you hypocrite. I have your henchman right here.

Palabras is quiet a moment. – I don't know who you mean, he says.

– He's filled me in on a lot of interesting details.

– Trust me when I say that I don't know who you mean.

– Shut your—

– I advise you to listen now, Piano Tuner. I have our little, what shall we call her, girlfriend here. I've heard the entire story, and it's very moving.

Erhard doesn't budge. – You... you better not...

– I'm not going to do anything. But unless you don't start acting sensibly, I'll seriously consider putting an end to her miserable existence.

– Let me talk to her.

Palabras laughs. – You're too good to be true. She's not very talkative, but if she were, she would doubtless miss your company. Now, for the time being, please do as I say.

– I'll do whatever you ask. Just don't harm her.

– I want you out here. Now. The harbour in Corralejo. And take that fucking boat this time. It'll sail you over here. Then we'll talk.

– Over here? Erhard manages to say before Palabras hangs up.

He walks along the water. He's kicked off his shoes and now feels the cool sand against his bare toes. The city and the bay are illuminated by colourful chain lights, and music of various kinds floats up beneath wispy white clouds. With each step he has to convince himself to continue; his body is worn out beyond all reason, and he can't imagine returning to his previous self again. It's like driving on petrol fumes with a motor that needs oil and tyres that are flat. If he arrives on time, it's only because he can't stop thinking of Mónica. For some reason, the image of her pale belly and the broken clay pots keeps cropping up in his head, and he lumbers forward, forward, as fast as he can.

He left Pascual in the delivery van, and doesn't figure he'll go anywhere. He needs to keep him around, like a trump card he can throw down if necessary. That Palabras refuses to admit he knows the man only serves to underscore just how much Erhard needs proof. He would have taken the van, but it would do no good to try to drive through the city during Virgin del Carmen. Most of the city is closed off to vehicles, and the harbour is teeming with people.

They've constructed pavilions on the beach where visitors at some of the coastal hotels can dine with a tremendous view, chatting excitedly and loudly. They're waiting on the high point of the evening: Carmen's final journey on the flotilla, followed by a massive display of fireworks visible all the way out in Majanicho. Walking along, he probably resembles one of the sand sculptors, and several euphoric people say hello to him, calling out *Holy Carmen*.

The beach leads up to the packed, chaotic promenade. Adults raise their wineglasses, kiss over empty plates, slurp the last sips of their daiquiris. Children crawl among chairs with dogs and cats, and street hawkers tie bracelets to tourists' wrists. There's more noise here, but also more light, and for a moment he fears being seen by a policeman standing hatless along the wall beside the jeweller's shop. But before long Erhard merges with the throng, and any interest in him as a person dissolves. A few hundred metres down the street, he walks past Azura and spots the Bitch standing behind the bar. Then he shoves his way forward and zigzags towards the harbour.

78

The red cutter chugs quietly out to sea.

The man behind the ship's wheel isn't nearly as frightening as Erhard had anticipated. He's focused on steering the vessel around all the small skiffs and inflatable boats filled with people watching the beach and the flotilla. A curtain of torches sets the entire beach ablaze.

Erhard's first guess is that they're heading to one of the large yachts anchored in the bay, but instead they pass through the cluster as if they don't wish to wake the sleeping boats, and sail towards the magnetic black dot on the horizon.

Isla de Lobos.

Unsympathetic and independent, loved by fishermen, birds, the occasional tourist, and, once in the 1960s, John Coltrane. Just a few months before his death, he'd insisted on giving an outdoor concert, along with the greatest jazz names of the age, on the rooftop terrace of the island's only cafe. Before that, Coltrane had spent some weeks alone on the island, living in a cabin with a view of a beach overrun with seals, the island's namesake. But the seals are now gone. One morning Coltrane saw a man walk across the water from Fuerteventura, a version of himself, he later said, a naked man with musical scores tattooed on his body from head to toe. Ogunde, Coltrane called him.

Tonight the island is like Corralejo's shadow side. Completely void of light and sound. A sanctuary of silence at the end of the ship's bow. And even though the cutter slices the water at a good clip, the island doesn't seem to grow larger or closer, but continually appears and disappears beneath the waves. Erhard leans sleepily against the railing and asks the skipper a lot of questions, but the skipper just chews on his cigarette and doesn't respond. All at once Erhard sees a thin wooden jetty protruding into the water, and the skipper eases the cutter alongside it with familiar caution. Then he throws a pair of slender ropes around the mooring poles and cuts the engine. Everything is quiet now, and totally dark.

Feeling inconsequential and small, Erhard almost forgets why he's here. Without hesitation he follows the skipper, who's stepped out onto the jetty, and feels the old wooden boards under his bare feet. Erhard has been here before, but not after sunset. All visitors are sent home in the afternoon. As though they could not comprehend the forces that rule this island at night. And now Erhard is about to find out.

They walk up the hill, following narrow paths lustrous in the darkness. At first Erhard thinks it's an optical illusion, but the crunch of his footfalls and the prickling sensation in his feet indicate that the paths are covered in mussel shells whose white mother-of-pearl glints faintly in the moonlight.

When they are on the other side of a ridge, Erhard gazes down at a little bay and a number of square buildings. Not houses exactly, more like bungalows next to the water. There are no signs of life. Only the churn of the sea: the surf pounding against the shore, perhaps a half-mile away.

The skipper finally stops and points towards the end of the path. It's unsettlingly dark, and Erhard's just about to ask what the hell he's pointing at. But the skipper's already gone, his crunching footfalls signalling that he's returning to his boat.

Stepping into the darkness, Erhard reaches for a railing of some kind. Slight variations of grey help him understand that he's approaching the cliff. Unreasonably, he expects to fall at any moment into a giant pit where he'll find Mónica lying pale, naked, and dead. But when he's close enough to the cliff to sense its warmth, he spots a small cabin between the cliffs, and a cabin door framed by yellow light.

– Go on in.

The voice is behind him. When Erhard recognizes it, he feels a sense of relief.

– I can still run away from you, Charles.

– Not as long as I have this. A bright light flashes in Erhard's eyes, almost blinding him. A pocket torch. As good as a weapon out here. Charles nudges Erhard towards the door, which opens from within. – Go in.

– What happened to you, Piano Tuner? You look like a foolish tourist.

Emanuel Palabras fills the doorway with his enormous bulk. He's wearing what looks like a red-and-gold circus tent. He notices Erhard's stare. – The Virgin del Carmen, he says, gesturing with his hand, as if Erhard has been invited to a party.

As usual, his entire entourage of Maasai girls are well represented, sprawled across wooden chairs, tables, benches, and the strange pieces of furniture that make up the décor. Eight women who look like sisters or cousins, all of them blacker than black. Palabras tries to explain why Isla de Lobos is the best place to be this evening, but Erhard doesn't pay attention. His gaze sweeps round the room to determine where Mónica is being held. A powerful lamp is fastened to a painted blue wall, the paint cracked and peeling. Hanging on the same wall is a torn old poster of the Spanish balladeer Pedro Jerez Segundo. On the far side of the room is a red door. An odd rapping sound emerges from behind it, like a banging water pipe.

– You're looking for your girlfriend. She's next door receiving special attention.

Erhard knows what that sort of thing means. Just as he's about to make a run at Palabras, Charles grabs his shoulder.

– Don't do anything you'll regret, Palabras says. Nothing will change if you assault me. I'm actually a rather patient man, and I have given you many, many chances to prove that you're not out to destroy everything for yourself and others.

– I want to see her. I want to see that she's OK.

– She's doing better than the last time you saw her, that much I can tell you.

Erhard recalls his last conversation with Mónica. How angry she was. – Don't touch her.

Palabras throws up his hands. Erhard stares at him. He can't fathom how a man he has known for as long as he has can be so criminally unscrupulous. – Why? Why are you doing this? Is it to show how powerful you are? Is it for the money? Or is it just because you're sick in the head?

– It's love. Nothing more.

– What's wrong with you?

– You don't understand, do you? Unconditional love. Devotion.

Erhard laughs. – Such fine words coming from you.

– 15 September 1995.

– Why do you say that?

The rapping continues. A grating sound. Palabras waves Charles over and asks him to make it stop. Charles shrugs, but hobbles off through the red door.

Palabras continues: – 15 September 1995. Your wife enters the living room to see why you're not coming to bed. Where are you? Where is her daughters' father, the man in her life? After all you two have been through? It makes her very sad, in fact. Did you know that, Erhard?

Erhard trembles as if every cell in his body is unstable, about to burst. – You have no idea. No idea what went on.

– All I'm saying is that you know nothing of love. The kind of love where one will do anything. Whatever it takes.

– Tell me what any of this has to do with love.

– Believe it or not, I am actually rather fond of you, my silent, guilty Piano Tuner. Year after year you've tried to help me, and you've never asked me for anything, neither my assistance nor my money. You're a true friend. And yet slowly, like poison, you turn my own son against me.

– I have never…

– He listens to you. Everything you say is correct, simple, and interesting.

– He didn't listen to me. He didn't care.

– So as a father, what does one do? Give up? Make sacrifices? Does he walk away from his family? Or do everything he can to keep the family together?

Charles returns and whispers something to Palabras.

– You're more twisted than I thought, Erhard says. – There are no excuses, none, for what you've done.

– No need to prattle on. My mother, may she rest in peace, used to speak of blame. But blame has never led to anything. Love, on the other hand. For the sake of love one must make sacrifices.

– These are people, Palabras. You can't just decide who lives and who dies. You're a criminal, and you'll pay for your crimes.

– That's exactly what I feared. Ill-considered and baseless.

– I have proof. It's in a safe place, and if anything happens to me, you'll read about it in the newspaper. I have a witness. He's implicated you multiple times.

Emanuel Palabras drops into one of the chairs, and he's immediately enveloped within four Maasai arms emerging from behind him. He grins. – I've told you not to play detective. You're not very good at it.

– I know more than you think.

– You're forgetting your own role in the matter.

– What do you mean?

– Where did you get the corpse?

– The corpse?

– The dead girl in Beatrizia's coffin. Who was she?

Erhard stiffens. They must have found Bea's body in the flat.

– She was the one you had killed at my place in Majanicho. The prostitute. I saved Bea from you. That's what I did.

Emanuel Palabras laughs. It unsettles Erhard, because the information genuinely seems new to Palabras – And how did that turn out?

– But I wasn't the one who killed her. It was you and your son and your disturbed henchman, Juan Pascual.

– From what Michel Faliando told me, you were the one who turned off the respirator. Even though he told you not to.

– She was suffering. She wasn't going to make it.

Palabras must have gotten his clutches on the doctor, Erhard thinks.

– Who is deciding who lives and who dies now?

– You're manipulating my words.

– Don't we all?

– So what now? Are you taking me out on the sea and throwing me overboard? You might as well. Whatever happens, the story will come out. A journalist is writing it as we speak.

– I do have an urge to drown you, I admit. Not me personally, of course. Charles. It would make everything easier. But Charles's leg still bothers him, and, in spite of everything, I don't wish you any harm.

– Juan Pascual says otherwise. He tried to strangle me earlier tonight. On your orders.

– You're not listening to me. I have nothing to do with this Pascual. And I've not asked anyone to kill you. I admit that I asked my friend at police headquarters to arrest and interrogate you, but I also got you out again. You said nothing to the young policeman. I couldn't have asked for more loyalty from you. I'd hoped you would hop on the boat this afternoon and we could get you to Morocco so you could live with a sweet little lady in a clay hut, but then you suddenly bolted. You ran from Charles and got a horrible haircut, and then you were gone. Next time I hear from you you're bloody raving mad and telling me I'm behind everything.

– You hired Juan Pascual, and you hijacked your own ship so you could get the insurance money. You killed your own son and gave me his goddamn job so you could keep an eye on me. You would have killed Beatriz, too, if you'd known she was alive.

Palabras sighs. – Show him, he tells Charles.

Charles nudges Erhard towards the red door. They enter a large room illuminated by another powerful lamp, on the ceiling, which throws light like in a brooding box. Like curious cats, the Maasai girls follow, clinging to Erhard and giving off an aroma of incense.

There is a wheelchair and an IV rack in the centre of the room, along with another chair. A person is sitting in the wheelchair. Her head is fastened to the headrest, and her bathrobe is wet with drool. A moment passes before Erhard realizes that it's Beatriz. His heart thumps. At once confused and happy, miserable and angry. He thought he'd seen her for the last time in the flat. He'd said his goodbyes. And yet here she is. Resurrected. Or resuscitated. There's no respirator. Instead she's breathing great gulps of air, as if the air is thin, and her head jerks up and down. She's trembling.

Erhard can't speak.

– Hello. A distant, tired voice behind the wooden door.

But Erhard sees only Beatriz. What she is. What he's turned her into. Her body, her name, her life. Everything is gone. Because he heard a voice that said *Help me, let me go.*

Palabras rests a hand on her shoulder. – Faliando contacted me because he was worried. Smart of him. He told me everything. That you'd hidden her, washed her, and everything else. Impressive, but also rather deranged, if you ask me. I'll never understand why you did it, but you must have had your reasons. You didn't fuck her, that much is clear. The doctor checked.

– I don't owe you an explanation.

– You could at least do your job and not get involved. When will you understand? I gave you an opportunity. But you destroy everything for yourself.

– Hello?

The voice again. This time it's accompanied by a heavy pounding on the door.

Palabras makes a sign to Charles to do something. – I thought you'd taken care of him?

– He should've gone out like a light, Charles says.

– Who's in there? Erhard asks, starting towards the door.

– Hello? Erhard?

Erhard recognizes the voice now. It's darker and gruffer, as if unused for months. But there's no doubt about it. It's his.

– Raúl? Raúl, what the hell?

– Erhard!

Charles blocks the door and fumbles to unlock the large, black padlock. – Be quiet! I've told you to be quiet.

– Why's he in there? Erhard asks, staring uncomprehendingly at the lock.

– Let me out, Erhard! Make them let me out.

– What the hell's he doing in there?

– Stay out of it, Palabras says angrily, poking his cane between Erhard and Charles to block him. But Erhard's already on his way over. He covers his head with his arms and throws himself against Charles with all his might. Unable to steel himself for the blow, the big man slams against the door, popping it from its hinges. Erhard and Charles tumble in a heap to the floor, and in the light filtering into the dark, narrow room Erhard sees Raúl – a changed Raúl wearing a tracksuit, with a beard and long, wild hair. He reminds Erhard of a thin, sinewy version of Saddam Hussein on the day he was pulled from the cave in Adwar. With a confused glimmer in his eyes and a crazed expression. Raúl glances at Erhard and Charles a moment, then uses Charles's cast as a launching pad and rushes from the room, as if he'd been waiting for just this opportunity. Erhard tries to stand, but has difficulty breaking free from the big man howling in pain beside him. His cast is broken apart, and his leg – paler than the cast – is sticking out. He shouts something Erhard doesn't understand. For the first time, Erhard wonders if the man is French or Flemish or something else. His skin is lighter than most Spaniards', his hair less curly.

Now on his feet, Erhard hears Palabras yelling at the Maasai girls for help.

– I'm coming, Charles says.

Erhard turns to see Palabras lying on the floor, his mouth and beard bloodied, looking weak and old. The Maasai girls put on his glasses, but they sit crookedly on the bridge of his nose. They hand him his cane, which had apparently been flung to the other side of the room. One of the girls also has blood on her lips. Charles hobbles towards them as if tugged along by an invisible rope.

– Let him go, Carlitos, Palabras says with difficulty. – No boat leaves the island tonight, so he can't go anywhere until tomorrow morning. He's a good swimmer, but he knows… that he can't swim that far in the condition he's in.

Charles stares at Palabras, then limps out the door.

– Carlitos, stop! Unable to shout, Palabras extends his hand. – Bloody obstinate employees doing what they please. He's always wanted to give that boy a thrashing. He's had his urges curbed these past few weeks, but he gets itchy every time there's an opportunity.

– What the hell are you doing? Raúl's your son. Why were you keeping him locked up? Didn't he want to go along with your plan?

– Be quiet, you fool. You understand nothing. The boy's behind everything. Don't you see? I've tried to protect him, to keep him away. I love that dumb boy, but he can't do anything right. He can't even steal from his own father.

Erhard stares at Palabras, trying to determine whether the man is speaking the truth or concocting more lies. Palabras's dark eyes behind his slightly smudged glasses seem tired, almost dry, as if he hasn't blinked in several minutes. – So what are you telling me? That Raúl was the one who hijacked the ship?

– Not him personally, but he was behind it. He knew the people who could get the job done. Someone helped him, of course.

– Juan Pascual?

– You keep talking about this man. I'm talking about the big fish. Hardened old men, I should say. Los Tres Papas.

One of the girls brings Palabras a glass of milk, which he quickly and soundlessly gulps.

– I thought you were one of Los Tres Papas.

Palabras hands the glass back to the girl and tries to laugh, but raises his hand to the wound on his mouth instead. – I wanted to be. Once. But they were too small-scale for me. Everything they do is illegal. I'd rather mix it up, get the best of both worlds.

He gestures at the Maasai girls as if they understand what he means. Maybe they do.

– So if it's Los Tres Papas, what about Raúl?

– Raúl is Raúl. When he was a boy, he stole my wallet and bought a cigar-cutter for me made of gold. He's always been like that, seeking to impress in all the wrong ways. But you helped him, you took the sting out of his pranks, made him stop and think. For some reason, he loved everything you said and did. But that girl over there, she made everything worse. He points at the wheelchair and what is left of Beatriz. – Because of her, he demanded more and more. More money, more power, a better job. He hated that job. Do you understand what I'm telling you? So I was warned. I feared this would happen. I tried to give him something to do, so he wouldn't do anything foolish, but then, well, this happened.

– She wasn't the one. She never asked him for anything.

– *Quién sabe.* Palabras throws up a hand. – The boy suddenly got too big for his britches, and he got stupid.

Erhard doesn't know what to believe. – So Raúl collaborated with Los Tres Papas on the hijacking?

– He carried it out for them, the little shit.

– How did you find out?

– When he began to speak badly of you. Saying that he knew you were working under the table and helped Los Tres Papas dispose of that double-crosser Federico Molino.

– Why did he say that?

– Because he wanted someone to put you in the hospital, I think. He knew that if he did it I would help you, and it would get messy. So he tried to convince me to deal with you.

Erhard settles in the chair beside Beatriz.

– Why?

– I didn't understand, either. I told him that I would look into it, but instead I began to investigate him.

– And?

– We sensed something was wrong when Mario, Charles's nephew, saw Raúl driving out to your place, even though you were at Raúl's flat. He pushed some girl off your roof.

– Mario? Thin guy with big teeth? Erhard recalls the young man who sat across from La Mar Roja the morning he ran into Raúl.

– He's not built like Charles, that's for sure.

– So Charles, or this Mario, went to Raúl's flat, beat up Beatriz, and dragged Raúl out here?

– Not quite. We didn't find out about Beatriz until you called the police. We followed Raúl when he and that other asshole returned to the flat and left a short time later. They were very busy, racing from the basement towards the harbour, obviously headed somewhere. When Raúl was alone in the car, talking on his mobile, Charles and Mario got ahold of him. We dragged him onto a boat and brought him here.

– The other guy was Pesce, Juan Pascual, Erhard says, mostly to himself. – What about the photo from the airport? The one the police mentioned, of Raúl on his way to a plane? And the passenger lists?

– Let's just say we helped them out.

Erhard wants to follow that train of thought, but it's pointless now.

Raúl didn't go abroad. He was here. There was no doubt. He came home from Majanicho after having killed Alina and, in a frenzy of anger and frustration, took everything out on Beatriz, bashing her skull right where he knew she was vulnerable. Hoping it was enough, he'd shoved her into the wardrobe.

– You need to take care of her. Erhard points at Beatriz. – It's your duty as a father-in-law. No matter what. See to it that she gets to a good hospital. Make sure she gets proper care.

– You can't make demands of me, says Palabras. Unconvincing.

– To some degree, I can.

Charles returns, his entire leg now jutting from the cast. – The boy's down near La Rasca. He's found a rowboat. I heard him shouting at Old Jorge.

– What about the motor boat?

– He didn't see it.

– So why don't you stop him?

– You told me to let him go.

– Not if he's fleeing the island!

– Fuck, Charles says. He turns and leaves.

Erhard drags himself out of his chair and runs after him. He hears Palabras shouting, but the darkness quickly swallows the sound. It's getting late. The air is warm, grey in the moonlight. He scans for Charles's white cast and his torch, which skitters like a finger across piano keys. They don't follow the path, but cut across rocks instead. Twice Erhard slips and falls in his bare feet, struggling to keep pace with Charles. Every step on the sharp rocks hurts, but he forces himself forward.

The coastline is around two hundred metres below Erhard; though the water is relatively calm, with just the faintest breeze from the south-west or west, the breakers seem unsteady. Erhard notices a few small cabins further down the coast, and he hears voices shouting from within them. Somewhere nearby, he hears shrill yelping from the Maasai girls, who're searching for each other in the darkness. Charles makes his way towards the cabins, calling out, Where did he go? and waving his torch.

If Raúl is rowing out of the little bay, Erhard thinks, then he'll head south-west. But the current will push him out to sea east of the island. Rowing against the wind on the open sea will be difficult. It will take time and energy to circumvent the narrow peninsula. But he's probably angry, and that will give him the strength to row like a madman for the first few hours.

Instead of continuing towards the cabins, Erhard turns northward and picks up the pace. The moon is now behind the island, and everything is dark, so he uses his intuition and sets his feet down uncertainly, hoping they'll find purchase in the soft earth. The crashing of waves tells him where the water is, and a gentle rustling indicates loose gravel and stone to his left. Judging by the sound of his bare feet against the rocks, the rock bed extends a little way.

He reaches the isthmus. From here, there's water on either side of him, and the rocks appear in varying shades of black. He moves carefully to the edge of the isthmus and gazes across the bay. It sounds as though Charles is trying to get another boat in the water. There's the putt-putt of an engine failing to start, followed by the word *Fuck!*, and then finally the engine roars to life.

The boat heads into the wind, southward. He sees Charles out on the water with his torch, and even though the light carries surprisingly far, it's clear that he's searching in the wrong area.

The voice he heard cursing came from somewhere ahead of him. From here there's no more than five metres of the isthmus remaining. Beyond that point, it merges with the wide, black Atlantic Ocean and there's no land from there to Africa. Erhard continues cautiously, trying not to fall. Above the chop of the engine he hears a strange thumping sound. Like clogs kicking a bucket, driftwood ramming a pier, or a man who doesn't know how to row a boat.

Raúl Palabras is attempting to row the boat away from the rocks, his arms and oars all a-jumble. He pushes and paddles. Off in the distance, the motorboat's engine begins to slowly fade. But Raúl's movements become more and more desperate. Erhard studies the landscape, considering which rocks he can step on to get to the rowboat quickly, but at that instant Raúl gives his rowboat a powerful shove and it drifts four or five metres into the current. In the faint glow of the moonlight, Erhard watches Raúl arrange the oars in the oarlocks and put all his weight into his rowing. It's slow going, but soon enough he's past the last big rocks and outcroppings, and nearly indistinguishable from the dark water.

Erhard wonders if he should call out for Charles in the motor boat. But he can no longer hear the engine. With a little luck, Erhard's shouts would be heard down at the cabins. But since Charles is out of earshot, too much time would likely pass before anyone from the cabins could relay the message to him by boat.

Erhard scales down the rocks, then feels the cold water on his feet. He lowers himself into a squat, then into the water, and his trousers quickly become wet. And his t-shirt. He walks along the craggy shore, but even that soon disappears, and he starts swimming towards the spot where he last saw the rowboat. The waves, which seemed like small ripples from above, now resemble hills crashing on top of him, and he struggles to inhale and hold his breath so as not to swallow too much water. He's not a good swimmer, but he's always been strong and durable. Yet now he feels the past few days on his body. For a moment he feels strong, but as soon as he's free of the rocks he's overcome by exhaustion and the fear of swimming out into the darkness. If only he could see the rowboat, it would be easier, but he can see nothing.

He has nothing to believe in now, he has no reason to be in the water, and yet he can't help but continue. To stretch his arms and shoot his body through the water. The water seems cooler, and the waves – now free from Isla de Lobos – are taller and saltier. He considers calling out to Raúl, appealing to their friendship and asking him to pull him into the boat. But he's certain that his shouts will only make Raúl row harder. He has nothing to gain by plucking Erhard out of the water. Their friendship is over, if it ever was anything more than a boy's attempt to replace his father.

It nearly strikes him in the head.

Something hard and black that suddenly flies past him. He lifts one arm and just manages to avoid the blow. It's a section of broken oar, the paddle and twenty or thirty centimetres of the shaft, water-logged and heavy. But it floats, and Erhard thrusts it ahead of him, using it as a paddle, his energy restored. He knows now that Raúl's not getting very far. The wind will carry Erhard, and maybe with this oar he'll manoeuvre closer to Raúl. With his feet, he begins to splash wildly. He can't hear the splashing, but the waves feel livelier, and some of his exhaustion abates.

The rowboat is close now, he can hear it, and also that strange thumping sound again. Briefly, over a wave, he spots the rowboat, then it's gone, then it appears again. It's approximately ten metres away from him. Raúl has lost his orientation, or he can't control his boat, because he's now facing Fuerteventura. He's sitting sideways to Erhard, who's swimming closer and closer. Soon Erhard hears Raúl cursing and talking to himself, shifting his oar from one lock to the other.

A wild wave heaves Erhard nearly to the boat. He hasn't even considered what he'll do once he reaches it, but he's so close now that there's only time to pursue *one* idea. The first that comes to mind.

When he presses the section of oar down into the water and lays all his weight on it, he feels the water forcing his hand and the paddle upward. He presses even harder and lets go, shooting the oar forward and upward, handle first. There's no time to aim for Raúl's head. There's just the intuitive movement and his will to make it happen.

The oar strikes the edge of the boat with a thud, then topples over the edge and drops into the boat. Erhard can't see what it hits, but he hears a howl and then sees Raúl on his feet, instinctively lashing out with the other oar and smacking the water beside Erhard. Erhard reaches for the oar, dogpaddling to stay afloat. But Raúl now has the section of broken oar and uses it to slash at the water. When he sees Erhard, his expression changes from one of fear to hatred.

– What the fuck do you want?

He slaps at the water with the oar, and it slams against Erhard's hand. A horrible pain shoots through Erhard's head. But his body is already consumed by exhaustion and pain, and forgets frighteningly fast. Raúl lashes out again, and Erhard leans back to dodge the blow.

Erhard tries to shout at Raúl, but his voice is gone. Though the water is relatively warm, it's still too cold to stay in much longer. You've got nowhere to go, he wants to shout.

Raúl wobbles on his feet, but he keeps slashing at Erhard.

– Swim away, Old Man. You'll grow tired and drown. Or you'll get hypothermia.

Whether it's what Raúl says or simply the truth, Erhard feels the exhaustion in his joints. The thought of having to swim back to land causes him almost physical pain, leg spasms. It's been years since he last went swimming. He was a good swimmer once. Ten years ago. Ten years. If he's going to survive, he needs to get into that boat before his body temperature drops.

Raúl stands rocking the boat, watching for Erhard's reaction. Then he slashes again, wilder, more aggressive. His blow rams one of the oarlocks that's attached to a long metal track; the track snaps and dangles over the edge, almost completely loose. Without the track, it would be nearly impossible to row the boat anywhere. Raúl bends forward to grab the track, but it's heavy and it sinks into the water, disappearing. He leans out, and the boat teeters to one side.

It takes Erhard a moment to recognize the opportunity. He swims around the boat. While Raúl's on his knees staring into the water, Erhard grabs the railing, yanking on it with all his might. The boat tips heavily, and Raúl falls forward and slams his face against the boat just before it jerks back. Erhard almost shouts *I'm sorry*, but he's glad to see the blow strike Raúl so clean and hard. Raúl goes down without a word, his foot sticking up. The night is quiet once again.

Erhard dogpaddles towards the bow and clutches it. Kicking his legs and hoisting himself up, he clambers head first. He falls across a sitting board and drops to the bottom of the boat, exhausted, but nevertheless revitalized by a final spark of energy as soon as the warm breeze dries his arms and legs.

In the back pocket of his trousers he finds the short plastic strip and fastens it around Raúl's feet and the remaining oarlock. He makes sure it's good and tight. Then he crawls across the seat and over to Raúl, who's sprawled out, unmoving. He takes Raúl's head in his hands to see his face and to slam it against the edge of the boat.

Raúl opens his eyes.

Erhard wants to look him in the eye when he bashes his head in.

A strange voice emerges from Raúl's throat. – I'm sorry. I love her. I didn't want to. I didn't want to.

Erhard lets go. He doesn't want to hear him. – Shut your mouth, you stupid boy.

– Everything I had was his. I wanted something of my own.

– You're not well. You need help.

– If you mean the whore, then…

– I mean everything. I mean the boy. Beatriz. Alina. Everything.

– Saving yourself isn't free, you said so yourself.

– Not that way, you shit.

Erhard grabs his throat, mostly to shake him, but also to choke the life out of him. If only he had enough strength to do so.

But Raúl rolls on top of Erhard, and somehow manages to scramble to his feet even though his foot is fastened to the oarlock.

Erhard is suddenly aware of the difference in their physiques. Even though he's been locked up for weeks, Raúl is still thirty-five years younger than Erhard. With an ordinary punch he could put an end to Erhard, tap the last of his energy reserve. But Raúl just stands there watching Erhard, his lips moving as if in prayer. Then he raises his arm. There's a rock in his hand – it must've been lying under the seat.

At that moment Erhard shifts to the other side of the boat.

Raúl is standing on one leg. When the boat tips he's forced to put his foot down to regain his balance, but with his foot attached to the oarlock he stumbles; his hand reaches out for something to hold onto but finds only air. He tumbles over the edge of the boat, ripping the oarlock free. The boat teeters a little, but quickly stabilizes.

A few seconds pass before Raúl emerges a few metres away, gasping for breath, coughing. He reaches for the boat, but he's too far away. He swallows water and tries to say something that sounds like *Wait.*

Just then, the fireworks begin at Corralejo.

It's the high point of the festival, when the flotilla bearing the figure of the Virgin Carmen is sent to sea surrounded by tea-light candles and flowers, and the city sings as fireworks explode in the sky. Larger and more ambitious than New Year's Eve. Erhard can hardly see the glow, but the booms split the sky in two.

I can't, Raúl seems to want to say, but water keeps lapping into his mouth. He splashes as if something's nibbling on him from below. Panic-stricken. Fearful. He slaps at the water. Erhard wants to tell him that panicking won't do him any good, but he says nothing. Just looks down at the man in the water. At the face disappearing in the darkness. Every thunderous clap from the fireworks pounds him, like a nail, deeper and deeper into the sea.

Only one of Raúl's arms is visible, the other hand is apparently underwater struggling to free his foot from the plastic strip and the oarlock. His movements push him farther away from the boat, but he doesn't realize that. He lunges and squirms, desperate for breath and swallowing water.

Finally Erhard offers his hand, stretching it as far as he can. He wonders how he might bring the boat closer to Raúl and get into position to drag him out of the water, but the oars are gone, and with both oarlocks in the water, there's nothing he can do. He can't create enough forward motion with his hand alone, so he offers it instead. He's nowhere near Raúl, but Raúl seems to notice the attempt. He looks at Erhard with salt-white eyes, his face dissolving.

I don't want to, Raúl says. Submerged.

Erhard stares at his hand before pulling it back. The one with four fingers. The narrower one. A nearly human hand.

Raúl sinks quietly.

Erhard is so shocked that he can't scream. All the treachery, loss, hatred, and love settles on him with such force that he begins to cry like a man without a past.

Then there's only the water. And the crackles and pops of fireworks in the sky far away, dying out.

LILY

28 February

79

She doesn't realize how relieved he is to see her. To follow Aaz to the door and let him into the house without a word. The anxiety he'd felt when he'd thought Palabras had kidnapped her and would harm her to punish him. He can't imagine anything more beautiful than her lively old face.

– Are you driving a taxi again?

– Not yet, but soon.

– Will you quit as director?

– Maybe. But I'll drive for a while, then see.

She tries to get his attention, but he's gazing down the corridor at the flowers, which he can see behind the kitchen window.

– So no more detective work?

– No more.

– What about the boy?

– I found his mother.

– You did?

– Yes.

– Was she dead? she whispers.

– No, she was very much alive. She owns a restaurant. A tough young lass, but she's all right.

Mónica grins. – You probably know plenty like her.

464

Erhard knows she's referring to herself, but he thinks of Annette and the time in his life that he could not stand her. The most difficult thing is to love someone who needs you; the easiest thing is to love someone who's not interested.

– See you at five o'clock, he says, then turns and heads down the stairs. She remains standing in the doorway, and he doesn't hear the door click shut until he reaches the end of the walk.

He drives a red Opel Corsa. It's Barouki's. He's borrowing it until he finds a used Mercedes with less than 90,000 miles on the odometer. He wants a better one this time. His plan is to start at Miza's in the mornings and only drive until lunchtime. Maybe some afternoon he'll go to the office to see if there's anything he might do. Barouki's very different than Marcelis. They even laugh at the same jokes.

The Opel Corsa rumbles towards Corralejo. On the right he sees Calderon Hondo, the pale triangle against the bright blue sky. The crater will always remind him of Juan Pascual, aka Pesce. Location unknown. When Erhard returned to the Hotel Olympus, the doors of the delivery van were wide open, and someone had set fire to the vehicle. It wasn't completely charred – the fire had been put out before it really got going – but it was nevertheless destroyed. There was no trace of Juan Pascual. Not even in his flat, which is empty; no one has been there for days. Pascual might have boarded a ship. He might be south of the Cape of Good Hope by now. A sailor knows better than anyone how easy it is to disappear in this vast world.

There's unrest at the airport. One of the larger airlines recently fired a quarter of its staff and discontinued all flights to the island. Thirty people have been sacked while politicians argue about how to boost tourism. The unions are picketing the airport, parking their honking cars in the middle of the road and not allowing taxis in or out, and the police are trying to clear the roads. It's all over the radio, and people are discussing it down at the corner kiosk where he parks now. He gets out of his car and cuts through the ally.

He waits ten minutes. Maybe fifteen. Then the cook comes out with the rubbish and sees Erhard. Erhard gives him twenty euros. The cook goes back inside.

*

– I figured it was you, she says.

Although she looks whipped, she doesn't seem as uncomfortable in his presence as the last time. She looks like someone anticipating a scolding. He considers giving her what she expects.

– Do you wish to know what happened to Søren Hollisen and your son?

She says nothing, just plops down on the rickety old stool.

– Søren Hollisen is dead. He sailed the Atlantic Ocean on a ship. Someone shoved him overboard, and he drowned.

Still she does not speak, just stares at the ground. He figures that her automatic smoking mechanism will kick in at any moment and she'll draw her fags from the small pack she keeps strapped to her waist, but all she does is fumble with the zipper.

– The dumb shit, she whispers. Her eyes are hard in her pale, powdered face. She's the type of person who hates the sun, who never spends any time outside. She dyes her hair black and paints her eyebrows, and she probably has a bunch of piercings all over her body. But she can't cover with makeup the fact that she's fragile and feminine, an angry little girl.

– He wanted to take the boy to Morocco, but fate had other plans. The ship was hijacked.

She looks up, troubled. – What do you mean?

– The ship's crew thought he'd gone crazy, but he just wanted to save your son, who was inside one of the containers.

She gazes ahead. Waiting for Erhard to continue. Waiting for worse news.

– Hollisen had hidden the boy in a car. When he tried to stop them from transferring the cargo to the second ship, the car slid from the container and plunged into the water. At least that's what I suspect happened.

– So the boy drowned?

– No. Somehow the car floated on the current, and it wound up at Playa Cotillo.

– What? she says, confused.

– It might have floated for a day and a half, before it washed up on the beach. The tidewater left it almost without a scratch. The police thought it had been stolen from a dealer in Puerto del Rosario. There was a lot of chatter about it here on the island. The boy in the cardboard box.

– Cardboard box?

– For some reason, Hollisen had put the boy in a cardboard box. Perhaps it was only temporary, and maybe the boy had been in the car only for a short time, but once the ship was hijacked it didn't really matter.

– I didn't hear anything about any boy in a cardboard box. I heard about a whore who'd abandoned her child in a car on the beach. There was talk of that right when I moved back. But I don't care about some whore's kid.

– It wasn't a whore's kid. It was your son.

She glowers at him as if she'll bite his head off.

– Is it possible that you gave birth to him on 23 October?

– No, it was 21 October. You think I can't remember that? You think I'm that dumb?

– Then why did Hollisen think the boy was born on the 23rd?

– Because I lied to him. I didn't want him to know. I was going to take care of the kid myself. Without him. I didn't need him. I'm not into men, you know? But then the kid started screeching and being difficult, and I couldn't take it any more. I brought it home from the clinic and found Hollisen, high as a kite as always. I didn't want him to think that he could have a kid handed over to him and just run away. I put the kid in his arms. Look what I've made. It's yours. He was angry that I hadn't told him. He said he could've helped me. Been with me for the birth and all the other shit men say.

He shows her the newspaper fragment with the text *rick 2310*. He found it along with the dried-out finger on his bookshelf in Majanicho after he moved home and began to clean up.

He figures that she'll ask him questions. Instead she begins to cry soundlessly. Tears roll down her cheeks. She crumples the fragment into a ball and tosses it into the rubbish bin. He's about to say something, but stops short.

– He loved that ridiculous film, and he kept talking about opening a cafe in Morocco. We saw the film together, in some theatre in Santa Cruz. Down near the water. That was before he realized I wasn't into him.

– Which film is that?

– The one with Humphrey Bogart. Where he owns a cafe called Rick's.

Søren Hollisen the dreamer. Erhard realizes to just what degree the man had tried to lead an extraordinary life only to repeatedly make poor decisions. This is how it looks, he thinks, when a man has to continually clean up after his own irresponsibility. But also how it looks when a man keeps believing that his luck will turn, that all hope is never lost. Until, of course, it is lost.

Erhard takes her hand. At first she's indifferent to his touch, but then she squeezes his four fingers until it begins to hurt.

– The boy was interred near Playa del Matorral, but I'm having him transferred to Oleana. Rick Hollisen's name is on the marker, but if you'd like, I can add your name as well.

Though she doesn't respond to this, she stops crying. – What about the people who did him in? Who pushed him overboard? It's all their fault, they are…

– I found the one responsible. He's been punished.

– What kind of punishment? A couple years at the Palace with free room and board?

– The police weren't involved. So no. He's dead. I watched him die.

She chews on that a moment. Then she releases his hand and clutches her belly with both hands. – But aren't you in trouble? Last time I saw you, the police were out to get you.

– A misunderstanding. I'm no longer of interest to them. Erhard thinks about the little computer gizmo lying in the tank at the restaurant, his video recording. It may not be up to date, but there's enough information there to build a case should it get into the hands of the press.

– You almost sound like my grandfather.

Erhard takes that as a compliment. – Then pretend your grandfather is telling you what I'm about to say. Get an abortion now. You must be at least three months along. Don't make the same mistake twice.

– I can't. I can't kill it.

– Yes, you can. You have to.

– I can't.

– Then don't. Have a kid. But for God's sake love it with all your heart. Love it like you would yourself. Love it like the child you once had. Love it so that it never feels alone.

– I don't want a husband, or a family. I'm not the mother type.

– Forget all that. Just be with your child. You don't need a husband or a family to love a child. There are many ways to be a parent. Find the way that best suits you. Just as Søren tried to find his.

The cook returns and looks at them. – Lily, a customer wants her money back. Frida's asking for you.

– I'm coming, she says. When the cook has gone, she scrutinizes Erhard. – Thank you, she says.

– I want you to have this, too. Erhard draws something from his pocket, and hands it to her.

She feels it in her hand before she understands what it is. – Where did you get this?

– I find things that are lost.

– Who are you? I can't figure out why you're doing all this.

– I'm just an old man with nothing better to do.

She puts on the ring, but it's much too large and she shifts it to her index finger; it glides on like something that belongs there. – Thank you, she says again. Almost in relief. She returns to the restaurant.

He drives home. He has forgotten how much he loves Alejandro's Trail, and the curve that makes his stomach lurch. He doesn't enter his house, but sits on a rock and turns his face up towards the sun. He notices the goats running about. Hardy's back again, though he hasn't approached the house. Soon Laurel joins him and they stare down the hill at Erhard. Today, Erhard's the one who walks towards them.

ACKNOWLEDGMENTS

One must be disciplined and a little crazy to write a book, and one must have patience and energy in surplus to live with a writer. I love my family for giving me the space I need. To my beloved P., who has helped me mature and challenged me more than anyone else. Thank you to good friends who always believed in my novel. Thank you to everyone who, with their interest and knowledge, has helped bring *The Hermit* to life: My editor K.; my agents; Nicole Callaghan in Fuerteventura; various sailors, taxi drivers, and piano tuners; and the cafe staff at the fantastic Louisiana Museum of Modern Art, who've poured my black coffee for five years and counting, because I don't have an office space, and simply love the view of the sea.